STINGER

OPERATION CYCLONE – BOOK 2

Books by Bill Fortin

Redeye Fulda Cold

Medellín Acapulco Cold

STINGER

OPERATION CYCLONE – BOOK 2

A Cold War Novel

with Rick Fontain

BILL FORTIN

Library of Congress Control Number: 2017902858

ISBN: 978-0-9964786-1-8 Paperback
         978-0-9964786-3-2 Hardback
         978-0-9964786-4-9 Ebook

This book was printed in the United States of America.

Published by Cold War Publications
February 2018

www.billfortin.com

Special thanks to the following individuals for their guidance. They helped set the tone and articulate this story.

A special thanks to my better half, Judy Fortin, who helped me allocate an immeasurable amount of time to the assembly of this project.

…and to my Mom, Dorothy Fortin, who passed at age 92. She was an avid reader and she loved the characters of both Bills (William Butterworth III, aka WEB Griffin, and his son William Butterworth IV). She was a pure joy to be around: her voice, her smile, and wonderful laughter. She was my very best friend and she is missed so very much.

I would also like to recognize three individuals who provided professional editing and design services:

On a specialized level of formatting and editing, I want to express profound thanks to my publishing supervisor, Donna Foley, who made this story better!

And special thanks to Stephen Walker of S. R. Walker Designs, who enhanced the *Stinger* cover with professional swiftness and skill.

Appreciation and recognition to Patty Wallenburg for formatting and type-setting.

Dedicated to the Real Deal

Colonel (Ret.) Luther R. (Luke) Lloyd

Trained as a Middle East specialist while serving in the U.S. Army, Luke holds an MA in Arab Studies from the American University in Beirut, Lebanon. Following his military service he lived and worked in Saudi Arabia and Egypt. U.S. assignments included the Current Intelligence Division, Defense Intelligence Agency (DIA) and the Office of the Joint Chiefs of Staff (OJCS) in the Pentagon, as well as the Political-Military Division, J-5 the Rapid Deployment Joint Task Force (which later became the United States Central Command at MacDill, Air Force Base), where he retired as the Division Chief.

He has published two educational novels: *Out of Darkness* in 2009 and *Baffling Puzzle* in 2012. His new book, *Friend or Foe*, offers insights into those who wish to kill us. He and his beautiful wife, Jeanne, live in Sun City, Florida.

"Joining is hard, belonging is earned,
and committing to those you serve with
will define you forever."

LTC THOMAS BROGAN

Contents

Part III   Three Years Forward – 1986

Part IV   The Ojhri Experience

Part V   Standing in the Cyclone

Author's Note

MANY PEOPLE FORGET that during our respective histories with Korea, Vietnam, and Afghanistan there was another theater of conflict taking place. An almost bloodless combat … a mental combat, but combat none the less. The Cold War, sustained mainly on the European landmass, was fought silently for well over 40 years.

On Christmas Day in 1979 the Soviet Union decided to try their hand at genocide in Afghanistan. This attempt at invasion would fail in a full retreat in February 1989. Some historians say that the proverbial beating of their feet back across the Amu Darya River, utilizing the infamous Friendship Bridge, signaled the end of the Cold War. I, for one, did not believe this to be the case. And since 2014, neither have the people living in the Ukraine.

Prologue

Early 1960s
Copper Mine
Ukraine, Soviet Union

ALEXEI GRIGORY LYSOTOVICH, Russian economist and politician, marched purposefully along the passageway. Lysotovich was deep in thought about what had just transpired. The lights in the passage were spaced few and far between. The sound of dripping water was constant. The noise that his feet generated, a crushing sound, made him nervous. The meeting had been a complete failure. However, he allowed a brief expression of relief to cross his face as the fresh night air made its way through the tunnel and touched him.

The relief was based on the fact that the men he had just met with were more hospitable than they might have been. They would have killed him, but shooting the messenger was not in their collective nature. If they killed the messenger, the government would never know what they were thinking and feeling.

Lysotovich found the main tunnel and followed the rail system embedded in the rock floor. He walked around several of the ore carriages that were bunched together near the mine's main entrance. Most of these wagons were overflowing with chunks of rock that would hopefully contain enough copper to warrant the collection effort. Lysotovich stepped out into the cold night. He stood for a moment, staring down at the buildings below.

The waiting Mark-1 Chaka, a black, four-door luxury GAZ M13, was parked between the main security hut and the larger construction trailers scattered around the yard. The vehicle, its motor idling, was converting its exhaust into a thick condensate that flowed close to the ground. The temperature this morning was well below freezing. The headlights came on and the rear window was being lowered as Alexei Lysotovich approached.

"Alexei," called Khrushchev. "Over here, please."

The driver's side door opened. A fit looking young man exited and scurried around the front of the car. His head constantly turning from side to side, he scanned the surrounding compound as he moved. He pulled the right rear door and held it with both hands as Khrushchev slid over, making room for Lysotovich.

"Alexei," said Nikita Khrushchev, pointing to the open area next to him, "come sit here beside me." Lysotovich entered the car but took a seat on a bench that faced Khrushchev.

"Comrade Khrushchev," said Lysotovich. He was concerned. "I did not expect to see you here!"

"Da, but I did not want to wait any longer for your report." It was a reproof that things were not moving as quickly as they should. "We are out of time, my friend. The Central Committee is becoming more disenchanted with each passing day. So, here I am. What were you told in response to our offer?"

"Comrade, I was planning to go directly to you when I left here."

"It has been four weeks since we spoke, Alexei," admonished Khrushchev.

"This was the first possible opportunity for a meeting. It seems our citizens no longer trust the government. They do not believe anything we say at this point, or what we say we are willing to do."

"Are they still meeting in there?"

"I do not think so. This location, I suspect, was chosen because it has more than one exit."

"I emphasize again how time-sensitive this issue has become. Mother Russia is on the brink—"

"You are preaching to the choir, Comrade. It was I who called attention to this situation almost two years ago."

"Ok. So what did they say to our offer?"

"It was not a good meeting, Comrade," replied Lysotovich. "Our proposed relief solutions would have fixed a simple problem a year past. The fix we offer now, at this time, they believe is no longer possible. And they believe that nothing this government says or promises is to be trusted. In any case, no one in their group was willing to consider any attempt on our part to correct years of economic injustice. There is no more confidence in what we say."

"Explain why they think what we propose is too little, too late," demanded Nikita.

"I can tell you what *this* site manager, *this* copper mine's administrator, has just related to me, and I'll try to quote you his exact words. He got very quiet when I finished outlining what we were prepared to do. He then said, "They pretend to pay us and we pretend to work. Nothing will change. What you offer is too little, too late, Comrade."

Khrushchev was quiet for a full thirty seconds. Finally, he said, "We had to try. So it is on to Plan B, Alexei."

"Sir, that at best is a short-term solution that will only postpone the inevitable," warned Lysotovich.

"Military conquest has always strengthened the soul of our country, Alexei."

"The sound of gunfire will not drown out the growling of their stomachs, Comrade."

"True, but we have never really been concerned with our citizens' meal schedules. Besides, there is nothing like a good war to take the common man's mind off of his personal predicament."

• • •

Born in April 1894, Nikita Khrushchev received his first career boost in 1939. Joe Stalin personally sent him to starve the people of the Ukraine. In 1953, Khrushchev became the Soviet Union's First Secretary of the Communist Party. However, in 1964, after 11 years on the job, he was succeeded by Leonid Brezhnev. Brezhnev saw to it that Khrushchev and most of his policies and proposals would be erased from the official Russian record. Brezhnev did, however, find merit in Khrushchev's idea of invading a neighboring country in order to raise morale at home, and years later put "Plan B" into effect.

On the last days of December 1979, took the Soviet Union and 12 percent of Mother Russia's Gross National Product, launching a military invasion into Afghanistan.

PART I

Cold Was the War – 1985

1

Dubai

Sheraton Hotel and Conference Center
Half Circle at the Main Entrance
United Arab Emirates
Friday 19 July 1985 1250 Hours

THE DRIVER OF the Mercedes pulled directly under the canopy. The hotel's master greeter pulled open the rear passenger door and extended his arm, directing me to a path to the glass-enclosed revolving door. His wide smile promised cooler temperatures. I stepped out onto the colorfully tiled footpath. One final scan of the doorman revealed no indication, not even a hint, of perspiration anywhere on this man. He was clearly not human. He must have been the offspring resulting from an alien desert experiment.

"Welcome back, Sir," said the smartly dressed door-keeper. The man had observably passed the course for playing on both sides of an air-conditioned environment.

"Looks like we're going to get some rain, Patrick," I joked, knowing full well that it hadn't rained in this part of the world for the last seven hundred years.

Laughing, Patrick politely offered his response. "I truly doubt that to be the case, Sir, but we can always hope for a miracle."

The tall, good-natured doorman, his uniform bright and crisp, stepped to the side. Patrick's prized possession was a full-length topcoat, most likely asbestos lined, I wryly surmised. Patrick's tailor was probably a former member of Apollo-7's spacesuit clothing unit.

I had made this same arrival several times in several days. I suspected that even if I picked up the pace, and ran for the door, my underwear would suffer the same fate as before. Anyone who has traveled to this part of the world knows what I'm talking about. Being completely soaked with perspiration by temperatures pushing past 47°C was actually a side benefit of the extreme heat. Surprisingly, I had started to look forward to the quick-freeze experience upon entering the zero degree temperature of the hotel lobby.

The condensation on my Ray-Bans prevented me from seeing the person behind the front desk. I asked to check messages, turning and leaning my back against the counter as my sight returned. I noticed the bustle of humanity in the lobby: the usual cross-section of celebrities, dignitaries, and business people filled this part of the hall. Local businessmen and several other categories of what the locals commonly referred to as the *out-of-towners*, such as myself, were the most common of all the sub-classes present.

"You haven't any messages, Mr. Fontain," said the front desk clerk in a refined British accent. I turned to face her as she said, "Do you want the same time for your wake-up call in the morning?"

"No, thank you. I plan on sleeping through until Monday."

She laughed as I turned from the counter and headed off across the lobby.

2
Elevator Etiquette

In the Atrium
Dubai – United Arab Emirates
Friday 19 July 1985 1305 Hours

THE DRESS IN the United Arab Emirates was a hodgepodge of western-style business attire with the occasional sprinkling of the traditional garb of the typical Emirati citizenry. With temperatures exceeding 123°F, the *kandoora* or *dishdasha*, an ankle-length white shirt woven from wool or cotton, seemed to be the favorite of the natives.

Many of the local women still elected or, in some cases, were still required to be concealed with an *abaya*. This black over-garment, when fitted properly, would cover most everything except the woman's hands and eyes.

It was also quite common to see the very rich and famous, as well as members of the well-connected royal class, out and about. This, I found, was the case no matter where you traveled in this city. Today would be no different.

Despite the crowded condition of the lobby there were only two other individuals waiting for the elevators when I walked up. The call button had already been pushed. In the next instant, the bell tone sounded and the light over the second elevator to my left announced its arrival. We shifted slightly as the doors opened to a full view of the car. Four outward-bound passengers scurried past us. The prominent looking Arab standing to my immediate left turned slightly and graciously motioned for me to enter the carriage first. His gesture was a refreshing bit of hospitality, I thought.

I entered the square car and turned completely around to touch the button for the seventh floor. I continued to move backwards, pushing my body up against the rear wall of the compartment. Staring out over the shoulder of the polite Arab gentleman, who had followed me into the car, I became alarmed and immediately assumed a combative stance. The man who had been waiting with us for the elevator was the cause of my concern. His movement and facial expression said it all. As he rushed to enter the elevator his arm sprang to an angled position just above his right ear. His hand clutched a large knife with a curved blade.

His intent became quite clear: he was going to bury this weapon into the Arab gentleman's back. I immediately set about removing the target.

I was now experiencing everything in a series of slow motion clips, a gift I've had since I was a kid. This concentration technique had proven beneficial in many fast-paced situations, from childhood football games to today's hair-raising encounter.

"Move," I shouted, pushing the man dressed in the *kandoora* to the right side of the elevator. I caught his look of total surprise as he slammed, face first, into the solid oak paneling. The attacker, a dark-complexioned foreigner dressed in a badly fitting, light-gray business suit, was intent on committing murder. His face was contorted with hate.

"Allahu Akbar," he yelled. My knowledge of foreign languages is limited, but I knew this meant, "Allah is the greatest!" Then he screamed again, this time in accented English, "Death to the devil." He lunged one final step into the car, plunging the curved knife into the space that just a millisecond before had contained his target. I pushed off the wall and extended the fingers of my right hand. I struck him, knife-like, directly in the throat. My left arm swooped downward and I chopped the assailant's weapon out of his hand. The knife fell harmlessly to the carpeted corner of the carriage.

The assailant was now kneeling in the center of the car, with both of his hands grasping at his throat; he seemed to be searching for some way to resume breathing.

The entire encounter took only seven seconds and had worked exactly as the Langley instructors had described. The attacker had dropped like a sack of rocks. His inability to inhale was about to become the least of his problems.

What happened next was truly disconcerting. The stunned Arab fellow seemed to have recovered completely from being slammed into the wall. He turned to center stage with a look that would have frightened George Patton. In one continuous motion, he moved directly behind the kneeling man and pulled out an even larger knife from somewhere on his person. He grabbed a handful of the man's hair. Pulling the head straight back, he made only momentary eye contact with his failed assassin. The Arab started at a point just below the left ear. Three of the man's fingers, lodged around his own throat, immediately tumbled to the floor. The blood-curdling scream that followed was quite brief.

The freed digits reached the floor in the same instant as the horrific spray painted the front of my pants and shoes. The wannabe assailant's throat was cut from ear to ear. The head was almost severed from the body. Playing the Good Samaritan had put me directly on the receiving end of this Arab surgeon's handiwork. The human heart generates amazing pressure.

"Jesus," I called out. This was my first experience in being behind the counter at a butcher shop.

You know that scene in *Star Wars* where Princess Leia announces, "It could be worse," and this huge fucking monster sticks his head out of the sludge and yells ARRRRRR … and Han Solo says, "It's worse"? Well, this assassination was not over by a long shot. No pun intended. Out of the corner of my eye, Assassin Number Two was moving at a fast clip towards us.

This man was determined to be with us also. Just as the doors were closing I saw him raise a gun towards us. The gun looked to have a silencer attached to its barrel. Three quick successive pops were heard. Two distinctive metallic strikes sounded on the stainless-steel doors. It was the second of the three shots that found its way through the narrowing opening between the doors.

The bullet entered the left shoulder blade of the Arab. The large caliber projectile spun him halfway around. His back now facing me, he began a slow twist to the floor. Grabbing the collar of his robe and pulling him close to me I was able to keep both of us standing.

With my free hand, I reached over and ran my index finger down the odd numbers on the left side of the column. The result was the illumination of every floor button from 15 through 3. The number seven was already lit.

We stayed huddled together and very still for the 28 seconds it took to arrive on the seventh-floor landing. As I guided my newfound friend out into the hallway the doors closed behind us. The sacrificial chamber continued its journey, programmed to stop at every odd level, all the way to the 15th floor. In the lobby below, the man with the silencer was watching our travel progress with great interest. This, as it turned out, was a complete waste of the little time he had left here on Planet Earth.

"We need," I said firmly, "to get some help. In the meantime, we can go to my room so I can take a look at that gunshot to your shoulder." I did a quick check of the carpet to see if we were leaving a trail. Convinced there wasn't any telltale sign of our travel, we shuffled along the corridor to Room 727.

"We'll be safe in here," I said. "At least until we can figure out what's going on down in the lobby." I pulled the key card from my shirt pocket. Placing it momentarily between my lips I glanced down to check the proper orientation of the card. Satisfied with the direction of the arrows, I snatched it from my mouth and inserted it smoothly into the slot.

The click was instantaneous as I pushed down on the handle. Raising my arm, I slammed the palm of my right hand on the wooden surface of the door, causing the key card to fall to the carpet just inside the door. This maneuver was done with more force than necessary. I kicked the card further into the room. The interior handle had thudded solidly into the rubber protector on the wall. The sound it made seemed to accentuate the urgency of our situation.

With one final glance up and down the hallway, I made sure we had not been followed. Nor was there any telltale evidence of our walk down the hall. I took hold of my new friend. Gripping his one good arm I propelled him quickly into the room. We stopped at the edge of the king-size bed. The door behind us had just clicked shut with a solid metallic finish. The Arab man, who had not said anything up to this point, asked, "You are an American?"

"Yes, Sir, my name is Rick, Rick Fontain. At your service, your Eminence," I replied, as always, with my very best first-greeting smile.

"You know who I am?" asked the injured man, his increasing pain apparent in his voice.

"Yes and no, but in either case I want your assurance that if you are ever displeased with my behavior you are to tell me immediately. I will then run from your sight."

The Arab chuckled at the witticism and said, "I owe you my life."

"Yes, Sir, you do. And a new pair of pants to boot. Who are these men who want you dead?"

Instead of answering the question he asked, "To boot?" Then, exhaling through clenched teeth, he said, "You seem to be highly skilled in self-defense methods."

My former Army colonel, Tom Brogan, once told me: some people get the elevator, while some only get the shaft. Today, that piece of sarcasm had a whole new meaning. "Well, self-preservation measures maybe, but in any case I have had several encounters with bill collectors over the years," I replied. "But, I must admit, this is the first time one came calling with a giant meat cleaver."

"Meat cleaver? Oh, you mean the scimitar. Even now you seem very calm and collected," he said with a note of suspicion in his voice.

"I assure you my pulse has tripled since we met in the lobby. And, I promise you it has no real chance of slowing down any time soon."

With both hands, I stabilized his stance. *"My, my, my," I muttered to myself.* I could plainly see the exit point of the bullet on the front of his shirt. If I had been standing just six inches further to my right in the elevator I would have been rewarded with the exiting bullet entering my own body. I gently pulled the injured Arab slightly forward and examined the entry point on his back, then turned his back towards the bed and gently guided him to a seated position. With the index fingers from each of my hands I ripped the robe wide enough to pull it down and around his waist. The sleeveless under-shirt was soaked in blood.

"Hmm," was the only response made by my new friend. And then after just a few moments of reflection he said, "Hand me the telephone."

I snatched both sides of the telephone from the nightstand and offered it to him. With great difficulty, he guided my hands holding the telephone to the center of his lap. His attempt to steady it enough with his one good hand failed. He couldn't get it done.

"Give me the phone; I'll dial the number for you. Tell me what it is." I sat down next to him and pulled the instrument back and sat it on the bed between us.

"Just dial zero and hand it to me," the Arab man ordered. He now was exhibiting signs of shortness of breath. He put the phone to his ear as the ringing started. I had a decent enough understanding of his side of the conversation from the Arabic I'd recently learned.

"Connect me to Hammad at once," he demanded of whomever answered. A few seconds passed and apparently someone named Hammad was on the line.

"I'm in 727; I've been shot and require medical assistance. Did you get the shooter in the lobby?" He listened for a full fifteen seconds. "Leave him confined in the basement and clean up the mess in the elevator." He listened again. "Good, the less attention to this event the better. Lock down seven; no one is to enter or leave this floor until we are sure we have everyone concerned with this. Get up here now."

He didn't attempt to end the call by hanging up in the usual manner; he just flung the handset without saying anything further. It sailed out onto the center of the bed. The hole in his shoulder blade was becoming more and more painful with each breath he took.

During the conversation, I had gone into my bathroom and retrieved a couple of washcloths that were stacked neatly in the basket set between the two sinks.

Just as his conversation ended I moved to the far corner of the bed and flipped up the comforter, grabbing a handful of bedsheet from the folds stuffed under the corner of the mattress. I used my small, square-bladed knife, kept in its miniature sheath hidden behind the head of my belt buckle, to quickly shred the sheet into large, wide strips. I placed the small towels on each side of the wound. I wound the cut strips around his chest and over and under his shoulder blade. Finally, I cut an additional strip of the cotton sheet and fashioned a makeshift sling. The whole procedure took less than three minutes. The washcloths, combined with the eight hundred thread count of the Egyptian cotton, seemed to please him.

The knock at the door came several minutes later as I was changing my pants. I pulled my pistol from the belt holster still installed on the bloody slacks. I walked to the door with my Walther *pistole* held in a position at the small of my back. My new patient watched me closely as I peered through the peephole.

I said, "Who's there?"

"Hammad," was the answer, so I pulled the door to a fully open position.

"Como esta usted, Hammad?" I asked in Spanish as the man flew past me. He ignored the greeting. I leaned out in the hallway, looking in both directions. It was quiet and empty.

"Sir, Hammad, your friend I hope, is here to see you," I said, closing the door and pressing my back to it. This announcement earned me a break in this fellow's stride. He turned to study my face but only for an instant. Moving quickly and swiveling his head from side to side, he checked behind the open door to the bath and quickly glanced at the far side of the room. Satisfied, he faced the man he had come to see. His boss was fully reclined, with his chin propped slightly on his chest. His eyes were open but his face was contorted with pain.

Obviously, this was the Hammad who had been summoned via the telephone call. I would later be told that his name was Hammad abid Ndakwah, HOS (head of security), for the injured man lying across my bed. Hammad immediately took a position, almost at attention, directly beside the bed. His right hand held a 9mm Beretta 92 pointing down towards the plush blue carpet. I held my Walther, a 7.62mm PP Zella, in a fully relaxed position at my side and slightly behind my right leg. The Walther had been a gift from a friend in German Intelligence.

Hammad turned for another quick security check and then immediately returned his full attention to his boss. I tucked the pistol in my waistband at the small of my back and folded my arms to watch the exchange between my two new roommates. I also allowed myself a quick mental image of my corporate colleagues who had invited me to attend a golf outing this very same afternoon.

Fortunately, for Hammad's boss, I had refused. It was a blessing in disguise for everyone except the would-be assassins. I suspected that my AT&T friends would be facing certain death via sunstroke at this very same moment. Playing golf in the UAE was almost as dangerous as riding the elevators at the Sheraton Dubai.

3

An Expert Opinion

Four Days Earlier

AT&T Office Complex – Conference Room 9 East
Dubai – United Arab Emirates
Monday 15 July 1985 1136 Hours – Friday 19 July 1985 1250 Hours

THE DUBAI AT&T team had asked for me personally, even though I normally worked out of our London office. The standard flight time from London to Dubai was six hours forty minutes. Mine was a short flight by most standards: the BA 747-400 managed the 3,401 miles in just a smidgen over six full hours. Normally, that would have been a piece of cake for me, but I was still feeling the effects of a 12-hour flight from Mexico City that delivered me to my London address only the previous morning. I have never been able to sleep on airplanes — it just seems like a good idea when flying to be awake for the crash.

I arrived at Dubai International Airport in the early morning hours. I was met, and driven directly to the hotel, by our local company transport. After a couple hours of sleep and a quick shower I was ready. Still, I had a vague, nagging feeling hanging around me. The idea of dropping an anvil on my foot to refocus my thought processes occurred to me. I descended to the lobby at 8:45 a.m., ready to go to work.

That day started like all the others I'd previously spent in Dubai, with the operative temperatures rushing towards 50° Celsius (120°F). There would be no chance of humidity in this city's immediate future. The local office manager again sent a car to deliver me to the ninth floor of the newly established AT&T offices. I arrived just before nine o'clock. I would repeat this same journey four more times during this week.

The days went by quickly — as had today's meeting, which had been cut in half by the arrival of the regional manager. He had flown in from Hong Kong the night before: Thursday the 18th. The strategy discussions, and ultimately my recommended proposal changes, needed his approval before we could proceed. Unofficially, this client had already indicated to AT&T that our solution should be modified to include certain engineering services. This was the sole reason that the local account team had requested my presence. I was London's Intelligent Building Systems expert.

Today, Friday, just before the noon dinner hour, the manager from Hong Kong held up both palms of his hands and halted the conversation. So, as far as I was concerned, the week's entire effort had been a complete waste of my time and, even more so, AT&T's.

Apparently, providing engineering services was a corporate taboo. At least that was the mindset of the AT&T general manager (GM) who formerly oversaw the Montgomery Ward catalogue desk. He cited the cost of doing business and the precedent it would set going forward. Engineering services simply would not be allowed. The GM had slammed both hands on the table and ended the meeting.

Unfortunately, the UAE and most other customers in this part of the world required engineering support services when purchasing state-of-the-art product. To do business in the Middle East, value added engineering had to be included. The creation of the 'Sales Prevention Center', managed and maintained in the mind of this specific manager, would prohibit us from doing business in the UAE … forever!

AT&T's post-breakup (with The Bell System) strategy in 1982 did not work out the way it had planned. Its attempt to enter the business of computer sales and services had all but failed, and it was quickly realized that the path to profitability would not be met in the U.S. domestic marketplace alone. Also, AT&T's manufacturing engine, Western Electric, was not and would not generate the required revenues unless new markets were approached. So, in 1983 the decision to enter the global marketplace was made.

To hit the ground running, partnerships were formed with valued added resellers in Europe, the Middle East, the Caribbean, South America, Mexico, and the Pacific Rim. The resellers identified as potential partners all specialized in the types of communication products that Western Electric could provide.

It became apparent to AT&T from the start that European Market Analysis, their one-size-fits-all approach, wasn't appropriate everywhere in the international marketplace and certainly not in the United Arab Emirates.

Promoting just the corporate widgets, not a full systems approach, would fall way short of what an owner or CFO expects at this high level of selling. Relationships in this part of the world were everything. It was customary. I had learned this the hard way and understood what this particular client was expecting. This week, I had explained this requirement ad nauseam. I had spelled out exactly what out shortcomings were as defined by this particular client's bid specifications. After all, selling techniques to owner/investor groups, and their very influential families, was very different than selling widgets to second and third tier telecommunication managers.

I'm Rick Fontain. I'm 36 years old and I've been out of high school for almost 20 years. It was after a full year of college at Loyola in Baltimore, and a full semester of ROTC under my belt, that I joined the communications industry. Part-time summer employment with one of The Bell System's core operating companies, C&P Telephone, provided me with the proverbial foot in the door. In April of 1968, while taking computer language and programming courses at Catonsville Community College, I was asked by my friends and neighbors to join the U.S. Army. I had been drafted.

Even after all of these years I still have an intense mental picture of the head of Howard County's Selective Service Board. She, Matilda G. Hodges, smile blazing, snuggled securely in her rocking chair, waved us a final farewell from the Board's wooden front porch. This well-rehearsed headquarters ritual was commonplace during the late 1960s. The chair seemed to pick up speed as 17 of Howard County's finest 1A classified inductees passed in review.

As we pulled out of the Board's parking lot I had thought of a quote from one of my favorite actors of the time: Jim Hutton, who played SGT Peterson in the John Wayne movie, The Green Berets. "… we can only imagine what gay adventure lies ahead," I remembered him saying. It was years later, while I was watching a re-run of this movie that I found my memory was mistaken. The actual quote was even more appropriate to what I had experienced: "With joyous memories, we leave the mystical city of Da Nang! What gay adventure lies ahead? Brother, this trip is going to make LSD feel like aspirin!" No shit!

"No shit." I say it all the time. This phrase, I've found, can be applied in almost any military conversation … and it is certainly appropriate inside any well-defined corporate culture. The Bell System was no different. As our leadership became more and more diluted with each divestiture, one facet of the culture hung stubbornly on, retaining all of its strength. I've named it the SPC, the Sales Prevention Center. I was not surprised to see it show up in force here in the UAE.

Despite the fact that my AT&T career was secondary to my real day job, my passion for Intelligent Building technology didn't miss a beat when I was called upon to perform for AT&T. My real family, the one that commanded my primary attention, was best known by the initials CIA.

The Central Intelligence Agency had recruited me for service when I was twenty years old in 1969. After a distinguished military service in the 3rd Armor's 1st/48th Infantry Battalion, I was told I had a natural talent for walking and chewing gum at the same time. This apparently was a prerequisite for being invited to play in the intelligence game. Having clarified that for you, I should explain that my assignment that week in Dubai was strictly to be an all AT&T affair. This meant no spy shit and absolutely no golf.

My corporate boss, not my company boss, had arranged for this project participation for me. The particular type of building construction that was being planned was tailor made for my developed engineering expertise. All of my recently published research on high-rise building systems would provide proof-positive that I was eminently qualified to work anywhere on the planet as a subject matter expert for systems integration engineering and the cabling for all intelligent building technologies.

The AT&T local account team could not sway the GM/SPC IC (In Charge) either … at least not up until that point. I was looking forward to my frozen underwear experience at the hotel when the lead account executive (AE) on my project grabbed me by the arm as I touched the button to call the elevator in our offices. He wanted to extend an unexpected, and unbelievable, invitation for that very afternoon.

"How about joining us for nine holes?" asked the smiling Dave Long. "The GM just agreed to continue the discussion off-line in a more casual setting."

I paused for fully five seconds before responding. "Thanks, but no thanks. I didn't pack my shovels this trip."

The head AE pursed his lips trying to understand the shovel comment when he finally understood and said, "The pro shop can fix you up with a really nice set of clubs. I thought you meant shovels for digging holes there for a minute … I meant to say nine holes of golf. If you join us—"

As he spoke, it occurred to me that the invitation seemed to be more of a request extended by Charles Bronson from the movie Death Wish 29. A relaxing afternoon on the back nine of Dante's Inferno Resort and Conference Center was not on my top ten list of things to see and do in Dubai. My refusal of the invitation re-emphasized my disappointment in the stalemate regarding reworking our project proposal. It also had everything to do with my complete lack of enthusiasm for the wonderful world of golf.

Cutting him off in mid-sentence I said, "I knew what you meant. I was just fucking with you. I never really have understood the attraction to the game. And I'm quite sure I won't change your boss's mind by succumbing to heat stroke out in the desert. Tell you what — he's here until Monday, right? Let's get together for some dinner this weekend and see if we can come up with some compromise planning to convince him that an enhanced offering is the only way we can win this client over. That is, of course, assuming he survives the golf outing."

"No problem there — he plays here all the time. I'll call you tomorrow morning to set up a time, OK?"

"Look Dave, this isn't my first rodeo out here. I suspect, no, I'll guarantee, that if we don't provide engineering support for this project we will kiss good-bye all future project opportunities. The history on this particular client indicates they won't consider doing any business with AT&T. Ever."

Processing what I just said, Dave's mind defaulted back to the beginning of the conversation. "The heat here is a dry heat," he replied in a subdued voice. He went on to say, "It's not at all bad once you get acclimated to it. I'll call you in the a.m. In the meantime, I'll rack my brain for a way to restate our requirements for this clien—" He stopped mid-sentence. A smile appeared on his face as he formulated a clever solution to our dilemma. "Tell you what. If by the 8th hole I haven't come up with a fix, I'll have the caddies bury him up to his neck in the sand just out of sight of the club house."

"Now you're talking Dave. If this gig at AT&T doesn't work out for you I have a friend who uses similar problem-solving techniques."

"That's good to know," said Dave, laughing at his attempt to amuse me. Seeing that I wasn't laughing, and was looking dead serious, he continued, "We'll think of something for sure. I'll call you tomorrow." The elevator arrived and I stepped in and selected the lobby button.

"Hey, Dave," I called, halting Dave who had turned to go back down the hallway. "Caddies may not be the best option. There may be better character choices from the ranks of the construction workers you see here along the highway. They are mostly Egyptian migrants, or so I've been told. They are probably much more eager and far cheaper in providing that type of service."

Dave turned to face me as the elevator doors closed. His facial expression seemed frozen in the moment. After all, I was just making a joke. I called through the closed doors, but I'm sure my words got through: "Sometimes brainstorming can be really helpful, Dave. Catch you later." I imagined that Dave stood there for a full 15 seconds before turning and starting his long journey up the corridor to his office.

As the elevator descended, I recalled a warning my AT&T boss, Joe Hauf, had given me just before I left the London office. He told me that July temperatures in Dubai were very much like the actual flame-heat generated by a blow torch. That thought, plus my preconceived notion that the game of golf had all of the allure of watching paint dry, confirmed for me that I'd made the right decision.

4

Cognitive Dissonance

Sheraton Hotel – Dubai
Penthouse Levels
Al Barsha 1 – United Arab Emirates
Friday 19 July 1985 1315 Hours

IT WAS REASONABLE to expect. Once the adrenalin calms, and the pain is managed, the human being in all of us starts the playback sequence. This will continue until we are comfortable and/or satisfied with the circumstances surrounding a near-death experience. Someone tries to kill you and someone shows up and saves the day. Well, we all know there is no such thing as a coincidence, especially when there is a possible preplanned, positive outcome.

My new best friend would be curious — perhaps suspicious is a better term — as to how I just happened to be in that elevator with him. It was while changing out of my blood-soaked shoes that it came to me. I had previously met this man whom I had just kept from being assassinated.

His name was Taisei, Maalouf Torki bin Taisei: a Malaysian citizen, prominent member of their cabinet, and probably the largest arms dealer in this part of the world. He was also the owner of this hotel. And as they would surely say at Langley (and any other organization dedicated to the unbelievable), this man now lying across my king-size bed was not going to believe that my being in that elevator was a coincidence.

19

Hammad, after conferring with his boss, announced that the party was being moved upstairs. He summoned four other individuals and a wheel chair just by speaking into what must have been a very expensive cuff link. I took it upon myself to lead the way at a hasty pace down the hall to the elevators. Each of the four security men followed me and took up a position so that they fully encircled their wounded boss. Each security man held a mini-Uzi with the collapsible stock at the ready; each weapon was connected to a sling worn underneath their respective suit coats. Their mission was clear; no one was to fuck with their boss for the rest of the day. At the end of the hall an elevator car was waiting with its doors locked open.

Hammad guided the chair with both skill and purpose. He marched the entire convoy into the open doors of the very same elevator car that his boss and I had witnessed being abused just a short while ago. I took my usual position along the back wall while the rest of band formed a defensive perimeter around their leader. Hammad held a key card up to a spot just above the numeric display panel indicating the floor levels. The readout on the display immediately changed to the letters "PH." I made a mental note to ask who the hotel used for their cleaning services. The elevator interior was spotless.

We arrived somewhere at the top of the building. The doors opened and all six of the players, including their quarterback, exited the car as one. I was the last to walk out of the car. The view of the penthouse interior took my breath away. A large atrium with a Tiffany-style glass ceiling rose thirty feet in the air. The room in miniature could shame most Catholic cathedrals. Even more impressive was an entire wall of glass at the far end that looked out over the downtown waterfront. This man's home was fit for a king.

A professional looking medical team complete with white lab coats charged into action as soon as the wheelchair hit the foyer. The team, consisting of a doctor and two nurses, rushed to take control of their patient. They quickly pushed the hurting traveler down the brightly illuminated hallway to the right of the elevators. Hammad followed his boss just a few steps behind. His four foot-soldiers went on defense, taking up positions across the access to what seemed to be the main hall to the private living quarters.

I moved across the bridge that connected the vestibule to the magnificent view of the harbor. The colored glass in the ceiling showered equally colorful light throughout the open space below. A very attractive woman walked up the wide staircase that joined the passageway at the middle. She introduced herself with both hands outstretched to receive my one. Observably of local parentage, her costume smacked of the decadence of the West. Her tailored fashion must have come from shopping excursions to some very expensive metropolises. Cities such as, New York, Paris, and London came immediately to my mind. It also occurred to me that with her resources she could probably have shopped in all three cities on the very same day.

"Hello, I'm Caitlin," she said with a very nice smile. "I want to personally thank you for saving my father. Our family will be forever in your debt."

"I'm very glad to meet you, Caitlin. My name is Rick, Rick Fontain. I'm just glad I was able to help your Dad get the situation under control."

"I've seen the videotape. You are being much too modest, Mr. Fontain. Please come in and make yourself at home. My mother and additional security are driving in from Abu — Abu Dhabi, that is. They should be here within the hour."

"Thank you, and please call me Rick."

"I will. Would you care for something to drink, Rick? Perhaps I could get you something from the kitchen?"

"That's very kind of you. I would very much like a glass of water. Perhaps a sandwich, if it wouldn't be too much trouble. I haven't eaten anything of substance since last night."

"No problem at all," she said, and led the way back down into a spacious lounge. There were four, large, white leather sofas facing a bubbling water sculpture at the center.

"Your home is magnificent." This was the understatement of the year.

"Thank you. We usually spend most of our time in Abu when we are in country, but I do like to spend time here whenever I can get someone to drive me down." One of the kitchen staff delivered the water and said that the food would arrive soon.

I had just taken a bite of the second half of the sandwich when Hammad appeared and announced that His Eminence requested my presence.

"Caitlin, could you watch my sandwich? I shouldn't be long."

"Of course, we will keep it safe for you," she said with a smile, "but I think I shall go along with you and see how Father is doing."

5

An Eagle's Nest

U.S. Embassy
25 Grosvenor Square, London
United Kingdom W1A 2LQ
Friday 19 July 1985 1010 Hours

THE TEMPERATURE THROUGHOUT the city had already climbed past 31° Celsius. The day, like most, had started with its usual measure of moisture. Bill Douglas's driver had picked him up from his flat in Kensington and delivered him on time for a get-together with his local British counterpart. The meeting's purpose was to finalize the arrangements for the Baltimore Symphony Orchestra to appear in concert at St. James Hall that coming November. Douglas's official role as Cultural Attaché required him to carry out this type of duty for dozens of like events each year.

His full name was William J. Douglas, and he had recently succeeded his former boss, David James, who had become the newly appointed U.S. Ambassador to the United Arab Emirates. Douglas actually wore two hats here in London. Like his predecessor, he was served by two separate but highly capable team operatives, each highly skilled. And, like his boss before him, he would spend 99.9 percent of his time as HOS (Head-of-Station), with a laser focus towards all matters important to the Central Intelligence Agency of the United States of America, best known as the C.I.A.

Douglas left the second-floor conference room and headed for the stairwell. He decided to skip the elevator, as the stairs would offer the only opportunity for him to exercise in the foreseeable future. As he entered the fifth-floor corridor he was met by one of his executive officers-cum-operatives Amelia Jane, who handed him a steaming mug of coffee by its handle and put a yellow and blue message center folder in his free hand.

"Thanks, and good morning," he began. "So it starts even before I get to my desk?"

"David thought you would want to see this right away," she confirmed in her perfect, lifelong English accent.

"What's it been, two weeks on the job, and he's conjured up a crisis already?"

"Ed McCall is on the phone with David right now in the conference center. He asked me to come and find you as soon as you were finished downstairs."

"Marvelous, I'm on my way. Did my briefcase make it up here yet? If so, pull the night traffic dispatches and put them in the safe, would you? Thanks, you're a godsend."

"It did, I will, and you're welcome. Oh! And your 10:15 is already downstairs," she announced. "Should I bring them up or wait to see how it goes with the Ambassador?"

"Them?" asked Douglas.

"Mohammed Abu Ghazala, Egyptian Defense Ministry, and Max Gresonine are in the conference center on one. Mr. Gresonine called yesterday afternoon and asked for 30 minutes."

"Do we have any idea what they want?"

"Max wouldn't say, but he did say it was important that you meet."

"Ok, I'll see what David needs. Bring them up to my office and I'll be there as soon as his Excellency makes known his need." They went off in different directions.

Bill Douglas arrived in the east hallway at the wall plaque marked CON5E. After shifting the folder under his left arm of the hand holding his coffee mug, he pushed open the door. Ed McCall, 42-years old and Douglas's number two in the Embassy, sat alone at the far end of the conference table. The light on the key set and the speaker phone volume control switch were both illuminated. Ed had been assigned to Douglas right after graduation from the farm in 1970. He was a 1965 graduate of Notre Dame University and had served a four-year hitch in the U.S. Marine Corps. He was recruited into the CIA in 1969. His file described him as intelligent and highly-motivated.

"Here he is now, Mr. Ambassador," announced McCall.

"David, Amelia Jane said there might be a problem?" Douglas walked around the table to the front of the room. It was a large room with seating for twelve. There was a screen at the far end mounted on the wall directly behind where Ed McCall was seated. There was an overhead projector installed on a cart that was pushed off to one side and a 16mm motion picture projector on another cart, but located on the outside wall just under the first of the four bulletproof window panes.

"Did you know that Rick was here in the UAE this week?" asked the Ambassador.

"Yep, he called me last Sunday and told me he was going to go help the local AT&T group in Dubai with a high-rise building bid specification. Why do you ask, has he eloped with the king's daughter?" asked Douglas, chuckling because he wouldn't put it past Rick.

"Wrong country, no king, but he did stop an assassination attempt this afternoon."

"No shit! Anybody we know?" asked Douglas as he tossed the folder onto the tabletop and slid into the chair next to McCall.

"Oh yeah, we sure do. Would you believe Maalouf Torki bin Taisei? This is the part of the conversation where you tell me what Rick is really doing in town, Bill."

"Come on David, you know me better than that. Rick is there solely on an all AT&T project. Nothing else, I assure you. And is this Maalouf Taisei the arms dealer we're talking about?"

"Yes, but that's not all he does. He's got Malaysian citizenship and is involved in a great many things. He's the Division Head of the Research Division for the Malaysian Prime Minister. He spends a great deal of time in Dubai but he owns property all over the world. And, of course, he owns the Sheraton Hotel where Rick just so happens to be a guest."

"This the same dude who reneged on our Afghan arms deal last year in Kuala Lumpur?"

"One and the same," confirmed the Ambassador. "It now appears that we may have an ace in the hole when dealing with Mr. Taisei and friends."

"You mean Rick? Do you know any of the details of the hit?"

"One of our Embassy staff was in the lobby when it went down around noon. It appears as if the attack took place in or near one of the elevators. Three, maybe four, shots were fired. Our guy on scene couldn't get close enough to see anything. Their security locked down the lobby and was seen dragging a man in one hell of a hurry through an Employees Only door. The entire incident was over in less than two minutes. There was no police involvement."

"How do we know Rick was involved?" asked Ed McCall, speaking for the first time since Douglas's arrival.

"Same embassy guy who heard the pops also knows Rick from his internship at State. He saw Rick walking towards the elevators just before the shots rang out," replied David James.

"Wrong place, right situation scenario," commented Douglas. "Who identified the target? Same guy?"

"No, the same embassy guy grabbed one of the bell hops by the arm as he ran by. He told our guy it was the owner who was attacked. We did the math and the rest as they say was just a simple phone call. Will Rick run a standard protocol?" asked James.

"He'll gather as much of the background for motive on the target and call in. He'll wait until he can get to a secure line, maybe the AT&T offices, or, more than likely, he'll decide that the embassy offers the most secure place to call out. Who's your Head of Station? Wase?" asked Douglas.

"Yeah, Joe Wase. He put people with eyes on-site just in case Rick shows up and needs a hug," replied Ambassador James.

"Good. Perhaps Joe can make a house call if Rick hasn't called in by supper time. All we can do now is wait and see," said Douglas.

"Good suggestion. I'll pass the recommendation to Joe. We'll call if we hear from him first," said David James.

"Right, ditto," replied Bill Douglas, and the Ambassador hung up.

6

Hammad's Henchmen

Dubai Sheraton – Penthouse Level
Master Bedroom Suite
Penthouse Level 2
Friday 19 July 1985 1455 Hours

CAITLIN AND I formed a new posse with Hammad and his henchmen and moved in formation up the steps and down the same hallway that her father had disappeared into just thirty-five minutes earlier. We took a small, private elevator up one level. The doors opened to a mini-version of the same luxurious appointments experienced downstairs.

Caitlin took the lead and walked from the foyer down three carpeted steps into a large living room that was staged on a balcony overlooking the center of the apartment. Because the apartment was built around an atrium, the cathedral ceiling was an impressive aspect of each level. The colorful cut glass in the skylight sparkled downward onto the wide spiral staircase.

This living space had a much warmer and more intimate feel than where we had just been. The black and tan furniture and wall hangings suggested a great deal of care was used in their selection. The leather sofas and chairs gave me the impression that if I sat on them I would sink deep into their depths. Everything looked very comfy and very expensive. Each piece of furniture was arranged around an extremely large, glass-topped coffee table. Holding up the glass were three, wooden, standing sea otters with their paws extended upward. Working together they were able to keep the heavy, thick glass level and in position.

"Are those giant squirrels? Do they work here full time?" I asked Caitlin on our way through the living room. She laughed.

"They are sea otters. Each one is carved out of driftwood that was washed up on Penang Island. It was a gift to my father from a business associate. This is my parents' private living quarters," she offered, and continued onward to the far side of the room where the staircase started its journey upward through the next two levels.

"When the end of the day comes, they find it calming to be able to escape all the hubbub of their business."

"My parents just push their dresser up against the bedroom door for privacy," I said in my best impression of being serious." Caitlin turned her head to see that I was smiling. I followed her up the staircase. One thing was for sure, Mr. and Mrs. Taisei had one very well put together daughter.

We exited at the top of the first landing. There was an elevator at the opposite end of the landing. We walked, in single file, directly across to a set of double wooden doors. The wood was teak I supposed. A carving spanning both doors depicted relatives of the otters working the coffee table downstairs in the living room.

Without waiting for an invitation, Caitlin tapped lightly and pushed at the forehead of the otter on the left panel. The door opened easily and she marched right in. I followed her at a quickened pace. Hammad, who was bringing up the rear, stopped momentarily to close the door and remained there with his back firmly up against it. The other travelers in the caravan remained outside in the hallway.

"Father," Caitlin asked as she arrived directly beside him, "are you going to be OK?"

Maalouf Torki bin Taisei's legs were elevated on two plush recliners in an elaborately furnished sitting area. Behind him was the entrance to the master bedroom. The large, canopied four-poster with a lace and flowered duvet wasn't what I expected to see in the bedroom of the number one arms dealer in the Middle East.

"Yes, yes, I'm fine, thanks to Rick here," replied Taisei, waving his arm towards me. As if he had read my mind he added, "My wife has decorated the room behind us."

"Your home is very nice, Sir."

"Then you understand, as a man I mean, that certain things are not in our control."

"Yes, Sir," I responded, laughing. "I take your point. Sir, shouldn't you be in a hospital? A shoulder gunshot is nothing to take lightly," I said with genuine concern. The entire medical team was standing on the far side of the room near the windows. They were watching the exchange with their hands clasped in front of their bright white lab coats.

"No, Dr. Asghar determined it to be, what was the term, Theresa?"

"A through-and-through, Sir," said the taller of the females on the medical team.

Well, so much for my male chauvinistic view of who's who in medical garb. And then suddenly I formed in my mind's eye the mental image of Dr. Janice Prasonio. She and I had fallen in love so many years ago — I was only 19. She had been killed. But still, after all of this time, like just now, I could just shut my eyes and look upon her face. When I turned to look at the doctor, she was smiling and looking directly back at me. And a very nice smile it was.

Dr. Theresa Asghar, MD, was thirty-two years old and spoke with a decidedly Boston accent. It turns out she had attended Harvard Medical School and recently completed a two-year residency at the Johns Hopkins Hospital in Baltimore. Doc Theresa was Mr. Taisei's personal physician. She went with him wherever he traveled. She was also drop-dead gorgeous and Caitlin's cousin.

"Nothing vital was damaged. It will be somewhat painful for a time but will not have any long-term effect on the movement of the arm. Your homemade field dressing kept the loss of blood to a minimum."

"That's good news, Sir," I replied.

"Father, Mother and the others will be here soon. Is there anything I can do in the meantime?" asked Caitlin.

"No, I can't think of anything right now. But I would like a moment with Mr. Rick. Alone."

Everyone started to move towards the door. Doctor Theresa patted my arm on the way to show her appreciation of my competence in dealing with Taisei's medical emergency.

"Caitlin, wait for Rick in the living room and see that Hammad has arranged for his new accommodations. And please make sure they meet with his complete satisfaction."

"Yes, Father," she said. "I certainly will." She reached for my hand and gave it a quick squeeze on her way out.

Maalouf waited until we were alone. "Come, and sit here beside me."

"Yes, Sir," I said, and took a seat at his side. His eyes were slightly dilated but seemed to sparkle none the less. He seemed to be relishing the idea of the conversation to follow.

"You know who I am?"

"Yes, Sir. I remembered on our way up here." This was only partially a lie. "We met briefly last year in Kuala Lumpur. March, I think. The Menara Maybank project was the occasion. We were introduced in the corridor outside the conference room by one of your construction managers. It was a Mr. Haddad, that is, if memory serves correctly? You were rather upset by a comment that one of the bidders had made."

"I do not remember our introduction but I do remember the meeting. Tell me, do all employees of Bell Labs carry Walther PBKs?"

"I don't know, Sir. I, however, find it comforting to do so when I travel internationally. It's a Walther PP Zella, Sir, not a PBK."

"May I see it?"

"Of course," I replied. I reached around and pulled the pistol from its holster under my jacket. I always traveled with two types of concealed carry — neither one of them legal. The one I preferred when out and about was a skeleton sheath worn on the inside of the belt at the small of the back. When speaking to an audience or traveling in a car I preferred the shoulder strap. I released the magazine into my left hand, then opened and locked the weapon, catching the cartridge in the same hand that held the magazine.

"You seem to handle that like a professional. A 7.65mm is an unusual load, yes?" he asked after reading the lettering imprinted on the frame of the pistol.

"Carl Walther manufactured this particular weapon in 1940. The 7.65mm can be substituted with 32 caliber ACP ammo. This particular Walther was a gift from a friend. A German friend," I said, and our eyes met as he handed back the pistol. I pocketed the free cartridge and slipped the mag into the handle, seating it with the heel of my palm. I released the frame lock, loading the weapon, clicked on the safety, and placed it back into the holster.

"And, what brings you to town — especially this time of year?"

"I was asked by the local AT&T account team to help out with the Etisalat Head Office Building project." Now comes the point in our new-found friendship that will determine if he trusts me or not, I said to myself.

"Ah, yes," replied Maalouf, warming to this welcomed piece of information. "It would seem we have a common interest in being in town at the same time."

"Sir," I asked for clarification, "are you bidding on this project?"

"No, we are here this week to run the bidding process for the Government."

"Sir, I'm certainly glad we ran into each other in the elevator."

"Young man, that is the understatement of the century," replied the laughing Maalouf Torki bin Taisei. Seemingly satisfied with my cover story, which in this case was not a lie, he patted my left hand and proceeded to tell me all about the upcoming bid on the building we had both come to address.

7

Party Crashers

Eleven Months Later

Pakistan – Towr Kham Copper Mine
Meeting with Saifullah Khan
31 Clicks NW of Landi Kotal
Wednesday 25 June 1986 1650 Hours

THE PAKISTANI MOVED to a better position from which to see outward from the main entrance to the mineshaft. Three high-velocity rounds had found their way into the main tunnel entrance. This is where he, his men, and the Americans had been told to wait. Two of his kinsmen had been taken out in the most spectacular hail of gunfire that he had ever experienced. This situation was definitely not described in the arrangement the CIA man had provided him when his services were solicited.

They had been standing just two meters inside the mouth of the tunnel. One of his tribesmen, a cousin, had his left shoulder completely torn from his body. He bled out in under a minute and a half. There was blood all over the tunnel walls near the main entrance.

The second round passed just to the right and six inches above the head of a seated Delta Force team member. The 50-caliber projectile hit the one-inch thick metal on the front of the first ore car. It cut through the material like butter. The bullet drove through the back wall of the car and went dead-center through the shoulder blades of a second member of his village. Holding his Enfield rifle within his folded arms, this Pakistani villager never knew what hit him. The oversized bullet exploded out the front of his chest, severing the antique firearm in two. The third shot embedded itself deep into the tunnel floor, sending chipped stone shrapnel in all directions. It was now clear that the meeting that had been called for this time and this location would have to wait.

Jim Pezlola, call sign ZERO, was the CIA man on loan to America's DIA (Defense Intelligence Agency) with the responsibility for coordinating the meeting. This was his third trip in as many months to Pakistan. Locating the relative of Maalouf Torki bin Taisei had been a challenge. Today was supposed to have been the final step in securing an audience with the Mujahideen leadership.

"You see anything?" asked Pezlola. Jim scurried toward the tunnel entrance and took up a position behind the third of the twelve Melcher Machine Works ore cars. None of the first three cars in line at the entrance were connected together and could be pushed by hand in either direction to provide minimum cover from the visiting sniper. The shooter must have been perched just outside the main entrance. The grouping of the three shots suggested the shooter lacked competence with this particular weapon. He was no professional.

"No, the sun is going down and the shaft entrance is facing directly west. The glare is making it impossible to see anything across the way," said Saifullah, the village elder and today's appointed tour guide. The good news was that the shooter was firing from an elevated post and wouldn't be able to see very far into the tunnel entrance. The bad news was that whatever the incoming monster rounds found would be destroyed.

Saifullah Khan was a local village chief who had been solicited as a go-between for the day's proposed meeting. "When we were told that everyone was to wait inside this tunnel I had not a good feeling," confessed Saifullah.

Today's meeting was supposed to be with the elders of the Mirdadzai Khudiadadzai tribe. Saifullah had worked with them previously and knew they were not friendly with the Russians. They controlled this district, Kakar

Sunzer-khels, with pathways that connected with Saifullah's district. They controlled the most direct routes to the Afghan border and the mountains beyond.

"Those shots sounded as if they came from a heavy SASR " said Chief Warrant Officer (CWO) Gary Lawson, call sign ONE, who had come up the tunnel behind Pezlola and was now crouched directly behind him. SASR was short for Special Application Scoped Rifle. Gary was also CIA and on loan to the Defense Intelligence Agency.

"They sounded like they came from a Barrett, or maybe a McMillan to me," said the slightly winded George Angerome, who had sprinted up the tracks from the back of the main tunnel. He was the Delta Force team leader with the call sign DELTA-1.

"Those companies you just mentioned have mass-produced a whole shitload of the .50 caliber monsters, First Sergeant," called out Pezlola. "The bastard doing the shooting is undoubtedly in an elevated position directly across from us. The grouping of the shots and the angle in the torn metal in this first ore car suggest the shooter can't see very far inside."

"He's positioned close by, for sure," offered DELTA-1.

"It'll be dark soon, so we can try to get down the trail to where we left the horses," proposed Saifullah.

"That's an excellent suggestion — unless of course he has a night scope. Any ideas on who cancelled our meeting?" asked Pezlola, looking directly at Saifullah.

Saifullah's response was slightly agitated. "Maybe, if I had to guess, I would think it would be Sardar Ansari Punjab. He may be the disgruntled party. He and his father reside in the adjoining district to the north and have aligned themselves with the new communist government in Kabul. Up to this point they have concerned themselves only with the transport of opium. Maybe Punjab finds friendship with the Russian intruders to be beneficial to his business."

U.S. President Ronald Reagan and the CIA had been trying for several years to arrange distribution and training in Pakistan, and safe passage into the mountainous regions of Afghanistan, for the Stinger weapon system. Touted as an equalizer by the U.S. Department of Defense (DOD), it was believed that Stinger would change the entire complexion of the Afghan struggle against their Russian invaders. The cooperation and involvement of the Pakistanis would be imperative in terms of putting Stinger into use against the Soviets.

The CIA had been made privy to the existence of Mr. Saifullah Khan and his district fighting force in Pakistan. After several months of searching, the CIA had finally found Mr. Khan. Their interest actually was in one of his family members — his sister. They had concluded that she would be their best chance for getting an introduction into the inner circle of the Mujahideen freedom fighters, the Afghan insurgents who wished to keep the Soviets out of their country. The specific group Pezlola and his colleagues were interested in was reported to be camped just across the border in Afghanistan. Saifullah had been called upon in his mountain village and persuaded by Pezlola to set up today's meet-and-greet.

Out of the goodness of his heart — and fifty thousand U.S. dollars, paid in advance for escort fees — Saifullah was going to enable the CIA to finally start a conversation with the Afghan Freedom Fighters. The key to the conversation was Saifullah's sister because she was the wife of Mustapha Ismail Taisei, one of the local commanders running a large Mujahideen military force. The CIA sought his council. They were happy to travel into the western mountains of Afghanistan to have that conversation.

Mr. Taisei and his fellow Tajiks had dedicated themselves to removing the invading Russians and the present, in-power, Afghan puppet government. They dedicated themselves to this mission, just as their ancestors had fought and died in countless battles over the previous several hundred years.

Mustapha also happened to be the nephew of Maalouf Torki bin Taisei. This was perhaps the most important fact to know about Mustapha. His uncle, the Malaysian real estate magnate, was now deep in debt to CIA operative Rick Fontain. Rick had run into Maalouf in his hotel elevator in the UAE. They had hit it off from the very beginning. This was usually the case when you save someone's life.

Pezlola's headset crackled, "ZERO, we got movement coming up the rear of the main shaft. Sounds like five or six individuals, maybe more," said ONE, Chief Warrant Officer, Gary Lawson.

"Swell, now what?" Pezlola whispered to no one in particular. "Get everybody back behind the last of the ore cars; put two guys up here to cover the front," he ordered into his throat mic.

"Roger that," replied Lawson from forty feet back. He turned and hurried back down the tunnel.

"Saifullah, we have movement to our rear," said Pezlola. "Did you know there was another entrance to this mine?"

"No, this is my first time at this place. These people coming towards us ... this does not necessarily mean there is another entrance. They may already have been here."

"True," acknowledged Pezlola. "Stay down and between the carts until we find out what we're dealing with." Two of the seven SFO-D (Special Forces Operations – Delta), foot-soldiers trotted past them and took up a defensive position fifteen meters from the tunnel's main entrance. All of the remaining members of Saifullah's group were told to pull back behind them. Pezlola's chaperones were a newly formed deployed Delta element based out of Ramstein Air Force Base in West Germany. Their sole purpose today was the well-being of the CIA operatives: Pezlola and Lawson.

"ZERO, we got an individual holding a lantern and waving a scarf about a hundred feet down the main corridor. He looks interested in having a conversation."

"Let's see what he wants. Wave him in. Be very, very careful, Mr. Lawson," said a suspicious Pezlola.

"Roger that." The CWO turned and said to the nearest Delta guy, "Okay, let's see what he wants. Bring him closer, Sergeant."

"Yes, Sir."

Sergeant First Class George Angerome moved briskly, bent over at the waist, following the rail tracks to the last of the rail cars. This one was all by its lonesome, separated from the others by at least thirty meters. As he quickened his pace he let his HK MP5 hang loosely from its sling, which was draped around his neck. He pulled a long, tube-shaped signal flare out of his leg pouch and with both hands twisted the flare into action. As the tunnel filled with the bright greenish light he stood and waved the person holding the lantern forward. The journey took about forty-five seconds to complete.

"You're CIA?" said the impressive figure in mountain warrior costume. He walked up and placed both arms on the chest-high edge of the ore car. The lantern was now hanging loosely inside the carriage space. It swayed gently back and forth from its wire handle. The shadowy glow exposed the well-weathered face of a deeply concerned citizen of Afghanistan.

"We have come to meet with a Mister Pee-zoola. Is he here?"

"Depends," said SFC Angerome. "Who are you?"

"My name is Taisei, Mustapha Ismail Taisei. My wife received word from her brother that my uncle, Maalouf Torki bin Taisei, has suggested we meet."

"Wait one, Mustapha Ismail Taisei," replied Sergeant Angerome, squeezing the switch on his throat mic. "Mr. Lawson, your four thirty appointment is here after all. He says his name is Taisei, Mustapha Ismail Taisei."

"Bingo! Bring him up front. Find out if anyone else is with him and keep them there. Stay frosty. Break. ZERO, did you copy that?"

"Roger that. Standing by," replied Pezlola.

"DELTA-1, here. Wait one," Angerome said, releasing the mic switch and turning his attention back to the man holding the lantern. "You have more people with you back there?" he asked, pointing down the dark passageway.

"Yes, there are nine of us and we are all armed to the teeth. I believe that is the appropriate expression for this situation, yes." Mustapha smiled wryly.

"Signal for the others to come forward and wait here. Put the lantern on the ground and come with me," said SFC Angerome as he tossed the half-burned flare into the nearly empty ore car.

Mustapha swung the lantern back and forth at eye level before placing it on the ground at his feet. Three other men came out of the shadows and huddled around the lamp. "Wait here until I return," ordered Mustapha as three members of Delta walked up to wait with his men.

"You said nine. Where are the others?"

"They are at the front by now. They will await my signal to approach."

"We took some fire earlier. They may run into some bad guys."

"Yes, we heard the gun fire. I'm sure the front entrance will be cleared momentarily," he said quite confidently.

They walked the sixty feet to where CWO Lawson was waiting.

"There are three more friendlies at the rear and five more out in front," announced Angerome.

"Thanks, George," said Lawson, and then addressed Mustapha's group. "I'll take you to Mr. Pezlola. Stay against the walls; we took some fire earlier."

"We will indeed. But you realize the walls are facing in the wrong direction for this technique to be effective, yes?"

They found Saifullah and Pezlola hunkered down by the second-to-last ore wagon that was very near the front entrance. Mustapha was the first to speak.

"Saifullah, Samira sends her best," announced Mustapha, referring to his wife, Saifullah's sister. "I'm Mustapha Ismail Taisei," he said, and offered his hand to CIA operative Pezlola.

"I'm glad we're finally able to meet," replied Pezlola. "It's been a long time coming. I'm Jim Pezlola and I've been sent here with a proposition from my President and a message from your uncle." He took a small, letter-size envelope from inside his field jacket and extended it to Mustapha.

"We expected representatives from the Mirdadzai Khudiadadzai tribe?" said Pezlola just as they finished shaking hands. It was more of a statement than a question.

"We just came from their camp. We were made aware of the meeting with Saifullah. So, we decided to come in person and save them the trip."

The sounds echoing off the chamber walls indicated the shooters were close. The noise was followed up by six or seven single pistol shots. Everyone looked towards the main entrance.

"I sent my men around to secure the front. When we arrived in the area we heard high-powered rifle fire." Mustapha walked to the opening and called out, "Suleiman, are we secure?"

The response came, "Yes, we are good to go. One is still alive."

Mustapha turned back to look at Pezlola, "As you probably can tell, my Mr. Suleiman was educated in your country — at the University of Meerieland. I think that is how you pronounce it. Anyway, do you wish to question the bad man?"

"Yes, we're all wondering how he got here," replied Pezlola. He then raised his right hand to his throat and activated the mic. "George, sorry, DELTA-1, the rest of the friendlies just rang the doorbell. Pack it up and move everyone forward. We'll be diddy-bopping out of here directly. Out."

"Roger that, ZERO. We're moving now," replied ONE who turned to DELTA-1 and with a head gesture he motioned everyone towards him. The three Mujahideen warriors just stood there. He turned to face them and with an exaggerated arm motion he got them to follow him down the tunnel.

Three armed men in local tribal dress entered the cave with a badly damaged and shirtless individual in tow. They walked up to Mustapha and pushed the man down at their leader's feet. The two other Afghans remained outside the entrance to keep watch.

"What is your name? Who sent you?" Saifullah inquired in a tone that suggested no matter how the questions were answered it would not end well for this man. He remained silent. The next words brought his head up.

"If you do not speak I will remove your testicles and stuff them down your throat." Pezlola was pondering the translation offered by Mustapha when one of the Afghans came in from the front.

"Mustapha, there is a large force moving this way up the mountain path. We should move from here as quickly as possible."

8

Amelia Jane

Three Days Later

Office of the Cultural Attaché – 5th Floor
25 Grosvenor Square, London, United Kingdom
Friday 27 June 1986 0945 Hours

THE ELEVATOR OPENED on five and I turned to the left and walked quickly towards Bill Douglas's office, formerly that of David James. Amelia Jane had just hung up the phone.

"Mr. Douglas, Rick Fontain is here and also, I just got a heads-up from the COMM Center that Joe Wilson's flight will be delayed leaving Andrews by two or more hours. He won't be here until well after midnight."

"Thanks, Amelia Jane," he called back. Welcome Rick and please ask Carrie to call down to the cafeteria to send up some coffee for us."

"Yes, Sir."

Carrie Ester Flouts was 43 years old, married, and the former personal secretary to David James. Bill Douglas had personally asked her (well, begged her actually), to remain in the same capacity for his new duties as Head of

Station (HOS) London. Carrie was a lovely woman, but my colleague Amelia Jane was the one who always turned my head.

It was when I was transferred to the AT&T office here in London in '83 that Bill Douglas filled me in on Amelia Jane Dancer Smythe. She was born in nineteen hundred and forty–six to Kendrick and Katie Dancer. She has a superior IQ of 149, attended St. John's College, Oxford, and married LT Commander Jonathan Smythe in 1967. Jonathan had been killed in July 1982 while trying to land his Harrier GR7 in severe weather on the HMS Invincible – a Royal Navy light aircraft carrier — at the start of the Falkland Islands dispute.

Douglas told me that Amelia Jane was being asked into government service the same week I was being treated for double pneumonia at Fort Bragg. (He seemed to think that this was tremendously funny.) Sir Keith Thomas Bolden, head of the MI-5, brought her into training himself.

Of course, if you believe in coincidence, or the tooth fairy, Amelia Jane's first assignment was to get a peek inside the manufacturing facility called the Ulan-Ude Aviation Plant. This facility was located in Ulan-Ude, Russia. The primary interest in this particular plant was a recently developed helicopter gunship designated as the Mil Mi-24.

Here's the coincidental (or not) part: in 1969 I ran a data gathering operation on the Czech border near the U.S. Army's training facilities at Grafenwöhr, Germany. The Mil Mi-24 was the target of an operation being conducted at a map point called One Tango. The then newly developed metal monster we were investigating was the very same machine being used by the Soviets in the mass murder of Afghan citizens.

Douglas hadn't told me, but I found out quickly that Amelia was full of surprises. Since leaving university she had become fluent in several languages. Amelia was also qualified on a wide variety of firearms with a category grading of expert marksman in all but the M79. The firing of a grenade launcher was frowned upon in sub-level-3, which was the basement area under the embassy. Also, in recent years she had taken it upon herself to become proficient in two flavors of the martial arts disciplines. You have got to love a woman with such an interesting choice of hobbies.

Amelia Jane was promoted and transferred into Mi-6 — Military Intelligence, Section 6 — as a case officer in 1979. She worked directly for

Sir Basil Duncan and ran several assets in Dresden. That is until one night in March of 1981 when it all had turned scary-bad. It was during an information exchange with one of her oldest developed assets that her time here on earth almost ended.

She was arrested and held for three weeks by the Stasi — German Ministry for State Security — at 35 Bautzner Straus. Mi-6 wrote her off and disavowed any knowledge of her employment. It was the American CIA, manning a listening post near Grafenwöhr, West Germany, that had monitored her arrest. David James, London's HOS at the time, was notified, and it was he who authorized a team to go in and rescue her. After a month of TLC in the American hospital in Nuremburg she returned to London.

In February 1982, she was approached by David and asked to work in his organization. Amelia Jane accepted and became one of his most trusted Administrative Officers. She hit the ground running, juggling projects for him on three landmasses. She was smart, competent, and very cool under pressure.

"Hello, Amelia Jane. How have you been? You're looking ravenous as usual." Amelia Jane was one of the few people who truly appreciated my off-kilter sense of humor.

"Thanks, Yank. You are to go straight in, and please tell Mr. Douglas that I'll be right there. I just have to run down to my office and grab some files off my desk."

Although we were close in age, from the very start I treated Amelia Jane with all the respect and affection of an older sister. We had become great friends over the last year — and we both seemed fine with that arrangement.

I went to Bill's door, knocked once, and opened it without waiting for a response.

"Hello, Bill. I came as soon as I got your message."

"Rick, sorry for the short notice but we just got Jimmy Pezlola's confirmation of his meeting with Mustapha Taisei."

Bill Douglas had just this year ascended to the position of head spook in London. He had first introduced himself to me in February 1969 as Alex Dobbins. We met again in Germany several months later and at that time he introduced himself as a Major Bill Carlstrum. I would find out later that his real name was William J. Douglas. Not much was ever disclosed about his background but his accent was decidedly American. Most likely he hailed out of the Midwest — maybe Chicago.

It was David James who had started the ball rolling on what we were about to discuss, but it was President Ronald Reagan who had first expressed the desire to utilize the Stinger weapon system to help Afghanistan repel the Soviet invasion.

Actually, it was just an extraordinary piece of luck (my saving his life, that is) that had put us in bed with Maalouf Torki bin Taisei, the largest arms broker in the Middle East. In today's meeting, the Mujahideen's acceptance of the CIA's offer to provide a game changing solution to the Afghan resistance force would be confirmed. Finally, Operation Cyclone would begin as soon as the final arrangement was reached with President Zia of Pakistan and his ISI.

"Did Jim make contact with Taisei's nephew?" I asked Bill.

"He did. He spoke directly with Mustapha Taisei. As soon as Amelia Jane arrives I'll fill you both in on what we're going to do next."

"She'll be right in. She went to pick up something from her desk."

9
Green Light

CIA Headquarters – Combat Systems Analysis
The Bullpen – 2nd Floor
Langley Virginia
Friday 27 June 1986 0515 Hours

JOE WILSON, CIA Department Head — Office of Russian and European Analysis (OREA), left the fourth floor via the stairwell. He traveled at a fast pace down two levels to a door marked with a giant black number '2' at its center. He exited and walked straight across the hall, pausing just long enough for the proximity reader to rob his ID card of the required information. The result was the familiar click of the electric lock. He pushed open the door and walked quickly through the area nicknamed "the bullpen". He wound his way around the maze of cubicles to the rear of the room and entered his office.

Daryl Russell, Department Head — Office of Mid-East Analysis (OMEA), was standing by the window pouring a cup of coffee from Joe's personal flask. He had come to collect the SAT (satellite) photos he'd lent-out the previous evening.

"You've been waiting long?" asked Wilson, as he sat down behind his desk.

"No, I just got here. How'd it go," he paused and pointed at the ceiling, "upstairs?"

"The President gave us the green light. I've got to go to London and brief Douglas's people."

"The Egyptians and the Israelis have agreed to the meeting in Kuala Lumpur. Depending on Douglas's timetable we can schedule the meeting as early as this weekend if necessary. The Mossad, in particular Director Admoni — is being particularly cooperative these days with the recent exposure of Mr. Pollard." Jonathan Pollard had sold classified information to Israel while working as a civilian U.S. intelligence analyst.

"President Reagan went bat shit when he found out about what Pollard and the Israelis had been doing. I guess Admoni wants to get back in his good graces. Also, POTUS acknowledges the simple fact—" started Wilson.

"—that the Israelis will provide the perfect cover." Russell finished the sentence for Wilson. "Their distribution channel, their setup through Egypt, is exactly what the doctor ordered," he added. Israel's world class scribing technique would remove any U.S. markings from the weapons, enabling the CIA to maintain its anonymity.

"And, of course, President Zia will be able to maintain that he wasn't involved," noted Wilson. "Plus, we keep control over the methods of transport, training, and, most importantly, the distribution of the weapons. All three phases will be managed directly into the hands of the Afghan Mujahideen ... with no ISI appointed middleman."

"Sounds almost perfect, don't it? The proverbial win-win for everyone except the Russians," chuckled Russell. "I hope Rick packs his dancing shoes. This whole Disney film script will turn into a giant frog-fuck if it's not managed right."

"It's a small world," said Wilson, laughing at his own wit. "Rick seems to excel at this type of operation. Besides, isn't it about time we provide some serious payback for Vietnam?"

"Oorah," said the OMEA Department Head, Daryl Russell.

10
A Fine Surprise

Fontain Residential Flat
30 Hyde Park Gate
Kensington, London
Friday 27 June 1986 2050 Hours

LEFT THE EMBASSY with Amelia Jane at 2030 hours. We walked up Binney Street to the Bond Street tube station, agreeing to meet with Joe Wilson as soon as word came that he had landed and was making his way from Mildenhall Royal Air Force Base into the city. The initial meeting would take place at the London Mayfair Hotel. We said our goodbyes and parted company on the lower level — each of us traveling home, but in different directions.

I made my way to Green Park Station and changed trains, getting off at Knightsbridge. The double-decker number 52 pulled to a stop just as I emerged from the stairwell. It was a very short trip up the Kensington Road and I stepped down from the rear of the bus even before it had come to a complete stop. I walked the short distance down the side street to my flat: number 30 Hyde Park Gate. The entire journey had only taken seventeen minutes.

As I made the turn into the Mews I quickly checked the area bordering the cobblestone pavers leading up to the entrance to my flat. I did one last check over my shoulder to examine the street I had just traveled. Everything seemed to be in the green. I pulled out two keys as I walked up to the front entrance. Inserting both keys at once, I pushed open the heavy wooden door and climbed the stairs, pocketing both keys on my way to my second floor living quarters. I heard the familiar sound of the front door hardware clicking into place as I entered the front hall of the flat. As usual, I pulled the drawer open on the marble top table. At the same time, my right hand went to the small of my back, to take the Walther out from its hiding place. Half way around I froze.

It was quiet. I stepped back to the opposite side of the hallway. An oriental runner ran the entire length of the passage. I turned my head to the right, which gave me a direct view through the living room. I could make out the furniture silhouettes and, well beyond, the triple set of the large glass sliding doors that framed the balcony and its furniture.

One of the reasons I had chosen this flat was that the backyard was completely private. Only the two tenants who lived here had access. I swiveled my attention to the rear of the flat and the far end of the hallway. There was a light shining under the closed door to the master bedroom. I was fairly sure I had turned it out before leaving in the morning. I was doubly sure that the door was wide open when I left.

"Jesus," I muttered. I edged my way down the hall, careful to place my feet soundlessly. I moved my hand with the Walther, pointing the business end at the ceiling. Just as I put my left hand on the doorknob it was suddenly pulled open.

"Mein Gott, Rick," screamed the naked lady. "You scared the hell out of me." Her head jerked suddenly backwards and the towel she had wrapped around her wet hair had fallen to the floor. My beautiful Hanna was standing before me. Since the day I first laid eyes on her Fraulein Hanna Gresonine had captured my heart. Standing five foot seven in her bare feet, her usually silky reddish brown hair was wet and matted. She squared her stance, looking at me through those deep-chestnut colored eyes.

"Hanna, good God what a surprise. Why didn't you tell me you were coming?" I asked, quickly putting the Walther back in its holster.

"There wasn't time. Uncle Max came into my office this morning and asked me on the spur of the moment if I wanted a ride on the embassy's courier flight. I said yes, and here I am. All I brought with me was what was in my go-bag."

"How did you get from the airport without any clothes?" I asked with a great deal of concern.

Hanna, knowing my personality, continued on — ignoring the absurd question. "You know the one I keep under my desk. The SAT phone wasn't working on the plane, so I called here when we landed. No answer, of course, but things are starting to look up, yes?"

"Mrs. Fontain, I'm sure glad you're dressed for the meeting," I replied. With that I scooped up my wife into my arms, our lips touching ever so slightly, our mouths parting just enough so that our tongues could greet one another. When we reached the bed, Hanna reached out and pulled back the comforter. I adjusted my stance and carefully kept the balance of my recent capture. With the English linen now exposed, I laid my naked wife down ever so gently.

"I've missed you," I said as I shed my jacket and started working the buttons on my shirt. I kicked off my shoes and slipped out of my dress pants, underwear, and socks all in one continuous motion — a feat I hadn't practiced in several weeks.

"Ambassador Heinemann, the German ambassador to the U.S., has arranged a temporary assignment for me at the consulate here." She said this as I slipped naked under the covers, pulling her close and snuggling her neck.

"When does the TDY start?" I asked.

"I'm not sure what 'TDY' is but what you're doing feels really nice."

"I was asking when your temporary assignment will start."

"The job will most likely start the first of next month. I'll know more tomorrow."

"How long can you stay?" I enquired.

"I've got to be back in D.C. on Thursday. The Ambassador has me hosting the BMW factory delegation on Friday."

"But as of the first of the month you'll be here full time? That's great, honey."

We stayed silent and motionless, kissing deeply for almost a full minute. I was the first to speak.

"I guess I'll have to buy Uncle Max a beer," I said as I rolled over on my back, pulling Hanna on top of me.

"I love you, husband," Hanna said as she rose slightly, lifting her hips just a touch and with her right hand reaching down and guiding me into her. We started very slowly at first. We moved as one, with our hips joined, in a slight clockwise circular motion. Slow at first, and then faster with the all too familiar end in mind. After a good long while Hanna suddenly froze and arched her back, letting out a cry that was mostly muffled as she buried her breasts and her face into my chest and neck.

"I love you, Baby," I whispered into her ear. "God, I'm glad you came." Hanna kissed her way down to my navel and paused, looking up towards my face.

"Did you mean just now, or were you referring to my jaunt to London?" she asked, not expecting an answer. Giggling, she continued her mission further down my torso.

I had Hanna's Uncle Max to thank. It was Max Gresonine (German BND, Federal Intelligence Service officer), who had encouraged the relationship from the start. In 1970, I was finishing up a tour with the 3rd Armor Division in Gelnhausen, Germany. At the time, I was also working for Bill Douglas and the CIA. During the final stage of our project, Operation Fulda Cold, a counterintelligence officer named James Pezlola, who also worked for Bill Douglas, invited me to dinner at a restaurant in downtown Gelnhausen. The restaurant, "Dining in Paradise," was owned and operated by Hanna and her mother. Hanna and I had hit it off from the very beginning and were inseparable during my final months in Germany.

It was Max who had arranged for Hanna to be offered a job in the German embassy in Washington, D.C. — a scenario that had unfolded quickly and was pretty unbelievable.

Of course, I ran all of my concerns through Bill Douglas on my last day of active duty with the Army. I had learned over the previous year that there was no such thing as Santa Claus, the Easter Bunny, or the good fortune of having someone you were in love with being transferred just 35.3 miles from your U.S. place of residence.

Douglas told me not to be concerned because he had it on good authority that Uncle Max truly admired what I had accomplished for the German Government during my tour. Douglas assured me that my future bride's kind and caring Uncle Max was just trying to show his appreciation for both of us. After all, we both had suffered similar tragedies in the late 1960s. Hanna's husband had been shot to death on a military assignment in East Germany, and my doctor girlfriend had been killed by a drunk driver in Nuremburg — not far from the hospital where she had worked. The 1960s had not been kind to either one of us.

Hanna and I were married in a small ceremony in 1973 at the Interfaith Center located in Columbia, Maryland. Both Bill Douglas and Uncle Max were present, as were a wide variety of relatives from both sides of the Atlantic. Also in attendance was an even broader spectrum of Army, BND, and CIA case officers who had traveled from near and far to attend the Fontain union. All wedding photographs were restricted to include only the immediate family members. The reception was arranged by Uncle Max and was held at the home of the German Consul in Washington, D.C.

11
Ringtone

Millennium Mayfair Hotel
Rear Lobby Reading Room
44 Grosvenor Square – London W1K 2HP
Saturday 28 June 1986 0140 Hours

AT 0140 HOURS, the irritating 25 hertz ringtone that the Brits send out from their Central Offices, announced the incoming call. I reached across the soundly sleeping (but still naked) Hanna and grabbed the handset just at the start of the second barrage. It was Amelia Jane reporting that Joe Wilson had landed and was twenty minutes out. She would send the embassy car to fetch me and deliver me to the Mayfair Hotel where my old friend Joe would tell us what he wanted done.

I asked the driver to drop me off two blocks from the hotel. An unsurprising London downpour started as I walked to the west entrance of the building. I chose this particular doorway because it was the furthermost from the main lobby's front desk and the prying eyes of the nighttime staff.

I had been here many times before on official AT&T business. There was a small sitting area located just off the rear of the main lobby. As I walked into the space I saw Amelia Jane and Joe Wilson seated towards the back of the room. Joe was sitting in one of two wing chairs facing a sofa. His trench coat was arranged across his lap and his travel case was parked directly beside his chair. His well-worn and saddle-like, overstuffed brief case, which should probably have been removed from service by Wells Fargo in the late 1800s, lay flat on the table in front of him. I took a seat beside Amelia Jane on the couch.

"Hi, Rick. Were your ears burning? I was just quizzing Mrs. Smythe on how your Pashto language skills are these days." Joe managed to mock my "language skills" every chance he got.

"Yesss, Sirrr, Mr. Joes, yous knows I barely gets by with just speaking *a-mare-I-can*," was my retort. "Now if you are looking for a real expert linguist," I switched to my best radio commercial voice that was an attempt to imitate my good friend Jack Swanson, "Amelia Jane speaks great Pashto and several other exotic but impossible to pronounce dialects."

"That's why she'll be going with you — so you don't insult anyone with a turban and an AK-47. And for that matter, any other type of weapon that may be pointed at your head," cracked Wilson. "How have you been, Rick?"

"Fantastic," I said. "So, I take it we can rule out a CIA invasion of Antarctica for this project?" Amelia Jane just rolled her eyes.

"Don't mind him, Mr. Wilson. He really becomes quite accommodating when he takes his meds."

"Let's go upstairs so I can fill you in on which tooth is the best in which to hide your cyanide capsules." Wilson turned his head slightly and winked at me. Poor Amelia Jane. She had to put up with both of us.

12

Paralleling the Landay Sin

Afghan Freedom Fighters
On-route to Mujahidin Base Camp
Konarha District of Afghanistan
Saturday 28 June 1986 0455 Hours

IT WAS STILL dark when Mustapha informed Jim Pezlola that they were entering the Konarha Province of Afghanistan. The almost-full moon was providing more than enough light for everyone to keep safe on the narrow footpath. Occasional breaks in the cloud cover offered random glimpses of the valley floor even farther below. They were high up on the mountain heading north-northwest. As they proceeded along the trail they were afforded an extraordinary view of the river Landay Sin. The main highway paralleling the river could be seen at times via the headlights of sporadic vehicles, mostly traveling towards the south.

The day's procession had been formed in haste. It was just the day before that they had escaped an ambush in an abandoned copper mine near the mining town of Landi Kotal. The cavalcade lead was made up of Afghan Freedom Fighters (Mujahideen). The CIA and their Delta Force guardian angels were in the middle, followed closely by Mustapha's brother-in-law, Saifullah, with his three remaining village combatants. Suleiman and one other were assigned to bring up the rear of the parade. The village men were asked to travel with the CIA and Delta Force group to the Mujahideen camp to ensure their safety should Pezlola's offer be rejected by the Mujahideen management.

The march changed direction just as the dawn began to paint their backs. The single-file troop left the upper trail and the magnificent overview of the river below. They picked their way down the back of the mountain. Within the hour, the journey would start upward again, but this time the heading was due west and deeper into the mountainous region of Afghanistan. The terrain became more uneven and jagged with every kilometer traveled.

Pezlola was pondering the sheer magnificence of the landscape and the fact that there was not much available cover from attack, if the need arose. Just as he was dismissing that particular thought from his mind, Suleiman, Mustapha's lieutenant, came from the rear of the line at a very fast clip. The University of Maryland Terrapin was beating feet to his boss who was near the front of the procession.

Mustapha, marching three back from the front of the line, had also heard the engine sounds now bouncing off the stone cliff above. Suleiman saw Mustapha turn and look back down the valley. Instead of proceeding any further up the trail he cupped his hands to his face and called out to his fellow warriors.

"Mustapha, gunships are coming up the valley!" shouted a slightly winded Suleiman.

Suleiman had stopped next to Pezlola. He raised his arm to Mustapha, who was already ordering everyone off the path. Pezlola realized he also heard the turbines. He depressed the throat switch on his RAP-4. "Sergeant Angerome, let's find some cover and get the old Bob Barrett's SASR locked and loaded. Focus on the sound of the unfriendly helos coming up on our six."

"Roger that, ZERO. Break. DELTA-2 and 3," Angerome called to Delta Force team members Deccan and Goschich. "You work your magic with the SASR." MSG Angerome released his mic switch, paused for just a moment and then raised his hand once more to his throat. "All other Deltas, secure in place and become invisible. Move it people, this is DELTA-1 getting low."

"Roger that." Taking the 50-caliber sniper rifle from his shoulder, Goschich yelled to Deccan with his usual calm, southern drawl to follow him off the trail. In just a matter of seconds everyone disappeared, as best they could, and remained very, very still.

Mustapha had made a beeline to where Pezlola and Lawson were hunkered down behind several large boulders. He proceeded to squeeze himself between his two favorite CIA operatives. It was not a moment too soon. The distinctive air-battering sounds of helicopter rotors grew very loud. The approaching gunships were making their way to center stage.

"Depending on their hangovers they may pass without seeing us ... but that is not usually the case," Mustapha sighed, accentuating the point.

What happened next was surreal. As the sound of the engines was being amplified by the hard rock surfaces above their heads, the Mil Mi-24 and two smaller birds of prey came into view. There were three helos traveling well below their usual cruising speed at an altitude of only 300 meters. The distance from the concerned citizens of Afghanistan to the three trolling Russian gunships was a very short seven hundred meters. The motley group was motionless. Each member was holding his breath, willing the iron monsters to pass them by without incident.

Suddenly, the Mil Mi-24, the lowest and closest, pulled sharply out of formation and climbed at full power away to the north. In a kneejerk reaction, the smaller aircraft, Mil Mi-8s, followed suit and circled off in the distance. In less than forty-five seconds the three returned, but this time the larger aircraft was at the center of the v-shaped wedge. All three gunships were facing the trail at the base of a sheer rock cliff.

"Uh, oh!" gulped CWO Gary Lawson, call sign ONE. He was peering through a small slit between the rocks. "Something just got their attention and it appears to be us." Pezlola peeked over the rock and saw what it was that Gary saw. The Russian gunships were hovering together about a half a click (kilometer) out, and at an altitude that seemed to be dead even with the motionless patrol members lying flat all along the rugged trail.

"Heads up, everyone," called Pezlola, depressing his throat mic. "Things are apt to get exciting in a moment. Stay quiet, hold your fire, stay put, and pass that word to the front." A group of successive double clicks was returned by Delta in rapid succession. Pezlola could hear Suleiman yelling orders in Pashto that he assumed meant everyone should kiss their ass goodbye.

The first of three rocket explosions hit thirty feet high on the rock wall above their heads. The second exploded somewhat lower, but its impact hit well beyond the last hidden member at the rear of the patrol. The third, however, hit directly on the path, just ten meters to the left of Lawson and Pezlola.

The shrapnel and pieces of rock instantly killed the two Afghans who were lying directly opposite the point of impact. One of the Delta Force members took a hit under his left armpit from a ricochet. Twenty-millimeter cannon fire commenced even before the sound of the last rocket explosion had dissipated. Six more rockets exploded mostly towards the front of the line. The Afghans were taking the worst of the attack.

Pezlola raised his head enough to look through the small space between the two boulders he was using as a shield. The Mil Mi-24 had moved to just three hundred meters from their position. The fire power demonstration went on for what seemed a small eternity.

"DELTA-1," said Pezlola, grinding his teeth into his throat mic. He had his right arm snug across his eyes to protect them from the stone splinters that were peppering the back of his hand. "Get Deccan and Goschich up and see if you can get a shot into that son-of-a-bitch. Target the upper cockpit windshield."

"Roger that," was the reply. "Break, break. You heard the man. Shoot the son-of-a-bitch, DELTA-2 – right the fuck now," he ordered. "DELTA-1, out."

Three days prior, just before leaving the ambush area of the copper mine, DELTA-1 (SFC George Angerome) had sent Delta Staff Sergeants Dennis Deccan and Pat Goschich, call signs DELTA-2 and DELTA-3, respectively, to retrieve the weapon of the sniper who had pinned them down in the mine shaft. The captured weapon turned out to be the Barrett M-82A1 complete with two bandoliers holding thirty-three rounds of .50 caliber ammunition, plus one fully-charged spare magazine.

"Pat, we'll do this on three. Spot me the target. Line us up," yelled DELTA-2, so he could be heard over the heavy raking action of the 20mm cannon fire.

"You got it." DELTA-3 began the count. "Two, three, go," he yelled, as he popped to his feet, throwing both his forearms flat on top of the boulder they were using for cover. Squaring his stance, he brought the single lens of the spotter's scope up and cupped it to his right eye. Holding it on target with his left hand he made one slight adjustment with his index finger. His right hand went to the switch on his throat mic.

"Target is at two o'clock; distance approximately three hundred fifty meters and hovering. Shoot the bastard," shouted DELTA-3 into his mic as well as into the ear of DELTA-2 as the cannon fire intensified all around them.

On the count of two, Deccan had chambered a round into the M82A1 and, just before the number three was announced, he had reached up and extended the pod legs on the weapon. On three he had risen to his feet only seconds behind Goschich. He immediately dropped the rifle down on the semi-flat surface of the boulder and pointed the barrel towards the Russian gunship. His left eye was slightly closed and his right eye was tightly cupped against the rubber eye guard of the scope. The view through the crosshairs brought the Mil Mi-24 very, very close. His right thumb pushed down on the safety release. He took in a full breath of air that smelled of pulverized rock and gunpowder. He slowly blew out. His finger moved inside the trigger guard, just barely touching the trigger itself.

"On target. Firing," he said, took in another full breath, and pulled the trigger three times halfway through the exhale.

13

A Buzzard's Fate

Russian Gunship Patrol – Air group ZK750
302nd Separate Helicopter Squadron
Konarha District of Afghanistan
Saturday 28 June 1986 0535 Hours

MAJOR MIKAEL VASDONAVITCH was the Section Commander of Air Group ZK750. His air group was part of the larger 302nd Separate Helicopter Squadron of the 5th Guard Motor-Rifle Division. This helicopter squadron had been relocated thirteen months before from the main Russian base near Kabul to the newly established airfield located just outside the town of Wama in the Konarha District.

Air Group ZK750 was on the last leg of the morning's mission and was within seven kilometers of their base, code name K561. The three gunships were cruising at an altitude of only 340 meters and were crawling along at 135 KPH. This formation strategy had become standard operating procedure, and it was designed to seduce the rebel force into engaging Russian aircraft.

The weather today was perfect for Vasdonavitch's mission. Unfortunately, there had been no contact with any rebel forces thus far and this patrol was almost over. He was running out of time to find something or someone to kill.

The Major's search and destroy mission had lifted off a full two hours before daybreak in hopes of catching a glimpse of one or more of the Mujahideen campfires. Vasdonavitch was the pilot in command, and this required him to be seated in the upper cockpit of the aircraft.

The largest gunship in today's operation, the Mil Mi-24 had been self-assigned to be in the most exposed position in the standard attack "V" formation. This configuration strategy was fully compliant with the standard operating procedures of Russian air-to-ground combat protocol. The heavier armored configuration of the Mi-24 would be positioned at a slightly lower elevation then the others. This would provide a slight shield for the other smaller and less armored Mi-8 aircraft from taking direct fire from the surrounding hills.

The helos proceeded through the last leg of their patrol through the largest of the mountainous passes in the region. Flying on the left side of the "V" formation, and ten meters below the others, the Major caught sight of a ground glint, a sparkle, just off to his left and halfway up the rolling hills to the left side of the aircraft. The area of the reflection was at the very point where the tree line met the sheer wall of rock that shot straight up for a hundred and fifty meters. Vasdonavitch knew full well that that area at the base of the cliffs was a trail known to be widely used by the insurgents.

His pilot's reflex was automatic and he immediately yanked the aircraft out of formation and accelerated away to the north and a much higher elevation. He called for the other two gunships to follow and join up immediately.

Once again, the three Russian gunships reformed in a hovering "V" shape, but this time the Mi-24 was at the center. They were facing the cliffs which were now over one-half kilometer from the suspected ground activity. This was the third time this morning they had performed this same maneuver. The radio order was given for all three gunships to slowly descend to four hundred meters and advance to within six hundred meters of the rock walls and the suspected targets.

At seven hundred meters, Major Vasdonavitch radioed the Mi-8s and ordered them to hang back while he closed the distance to five hundred and fifty meters. It was at this point that he opened fire on the area located at the base of the cliff wall.

The first volley came from the rocket pod mounted on the right side of the fuselage. He then moved his selector switch to guns and proceeded to sweep the base of the cliff with 20mm cannon fire. He moved the nose of the aircraft first down the path to the left and then slowly walked it back up the trail in the opposite direction.

The Major had just about decided that it was a false sighting and was about to break off contact. "ZK5, looks like another false alar—" was the partial message sent, but Vasdonavitch stopped abruptly mid-sentence.

Two individuals had popped up behind one of the larger boulders on the back side of the trail. One of the individuals was pointing a large, scoped weapon directly at him.

The Mil Mi-24 was hit by all three .50 caliber projectiles. The first and the second shots stunned Major Vasdonavitch greatly. One shot hit the metal roof just above the bubble-shaped windshield. The sound was deafening. The metallic impact of the armor-piercing ammunition ricocheted up into the case-hardened blades above. The second round hit just below the right side of the lower windshield of the co-pilot/gunner. This penetrated and completely destroyed some of the more important cockpit electronics. The third report was not heard by the Major at all.

This round came through the left side of the windshield and entered the right eye socket of the pilot. The sheer velocity of the steel-tipped projectile caused Vasdonavitch's head to disintegrate inside his helmet. The slug blew out the back of the Major's headgear and continued harmlessly through the bulkhead into the main cabin of the aircraft. The gunship turned sharply downward and violently to the right. The aircraft's downward push was immediate, spectacular, and final.

The speed of the crash was a direct result of an involuntary muscle spasm response by Vasdonavitch's death grip on the cockpit controls. The cyclic stick was yanked all the way to the right, the collective lever twisted itself to full military power, and the anti-torque pedals suddenly were without the necessary pressure for a lifesaving solution. The downward pressure on the rotor blades at this point was enormous. These facts, when combined with the extremely low altitude of the gunship, flung the iron bird like a pub dart, nose first into the ground. The resulting explosion and huge fireball would be documented in the historic record as being heard and seen by the Russian ground crews that were located over seven kilometers to the northwest at the air base designated as K561.

PART II

Three Years Earlier – 1982

Fort Bless Texas – White Sands New Mexico

14

The Right Stuff

The Whitehouse
1600 Pennsylvania Ave.
Washington, DC
Saturday 11 September 1982 1850 Hours

THANKS FOR COMING to see me, General," said President Ronald Reagan in his signature low whisper of a voice. "Since I got this job, working weekends has become the norm. If you would just take a seat right there," said the President, and pointed to one of the chairs positioned at the front of his desk.

As General Gerald Bushman, head of the Department of Defense (DOD) and Defense Intelligence Agency (DIA) sat down, POTUS added, "Now, I hope I haven't ruined your plans for this evening, Gerry."

"Of course not, Mr. President; I was just leaving my office when I got your message," replied Bushman.

"And how are things at DOD?"

"I'm searching for the right adjective, Mr. President," said the General with a twinkle in his eye.

The President chuckled at the response and asked, "How about a cup of coffee, Gerry?

"No thank you, Mr. President. I find these trips to this part of D.C. to be quite stimulating in and of themselves without adding any caffeine to the equation."

The President laughed and nodded his agreement. "Or, better yet, Gerry, how about coming upstairs for a drink?"

"Thank you, Mr. President. That would be very nice."

"Let's get out of here then," directed Reagan as he moved to the door. He placed his hand on the knob and turned towards the General and said, "I'll make this request as quick as I can, Gerry. Are you familiar with Executive Order 12633 that was issued in December of last year, regarding the use of the Stinger weapon system in Afghanistan? Code name Cyclone?"

"I am, Mr. President."

"Good," replied Reagan, and pulled open the door to the waiting face of his Secret Service protection. "Then you also know that the CIA, for one reason or another, has been dragging its feet in providing support to the Afghans," continued the President in his normal, conversational tone.

"As I understand it, the CIA has aligned itself with Pakistan's President Zia and his ISI. The flow of weapons into Afghanistan is being controlled by Zia's people, not CIA."

"That's my understanding of the situation also. Strange don't you think? It would seem to anyone looking in from the outside that the CIA was content with the present arrangement. The question is why?"

"Why are they content, or why are they placating Zia?" asked Bushman.

"Both good questions. The ISI is providing just enough aid to the Afghans to keep the Soviets bogged down. As I see it, the aid will never be enough for the Afghans to gain the upper hand. It's time for us to get off the dime and put the types of weapons needed directly into the hands of the people doing the fighting — and the dying. Wouldn't you agree, General?" asked the President as they entered the waiting elevator.

"Yes, Sir, I believe you've summed it up nicely. What is it that you want me to do, Sir?"

"Hold that thought until we get to the residence. I wouldn't want to say anything that would make my protection detail faint," smiled the President, as the Secret Service agent accompanying them remained completely stoic. The President's sense of humor was world class.

Nancy Reagan, and another member of the protection detail, was waiting in the vestibule when the two men arrived in the residence. Nancy stepped forward and kissed her husband on the cheek. She then turned her attention to the General by placing her hand on his right arm.

"Where did he get you from, Gerry?" she asked.

"I just happened to be passing by Mrs. Reagan."

"Right, and it is true that the moon is entirely made of blue cheese." She switched gears. "We've known each other for a while now, Gerry. Do please call me Nancy."

"Yes ma— Nancy, of course," replied Gerry.

"Let's sit over here." The President pointed to a leather sofa facing the fireplace. "What would you like to drink, Gerry?"

"Scotch, Sir. Single malt if you have it."

"No problem," replied Rawhide as he walked to the bookcase wet bar on the opposite wall. "Ice?" he asked, holding up an empty glass.

"Neat, if you please, Mr. President."

"I'd like to put you in charge of Operation Cyclone, General," Reagan said, handing over a glass containing a generous helping of Glenlivet 33 Year (Signatory, 1981). "The CIA will continue to manage and funnel ammunition and arms into Pakistan. The specialized weapon systems, such as our Stinger — our surface-to-air-missile technology — will now be completely under your shop's management. How you go about getting it done is totally up to you. The fly in the ointment will be President Zia's concern that Russia will do to Pakistan what they've been doing to Afghanistan. Since the invasion started in '79, both sides have pretended to not know what the other has been doing."

"Yes, Mr. President."

"I've already informed Bill Casey over at the CIA that DIA will be taking over the lead on this. I made sure he understands that any and all Afghan CIA resources presently in place will remain focused for the duration. Also, all required logistical assistance from the CIA going forward will be made available upon demand."

"Thank you, Mr. President."

"Gerry, I hope you understand that I'm not just banging on the microphone. I want this to be a real solution. Operation Cyclone is not only important to America, but to all the people around the world who are willing to stand up to the evil empire."

"Yes, Mr. President. Sir," Bushman added, "the Pakistani leadership, President ZIA and his ISI, have to this point dictated the quantity of arms and the speed of provisioning those arms to the Afghans. And so far, our CIA has acquiesced to this philosophy. If this had been any other country but Afghanistan being forced to resist with what they've been given ... well, Sir, it would be all over but the shouting by now."

"Stinger," said Reagan thoughtfully, "I have been told, will make all the difference in the Afghans' fight against the Russian invaders."

"If they're trained properly and shown how to strategically deploy it they'll be able to drive the Russians out of their country, Mr. President. What the Russians don't yet understand is that the Mujahideen are not concerned with politics. They are only focused on one thing: getting the Russians to leave their country. And, if that requires throwing rocks or killing soldiers with their bare hands, then that's what they'll do. Stinger will even up their fight. Hell, it may even win them the war."

"You believe that, Gerry?" asked the President. "This technology is capable of defeating the Russians?"

"Yes, Sir, I believe that will be the result and I have just the person in mind who can make that happen."

"Oh? Anyone I know?"

"His name is Rick Fontain. He headed up a Redeye team in Germany in '69. He ran several OPs for the CIA in connection with Soviet aircraft capabilities. In particular, the Mil Mi-24, their most deadly attack gunship. Neutralize this one component and the entire momentum will shift to the Afghans."

"Where have I heard that name before?" asked the President.

"He met with Congressman Wilson in '82. Zia shut the CIA down for unknown reasons. All efforts since then have failed. If any new opportunities have presented themselves since that time, I'm not aware of them."

"Are you ready for another drink, Gerry?"

"No, thank you, Mr. President. I've got one more stop to make before I go home. With your permission, I'll get started on this right away, Sir."

"Good. Keep me informed, Gerry."

"Yes, Sir. Goodnight," said General Bushman. He finished the last swallow of his drink and placed the glass on the coffee table in front of him.

The White House
Washington, D.C.
Stalling the Solution – 1982

Greenlighted by President Reagan in December 1982, Operation Cyclone had not made any progress for almost one year because of the stalemate by the Pakistani government. It wasn't so much that Pakistan objected to the U.S. Government's efforts to arm and assist the Afghan rebels, but rather their determination to control every aspect of weapons and ammunition moving through their country and earmarked for Afghanistan.

Whether this was done as a self-preservation technique or was just plain old-fashioned corruption of the system, the U.S. CIA didn't seem to be concerned either way. What started out as a management program to protect President Zia's government had become a bottleneck of control and power concerns. It had been almost four years since the Soviets invaded Afghanistan. Instead of becoming more efficient, the supply lines were becoming less and less productive. Fewer and fewer supplies were making it all the way to the front lines in Afghanistan. What had been genuine concern over the plight of Afghanistan was becoming more politicized every day.

The injection of Stinger technology into the war would pose problems on several fronts. First, for a sophisticated weapons system to be effective in this particular theater of operation, both operational skill and combat leadership needed to be present. Second, all top-secret weapon systems require a guarded and well thought out distribution plan. This was definitely true of Stinger. The agreement to proceed was never negotiated and Operation Cyclone had gone cold.

A development in January 1984 — an invitation to a meeting in Kuala Lumpur from a General Akhtar Abdur Rahman Khan of Pakistan to the CIA — presented the opportunity for a possible solution to be found to put the wind back in the sails of Operation Cyclone. However, the meeting was cancelled at the last minute by Maalouf Torki bin Taisei. No explanation was ever given.

Several attempts by the CIA to follow-up with General Khan failed. Their file on Khan, ISI's Director, Intelligence – Internal Services, confirmed his original claim that President Zia had given him the authority to negotiate a solution to inject Stinger into their neighbor's war. It was necessary to find a way that was acceptable to both the American CIA and the Pakistani leadership. It wasn't until July 1985, when I ran into Mr. Taisei in the elevator at his hotel in Dubai, that any progress had been made in setting up a meeting to discuss the Stinger weapon.

In a perfect world, I would be the subject matter expert who would fly in and interface with the Pakistan Intelligence Services (ISI). It would be the technical presentation that would wow them into accepting the CIA's terms and conditions.

And because we asked nicely, the ISI would provide the Stinger missile a safe haven for the training of the Mujahideen shooters. I could also expect a focused and unique distribution plan. And, once that was agreed upon, I could expect and receive safe access for the Stinger missiles into the mountainous regions of Afghanistan. Unfortunately, there is no such thing as a perfect world.

15

The Perfect Cover

Engineering Support Services
Operations Center – EAST
Cockeysville, Maryland
Friday 17 September 1982 0820 Hours

THE YEAR WAS 1982. This was my third, and hopefully the last, in the series of Bell Labs' on-the-job-training assignments. Each of these projects had provided the necessary hands-on experiences for my systems engineering education. My work life inside the vast corporate services network had been the most satisfying and rewarding thus far.

The start of this morning's activities would mark the beginning of a six-month rotation inside Network Systems Engineering Services Operation Center East. I was assigned to the Cockeysville, Maryland location not only for its East Coast proximity to Langley, Virginia but because it was known that this particular center's services were soon to be offered on the world stage. I was being groomed to play an important role in this corporation's move into the international marketplace.

Yet another reason for my presence in Cockeysville was the recent finding authorized by the President. The United States was going to kill some Russians. There was finally going to be some payback for our airplane drivers who lost their lives in Vietnam. Both the CIA and the DIA were gearing up to support the freedom fighters in Afghanistan.

The Defense Intelligence Agency was the main coordinator for the foreign military espionage organization of the United States. They operate exclusively under the jurisdiction of the Department of Defense. President Reagan's Executive Order 12633 in December 1981, code name *Operation Cyclone*, gave the intelligence communities a mandate to assist the Afghan people against the Russian invasion of their country. This had been seen by some as a movement that was two years late and many dollars short of possible.

A phone call I received at home the previous evening provided a heads-up for this morning's schedule. I would receive a call, I was told, about a project assignment that was activated the year before but had suddenly gone cold. The CIA was moving slowly in its participation to support the Afghan people being terrorized by the Russians. I found this perplexing. How could a Presidential finding be ignored?

I wouldn't be officially listed as an *illegal* until the end of this AT&T training assignment. (In espionage, agents under non-official cover, called "NOC", assume covert roles in organizations without official ties to the government for which they work. They are also known as "illegals".)

Why there had been failure to support the Afghans would be interesting to know. I wouldn't hold my breath waiting for the explanation. I was told, however, that the lack of support might have gone on indefinitely had it not been for a little known, but determined, Congressman from the great state of Texas.

The head of the DIA, Lt. Gen. Gerald Bushman, told me that his office had been approached by Congressman Charlie Wilson. Wilson was looking for a method to shoot down the Russian attack helicopters. The Russian invaders in Afghanistan were conducting mass murder. The primary instrument being used was a gunship with a factory designation of Mil Mi-24.

Little had the Congressman known that just that past week the President had tapped the General's office to provide the very thing that Charlie wanted done. A recently prepared CIA report revealed that the main instrument being used in the rape of Afghanistan was a Russian aircraft known as the Mil Mi-24. My name had immediately flashed into the general's mind.

In 1969, then Sergeant Fontain of the 3rd Armor Division, I had run a successful Redeye surveillance action called *Sparrow View*. The OP had taken place at Tillyschanze on the German border with Czechoslovakia. The purpose of the task was to capture the engine infra-red and heat signatures of the newly developed Russian attack gunship that was given the NATO code name "The Hind".

The briefing documents given to me in June of 1969 described the Mil Mi-24 as a large helicopter gunship with both attack and low-capacity troop transport capabilities. It was reported to have been developed by the Mil Moscow Helicopter engineering and manufacturing facility. Since its formal introduction onto the world stage in the early 1970s Soviet pilots have affectionately nicknamed the Mi-24 the "flying tank". The unofficial nicknames in 1969 were "Crocodile" and "Drinking Glass" because of the flat glass plates defining the dual cockpits located on the nose of the metal behemoth.

General Dynamics, in conjunction with Bell Labs and Lockheed, had devised a method to record aircraft engine signatures. The extraordinary device was a modified version of the very portable Redeye shoulder-fired, guided missile tracker/trainer system. Specifically designed as an aimed sensor array, its specialized targeting software was designed to apprehend infrared and heat engine profiles.

My knowledge of both Redeye and the Mil Mi-24 was why General Bushman immediately earmarked me for this project. The more significant reasoning for involving me was the little-known fact that the Stinger missile system was actually the second generation of the Redeye weapons program. I was read into Operation Cyclone and was assigned to interface and coordinate with the General Dynamics and Raytheon Corporation's Stinger manufacturing and training facilities.

It was on March 6, 1968 that Lt. Gen. Gerald Bushman, USMC, while serving in Vietnam, was nominated by President Richard M. Nixon to become the Deputy Director of the CIA. The very next year DDCI Bushman was charged with the modification of NATO's War Plan MC 14/3C, Western Europe's response to a Russian invasion. Several major operations were implemented that year and I was involved in all of them.

General Bushman was also Janice Prasonio's grandfather. Doctor/ Captain Janice Prasonio and I had fallen head over heels in love with each other just as *Operation Sparrow View* in 1969 was concluding. It was a short-lived romance, however. A drunken German truck driver broadsided Janice's car just three blocks from the U.S. Army hospital in Nuremberg where she was assigned. The General and I had remained quite close over the years.

On the morning of September 17, 1982, I had arrived especially early to my Cockeysville office. The General had told me to expect a call from Daryl Russell – Russian Desk – between 0800 and 0830 hours. The call came at exactly 0820 hours.

Daryl and I had also become friends during the CIA-sponsored operations in Germany. Since then, Daryl had overseen my CIA training and coordinated my field assignments with the management at Bell Labs. Our homes in Maryland were just a few miles apart and our two families got together socially quite often. Hanna and Daryl's wife, Darcy, had become the very best of friends over the years.

I had just refilled my coffee mug and was winding my way back through the maze of gray metal desks. My assigned space at the center was located towards the back wall on the south side of the building. The double electronic ringtone was sounding on the 2500 station set as I approached, indicating that an outside call was about to arrive.

"Good morning. Fontain speaking," I answered. It was Daryl Russell.

After a brief conversation to catch up and define what needed to be done, Daryl added a third party to the call. The Raytheon Corporate Executive VP, Barry Flax, came on the line. Barry was also an old acquaintance. He and his former company, General Dynamics, had participated in the 1969 CIA operation that became known as *Aim of the Sparrow*. It was a remarkable exhibition of Redeye missile technology that demonstrated America's commitment against the threat of a Russian incursion into Western Europe. The spectacular display took place high over OP (pronounced Oh Pee) Alpha, located at the midpoint entrance to the famous Fulda Gap, the gateway of countless invasions of Western Europe from the East.

"Well, I'll be damned! I couldn't believe my ears when my secretary announced who was calling so early in the morning."

"Barry, it's good to hear your voice. How have you been?" I asked.

"Hey Barry, it's Daryl; it's been way too long, man."

"You two still working for my favorite Uncle?" asked Barry.

"Now you know better than to ask that. We could tell you but then we would have to kill you," I replied, laughing at my own corny wit.

"Barry," said Daryl, "I know you're a very busy man so I'll get right to the point. Rick needs to get into your FIM-92 course, preferably the one starting on the twenty-first."

"Jesus Christ, Daryl, you're not talking about the twenty-first of this month, are you? This coming Monday is what you mean? Why didn't you just wait until Sunday night or even Monday morning to call?"

"Hey *Bear* ... it's only Friday. You have all weekend to make it happen," I teased.

"That's very funny, Rick. I see you haven't lost your sense of humor."

"Sorry for the short notice, Barry," Daryl quickly interjected, "but this just fell down on us from Mt. Olympus. Rick needs to update his bedside manner on Stinger. He doesn't need to become a subject matter expert by next week, but he does need to be able to *talk the talk* and articulate which end of the tube the missile shoots out."

"Oh, I assure you, Daryl that he knows what end the missile pops out. The first time I had the pleasure of meeting him was just after he had destroyed one of my very expensive jet target drones."

"Barry, he needs to be brought up to date on Stinger's recent software updates and be able to describe its finer features to eager students in an outdoor classroom setting. There are people who are highly pissed at uninvited Russian military employees who have taken up residence in their country."

"Come on, Bear," I wheedled again. "I have it on good authority that you practically run the Raytheon Corporation."

"Is that so, Rick?" replied Flax. "I hadn't heard that. Daryl, what number can I get you back on?"

"Call Rick. I'm unreachable 'til Tuesday. I'm walking to the transport as we speak. Rick will know how to get hold of me if necessary. Rick, give Barry the best number to call you back on. Barry, I can't express how much we appreciate you doing this."

"Just like old times, right, Bear? You want my office number or my home number?" I asked.

"Give me the home number. I won't be able to set it up until late this evening."

"That number is 298.5766. The Maryland area code is three zero one. The machine will be on if I don't pick up. Are you in El Paso next week?"

"You said 5566?" Rick could hear Barry scribbling the numbers down.

"No, it's two nine eight five seven six-six."

"Yeah, I'm in all week," replied Barry. "Do you have a place to stay or do you want me to arrange quarters at the school?"

"No to both. I don't want to mix with the students outside of class. I'm open for any suggestions, Bear."

"We have a house leased outside of Bliss. When I call to confirm the course availability, let me know your flight information. I'll have a friend of yours pick you up."

"Thank you, that's very nice of you. A friend?" I inquired.

"You'll see," replied Barry.

"Oh, I almost forgot to ask: is civilian attire permitted or should I scrounge up some fatigues?"

"Civvies are OK. We've had several groups come through the course from NSA and DIA. One of the men came dressed in a dark, three-piece business suit. As you can imagine, he didn't fare very well out in the desert." The heat experienced at White Sands during the live fire training can duplicate, almost to the centigrade, playing nine holes of golf in Dubai.

"OK, I guess that does it," Daryl said, laughing and moving the conversation to a conclusion. "Thanks for dealing with the short notice, Barry."

"OK, you two. I'll be in touch, Rick." The line went silent.

Barry had disconnected from the call. Daryl went on to say, "I'll get Coover to call your boss down there and explain the sudden trip requirement."

Don Coover was a third level manager in Bell Labs. His office was on the Holmdel campus in New Jersey. He was one of only four corporate people who knew about my connection to the CIA.

"OK, let me call Don first and get our story straight. Some kind of a cabling project in New Mexico I would think is the way to go. I'll let him know you will be phoning in the project request."

"That sounds good. Do that right after we hang up."

"Will do," I said. "I'll leave word with your office as soon as I hear back from Barry."

"Good luck in El Paso," said Daryl and clicked off.

I immediately walked over to the Engineering Center's administrative assistant, Dorothy Mathieson, to solicit her expertise for arranging travel through Carson Wagonlit, the official corporate travel agency. The request produced a TWA ticket to El Paso County, Texas. My five exciting days inside the U.S. Army's professionally-staffed Raytheon FIM-92 Stinger training center was about to be under way. The date and time for the return trip had been left open-ended per the instructions of DHIC Russell.

16

The Reunion

US Army Stinger Training Center
Course: FIM-92
El Paso, Texas
Sunday 19 September 1982 1435 Hours

I T HAD BEEN a little over fourteen years since I had been in El Paso County, Texas. The last time I had landed at this particular airport was the summer of 1968. I had arrived in Texas for the first time armed with my newly acquired secret clearance and a special set of orders assigning me to the U.S. Army's newly formed FIM-43 course. The Military had received the world's first shoulder-fired guided missile system and was in the process of training a select number of people to literally launch the technology.

The amazing weapon system had been created by the General Dynamics Corporation for deployment into a very cold war. The tri-week course of instruction consisted of one full week in the classroom being versed in the miracle of the missile. There were two additional weeks of hands-on training that took place in the wilds of the White Sands Missile Range in New Mexico. All three weeks were tailor-made for the shooter to become proficient in destroying multimillion-dollar enemy aircraft. Of course, the survival of the Redeye Gunner while being strafed, bombarded, and shelled was always a major concern and the most exciting part of the training.

In 1968 General Dynamics delivered to the military establishment effective, relevant, and affordable products and services. All training was held at Fort Bliss and the White Sands Missile Range, respectively, and all products were designed to scare the crap out of any airplane driver anywhere in the world of war.

This new missile technology was being delivered to the U.S. Army for the first time — hence the requirement for the development and training of personnel on the man-portable, surface-to-air, missile system. This, of course, required continuous hours of study under one 20-watt light bulb. The light was strategically located in the center of the barracks ceiling. The room itself was equipped to accommodate 80 plus students. Some say that this one feature was solely responsible for the development of the miracle drug called Visine.

Hence, the name Redeye was established. It isn't quite clear how many students went blind reading Redeye manuals. Other sources suggest the name Redeye was actually a reference to the infrared sensor array installed in the nose cone of each missile. (Those sources happen to be correct.)

The FIM-92, nicknamed Stinger, replaced Redeye in 1975, and had become the next generation of hand-held, ground-to-air weapons systems. Not only was Stinger faster than its predecessor, its enhanced software packaging enabled it to be customized for a wide variety of combat solutions. This new set of features was what I needed to digest in order to be successful in my new career assignment as a missile salesman in the Middle East.

17

Homecoming

1968

1983

El Paso International Airport
El Paso County Texas
Sunday 19 September 1982 1550 Hours

THE TWA DC-9 touched down on 26R at 1530 hours, which was twelve minutes ahead of the expected arrival time. The pilot taxied the aircraft through the third exit ramp. He then proceeded to trot it half-way down the service drive, turning the aircraft directly towards the closest terminal. From my window seat, I saw that there were several nice touches added since my last visit. A huge letter "B" protruded from the brand-new roof of the building that the aircraft was approaching.

In 1968, on my maiden voyage from the Advanced Infantry Training Center at Fort Dix to this very same airport, all aircraft were forced into the long-term parking pavilion located 170 miles from the wooden shack holding an informational sign naming it for what it was designed. Baggage Claim was well named — but only for the lucky few who would actually find their luggage.

In 1968's El Paso, passengers who survived the rather lengthy walk across the tarmac to claim their luggage were asked to wait behind an electri-fied metal fence. To this day, I'm still not sure if it was meant to keep people out of the baggage claim area or to keep the trained luggage stackers from escaping. In either case, what the stackers created was a work of art. Truly something to behold: an un-scalable pyramid constructed out of recently delivered luggage. This provided each and every arriving passenger a complete view of the ordeal they were about to experience. What made it really interesting, for the civilians especially, was that all newly arrived luggage was placed on the very bottom of the heap. Bags that had been unclaimed for the past ten years were always moved from the warehouse and stacked neatly on top for each new incoming flight.

Today, however, I smiled inwardly as the aircraft pulled into one of the brand-new jetways for Terminal B. As I departed the aircraft into the modern airport complex I almost chuckled out loud at the memory of the old airport's baggage claim ordeal. This earned me a curious look from the good-looking flight attendant manning the cabin exit door.

"It's OK," I said. "I just remembered I didn't pack any underwear."

"I never pack any either," she whispered and smiled broadly at me as I exited into the jetway.

"No shit," I said to myself, and continued laughing all the way up the gangway and out onto the main concourse.

I had carried on a single piece of luggage and a briefcase for this trip. I followed the signs and proceeded directly to the front entrance of the airport. Barry, the Raytheon VP, had arranged for "a friend" to meet my plane and transport me to a Raytheon guesthouse, which was described as being "not far" from the Fort Bliss Main Post.

I walked outside into the warm Texas sunshine and stood under the large lettering spanning the roofline which identified El Paso as the *Home of the Sun Bowl*. For a Sunday, there wasn't much car or foot traffic for this time of the day. Off to the right side of the half circle driveway there stood a tall, well set up individual wearing a black Stetson cowboy hat. He was standing next to a late model, white Chevy Suburban. He was holding a clipboard at chest level, and on it large block letters spelling "FONTAIN" were clearly displayed.

"Hi, I'm Fontain," I said to the cowboy chauffeur as I walked up on the individual holding the sign. "Thanks for coming to pick me up on a Sunday."

"No problem at all, Rick. I was delighted to hear it was you who was coming in this afternoon."

"Oh, how so?" I asked with some of my apprehension radar coming online with the unexpected comment.

"Andy Davis, Rick." He touched the brim of the Stetson slightly and extended his hand towards me.

"Good to meet you ... Andy. Oh, my God. I'll be damned! It's you, Sergeant!"

"Yep, it's me alright. But it's just Mister now-a-days, Rick. Our destiny, young man, is what I suspect to be true. We are damned if we do and damned if we don't."

"I surmise you have inhaled way more than your share of rocket motor fumes, Mr. Davis."

"I have always admired your quick grasp of the situation, PFC Fontain."

"How was your all-expense paid trip to the Aleutian Islands, Andy?" I asked the former Sergeant First Class Andy Davis, who was now laughing loudly and completely enjoying the exchange. Andy pulled open the rear passenger-side door and tossed my carry bag and briefcase on the leather seating.

Andy had been the Instructor/Spotter (cadre supervisor) on the day I had earned a slot to live fire the infamous Redeye weapon system. The FIM-43 course in 1968 gave the firing privilege to the five students who had scored the highest grades. Andy had tapped me on the shoulder and shouted the words "*shoot, shoot, shoot.*" This one event had changed both of our lives, forever.

Andy rounded the front of the Chevy truck, pulled open the driver's side door, stepped up on the running board, and slid easily into the driver's seat. He started the engine and eased us out onto the airport turn-about. He took the first exit ramp towards the west, which dumped us down onto Montana Avenue.

"PFC Fontain, your $400,000 'kill shot' on Barry Flax's target drone changed my entire military career."

"*Oh boy, hear it comes,*" I thought, and pushed my ass deeper down into the comfort of the bucket seat.

"Well, by the looks of the hat you're wearing you must have abandoned your desire to outshine Audie Murphy. Did you up and quit the Army to join the rodeo?" I asked.

"Not really, but there are those who work for GD-Ray that would say it is very much like being in the rodeo," replied Andy, laughing.

"GD-Ray?" I asked.

"General Dynamics-Raytheon," explained Andy, who turned to smile in my direction. "It's hard to imagine, but the corporate world uses more god-damn abbreviations than the Army ever did."

"I'm sorry for having left you at the altar that day, Andy. But they whisked me away to Fireman School at Fort George G. Meade. I still have the rash from the asbestos underwear that they made me wear."

Andy looked over at me and said, "I see you still have that wonderful gift of gab. Just the right amount of bullshit delivered in a tone with such sincerity. It's no wonder Barry wound up thanking us for shooting down one of his very expensive toys."

"Barry told me that you were doing very well as his corporate 'dog rob-ber' when we ran into each other in Germany in sixty-nine. He said you were very good at making problems disappear."

"He told me he ran into you but didn't elaborate."

"I told him what you said our choices were the day we met him. As the burning drone was put out by the Air Force's Fire Rescue service, you had listed our somber choices. One, repairing of mess kits in the Aleutian Islands or two, a cushier assignment lashed to a modified tow-array on one of Barry's remaining target drones." Andy and I had thought our asses were grass because of a mistake I had made. Because he was smart, and kept his cool, Andy had turned the proverbial lemon into lemonade.

"Actually," Andy replied, chuckling, "as it turned out there was a third choice. Barry had me assigned as the Army's liaison officer coordinating between the school at Bliss and General Dynamics-Pomona manufacturing facility."

"No shit. You said officer? You took a walk on the dark side?"

"CW3, Chief Warrant Officer, retired. Now I work directly for the man."

"I'll be damned. You look great. Whatever you are doing now really seems to agree with you."

"It does and I have you to thank for the opportunity."

"Right," I said, laughing. Not sure where this part of the conversation was heading I asked, "How so?"

"Barry returned to the school for the second time after some big hush-hush operation in Fulda. I think the timeframe was towards the end of 1969. The next day he asked me to take on additional responsibilities within his corporate group. I was already coordinating all of the Bliss school activities for him. He pulled some strings, got me promoted, and took very good care of me until I retired three years ago. I'm head of security at Raytheon now. I think that day in the desert changed everything. I have you to thank for all of that." The Suburban took the next exit which was marked RT-478 north.

"Come on, Andy. Really?" I asked.

"Barry told me a few years after I went to work for him what you did and said about that day in the desert."

"Look Andy, I'm sure Barry came to you because he realized what a standup guy you are."

"Maybe so, but Barry repeated word for word what you told him. You know he is your biggest fan?"

"He told you I thought you were gay?" I offered up in a half serious tone. This caused Andy to whip his head around to look directly at me. Of course, I was smiling my biggest.

"There it is again. I think you missed your calling as a stand-up comedian."

"Seriously Andy, what I should have done years ago, was to seek you out and personally thank you for standing up for me that day."

"You did that same day — several times, if memory serves me correctly. But, besides that, there is another event that I can't begin to repay."

"You lost me, Andy. Now what in the hell are we talking about?"

"Does the name Staff Sergeant Mike Davis ring a bell?" Staff Sergeant Mike Davis, an Army Green Beret, was a member of the A-team who was wounded, along with several others, in a hairy landing zone (LZ) in northern Laos.

"Yeah, I know Mike. Good guy. You two related?"

"He's my brother. And he told me how you behaved in a hot LZ."

"You should know that I was the only non-professional at the party that day. I believe it was Mike who pulled my dumb ass back in the chopper. Andy, you know Mike could get himself in a lot of trouble for telling you stories about that particular road trip."

"In '73 he got dinged and was home on leave. He came down to Bliss to visit and we spent three days catching up. I told him about my job. I told about the circumstances surrounding my good fortune and I mentioned you by name. Well, Mikey stopped taking a pull on his beer and very softly uttered the words, 'No shit.' Then he started laughing and couldn't stop. He finally calms down and in a very serious tone says that if it is the same guy, we are both privileged to be acquainted with one of the craziest motherfuckers ever to walk the earth."

"Andy, I can't tell you how many years I spent thinking that mother was only half a word."

"What?" asked Andy, not understanding the comment.

"Never mind, Andy. It is truly a small, a very small, goddam world."

"You got that right, Rick."

"I have pondered long and hard the good fortune of having crossed paths with soldiers like you and Mike. Let's change the subject, shall we?"

"For now, Rick, but I would like a rain check." Andy guided the Chevy down the off ramp and north onto SR-54.

"We're going out to an area called the Devil's Tower. The house is being leased to the DOD from one of the big muckety-mucks who manages the Intel Research Labs here in El Paso."

"Is Barry in town?" I inquired.

"He'll be in later tonight," replied Andy, and then was silent for almost a minute.

"Anyway," said Andy, starting up the conversation once again. "Barry got a phone call last night from corporate. The board has directed him to receive three VIPs this week, one of whom is a congressman from Texas. Any idea what that's all about? Or, for that matter, why they're coming all the way down here for a sit-down?"

"No, haven't got a clue. But it does sound interesting," I replied.

"General Bushman, DOD/DIA, that's the Defense Department's intelligence agency, called Barry on Friday afternoon. Barry said he started off the conversation by thanking him for arranging the course time. He then gave him a heads up on the corporate arrangement. Can you shed any light on that?

"I know the General. If he's paving the way for these people, then the visit is being sanctioned by the highest levels of government."

"So, you're not going to tell me?" asked Andy lightly.

"Andy, let's get something straight. The people we work for require us to remain professionally stoic at all times. It means that we only share information on a need-to-know basis. Having said that, I confess to you that it appears you have way more information about this week's activities than I do. I was told I was coming down here on Friday morning and that's all I was told."

This wasn't the whole truth, but for the purpose of this conversation it would have to suffice. According to the General, the President was a bit miffed with the CIA. I had been read-in on Operation Cyclone by the CIA almost one year ago, to the day. I had not been told anything more on the subject until the previous Friday. The President of the United States wanted to get off the dime and arm the Afghan Freedom Fighters with the types of weapons that would assist them in removing the Russian invaders from their country. Stinger, in a trained hand, would go a long way towards accomplishing that objective.

"Rick, I'll respect that, but know this. I've already been told by Barry that it's been decided that I'll be going with you to assist with setting up the logistics of deployment and the training."

"No shit. Any idea where that might be?" I replied, laughing.

"Like you don't! But once we all get on the same page let's start sharing, shall we?"

"You got it, Andy. Perhaps the congressman will shed some light on what's next."

"Nah," replied Andy, "they are all a bunch of trained liars. The best we can hope for is a smile and a quick stab in the back." Andy turned the Suburban onto Titanic Avenue, heading due west toward an area known for its magnificent view. "The residence is located at the end of this road. I think you'll find it rather charming."

"Oh, did Barry hire a flock of French maids?" I chuckled. As the rugged, but beautiful, countryside went zooming past I added, "It really is beautiful here, isn't it?"

"Son, you just hold that thought."

Barry's Retreat
2097 Devil's Tower View
El Paso County Texas
Sunday 19 September 1982 1640 Hours

Andy guided the Chevy between the two massive, cut stone pillars as the wrought iron gates eased into a fully opened position. There was a fourteen-foot fence that surrounded the mountaintop complex. The sections of fence that extended outward from both sides of the huge pillars also seemed to be constructed out of wrought iron. I saw three separate buildings appear through the windshield. The landscape engineering perfectly complemented the natural terrain. The devil was a long way from home in this high elevation property.

As we ended our journey up the seven-hundred-foot paved driveway, Andy pulled directly in front of the center bay door of what was recognizably a carriage house/garage. There were three, twelve-foot-high, double-wide bay doors crowned with a cedar-shake, hip-style roof. Four large, abbey-style dormers protruding outward suggested that a large living space resided above.

"You weren't kidding about the view," I said, but Andy had already exited the vehicle and was pulling open the rear passenger door to get my carry bag.

"You say something, Rick?"

"I said you weren't kidding about the French maids. Old Barry is really in high cotton this time."

By the time I climbed down from the Suburban onto the courtyard pavers the gates had returned to their normal closed position. The main house was located off to the left side of the carriage house. A paver walkway of a contrasting color wound its way up from the driveway to the front entrance. There was a third, very large, A-frame structure further off and slightly lower to the left of the main house. The second level of the A-frame faced directly towards the city of El Paso, and was constructed almost entirely out of glass.

"What a gorgeous place, Andy," I said as I pried my bag from his hand. Andy acquiesced and pointed towards the walkway and the main entrance of the villa. The view, as well as the house, was indeed spectacular.

"Wow, is that the city of El Paso way over there?"

"Yep, and it's even prettier at night — that is, when all the lights come on. Let's go inside."

One side of the double wooden doors was pulled open as we approached the portico. Andy stepped to the side and motioned for me to enter.

"Consuela, this is Mr. Fontain. He'll be staying with us this week."

"Si, Senor Flax told me yesterday to take very good care of you."

"Thank you. That is very nice of you. Please call me Rick, Consuela."

"Si, Senor Rick. Follow me and I'll show you to your room. I have it all ready for you."

"Thank you. Andy, are you going to hang around?"

"Yeah, I'll be here a while. The boss has promised to call when he gets close."

The Devil's Tower
2097 Devil's Tower Circle
El Paso County Texas
Sunday 19 September 1982 1710 Hours

The Devil's Tower estate was constructed in 1978. Its purpose was to provide a secure conference center and safe-house environment for a select number of corporate and government agencies. At present, the compound was being utilized and managed by the Raytheon Corporation.

There were three separate buildings on the campus. The main villa consisted of four levels. There were fourteen guest rooms with baths, including four VIP master suites, located on the top two levels. The first floor was dedicated to the complete entertainment experience. Every creature comfort was considered in the design. A huge gourmet commercial kitchen could prepare for and attend to twenty-plus hungry inmates within its own dining alcove. There was a first-class home theater that provided leather recliner seating for twenty-four (three rows of eight, with center aisle), a game room boasting three regulation-size pool tables, and a fully equipped spa and exercise center located in the basement level.

Also, there was a large swimming pool that could be accessed from the rear of the second-floor landing. The house was nestled into the top of this mountain property, and the space for the pool was carved out of rock directly behind and slightly to the left of the main house.

The three-bay carriage house situated to the right side of the main house held a dual function. The second level provided office space and two additional apartments for the security staff. The AT&T Dimension PBX System cabinets and cross-connect frames, a security surveillance center displaying twenty-four CCTV monitors with 19-inch, rack mounted VCRs, a shitload of perimeter sensor status panels, plus the motorized gate controls and intercom, were terminated here and monitored around the clock.

The third building, called the executive conference center, was the large A-frame structure situated just ninety meters to the left of the main house. A wider walkway was attached to the main house at two locations. One avenue of the stone path led directly to the dining facility located just inside the kitchen side entrance. The other wound its way around to the main driveway. There were two large classrooms plus a first-class lounge with a fully stocked bar on the first level. The second level was configured with eight, first class executive suites with all the comforts of home, including color TVs and tile floors throughout. Seven of the rooms were occupied this week by personnel from three, non-English-speaking countries. None of them, however, were visitors from Afghanistan.

I bounced down the staircase and headed towards the rear of the foyer. I could smell something wonderful cooking as I moved down the main hall-way. The marvelous aroma reminded me that I hadn't eaten since breakfast. I found Andy just outside the large lounge, in a room that had the look and feel of a European men's club. He was standing in front of a large marble structure nursing a beer. As I walked up I could see three pool tables lined up in the center of the adjoining room.

"There you are. I was getting worried that you got lost," said Andy.

"This place is certainly large enough to do just that," I replied as I slid onto the bar stool next to where Andy was standing.

"How about a drink?" asked Andy.

"One of those looks good," I said, pointing at Andy's bottle of Coors. "We can't get any of that on the East Coast yet. Any word from your boss?"

"He called a few minutes ago," Andy said as he walked around the business side of the bar, opened the ice chest and pulled out a beer. "His ETA is about an hour. You want to wait and have dinner together or would you rather eat now?"

"No, I'm good. Besides, I don't want to be hugging the little bastard on a full stomach."

"Outstanding. I think he's pretty excited about seeing you, too."

"What's this bar made out of? Marble?" I asked.

"Funny story: the original owner who built this place had it removed from a church renovation in Italy. It's supposed to date back to the fifteenth century. Do you see these little glass covered holes in the marble? Supposedly, they contain the relics of saints."

I looked down at the bar top, raising both of Andy's hands about six inches off the marble to examine what he'd just described.

"Well, this is my first time committing mortal sin by just drinking a beer, Andy."

I got off the bar stool, took a sip of beer, and backed up to examine the entire structure. Sure enough, it was a complete church altar. Actually it was three separate alters rejoined into one, which had been converted into a very good looking and functional watering hole.

"How about a snack while we wait?" offered Andy, who seemed to be fumbling with something down towards the floor.

"That would be wonderful." I sat back down. "What are you doing back there?"

"There's supposed to be a toe-kick button down here that calls the kitchen." Just then Consuela came strolling in with a tray held high above her head. She lowered it and placed it on the bar in front of where I was sitting.

"Here is something to munch on before dinner. It is my special layered buffalo chicken nachos with creamy gorgonzola sauce. I hope you like it."

"Consuela, you're a life saver. I was about to die from starvation," I said, picking up a nacho and popping it in my mouth. "These are good." I picked up another and put it quickly on top of the one already in my mouth.

"You're a mind reader, Consuela. I was just trying to call the kitchen," said Andy.

"Si, Mr. Andy," she said and went behind the bar to where Andy was still standing. "The copper plate," she said and pointed towards the base of the bar. "You just tap it with your foot, and it will signal the kitchen."

"Thanks. I've seen Mr. Flax do it several times but always from the far side of the bar."

"You're welcome. Will you wait for Mr. Barry to arrive before having dinner?"

"Yes, if that is OK with you?" asked Andy.

"Of course. Just let me know when you are ready," she said and left the room after nodding slightly at me.

"Is this a private party or can we all join in?" asked the tall, silver haired gentleman standing in the hallway entrance to the bar. There was another, younger man standing slightly to his rear who was scanning the room quietly, conducting his own personal threat analysis.

The older man was very well known to me. His name was Lt. Gen. Gerald Bushman. The other individual was definitely CIA, but I drew a blank as to who he was. I couldn't quite place a name with the face.

"Sir, this is indeed a pleasant surprise. We were just about to go pick up Mr. Flax," I said and put my hand out towards the general. The hand was ignored and I received a warm embrace.

"Rick, this is Mike Vaughn," said the General, indicating the man standing behind him.

"Bingo. I knew I knew the face," I said to myself. *"Now I know where we met."*

"He's going to audit the FIM-92 course this week," continued the General.

"Mike, glad to see you again," I said and shook his hand. "I think we were at the farm together a few years back."

"June, seventy-nine," replied Vaughn. "Surveillance Detection Avoidance training, right?"

"Yeah, that sounds about right. The Pilgrims of Williamsburg will never be the same," I replied.

"How so?" asked the General.

"Mike stole a costume from one of the re-enactors in Williamsburg. I think it was a Pilgrim, and Mike here left him half naked on the men's room floor."

"He was the Town Crier, you idiot, not a Pilgrim," admonished Mike.

Not to be chided, I added, "This, of course, was not what our instructor expected of young men studying to be super spies. The fact that we managed to avoid being arrested saved us from being thrown out of the agency."

"I'll have you know I traded that Town Crier my very best and very expensive Brooks Brothers sports jacket."

"I think it was stealing his pants that upset him the most," I countered.

"Bullshit, I gave him my slacks as well. He seemed all right with the trade at the time," replied Vaughn, who had stopped laughing and was getting noticeably upset with my version of this story.

"OK, you two," said the General. He was laughing at the exchange. "You can update your after-action reports later. Right now, I need a word with you, Rick."

"Sir, this is Andy Davis. He works for Mr. Flax," I said.

"It's an honor, Sir," said Andy, as he walked over and shook hands with the General. He then turned to face Mike Vaughn. "Mugging a forefather, huh?"

"And this is Mike Vaughn, the famous Pilgrim mugger," I said as Andy and Mike shook hands.

"Town Crier, here. Glad to meet you Andy," said Mike.

"Andy, where's a good place the General and I can talk?" I asked.

"The theater is right down the hallway on the left. It's quiet and private"

"Let's go have that chat, Rick. Mike, you stay here with Mr. Davis," said the General.

"Yes, Sir," replied Mike the Pilgrim Mugger.

As we walked down the hallway the General asked, "How's Hanna?"

"She's good. She's been given more responsibility at the embassy. She seems quite happy."

We entered the room through the front entrance and took the two center seats. One word came to mind as I looked around the room. Plush. The rich pile carpeting, the leather recliner seating, and the huge screen built into the front wall all screamed extravagance.

"Rick, this project has been stalled for a little over a year. I haven't been officially told yet, but we may be asked to stand down one more time while we try again to negotiate with President Zia."

"Sir, should I reschedule this training?"

"No, take the course and finish with your assignment in Cockeysville. We'll reset our timeline for injecting Stinger technology into Afghanistan once Pakistan drops their insistence on control of the operation."

"What kind of timeframe do you expect, Sir?"

"We're hoping the good Congressman Wilson will plead our case with President Zia once he understands the DIA and CIA mandates on this weapons system. We'll continue to insist on absolute over watch for this weapon. I'm afraid there's not any wiggle room on this point with the DOD. Did Barry tell you the Congressman was coming down here this week?"

"Andy told me on the way from the airport. Who's he meeting with? Are you here to greet these VIPs?"

"No, and it's just the Congressman and some of his staff. I've been asked to keep an arm's length from the Congressman. That's why I brought Mike down here from D.C. He sits on the Iran/India desk. He reports indirectly to a fellow named Gust Avrakotos. You know who he is?"

"Never met him, but Douglas says he's one capable guy."

"He is that, and then some. Up until these past few months no one at the Agency has taken Wilson seriously. Gust, on the other hand, has really hit it off with Wilson. He's been the only ray of sunshine in the Congressman's long but disappointing relationship with the CIA. They have two things in common: the plight of Afghan people and an insatiable desire to kill Russians."

"Do you want me involved with the meeting with the Congressman?"

"Yes, we might as well get the two of you interacting." He continued, "Pakistan has consistently denied that they are providing military assistance to Afghanistan. Zia knows he's walking a fine line with the Russians. He doesn't want them coming across his border."

"Makes sense," I said. "How do we resolve the management and control issues with Stinger?"

"We are aren't sure they can be resolved. Getting Zia's approval will be only half the battle. The Pakistani ISI, military intelligence, is actually the group insisting that they be allowed to say who gets what and when."

"Can the Congressman help with that conversation too?"

"Perhaps, yes. Perhaps, no. That's why I asked for Mike Vaughn to attend this week. He has an excellent understanding of the top people in the ISI. Once we get to second base with President Zia we'll be better equipped to lay out a strategy for a meet and greet with some of those folks. Or, better yet, bring them here for a sit-down."

"Yes, Sir, I'll feel the Congressman out to see what he thinks our chances are with President Zia. Andy told me that Barry has asked him to make himself available to set up the training once we get that far in the negotiations."

"That's good to know. Mr. Davis comes highly recommended from the Bliss Training Command."

"OK, Sir. I think I have an understanding of what you want done."

"I know you'll do what you do best, Rick."

"What's that, Sir?"

"Selling ice cubes to Eskimos and water to the drowning. On a serious note, Rick, I believe Charlie Wilson is our best and perhaps our only chance to pitch our requirements. Without their acceptance, there's no way in hell we will ever relinquish control of this type of weapons system to the Pakistani military. You may want to work that into the conversation with Wilson."

"Roger that, Sir. Is he coming here, or is he going to show up at Bliss?"

"Mr. Flax is the best one to ask about that. He'll be playing host to the Congressman and his entourage," said General Bushman.

"Entourage, Sir?" I asked.

"You'll see," said the head of the DIA, just as we heard a quick knock and the door was pushed open.

"Sorry to interrupt, Sir, but Mr. Flax is 30 minutes out. I need to go pick him up."

"No problem, Andy. We were just finishing up," replied the General. "Can I get a ride with you to the airport? I need to get back to Washington tonight."

"Yes, Sir. The car is right out front when you're ready," replied Andy, pulling the door closed as he left.

"You OK with this, Rick?" asked the General as he rose to his feet. "Your ace in the hole is the capability of the Stinger to shoot down Russian gunships. This fact alone should make Wilson want to plead our case to President Zia. So be your usual charming self and convince the Congressman to get us in the game."

"Yes, Sir. Three bags full, Sir!"

"Come on, Rick. We can continue our conversation in the car."

The Entourage
El Paso International Airport
Sunday 19 September 1982 1810 Hours

Mike was on the phone when we walked back to the villa's bar. He put his hand over the transmitter and asked to stay behind. I took a couple more of Consuela's hors d'oeuvres from the tray on the bar. I waved goodbye to Mike as I hurried up the hallway. The General was already in the car when I arrived at the carriage house.

Andy drove directly to the airport's central terminal drop off point. The General and I had gotten out together and walked a short distance from the Suburban. There was a United States Navy C-40A, a variant of the 737-700C, parked at Gate A-23. This would deliver Bushman to Andrews Air Force Base, allowing him to keep his next scheduled meeting at the White House. Afghanistan was not the only iron in the fire this day in 1982.

"Rick, touch base with me when you get back. If something comes up that you can't handle, get Daryl or Mike Vaughn's boss to locate me."

"Yes, Sir," I replied, and we shook hands. The General walked into the terminal.

Andy and I drove away from the main terminal and continued to the second exit ramp, which took us to the ring service road that encircled the entire runway complex. We followed the security fencing for what seemed to be a good mile and a half. A gated entrance appeared in the fence line. The sign mounted on the gate displayed the words *Entrance for Private and Business Aircraft Owners*. Andy utilized a security gate keycard to gain access. This part of the airport housed thirteen medium-size hangars for privately operated aircraft. Service ramps connected this brand-new facility with the airport's three main runways. He drove the Chevy to the rear of hangar building number 11.

"This is it," said Andy. "Let's go inside and see if Barry remembers who you are."

"I'll have you know I gave him his very first ulcer. I'm sure he'll remember me."

We entered through the rear service door. The lights in the hangar were all on and operating at their highest intensity. The doors at the front were completely closed. The hangar floor was large enough to accommodate at least three, medium-size aircraft. Tonight, there was only one in residence. It was a Gulfstream, and a very new one at that. The large corporate logo of Raytheon and the model designation G-IV were displayed just under, and slightly to the rear of, the cockpit window.

The fuselage door was wide open and the steps were deployed. We could see six individuals standing near the wing as we walked up to the aircraft. Two of these individuals were in uniform and I surmised they were part of the crew. A young woman in the same type of uniform, possibly the flight attendant, was descending the steps of the plane just as we arrived. All three of the crew said their goodbyes and started walking towards a glassed-in office located in the front right corner of the hangar.

Barry Flax turned his attention to Andy and me when he heard us announce ourselves as we walked up. He shook hands with Andy first and then grabbed me in a bear hug that almost succeeded in lifting me off the floor.

"Jesus, Barry! I'm glad to see you too. Put me down before you give yourself a hernia," I complained in a voice that sounded similar to that of someone being deprived of oxygen. The other three individuals were watching with great interest. There were two men holding crystal glasses filed with what appeared to be, and smelled like, scotch whiskey. The older man and taller of the two was laughing at the exchange. The third person was female, blonde, and could only be described as drop-dead gorgeous.

Andy was also laughing as Barry released me. Introductions were made all around. Six-foot, five-inch Charlie Wilson, the junior congressman from Texas, drained his glass and sat it on the wing.

"Rick, Andy, this is Congressman Wilson," Barry announced rather formally.

"Glad to meet you both," said Wilson, extending his hand first to me and then onto Andy.

"Yes, Sir, Congressman Wilson. I'm very glad to make your acquaintance," I offered right back.

"It's very good to meet you, Sir," added Andy.

"Seeing's we're all going to be in meetings together this week, please call me Charlie. Who do you work for, Rick?"

"Sir, I'm on loan from Bell Labs and I have an assignment to the AT&T Engineering Center in Maryland."

"That's an interesting assignment — I didn't know that AT&T was in the business of shooting down airplanes," he said wryly. "This is Ellen Lang, my press secretary," he added, half turning to the gorgeous blonde.

I guessed Ellen Lang was what General Bushman meant by "entourage".

Andy and I both smiled and nodded towards Ellen as Charlie continued. "And this is Dave Shatner, my office manager." Dave walked forward and shook hands with both of us.

"I'm glad to meet you both," said Mr. Shatner. "The congressman insisted I accompany him on this trip. He thinks I don't get out of the office enough."

"It's true, David. The last time you left Washington was when Eisenhower was President."

"Right. Well I'm here, and I'm very glad to meet all of you."

Andy and I grabbed Ellen's and the Congressman's luggage as Barry and Dave grabbed their own bags. We started moving towards the rear of the building and the parking lot.

Senator Charlie Wilson
2097 Devil's Tower Circle
El Paso County Texas
Sunday 19 September 1982 1945 Hours

Once we got underway, Andy called Consuela from a phone in the dashboard of the Suburban. A Motorola DynaTAC 8000X had been installed in each of the Raytheon pool cars. I had met Martin Cooper, the inventor of this technology, at a Bell Labs Seminar in 1979. Mobil telephone technology was still in its infancy stage at this time.

I was fast becoming a gadget junkie ever since my induction into Bell Labs in April 1975. I had been fascinated by the latest products that were being tested before they were introduced into the marketplace. I would install a variant of this same technology in both of the family cars in 1987.

"Sir," announced Andy, half turning his head towards Barry who was seated in the front passenger seat, "everything is ready for our arrival. Consuela has set the dining room for seven. She can start to serve with twenty minutes' notice."

"Thanks, Andy," replied Barry. "Why seven?"

"Mike Vaughn got invited over the weekend by his boss when he found out that Congressman Wilson was coming down here for a sit-down." I made the comment very casually, hoping to play down any negative interpretation of Mr. Vaughn's presence.

"Nice try, Rick," replied Wilson from his middle seat position next to Ellen. "I requested that the CIA be here to tell me to my face why we can't get this weapon in the hands of the Afghan Mujahideen. They've been dragging their feet for quite some time."

"Sir," I paused slightly before continuing, "it's not the CIA dragging their feet. It's the DIA. They have control over the distribution and training requirements of this top-secret weapon system. They're the ones causing the delay."

"What has Bell Labs got to do with this conversation?" asked Wilson, turning slightly to look at me and resting his arm along the top edge of the seat, behind Ellen's shoulders. He found a lock of Miss Ellen's long blonde hair and immediately began to coil it around his finger.

My eyes moved from Charlie's finger back to his eyes. He was smiling at me.

"I was brought in because of my involvement with this technology since it was first introduced in sixty-eight. I have firsthand experience in its software development, as well as tactical field deployment and training requirements. I also have had the distinct pleasure of shooting down one of Mr. Flax's very expensive jet target drones."

"No shit," replied the impressed Charlie Wilson. "You're just the guy I've been looking for."

"Yes, Sir," I said, acknowledging the congressman's acceptance. "I also have a working knowledge of the Russian gunship known as the Mil Mi-24, a truly evil piece of hardware, Sir."

Once again, the congressman from Texas uttered the words, "No Shit," and went on to say, "Just where in the hell have you been hiding for the last year and a half, Mr. Fontain?"

Smiles appeared on both Barry's and Andy's faces almost simultaneously.

"Sir, in the next couple of—" I was cut off mid-sentence by Wilson.

"Rick, please call me Charlie and stop all that 'sir' shit."

"Yes S—OK, Charlie. If you can stay for a day or two to receive the technical overview on Stinger you'll acquire a better understanding of what a great asset we have. We all want to kill some Russians. And if you and I can convince President Zia to accept Stinger on our terms the 40th Army and the Russian military in general are all going to need a *shitload* of new gunships."

The Re-Cap – A Good Sense of Killing
El Paso County Texas
Tuesday 21 September 1982 2230 Hours

Congressman Wilson stayed until mid-week at the Devil's Tower. He had come to get a briefing on the Stinger weapons system and had received quite a bit more. He also wanted an explanation as to why the Defense Department and the CIA were dragging their feet for the deployment of an antiaircraft weapons system that would change the outcome of the Russian invasion of Afghanistan.

I suggested, and Andy and Mike agreed, sparing Wilson all of the classroom mathematical bullshit. We started on Monday morning right after breakfast with the historical background of the older Redeye program and wound the timeline all the way up to the present-day parameters of the Stinger program. Andy suggested that the discussion would be greatly enhanced if the graphics available in the classrooms of the nearby Conference Center could be added to the conversation.

By Tuesday afternoon, there was a lull in the discussion. We had just returned from a live tracking exercise at White Sands. Everyone had gotten in on the activity of tracking and shooting at a live target. Ellen, the focal point of Charlie's entourage, had used the trainer to score hits on both of the Navy F-16 aircraft that were providing the day's entertainment. Even Charlie's office manager did OK, but you could tell he was preoccupied with the more pressing issues of Charlie's real day job.

Consuela had packed everyone a lunch, which we ate on our one-hour and ten-minute trip back from the firing range at White Sands. Everyone went to his or her rooms to shower, rest up, and do our own things. We all met in the bar before dinner. The food served at each and every meal had been good, and there was plenty of it. Charlie and I broke away from the group after what would be our last dinner together for quite a while. We excused ourselves and went out by the pool to enjoy one of Barry's very special, and extremely illegal, Cuban cigars. Charlie carried with him a glass full of ice, dark with Macallan 25.

I looked directly at Wilson. I could tell he had mixed feelings regarding what he was about to say.

"So, Charlie," I started the conversation. "Did you get what you came down here for? Have we covered everything you came here to discuss? Are there any other issues we need to go over before you leave tomorrow?"

Charlie didn't answer right away. He turned his head and peered out towards the view of the city of El Paso off in the distance. He put the Cuban between his lips and took a long pull. He then proceeded to blow smoke rings towards the lights of the city.

"Yes, I think you've given me everything I came for," said Wilson. "Additionally, you've raised some issues I hadn't considered. Zia, being a man who isn't easily swayed, for one thing. Plus, his generals will be even tougher nuts to crack. Rick, Stinger can change everything for the Afghan people." Charlie shook his head, thinking of what it would take to get Stinger into the Afghans' hands.

"Congressman ... Charlie, we both know that the key to a win-win scenario lies with President Zia and his ISI Inter-Services Intelligence staff officers. If we can't get their buy-in, little can be done to move this issue forward with the DOD. Quite frankly, if we can't keep control of the distribution of the weapon and implement the necessary training criteria it will be my recommendation that Stinger remain on the shelf for the duration."

"Then you and I need to find a way to convince them," replied Charlie Wilson.

"The people I work for won't bend on this either. Even a hint of the possibility that this weapon could get out in the open is too horrific to even think about. Even more importantly, we, as Americans, must always consider our country and our citizens first and foremost. And if that requires giving a pass on an opportunity to kill Russian gunships, so be it."

"Well Rick, that would be a damn shame, wouldn't it? Don't give up hope yet. I may know just the person who may be able to intercede on our behalf."

"Oh! Are you on a first name basis with the prophet Mohammad?"

"No, but I think the person I'm thinking of has that honor," said Wilson confidently. "She indeed may be just the one to pull this off for us."

"That would be outstanding, Charlie," I replied. "By the way, we have another little issue with Zia. Did you know that he's building a nuclear weapon?"

"Yeah, but let's work on one trouble at a time, Rick."

"You're the boss, Charlie."

PART III

Three Years Forward – 1986

Nangarhar Providence Afghanistan

18
Thirty Seconds After

Moving Northeast in Nangarhar Providence
Aftermath of Russian Gunship Encounter
Nangarhar Mountain Pass
Saturday 28 June 1986 0501 Hours

OLY SHIT," SCREAMED Staff Sergeant Dennis Deccan. He stood straight up, pulling the Barrett .50 CAL weapon from the top of the boulder and holding it firmly across his chest. DELTA-3 was standing next to him. They both were frozen in the moment looking at the huge fireball and the thick black smoke rising from the canyon floor. Almost immediately, the voice of Pezlola sounded in their headsets.

"Everyone move it NOW. Up the path people. Follow the Afghans up the trail," yelled ZERO.

"DELTA-1," commanded ONE (CWO Lawson), "drop two shooters to the rear. Let's go, let's go people. This smoke isn't going to last forever. Move out."

"DELTA-3 and 7," said Sergeant First Class George Angerome, squeezing his throat mic. "Drop back and cover Mr. Khan and his people. Watch our six until we can get off this trail. This is DELTA-1, out."

"Roger that. Three and seven are at your six. DELTA-7, out."

The thick black smoke from the Mil Mi-24 was rising high in the sky and blowing back towards the cliff wall. It would provide excellent cover for traveling the short distance needed to escape through a place in the cliff wall that Mustapha said was nearby. This secret passage would take them west into the valley beyond.

Mustapha Ismail Taisei stepped out of the single file procession once his men reached the narrow slit in the cliff wall. They had lost two men in the hail of cannon fire. They carried both of their dead comrades to the thin exit point in the rock. With one man on each side of their fallen comrades they side-danced each body upright into the narrow crack in the stone. Mustapha stood there surveying the last of his people into the slot as the first of the Delta Force arrived. He suggested that they remove their packs so that they could better negotiate the narrow opening.

"Mr. Pezlola," Mustapha said to the approaching, and slightly out of breath, CIA man. "Remove your pack, Jim. Did everyone in the rear survive the attack?"

"The prisoner is dead. He took some shrapnel in the back of his head from one of the rockets."

"He is a lucky man. He would not have survived what was waiting for him at our camp. Come. Let's get everyone off this trail."

Squeezing through an eighteen-inch crack in the cliff wall gave Pezlola a feeling of complete helplessness. The fact that he had skipped breakfast made Jim grateful for the perceived additional clearance. Pezlola was not sure if being slightly out of breath was caused by being out of shape or if it was a result of the altitude. Maybe it was a little of both. Turning his head back towards the entrance, he confided to Mustapha, who had followed him into the passage, "I sure hope this space gets wider."

"The pathway will become much broader after another fifteen meters," said Mustapha.

"Good to know; walking sideways all the way to Kabul could get tiring," said Pezlola, lifting his head straight up as he continued to slide along the narrow opening. The rock wall six inches from his nose shot several hundred meters straight up to the sky. "I suspect," he added, "if you didn't know what to look for from out on the main trail you could walk right on by and never know this was here. A real secret passage, yes?"

"A shortcut," answered Mustapha laughing. "It has been used for over a hundred years by the locals."

"I think you should not recruit any heavy-set warriors," the CIA officer dryly suggested.

"I don't understand" replied Mustapha. "What is—? Ahh! I see what you mean. We would be forced to leave the larger men out on the main trail, yes? Ha, ha!" The two men were now shuffling side by side sandwiched in stone.

"Perhaps there's a more appropriate term for this gift from Mother Earth."

"And what is that, Jim?" asked Mustapha.

"Are you ready? It should be called a narrow escape."

"Ahh ... I understand this.... It is a play on the words, yes?"

Then Pezlola said, "Yes, I was making fun but it will only be funny if you're telling the truth about it getting wider in the next few side steps."

After progressing twelve additional meters along the narrow slit in the mountain it widened to a whopping two meters. The passageway was now pitched downward at a fifteen-degree angle. The column of warriors continued their march in single file for almost an hour.

Suddenly, the pathway walked them right out onto a valley floor with a temperature that was much warmer than the mountain out of which they'd emerged. Pezlola stood at the edge and looked out across a valley that was rich with meadow grass and huge patches of flowers for as far as he could see. There was a tree line that tapered up both sides of the gorge. Above the trees was a sheer rock wall jutting down both sides of this canyon, worthy of being in Shangri-La.

"This is a very special place, Mustapha," said Chief Warrant Officer Gary Lawson, who had just walked up from the rear of the parade.

"Yes, and, because of how it is sheltered between these two mountains," Mustapha replied, "the temperature here is quite conducive for growing things throughout the year." He said this tongue in cheek. His American audience was more than aware of what he meant. The growing of opium poppies was one of the main sources of income for the Mujahideen in 1985. This valley was being utilized to generate part of that needed income.

Lawson continued, "Saifullah says we're not far from your camp?"

"That is true. Come, let us continue. We still have several kilometers to complete. Please tell all of your people to walk directly behind the person they are following. We would not want any unfortunate accidents to occur, if you take my meaning."

"We do indeed," replied Pezlola. CWO Larson and DELTA-1, George Angerome, who had walked up on the conversation, both started to scan the ground around their feet. Landmines make no friends.

"I'll make my way to the rear and remind Saifullah of the trail conditions before we proceed. He has been here many times but it never hurts to refresh his memory, yes?"

"Definitely," replied DELTA-1. "A really good brother-in-law is hard to find. Especially if he is suddenly exploded into many pieces."

19

Meeting the Management

Mujahidin Base Camp
Saturday 28 June 1986 1615 Hours

CWO LAWSON POINTED towards the overhanging wall and muttered the words, "Jesus, would you get a load of that?"

The stone-faced cliff extended straight up for over 300 meters. The gray rock surface was marked haphazardly with patches of greenery halfway up the mountain. What appeared to be a walled boundary marking the end of the valley floor was actually a huge open cavern. As they got closer to where the base of the cliff should have been, the light from hundreds of Mujahideen campfires provided an eerie glow throughout the huge space. This cavern was truly a wonder of nature.

"Pass the word to DELTA-1 to hold up at the entrance; you and I will make our manners with the management of this resort," said Pezlola to Lawson. "I'll pass the word when it's safe to approach the front desk to check-in."

"Roger that," replied ONE. He pressed his throat mic but the unit was dead. The batteries needed to be changed. He turned and signaled with his hand to DELTA-1, who was only twenty feet away.

The Afghan escorts, who were walking out in front of the group, had already disappeared into the void under the cliff. The ledge height was an impressive 10 meters in places. The uneven opening was stretched along the entire base of the natural, sheer rock fortification. The architect of this encampment was obviously commissioned by God, thought Lawson. The friction from a river or a glacier or a combination of both had carved out a space that was housing a very large Mujahideen force. It was obvious to Pezlola that this headquarters renovation contractor must have worked long into the night. Even though the contracts were signed 10,000 years before, it had been brought in on time. The Mujahideen tenants seemed to be completely on board with the inside accouterments and the specifications of a long-term lease. The choice of this location for this particular camp was obvious.

DELTA-1 walked up next to CWO Lawson, who had walked back outside to greet the portion of the patrol just emerging from the tall meadow grass.

"You could hide an entire army in there," exclaimed SFC George Angerome, awed by the massive opening under the cliff.

Lawson guided everyone up to the edge of the overhang. "ZERO wants everyone to hang here until we make our manners. 10-4."

"Roger that, Sir," replied DELTA-1. "OK, everybody hold up here. Take a knee and keep eyes all around."

The Mujahideen headquarters was impressive. The base of the cliff from a distance, and certainly not from the air, gave no indication what was camped under this mountain. The jagged height varied in both directions for several hundred meters. The massive overhang could accommodate the population of a small city.

Lawson walked back and stood next to Pezlola. "Well, this is one for Ripley's."

"You're right, Lawson; they've hidden an entire army in there," said an amazed Jim Pezlola, nodding his head towards the large Mujahideen group gathering and moving towards them.

"You have arrived," said Ali Mohsen al-Ahmar, who was the Mujahideen District Commander. Mustapha Taisei and Saifullah Khan were standing just behind the man. They had gone immediately to the far end of the encampment to announce the arrival of the Americans.

"Thank you very much for receiving us," replied Pezlola. "It's been a long-time desire of my President to offer our assistance with your fight against the Russian invaders." Pezlola had prepared several responses for this moment. This was the one he had hoped to deliver. Oh, God, please don't shoot me, Sir, was the last and least favorable on his list.

Mustapha had told Pezlola that this base camp was one of the largest in this part of Afghanistan. Out of the 900 plus men encamped here, over 100 Mujahideen warriors had followed their leader to greet the recent arrivals. They gathered around al-Ahmar, waiting for the decision of their leader. Pezlola wondered whether they utilized a simple thumbs up or thumbs down in their decision-making procedures. ZERO couldn't tell from the many facial expressions of the onlookers.

The conversation that was about to take place would be easily understood. There would be the utterance of one of two simple, three-word phrases by al-Ahmar. The phrase he chose was important because it would start or end Pezlola's mission. With the first of the two possibilities, Ali Mohsen al-Ahmar would spread his arms and simply say, "You are welcome". With the second choice he would yell at the top of his lungs, "Kill them all". The hair on ZERO's neck was behaving as it had when he was a kid and watching any one of the many horror movies he favored.

For the moment, the crowd was perfectly silent. All eyes were following the exchange of the Americans with their management. The motionless faces sent a chill up Pezlola's spine. The greeting by the Mujahideen leader was just milliseconds away. Pezlola realized that at least some of the onlookers would be disappointed if the decision was made to welcome the Americans. This, of course, would mean that they would not be allowed to eat them.

Pezlola's body went lax with relief as the magic words were uttered and he and his men were welcomed with open arms. As the decision was passed into the crowd, smiles appeared on most faces. He could see beyond the crowd the many campfires sprinkled everywhere throughout the cavern. Next to one of the larger fires stood Mustapha. He was smiling and nodding at Pezlola. Jim made a mental note to write a comment in the margin of his report to his handlers at Langley: the Russian military in Afghanistan were in for a great big, fucking surprise. Operation Cyclone would now go forward.

20
Slightly Late

Third Floor – Conference Room 3C
25 Grosvenor Square, London United Kingdom
Saturday 28 June 1986 0905 Hours

CHARGED OUT OF the Bond Street tube station. I was making very good time. The lost seventeen minutes this morning were gone forever … but certainly not forgotten. Hanna had made sure of that. The only problem was that I was now late for a meeting being led by my boss, Bill Douglas.

I entered the embassy compound at full gallop. Climbing the front entrance steps two at a time, I pulled the heavy plate glass door outward and zipped into the lobby atrium. Mr. Haralson was on duty behind the counter. He made eye contact with me, holding up three fingers on his right hand. He then formed the letter "C" with his index finger and thumb. I nodded my understanding and darted past the bank of elevators to the stairwell.

Conference room 3C was at the opposite end of the hallway from the stairwell entrance to the third floor. Taking a very deep breath I paused for just a second before pushing open the frosted, floor to ceiling, glass door. Bill Douglas greeted me immediately.

"Good afternoon, Rick," he said in a tone that indicated that he was not amused. "You have trouble finding the embassy?"

"Good morning, everyone," I replied, not directly responding to Head of Station (HOS) Douglas who was standing at the front of the room next to a powered-up 35mm slide projector.

"Sorry for my late arrival," I said with my head down and my eyes low.

The slide on the screen was displaying the downtown area of the city of Kuala Lumpur (KL), Malaysia. I took a seat next to Amelia Jane at the rear of the room. Only five of the sixteen chairs were occupied around the large, oval table. Actually, the head count was six; it would be a big mistake not to count the standing Bill Douglas.

I returned the nod of everyone who had turned momentarily to face me. Everyone but one returned to face HOS Douglas. A person I didn't recognize was seated at the right front side of the table. He held his stare with a smile a good bit longer than the others before returning his attention to Douglas.

The HOS slapped the screen with his wooden pointer. The sound it made reminded me of the *Sisters of the Iron Underwear* at St. Marks Elementary School. To be specific, Sister Marie Charles had made the sound famous. Her nickname was Chopper Charlie. The slapping noise just heard was an exact replication. At four-feet, eight-inches in height, she — and her lightning fast wrist action — had amazed me, and my fellow classmates. The sound of a single strike was generated by any wrong answer. Multiple strikes would occur with the second incorrect response. Her custom pointer, made of hickory, struck the center of our collective soul with all the force of a whaling harpoon. The sound of a Tommy gun being fired on fully automatic would result if ignorance prevailed. Chopper Charlie would happily have mowed each of us down.

Douglas drew everyone's eyes to the location of the building where our proposed meeting was to be held. The place was The Majestic Hotel. The purpose of the meeting, and I'd be the first to admit this to anyone asking, was not well defined. Of course, it is well documented that every journey begins with the first step. It just seemed that lately Mr. Douglas had us all standing on a cliff's edge. The command to remove our blindfolds would signal the start of his next exciting project.

The logistical nightmare of securing a multitude of permissions from an array of characters in four different countries was the task at hand. Without a doubt this would be the most complex undertaking I had been involved in, to date. Thank God, the stated purpose of this morning's meeting only concerned two of the four countries: Egypt and Pakistan. The end goal was to provide a means for the Afghan Mujahideen to be able to kill a whole bunch of Russian government employees — and the machines they fly around in.

"This property," Douglas tapped the map, "is owned and operated by Maalouf Torki bin Taisei." The address of No.5 Jalan Sultan Hishamuddin was posted in a text box with an arrow pointing at the map coordinates. "As you can see, The Majestic is very near, if not exactly at, the center of the city."

I had run into Mr. Taisei in his elevator in Dubai just a little over three months before. That unscheduled meeting had taken place in a hotel property also owned by Mr. Taisei. As a personal favor to me (I suspect that saving his life had something to do with him granting me three wishes), he had agreed to set up a meeting — and issue motivational invitations to attend to individuals who in the past had been reluctant to play ball with the United States regarding helping Afghanistan.

These key decision makers were critical to our intent to place the Stinger weapon system into the hands of the Afghan warrior. This not only included the guys from Pakistan's ISI but would also include several individuals from both Egypt and Israel. The meeting was scheduled to take place early the following week. That is, of course, if the good Lord was willing and the rivers didn't rise!

"The meeting date is Tuesday, October 15," said Douglas. "That gives us a little over six days to prepare. As of this morning the exact time has not been determined. Our KL embassy folks will provide security to and from the airport. The HOS, Jasper Duncan, will supply us with five additional people: three men, and two women. This additional staffing will provide premise security and run the communications once we're inside The Majestic. Mr. Taisei's people will provide an additional layer of security on, and/or above, the concierge floor on eighteen. We have been tentatively told that the meeting will take place somewhere above the eighteenth floor. Questions?" asked Douglas and looked around the table. There were none.

"Rick," called Douglas, "do you have anything to add?"

"Yes, Sir," I replied, getting out of my chair. I proceeded to the front of the room. Only a few hours before, Joe Wilson, Amelia Jane, and I had gone over the proposed scope of potential meeting topics in Wilson's room at the Mayflower.

"Good morning, everyone," I said, taking the pointer offered by Bill. Douglas took his seat at the front on the left side of the table, directly across from the gentleman I didn't recognize.

"A point of interest for everyone: the U.S. Embassy is here." I pointed several blocks away, to the north of the hotel.

"I've found on more than one occasion that having a Plan-B in place is very soothing for the soul," I said as I scanned the faces looking carefully at me from around the room. The only people in this room whom I knew for sure would be attending were Amelia Jane and myself.

"If for any reason, once we enter the hotel, the need to abort is forced upon us — during or upon leaving the conference — we'll take everyone out the back of the property here," I said, pointing to the alley intersection. The rear of the hotel offered a direct pathway towards the north.

"Because of the way the property is sloped, the loading dock egress can be accessed only from basement level B-1."

"Our drivers — because there isn't any underground parking — will be stationed in the half circle at the front of the hotel. At the first sign of trouble they will move to the rear of the complex, here," I said, moving the pointer towards the hotel's backstreet. "This alley runs parallel to Jalan Sultan Hishamuddin, along here all the way to the park, here," I said, pointing to a spot just across from our Embassy.

"If they are not in position when we exit the hotel, here," I said, pointing again to the back end of the hotel property, "we would then proceed on foot to the far end of the loading-dock landing." Tapping the screen, I continued. "Once down in the alley we will make our way to here," I said. I pointed to where the road ended at the Masjid Negara Park. "We will continue on foot north through the park and cross under the Jalan Damansara, here," I said and lightly tapped the exit point just below the south gate main entrance of the U.S. Embassy. "People, this is Plan B. It can't hurt to have one, just in case someone crashes our party."

"Rick's caution is well-founded," said Joe Wilson, who had spoken for the first time since the meeting started. "Our people in KL tell us that the Russians have eyes and ears just about everywhere in and around the city. For the last several months Langley reports that the Russians have doubled their number of assistant cultural attachés in both KL and Singapore."

"Why is that, Sir?" asked Amelia Jane.

"Max, do you want to take a stab at that? This may be a good time to explain why we are meeting in this particular city."

"Yes, I would," replied Max Gresonine, standing and turning to face the others. "KL is the center of all of Mr. Taisei's businesses. For years now the ISI has been a major client—"

"Max, first, could you explain why the KGB has an interest in the activities of both Kuala Lumpur and Singapore?" interrupted Amelia Jane.

"Yes, that's what I was about to describe for you," replied Max. "The simple answer to that question, Mrs. Smythe, is that both Singapore and KL offer a neutral stage to a wide range of Mr. Taisei's international clients, with KL being slightly more relaxed than Singapore. Most of the players involved in this project do not play well together on the public stage. What KL provides is a sanctuary of sorts, to countries that need to debate issues that cannot be discussed through normal channels. The Russians, on the other hand, have known for some time that the Afghans are being supported, if not directly, then indirectly, by Pakistan and other outside sources. We suspect that their increased presence in Malaysia is to gather intelligence on Mr. Taisei's organization."

Max continued. "As some of you already know, Maalouf Torki bin Taisei is financially well off and holds a position of importance as the Deputy Minister of Transport in the Malaysian Government. What most people do not know is that he is the largest arms dealer in the Middle East."

"OK, but as I understand it we were all set to meet last year around this same time but he reneged at the last moment. Right?" prodded Amelia Jane. "What makes you think it won't happen again?"

"Let me give that a try, Max," I offered. "A good question, and a point well worth exploring, Amelia. Ed, did you pull the file I asked for?" I reached in front of Douglas for the folder.

Ed McCall, the other Executive Officer to Bill Douglas, handed a blue and white striped folder to me. "Amelia Jane, I had Ed ask Langley to pull the after-action results on the failed meeting date last March in KL. On a hunch, I asked that the results be analyzed for a 72-hour period. The parameters I asked for were the twenty-four-hour segments before, during, and after the failed meeting date. The requested analysis was to include lists of traffic accidents, emergency room activities, and three days of newspaper current events in and around the city. There was a report of a drug overdose victim who was admitted to the Sentosa Medical Centre. The individual was listed as DOA the morning of March 6, the same day as our proposed meeting. The deceased's last name was Rahman. Wife number two of Mr. Taisei has that same family name."

"So, you think this is what caused the meeting to be cancelled?" asked Amelia Jane.

"Yes, it's a good bet that that's what caused the cancellation. Maalouf's sudden change of heart had nothing to do with you last year," offered the nameless man seated directly in front of me. "It was due to this most unfortunate event."

"My question then is, why didn't we follow up and request another meeting?" asked Amelia Jane, her irritation showing.

"Short answer," I replied. "We assumed we were the ones at fault. Until I confirmed my suspicion with Dr. Asghar last night, we just supposed we were somehow the cause of Maalouf's sudden mind change."

"That's good to know," offered Max. "It will allow us to pursue our requests without the worry of an assumed hidden prejudice."

"That's true. And, we have his personal assurance that he will help us all he can to make our terms and conditions to Pakistan and President Zia understood," I added.

Max moved from the table and walked to the projector. He pushed the switch, killing the lamp. He then came and stood beside me at the screen

"When David James came to me last year asking for my help I knew that the solution we would seek would not come easily. I made a checklist, a matrix of tasks if you will, that would be necessary for this project to succeed. For Germany, it was easy to join you. Our interest in seeing America succeed with Operation Cyclone is viewed by us as the first crucial step in ending the Cold War in Europe." Max paused briefly and raised his head to examine the ceiling tile.

"The purpose of the meeting next week," Max continued, "will be to detail the requirements for all of the essential players. And, as you all may suspect, there are many personalities with diverse interests that need to be involved in this operation. To say that this undertaking has somewhat of a complex nature would be a major understatement."

Max paused, turning his head to peer out the window. He seemed to be thinking how to phrase his next recommendation. Finally, he looked back towards the five faces with eyes on him and said, "The Stinger weapons system in the hands of the Afghan Freedom Fighter will change the way the world will view the Soviet Union. Yes, this will be a very complex operation. And, any one of the players we solicit could cause us a setback. However, if we succeed, we will change the world for the better. And I'm not just talking about Afghanistan."

Joe Wilson spoke up next. "Congressman Wilson believes that President Zia has made up his mind to openly support the Afghans. As most of you know, for the last several years Zia has been playing his cards close to his chest. His sole reason for doing so was to not publicly irritate the Russians."

"Charlie Wilson and his very good friend, Joanne, were recently able to convince Zia of the importance of Stinger in winning the fight in Afghanistan," I said.

"What about the ISI?" asked Amelia Jane.

"Mike Vaughn has it on good authority, probably from his boss," replied Joe Wilson, "that Zia has sent a written order to his ISI organization directing its management to support the Stinger program."

"To what extent?" I asked.

Joe went on to say, "Zia has blessed, and given the go-ahead to, the head of the ISI, General Khan. Our concerns on the control and distribution protocols have been approved and will be complied with. As you know, the game would have been called without it."

"So, we can expect ISI participation for Tuesday's meeting?" I asked.

"You can," replied Max. "The ISI will be represented in KL."

"Why do you think the sudden willingness to cooperate?" asked Ed McCall.

"Good question, Ed," said Wilson. "Zia knows if Afghanistan falls then Pakistan will be next. Perhaps he sees the handwriting on the wall."

"Pushback?" I asked.

"There will be some ISI hardliners," affirmed Wilson, "who will continue to oppose this change."

"Giving up any part of the control and the distribution channel will be a real point of contention going forward," said Bill Douglas.

"For that matter," said Wilson, "our own CIA man in Pakistan will take issue with this latest policy change. The Islamabad station chief has supported and probably designed the means and mode for distribution and control of weapons and ammunition."

"But why?" asked Amelia Jane.

Max spoke up immediately. "The black-market corruption in the distribution channel is world class. The CIA, the other CIA, has a very different result in mind for Afghanistan."

"Which is?" I asked.

"Their goal," said Max, "from day one, has been only to keep the Russians bogged down in their fight with the Mujahideen. Their policy is to only allow a calculated number of arms and ammunition sufficient to contain the conflict, but never enough to win."

"You can't be serious," exclaimed Amelia Jane.

"I'm afraid Herr Gresonine is correct," interjected Joe Wilson. "The program that establishes Stinger as a separate support channel will cause ill-will inside the ISI and with a certain group in Langley."

"Bill, please tell me this ain't so," I implored. "How in the hell could Bill Casey subvert a Presidential finding?"

"In short: he didn't," replied Douglas. "Did he know what his HOS in Islamabad was doing? Yes, and no. And he was being told that the Mujahideen could not win."

I said, "So when Charlie Wilson shows up and starts rocking the boat, Bill Casey is forced to side with his HOS."

"Correct," replied Joe Wilson. "And the folks skimming huge amounts of product from the distribution channel realized that Stinger would be bad for business."

"Bad for business," I repeated with disgust. "That, despite the fact that the Russians may soon come through the Khyber Pass and kill them? Am I the only one here who's read Catch-22?"

"President Zia was aware of the corruption," said Bill Douglas. "In March, he sent word to us, through Gust Avrakotos's people in Pakistan, requesting to revisit the terms and conditions of Operation Cyclone. Gust's communication came in last night's dispatches. Zia has assured us that the ISI will fully support our request to supply and manage Stinger directly into the hands of the freedom fighters of Afghanistan. The two Generals he appointed will attend the logistics meeting in KL. They have the complete confidence and authority of President Zia to implement what we require."

"Mike Vaughn's message I received this morning indicated the ISI issue will be resolved in the short term and they'll cooperate fully going forward," said Joe Wilson, who appeared and sounded slightly sleep deprived.

"It's already been resolved," Max Gresonine announced, having read a note just then passed to him by Mrs. Flouts. "Apparently, Zia's solution wasn't very pretty," Max continued. "But we have positive confirmation that those ISI officers who are now assigned to assist us are committed to helping us in any way necessary."

"What in the hell did Zia do? Get all of the hardliners transferred out of the ISI?" I asked.

"He transferred a few individuals into the afterlife," replied Max dryly. "Everyone not electing for a transfer became very enthusiastic about support-ing their President's wishes." Max casually folded the note that described Zia's solution for better management. Putting it in his pocket he said, "This will help, but we still need to convince the Israelis and the Egyptians to provide a discreet means of transportation, plus a Stinger package that is completely devoid of U.S. markings."

"Baby steps, Max," I said. And then I whispered to myself, *"God, I love it when a plan comes together. Or not."*

Mr. Ghazala
US Embassy – 5th Floor
25 Grosvenor Square, London United Kingdom
Saturday 28 June 1986 1135 Hours

The meeting had lasted an additional hour and a half. I followed Amelia Jane back to her office on the fifth floor. We were standing in the hallway near Bill Douglas's office entrance when he walked up with Uncle Max, Ed McCall, and the unnamed person from our meeting.

"Good, you're still here," said Ed McCall. "Let me introduce Mohammed Abu Ghazala from the Egyptian Defense Ministry. He is here at the request of Mr. Taisei."

Mr. Ghazala's was a firm and sincere handshake. "I must apologize for ogling you this morning, Mr. Fontain. I wanted very much to see and meet the person who saved my brother from being assassinated."

"Please, Mr. Ghazala, call me Rick," I said. "And I would never pass up a chance to be ogled." Amelia Jane immediately glanced down at her shoes and noticeably shook her head from side to side. "You did say *brother*, didn't you?" Amelia Jane delivered a quick, unobserved kick to the back of my left shoe.

"Yes, Maalouf and I share the same mother but we had the experience of very different fathers."

"Good to know, Mr. Ghazala. What brings you to the city of no sunshine?" I inquired.

"Actually, I'm assigned to our Embassy here. Maalouf called me and wanted me to assure you and your government that arrangements are being made to stage, scrub, and transport the Stingers into Pakistan. Right now, we think the best way to do this is through our organization in Egypt. Also, the existing transport channels set up by the Israelis are the proven way to go."

"That's great news. Please pass our thanks to your brother, Mr. Ghazala," I said.

"I certainly will. Moreover, please call me by my first name, Mohammed. On the other hand, if you prefer my nickname, it is pronounced from the first two letters: just plain Mo. Dr. Asghar told me that today everyone needs to have a nickname."

"She's right, and tomorrow, also, 'Just Plain Mo'," I replied. This got me a second kick from Amelia Jane. "Will you be attending the conference in KL?"

"The nickname is Mo, not—" Mohammed, trying to explain the misunderstanding, was cut off mid-sentence by Amelia Jane.

"Please excuse just plain ol' Rick," said Amelia Jane. "He gets easily confused when people speak to him in English."

"Oh?" replied Mo.

"Sorry Mo, I was just having a little fun with your nickname. Will you be going with us to KL?" I asked.

"Most likely I'll be joining you there. I have a meeting in Cairo on Saturday with the Israelis."

"Have you and the Israelis worked this type of project before?" I was genuinely curious.

"Oh yes, we do a lot of business together. Under the radar, I believe is your term, yes?"

"I think that would be one way to describe it, Mo."

"In either case, I'm glad to have had the opportunity to finally meet you, Mr. Rick."

"Likewise, Just Plain Mo," I said, and everyone laughed, including Amelia Jane. "Have a safe trip to Cairo. I'll look forward to seeing you in Kuala Lumpur next week."

"Thank you, and goodbye," said Amelia Jane. Ed McCall, who had just joined us in the hallway, volunteered to escort Mo to the lobby.

"Where is Joe Wilson?" I asked Mr. Douglas.

"He got a call when we were leaving the conference center. He said he would come up here before going back to the hotel. Do you need to talk to him?"

"No, but you can ask him to invite either Mr. Avrakotos or Mike Vaughn to make an appearance next week in KL. Some serious eye-to-eye contact with the new ISI guys might go a long way in our newly formed relationship."

"I think that's a good suggestion," replied Douglas. "I'll ask. Gust has been close with most of the ISI worker bees in Islamabad. And Mike has been working the Pakistan Desk for the last year. I'll call you later and let you know what he says."

"Thanks, I'll be at home, not in the office. Max brought Hanna with him from D.C. last night. Would you touch base with Joe Hauf and give him a heads up about next week?" Mr. Hauf was my AT&T boss in the U.K. He was one of the four non-CIA individuals, and the only one in London, who understood that my real day job was with the CIA.

21

Guns & Bagels

NIA Mossad Safe House – National Intelligence Agency
Trumpeldor ST – Beach Front Area
Tele Aviv, Yafo, Israel
Saturday 28 June 1986 1925 Hours

SO, THE AMERICANS are finally moving forward," remarked Nahum Admoni, Director of Israel's Mossad.

"Yes, that is why I asked to see you. Mr. Taisei would like your assurance that you will not withhold support this time around," replied Mohammed Abu Ghazala.

"You know, it was not we who made the threat. It was the ISI. And you know the risk we were all faced with. Besides, it really doesn't matter now, does it?"

"Correct. It appears that President Zia has made up his mind to openly support the Mujahideen," replied Mohammed.

"Well, if the American Stinger lives up to only half of its reputation…." Admoni paused to stare out the window that overlooked the shoreline.

"I was shown a capability report in London. The data on the statistical kill ratios are charted in the ninetieth-percentile range. If this weapon is introduced into the fight properly it will go a long way in changing the outcome of the war."

"If," replied the Mossad leader? "I just hope Zia's caution hasn't cost him."

"Cost him what?"

"The Russians are not stupid," replied Admoni. "They have known for some time that he has sheltered the Afghan leadership."

"True. But perhaps his luck will hold for just a bit longer. In any case my brother's main concern is our nuclear investment."

"And rightfully so. Is it still your intention to move the scrubbed Stinger tubes to Peshawar after they are processed?"

"No, they will be warehoused within the ISI Ojhri Camp. Our depot in Nasr City is setting up to scrub the weapons. I would like your personal assurance that the transport channel will be made available to the Americans as long as they require it. Also, Mr. Taisei requests that your man in Cairo come to KL next week."

"For what purpose?" asked Admoni.

"His presence is required to reassure the Americans that nothing is being left to chance."

"I'll call before you leave. What else?"

"That's it. Oh, and Mr. Taisei says the uranium will arrive in Karachi on the 22nd."

"Good, General Khan will be pleased. Now, how about that drink I promised you, Mohammed?"

22
Incognito

Mildenhal NATO RAF
C-9A Nightingale/Sky Train II
United Kingdom
Saturday 28 June 1986 2345 Hours

"RICK," QUERIED AMELIA Jane in her precise British accent, "do we know who, and where in the hotel, we will be meeting?"

"Yes, and no," I replied. "The details have been withheld. Just after I put Hanna on her flight at Gatwick I called Mr. Taisei's HOS this afternoon, Mr. Ndakwah. The location and start time haven't been finalized.

"What's the reason, pray tell, for all the cloak and dagger?"

"Due to the diversity of the many personalities attending, and in some cases lack of moral character, the attendees, I was told, might ask some of their friends to crash our party."

"Oh, and what does your Uncle Max have to say about that?"

"He told me last night that our new pal Mo has expressed the same concern to his brother. Nevertheless, Maalouf told him that KL was still our best chance for getting all of the players we require into the same room. This, as I understand it, is our best hope for getting Spring Training started."

"Oh, God. There you go again with your American sports analogies."

"Would you rather I use the favorite British past time?" I asked.

"Which is?" asked a suspicious Amelia Jane.

"Mud wrestling, of course. I'm surprised you didn't know that."

"Seriously, Rick, how can we protect ourselves and everyone attending if some of the people can't be trusted?"

"We can't. Nevertheless, Bill Douglas thinks it's the best chance we're going to get. The designated location and the people selected to attend present our best opportunity to reach an agreement. If there's a possibility that we can finally strike a deal to get Stinger into the hands of the Afghan freedom fighters, then the risks are worth it.

The plane we were traveling on was an USAF C-9A. The NATO medivac flight designation was Nightingale/Sky Train II. The flight was scheduled three times per week. That night, it left the UK on time from the RAF base at Mildenhall for its programmed destination: the U.S. Rhine Main AFB in Germany. Hanna's Uncle Max took the liberty and booked us on a Lufthansa Frankfurt/Main (FRA) to Kuala Lumpur (KUL) flight that would depart 55 minutes after the scheduled touchdown. The timing would be tight, but FRA's main terminal building was only a stone's throw from where we would land.

A plain, white van with large blue lettering pulled up to our aircraft even before the engines had completely wound down. We stepped down on the tarmac and were directed toward the side door of the van. For just a brief moment I saw what was stenciled on its side: Airport Catering Service. The door was thrust open and a smiling Max Gresonine waved us inside. The rear of the vehicle was open just long enough for our luggage to be stowed.

The van followed the service apron around to the commercial side of the airport. We pulled up next to a Lufthansa 747-400 that would take us to KL. Max told us to remain in the van until he checked the boarding arrangement. He returned in a few minutes' time and handed baggage tags to someone from the ground crew, directing them to put our luggage in the hold of the aircraft. He reentered the van, slid the door closed, and turned on the dome light.

"Here are your tickets, passports, baggage receipts, and two forms of picture IDs."

"Siemens Telecom?" I asked, making eye contact with Max.

"Yes, there is a Communications Expo going on at the Hilton. Both of you are registered."

"How do we get to the Majestic Hotel from the airport?" asked Amelia Jane.

"Once you clear customs in KL you will be met by Taisei's transportation people. The weapons you requested will be made available once you depart the airport. They will then take you directly to the Majestic."

"Thanks, Herr Gresonine. Arriving incognito at Subang is much appreciated," said Mrs. Smythe, referencing Kuala Lumpur's international airport.

"You are both very welcome. But seeing how we will be working together for the next several months, how about if you just call me Uncle Max?"

"It's a deal, if you'll call me Amelia?"

"OK, then it's settled," smiled Max and handed an envelope to me. "These are the people expected to be at the meeting. The backgrounds on the two Afghan men indicate that they can be trusted to do what we require. However, there are still factions within Pakistan's ISI that do not want to relinquish control of the distribution channels into Afghanistan. Some of these people may be on the Russian payroll."

"Understood, Max," I said. "What about the Russians in KL?"

"Up to now they haven't been a problem. The Egyptians and the Israelis have been the real concern. They are true chameleons — especially when it comes to making money. Their people in the transport and manufacturing channels can be easily bought. And that is why the Russians, in this case the KGB, have become the greatest danger in the equation."

I took the three sheets of paper from the envelope. "I don't see our new friend Mr. Mo on the list. Did he renege? Or, did his brother ask him to abstain?"

"Neither, I think," replied Max. "Number five on the list runs the depot facility in Nasr City in Egypt. He's ex-Egyptian military, very well connected within government circles, and comes highly recommended by the Israelis. Mr. Ghazala has been fully briefed on what we require."

"Which is?" asked Amelia Jane.

"The facility in Nasr City will remove, before shipping, all external markings on the Stinger tube and sight array. It will replace the characters and graphics with Serbian Cyrillic script."

"What about what's inside the tubes?" Amelia asked as I passed the list to her.

"Not feasible," I said, "without risking damage to the weapon. Check out number nine on the list: Dr. Theresa Asghar is a last minute walk-on and a fully vested agent of the Mossad."

"How you know that bit of information, I'm sure would make an interesting story. Yes?" Max almost whispered.

"Will she handle the transportation issues?" I asked, not offering my source.

"Yes, and from what I was told, she has requested and received permission to attend from Admoni himself. She also made the case that your role at AT&T should be protected."

"Why would she want to do that?" I asked.

"When I asked that same question I was told that Mr. Taisei is a very important business partner. And besides the fact that he's her uncle, she really has become quite a fan of yours."

"That's probably true for all of us, Yank," said a smiling Mrs. Smythe.

"I'll be damned," I whispered. In my normal speaking voice I said to Max, "You know she had access to some 3AD background files on me? You care to comment on that tidbit of information, Max?" I was referring to files kept on me from my days in the U. S. Army's 3rd Armor Division

Ignoring the question, Max said, "OK, that's all I have for you two. You better get aboard." We all stepped out onto the asphalt. Max pointed to another catering truck that had just pulled head-in and taken a position under the forward-most cabin door of the 747–400.

"See that man waving to us? Go to him and he'll get you seated on the aircraft. Godspeed," said Max.

"Thanks, Max," I said, and shook his hand with both of mine. He held on a moment longer than necessary. He started to say something but stopped. He gave Amelia a hug and a peck on the cheek and then pushed us off towards the waiting van.

We stepped up into the rear of the truck and when I turned to help Amelia I saw the lorry we came in was already backing out onto the service way. As soon as we had both sets of feet safely inside the van, the body of the vehicle separated from its frame and scissor-lifted its way up three stories to the forward cabin door of the 747-400.

23
Betrayed

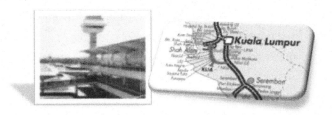

Subang International Airport – Car Park – Top Level
Subang Jaya, Selangor
Kuala Lumpur – Malaysia
Sunday 29 June 1986 0535 Hours

THE LUFTHANSA 747-400 arrived right on time, utilizing a landing technique that most pilots would refer to as a greaser. After we collected our luggage from the indicated conveyor belt, we nodded at one another and selected different customs lines from which to have our documents examined. The foot traffic exiting the customs area at this time of the morning was very light, and when we entered the main concourse, there were perhaps only forty to fifty people waiting for those arriving from other countries. A middle-aged Chinese man, typecast right out of the James Bond film, "Goldfinger," was standing at the far end of the small group. Wearing a black suit and a chauffeur's hat, he held a sign at chest level that said "Siemens Communications".

I raised my right hand as we walked toward him, to indicate we were the people he had come to transport. He gave us a deep nod of the head and stepped forward to take charge of our luggage. Still silent, he pointed towards the exit and the South Car Park. The ten-minute walk took us to the roof level of the garage. At this time of day there were fewer than ten vehicles parked up this high in the facility. The trunk popped opened and our bags were loaded. Before he closed the trunk lid, he pointed to each of our brief cases. Amelia and I both shook our heads indicating "no".

The passenger rear door was opened for Amelia and I went to the rear driver's side door and got in without assistance. The driver circled the front of the car, got in, and immediately started the engine. He made a slight adjustment of the rear-view mirror, put the car in gear, and proceeded slowly towards the exit ramp. His eyes flicked back and forth from the mirror to the road. He seemed nervous.

"Have you worked for Mr. Sorelly at the Majestic for very long?" I asked. This caused Amelia to turn her head and give me a puzzled look. I pulled my briefcase up on my lap and clicked open the locks — one on each side. The lid of the case held a variety of office tools such as pens, pencils, erasers, a pad of loose-leaf paper, and a gold letter opener. The letter opener was a parting gift I had received from the engineering group in Cockeysville before I transferred to AT&T International. I nodded my head slightly towards the driver's head-rest. There was a drop of fresh blood that was apparently only visible from the rear seat. Whoever had cleaned up had not done a very good job.

"Yes, I have worked for Mr. Sorelly for over a year," replied the Chinese man.

"That's funny you should say that. There really isn't anybody with that name — Mr. Sorelly that is — who has ever worked at the Majestic."

As soon as I uttered those magic words, the driver jammed on the brakes, stopping the car on the ramp between floors two and three.

His right arm came up holding a Glock 17. He was turning in his seat in order to point the gun in our direction. He was halfway into the turn when I leaned forward, catching his gun hand with my right. Within the same instant my left hand plunged the letter opener a good five inches into his right ear. He died instantly, but the Glock went off, shattering the side passenger window next to Amelia Jane's head.

"Good God, Rick," yelled Amelia Jane. "Give a girl a little warning, will you!"

I read somewhere that the quietness after a kill can only be described as deafening. However, that moment was short-lived. The silence was broken by the sound of a vehicle skidding to a stop somewhere behind us. Car doors were being opened and slammed shut. I dove forward over the seat, prying the Glock out of the driver's hand. I tossed it over the headrest and on to the seat next to Amelia. I reached across the steering wheel and grabbed the door release. I leaned back and, with both feet, pushed the unemployed driver from the car. I snatched the letter opener from his head as he exited the vehicle and tumbled onto the concrete ramp.

"Get down ... hold on," I yelled, pulling down the shifter. With the car in gear, and using the steering wheel for leverage, I swung into the driver's position. I pressed the accelerator all the way to the floor. The car lurched forward just as the shots rang out. The massive implosion of the back window interrupted several of the metallic thuds pounding the metal of the car's rear end. Beads of glass rained down on top of Amelia Jane and peppered the back of my head.

Amelia was lying across the back seat clutching the Glock against the center of her chest. Her right-hand index finger was extended along the trigger guard. She clamped her left hand over the slide and pulled back slightly to check if a round was chambered. Without bothering to look at who was trying to kill us, she raised the weapon, pointed it towards the rear and squeezed off five quick shots in just a little over three seconds. She was aiming at no one in particular. At that point we simply hoped to make our assailants just a tad concerned about continuing to try to kill us.

After what seemed like a small eternity we reached the ground level of the garage. Just one last turn would bring the main exit into full view. I reached up and adjusted the mirror by tapping it with my index finger. We were still being followed by a light gray Mercedes. Our pursuers had ceased tailgating us. However, as both vehicles neared the exit, the trailing car increased its speed.

"Ten more seconds and we're in the clear," I yelled. "How many rounds are left in the clip?" I heard the clip release and with the sound of a slap we were back in business.

"Nine or ten in the clip and one in the tube," replied a calm, business-like Mrs. Smythe.

We hit the bottom of the ramp at 50 Kph. It was way too fast to negotiate this last turn. We skidded sideways and slammed into a concrete barrier and the car stalled as it came to a sudden stop. The driver's side of the car was now facing towards the ramp that we had just exited.

"You OK?" I yelled.

"Define OK," she said in a now highly agitated voice. "Where did you get your bloody driver's license?"

"Hand me the gun, now." Amelia handed over the Glock butt first. I grabbed it and pointed it at the ramp exit just as the Mercedes sedan came flying around the last bend. Gripping with both hands and resting my forearms on the open window frame, I emptied the remainder of the magazine into the windshield of the oncoming vehicle.

The driver's head exploded. The tiny holes in the windscreen were coated with a bright red liquid. The vehicle did not attempt a turn and crashed straight into a support column. The only other passenger in the car, who apparently did not have his seatbelt fastened, was halfway through the windscreen, lying completely still on the bonnet of the car. They both appeared to be quite dead.

"Hold on while I see if we can get this pile of junk to move again." I turned the ignition key and after a full fifteen seconds of cranking, with my foot pumping up and down, the engine finally caught with a roar. I pulled away from the wall and slowly headed for the exit. There were perhaps 10 or 20 people milling around the parked cars on this level. Everyone was moving in the direction of the accident. All of the onlookers were ignoring us while wisely keeping their distance from the crashed Mercedes. We exited the garage on the opposite end of the building.

"Amelia, pull the SAT phone from my briefcase. Hit six on the speed dial. Ask whoever answers for Hammad. We need to get rid of this car and we need to do it ten minutes ago."

"3066," was said by whoever answered the call.

"Mr. Ndakwah, please," Amelia requested.

"Wait one," and 15 seconds went by.

"Hammad," said the person who came on the line.

"Rick Fontain would like a word with you, Mr. Ndakwah," Amelia Jane said and passed the SAT terminal to the front seat.

"Hammad, we were attacked at the airport. We escaped but need to get rid of what we are driving. Can you help us?"

"Where are you right now? Where is the driver?"

"We are on the main road leaving the airport. We're just coming up on the North-South Expressway. The Chinese man who met us at the gate is dead."

"Chinese…. The next exit will be Jalan Duta. Take a left at the end of the ramp and then an immediate right. Go 75 meters down the alley and you will be met by one of my people."

"No offense, Hammad, but are you sure this person can be trusted? The driver who picked us up tried to kill us."

"Yes, you can trust him. He is my son. His name is Aragón. Now hurry and get off the main highway. I will come for you immediately."

"Will do. Thanks, Hammad," I said, and pressed 'end call'.

"Did you hear any of that?" I asked Amelia.

"Yes, I did. Can we trust him?"

"I don't think we have a choice at this point."

The Majestic Hotel – Concierge Level Suite 1800
No.5 Jalan Sultan Hishamuddin
Kuala Lumpur, Malaysia
Sunday 29 June 1986 2340 Hours

"I'll get it," I said as the door chime was going through a strange rendition of the Lone Ranger's theme song. I peered through the peephole. It was Hammad and the gentleman listed as number seven on the list of attendees for Tuesday's meeting. I had not spoken with him for a little over a year. My personal code name for him was *Pilgrim Mugger*. He was better known as Mike Vaughn.

Mike's primary expertise was analysis. For the previous three years, he had been jockeyed back and forth between the Afghan/Russian and Middle East desks at Langley. On paper, he worked for Joe Wilson; however, a strong dotted line assigned his soul to Gust Avrakotos and the Afghan prayer group.

Gust and Congressman Charlie Wilson had become close buddies. Charlie's campaign had been pushing a number of government agencies, including the DIA and their own CIA, to get the right type of arms into the hands of the Afghan freedom fighters. Since March of '83 most of his and

Gust's efforts had been ignored. The good Congressman had on more than one occasion described the success of their efforts as akin to pushing a rope up a wild hog's ass.

"Hammad, Mike … come on in and join the party."

"Rick, it's been a long time. I heard about your transportation delay at the airport. Are you two alright?"

"Yeah, we're good. Speaking about the airport, Hammad, do you have any news on the bad guys?" I asked as I guided everyone towards the living room.

Suite 1800 was decorated in traditional Malaysian colors and fabric choices. Most of the seating was fashioned out of large bamboo piping which was lashed and lacquered to an exquisite finish. The colorful pillows were fitted perfectly on each piece of furniture. If comfort were the key to guest satisfaction, this hostelry would get an "A" rating.

"Everyone, you have met Mr. Ndakwah …"

"Please everyone, call me Hammad."

"And, this is Mike Vaughn. He's still wanted in Williamsburg, Virginia for the mugging of their head Pilgrim a few years back. Mike, this is Amelia Jane," I said, pointing to the sofa at the far side of the room. "Caitlin and Theresa," indicating the occupants of the chairs that were located just to the left of where Mike was standing. "And the gentleman standing at the bar is Maalouf Torki bin Taisei, the owner of this fine establishment."

"I'm very glad to meet all of you," Mike said. "And for the record, it was the Town Crier, not a Pilgrim."

Everyone was quiet for the moment, not knowing just what to say. So I said, "Mike, they don't seem to believe you either. Come on over to the bar and we'll bring you up to speed on our project. Hammad, what did you find out?"

"Mr. Rick, so far the men who attacked you at the airport have not been identified. We have been able to access Subang's security video feed files. The man who posed as your driver has not been identified. We are making additional inquiries but nothing so far has turned up. My sources suspect," Hammad stopped and swallowed hard before continuing, "he may have been working for the Russians. All of the chatter seems to point directly to the KGB."

"Swell," I said. "Do you have any idea where the leak came from?"

"No, not yet, but I've been assured we will have more information before morning. My driver, the one who was supposed to meet you was found in a trash bin about six blocks from here ... he was ..."

"I'm very sorry for the loss of your man, Hammad," I said.

"Rick," said Mike Vaughn, "I need a moment of your time in private."

"Sure Mike, we can go into the master suite. I tried to get Amelia Jane to sleep in there but she was afraid she would drown in the oversized bathtub. Apparently, she can't swim." Amelia, who was sitting with Caitlin and Dr. Asghar, stuck out her tongue as Mike and I marched passed them.

"What's on your mind, Mike?" I asked as I pushed the door shut.

"Wow, this is really nice," said Mike as he turned to face me. He reached into his jacket pocket, produced a sealed white envelope, and handed it to me.

"This is from Gust. His source in Peshawar said the Russians were aware of a meeting here in KL. They only knew about a meeting — not about its purpose. Still, they also know that Mr. Taisei has been supplying munitions into Pakistan for quite some time. So, they're curious."

I tore open the end of the envelope and pulled out a single sheet of paper. It was hand written and it was signed with two large cursive letters "GA" (Gust Avrakotos). The single paragraph was short, simple, and straight to the point. "Fuck me," I whispered. I turned and walked to the doors, jerked open the right side, stuck my head out and called across the living room. "Theresa, can you come in here?"

"What's up?" she asked as she came into the room.

"Close the door," I said. She pushed the door and it closed with a solid thud.

"Read this," I said. Mike took a seat on the large bench at the base of the king-size bed.

"Where did you get this? Who in God's name is GA?" Theresa was agitated.

"Gust Avrakotos, surely you have heard the name in your travels? Is the individual mentioned in that note on your staff?"

Theresa looked down and reread the note, hoping it had changed from her first understanding.

"Does it surprise you that his brother has been working for the Russians in Pakistan?" I asked.

Mike got up, walked over to Theresa, took the paper from her hand, and said. "He was apprehended breaking into a weapons depot in Mankera Tehsil. It was during his interrogation that his ties to KL were uncovered."

"How do you want to handle this, Rick?" asked Mike.

"Theresa, do you have any suggestions?" I deferred to her.

Without saying a word, she opened the door and walked to the bar. She whispered something in Hammad's ear. Hammad's expression went from a smile to one that would kill. Hammad asked Mr. Taisei to be excused and left the room in a hurry. Theresa then went to the couch where Caitlin was seated and said, "We need to go. Now." On their way to the door, Dr. Asghar put her hand on Caitlin's arm to pause their progress. She walked over and stood in front of me. "This shouldn't take long to correct. I will come and get you when we are set up downstairs. I'm very sorry about this."

"Shit happens," I said as Maalouf Taisei walked over.

"Sir," said Theresa to her uncle, "a member of my staff has betrayed us. We have reason to believe that he is the one responsible for causing the murder of Hammad's brother. With your permission, I will return Caitlin to her quarters and I will personally conduct the interrogation."

"You will keep us informed, yes?" asked Mr. Taisei.

"Of course," she said and ushered Caitlin out the door before I could say *KGB Bastards*.

"The driver that was murdered was Hammad's brother?" I asked.

"Yes. They were very close. Hammad is blaming himself for asking him to go to the airport to pick you up."

"Sir," I said to Taisei, "this could get a lot nastier before we complete our business on Tuesday. I suggest we go on offense."

"What do you suggest, Rick?"

"First, I propose we move the location of the meeting. We're too exposed here. Any suggestions?"

"Genting Highlands," was his immediate response. The only thing I knew about Genting was that it was the only place in Malaysia where gambling was allowed. It had been built by an old Chinese gentleman. The distance from KL was an hour's drive via the Karak Highway. That was the extent of what I knew. I looked at Maalouf, raising my brows in a request for additional information.

"I have a home above Genting. It is very private and very secure. It was the site of the first casino. I purchased it from an old Chinese, Wong Ng, about ten years ago."

"Amelia," I called. "A word if you please."

Consulate General of the United States
Unmmu Hurair 1 – Al Seef Road
Bur Dubai – Dubai – United Arab Emirates
Monday 30 June 1986 0545 Hours

"Bill, sorry to bother you at home," said David James. "Joe Wase, HOS for UAE just got off a call with our HOS in Cairo. Ahmed Zadawi, member of Egypt's General Intelligence Directorate, was killed leaving their facility in Nasr City."

"Number four on the list to attend tomorrow's meeting! What the fuck is going on?" exclaimed Bill Douglas. "Rick called me a half hour ago and told me about the murder. He said Dr. Asghar found out about the plot too late to warn her people on site."

"How did she come by this information?" asked David.

"She got it from a member of her medical staff, a male nurse, that the Russians were aware of the meeting tomorrow and that they had been given the names of some of the attendees."

"Only some, not all?" asked David.

"According to Rick, the nurse didn't know all of the names, but that doesn't mean the Russians don't."

"What else did Dr. Asghar find out?" asked the Ambassador.

"That's about it, I'm afraid. Rick said she was in a hurry and the man died before she could recap. She apologized for the error."

"A member of the Mossad expressing regret; that's a first," observed David. "I've put a call in for General Bushman. He'll need to brief the President."

"Rick has folded the tent in KL. They're moving the meeting to Genting Highlands."

"The General will want to add you in to the call, Bill," said David.

"I'm leaving for the Embassy as soon as I get dressed. I'll give you odds that the President will not pussyfoot around with the Russian shenanigans of the past several days. I suspect the gloves will come off. Thanks for calling, David."

"Watch your back, Bill. Ivan has become very frisky lately," said David James, and the line went silent.

"A very good point, David," replied Douglas to himself. He went to his closet and spun the dial on the safe. He took out the Beretta and its holster, pulled the strap around his neck, and snapped it to a place on his belt. He put on his suit coat and examined himself in the mirror. He then went down the stairs and out to his waiting car and driver.

24

The Oval

The Whitehouse
1600 Pennsylvania Ave.
Washington, DC
Tuesday July 1 1986 1750 Hours

GENERAL BUSHMAN MARCHED down the hall on the wrong side. His pace seemed excessive to those who encountered him. His dark blue three-piece business suit, accented with a light gray pin stripe, was a surprise birthday gift from his wife. He liked the cut and the texture of the suit's material, for sure, but it did not come close to his preference for the look and feel of being in uniform.

It had been purchased from a shop called Hackett's Tailors. It was located directly next door to the Sir Isaac Newton House on Jermyn Street in London. Coincidentally, 88 Jermyn Street was the home of the AT&T Network System's Engineering Group, and, of course, the office of Rick Fontain.

As Bushman approached the administrative area just outside the Oval Office, the President's personal assistant, Peggy Grande, addressed him.

"General Bushman, the President is expecting you. Please go right in

When she pushed the slightly curved door open, the General could see Rawhide sitting behind his desk.

"Thank you, Ms. Grande," Bushman said, and nodded at the Secret Service agent as the agent pulled the door shut, leaving him alone with the President.

Reagan looked up immediately, stood, and came around his desk to shake hands with the man he had come to both respect and rely on. After a brief exchange, the President guided Bushman to the sofas located at the center of the room.

"I've asked Don Regan to sit in on this. He should be here any minute. Coffee?"

"No thank you, Mr. President. I've already exceeded Mary's two cup rule today."

"The facts as I understand them are, number one: the Russians have attacked two of our people in Malaysia, and number two and probably the most troubling: an Egyptian government official has been murdered outside of Cairo," said the U.S. President. This was said just as a Secret Service agent opened the door on the opposite side of the room. The Chief of Staff entered at a fast pace and was immediately waved into the discussion.

"Nasr City, Mr. President. He was attacked leaving their munitions refurbishment facility in Nasr City," said General Bushman as he stood to the outstretched hand of Donald Regan, Chief of Staff.

"Mr. President, Sir, sorry I'm late. There don't seem to be enough hours in the day anymore," he took a seat next to General Bushman.

"From what Gerry has just told me, it would seem an immediate change to Operation Cyclone is necessary."

"Yes, Mr. President. Joe Wilson, at CIA, has relayed information received from Ambassador James. The Ambassador reported that an additional attack had occurred and more were expected. This was the second occurrence in a 24-hour period."

The President was clearly angry and frustrated. "First let me say that Brezhnev, and now Gorbachev, would have to be deaf, dumb, and blind not to know that Zia, since the start of their murdering escapade, has been supporting the Afghan rebels. Am I, right?

"Yes, Mr. President," was the simultaneous response.

"So, all of this skulking around making sure we're not identified as the provider of Stinger missiles to the Mujahideen ends right now. General, you are to inform our team in the field that the preparation and scrubbing of USA markings is no longer a requirement. As of this moment I want President Zia and his ISI folks in agreement to accept direct shipments of the Stinger missile. Same rules for their implementation as before."

"Yes, Mr. President," replied General Bushman.

"The CIA tells me that Gorbachev is not in favor of continuing the military takeover in Afghanistan. He has publicly voiced his objection. The CIA says that he has set a timeline for the military to succeed or to conclude their occupation. His mandate for a complete pull-out will take effect if present operations fail to produce the desired result in the short term. I think he's looking for a way out of Afghanistan. I also think Stinger will present him with that opportunity."

"That's very possible, Mr. President. However, at this point in the conflict, a Russian victory is still very much a possibility," countered the General.

"Well, if only half of what I've been told about Stinger turns out to be true, Gerry, the Russian military and Mr. Gorbachev are in for a great big surprise. Perhaps now that the gloves are off we'll be able to speed up their timeline for them. Giving the Russians some true-life incentives will finally provide some payback for Vietnam."

"Yes, Mr. President," was again the dual response. The payback for Vietnam had been a long time coming.

25

Sultan Abdul Aziz Shah Airport

Car Park – Ground Level
Subang International Airport
47200 Subang – Selangor, Malaysia
Wednesday July 2 1986 1550 Hours

THE LIGHTWEIGHT BULLETPROOF vest, I was told with a wink of Theresa's eye, was an experimental version presently under evaluation by the Mossad. She coerced me into wearing it and I was already sorry that I had acquiesced. A steady stream of sweat started almost immediately to trickle down the small of my back. I was seated in the rear passenger side of a black Toyota Land Cruiser. We were parked head-in on the ground level of the car park, directly across from the entrance to Subang's main terminal.

From my position in the vehicle, I could see directly across the walkway that connected the garage to the terminal. There was a slit in the car park's concrete wall that provided an excellent view. Seated next to me was Theresa Asghar, the resident Mossad agent, and personal physician of our in-country host, Maalouf Torki bin Taisei.

On the passenger side, seated directly in front of me, was Hammad Ndakwah. He was Mr. Taisei's Head of Security and the brother of the mur-

147

dered driver who had been found in a trash bin six blocks from the Majestic Hotel. The Motorola handheld COMM (communications) link that was lying on the seat between us squealed briefly, letting us know that the staged pickup of the Pakistani ISI generals had been completed.

All members of Hammad's staff were making their way to the main concourse. From there, this group was scheduled to exit the main terminal and cross the apron to the pickup area. All four of the individuals were playing their assigned parts very well. They even had brought fake luggage with them. The second call came five minutes later as they approached the bright, sunlit sidewalk. The motion controlled sliding glass doors parted and they moved at a steady pace to the waiting hotel car.

There was a light tan, 1984 Opel Rekord Sedan with its motor running parked on the Subang airport roadway. It was positioned a good fifty meters down and to the right of the main terminal drop-off point. The vehicle sported four occupants: two in the front and two in the back passenger seat. Directly behind the Opel was a late model white Mitsubishi panel van. The driver and the passenger were the only visible occupants.

Hammad spoke first, "Watch from here, Doctor," he commanded. "Let's go," he said to the driver. Both doors of the Land Cruiser opened and both men rounded the vehicle parked next to them and headed for the zebra-striped walkway that led the way from the car park to Subang's main terminal.

Instead of crossing the driveway, Hammad and company turned to the right as they exited the car park. They walked casually along the sidewalk until they were directly across the road from the vehicles of interest. The occupants of the vehicles were parked curbside and were entirely focused on the four individuals who had just exited the main terminal.

Hammad turned towards the vehicles and picked up the pace. Hammad and the driver unbuttoned their suit coats and let the sling take the full weight of their .45 CAL ACP Uzi machine guns. These particular weapons had been upgraded with a conversion kit manufactured by Vector Arms. This modification allowed the Uzi to accept the same style 30-cartridge magazine as the US Army's M3, better known as a "Grease Gun". Everyone attending today's gathering was carrying two spare magazines.

Hammad headed directly towards the driver's side of the Opel, while his driver, Ahmad Haqq, adjusted his angle of approach and walked towards the van parked directly behind. The driver of the van recognized the coming threat and laid on the horn. But it was a split second too late. At a distance of five meters Hammad crouched slightly, bringing the weapon up level with his chest. Mr. Haqq repeated the same movement. Hammad fired first, emptying half of the magazine into the front seat of the car. The occupants of the front seat started to jerk uncontrollably. Blood, tissue, and brain matter splattered everywhere within the vehicle. The faces of the two rear occupants registered pure horror as Hammad turned his attention to them.

Mr. Haqq altered his trajectory slightly bringing his weapon up directly in line with the driver's side window of the van. With his weapon on full automatic, he emptied his entire magazine into the front of the van. The result was so devastating that it was hard to recognize that the former occupants were ever human. Without breaking stride, he continued on his way alongside the vehicle. Mr. Haqq, once the magazine was emptied, pushed the release and flipped the position of the taped together magazines. With his left hand, he pulled back on the charging handle. This action immediately allowed him to empty the second magazine into the side panel of the truck. As he moved to the rear doors of the truck he was joined by Hammad. The yelling and bloodcurdling screams had ceased halfway through Mr. Haqq's second clip.

Hammad and Mr. Haqq recharged their weapons as they arrived at the rear doors of the van. Hammad brought his weapon up as Mr. Haqq dropped the weight of the UZI onto its sling and pulled the right-side door to a fully opened position. There were five more individuals contorted in a variety of poses throughout the cabin. Everyone was quite dead.

"Good," said Hammad. "Let us get back." Hammad dropped the Uzi and buttoned his jacket. Mr. Haqq pushed the door closed, straightened his coat and followed Hammad across the street, turning several times to see if they were being followed. All pedestrian traffic had disappeared from the sidewalk. In the meantime, the four individuals who had come out of the main terminal building, as planned, got into the waiting Majestic Hotel limo and were slowly pulling away from the curb.

Meanwhile, back in the Land Cruiser: "Uh-oh, we have more bad guys," I said to Theresa. A black, four door Mercedes 190D drove past the rear of our head-in parked vehicle. The car had come from our left and stopped just ten meters from where we were parked. The driver was waving his hands in the air and pointing at the hotel limo that was heading out of the airport. The driver's side door was dead even with the entrance to the crosswalk that lead to the main terminal.

"You ready?" I asked. Theresa nodded and we opened our respective doors at almost the same time.

I wasn't wearing a jacket. The strap of the MP5 was draped over my right shoulder. Hammad's personal Walther PBK was in a paddle holster on my right hip. The rear driver's side door was the first to open as I approached. At the five-meter mark I brought the Heckler & Koch up and pushed it towards the target until the sling was tight.

A left leg was thrust out of the rear driver's side door and firmly planted down on the concrete slab. Next a head emerged and it began to immediately swivel back and forth, taking in the lay of the land. In his left hand, he held a KH-23 (Russian Drozd detachable stock shotgun) and in his right hand he held a Tokarev TT-33 (Russian 7.62 X 25mm silent pistol). He saw me approaching and immediately pointed the pistol in my direction.

On my way, I selected the middle of the three semi-automatic positions with my right thumb. I depressed the trigger three times in a measured, half-second timeframe. The result I wanted came on the third shot. The first went high into the front seat headrest; however, it wasn't a wasted shot. The bullet went through the padding like butter and entered the driver's skull, exiting through his eye socket. The second shot came very close, but no cigar. It was still slightly wide of its intended mark. It did, however, manage to dig into the very top of the right shoulder of the individual trying to exit the rear seat. They say three is the charm: the head shot hit just below the left eye and exploded out the back of his head.

In the very same moment I found myself thrown backwards. There was no sound. My breathing had stopped. The back of my head hit the pavement hard. The one shot he managed to get off was from the silenced Russian pistol.

"What the fuck?" were the exact words being displayed on the brightly lit wall in the back of my mind.

Theresa's Uzi barked several times with three to four shots per second. And then all got very quiet. The next thing I knew, Dr. Asghar was bending over me, telling me to breathe. She ripped open my shirt. She placed her left hand behind my head and tilted it forward to show me that the vest had saved my life. The bullet had struck me just below my left nipple. It had flattened out and was stuck to the material like a tick to a hound dog's ear.

"Can you walk? We've got to leave here, now," said the doctor with her best, but rushed, bedside manner. Hammad, who had run up on the scene, took hold of me on one side and Mr. Haqq on the other. They pulled me to my feet and guided me to the Cruiser. In less than 30 seconds we were backing out of our parking space. We exited the car park on the far side of the building. As we continued on Subang's main drive, five police cars with lights and sirens blazing were rushing towards the main terminal. Hammad turned in his seat to see how I was doing. Theresa had helped me remove the vest. There was a large bruise the size of a silver dollar on my torso. She told me that I probably had cracked a rib.

"No shit," I whispered back. I had been saying that a lot lately.

26
Genting Highlands

Awana Genting Retreat
Titiwangsa Mountains Elevation 2,183 m
Northern Malaysia
Wednesday July 2 1986 1950 Hours

"IT'S BEAUTIFUL HERE. The view is magnificent," said Amelia Jane to Maalouf Torki bin Taisei. He had walked out on the rooftop veranda and stood beside her. They were at the railing, facing west.

"The mountains you see there," said Maalouf, "where the sun is setting between them — the peaks are called Barisan Titiwangsa. We are high enough here so that on a clear day you can see all the way into the Strait of Malacca. Do you know about an occurrence that is called ... the Green Flash?"

"Yes indeed," replied Amelia. "My husband and I honeymooned in the Cayman Islands. We stayed on what they call their Seven Mile Beach. A direct line of sight all the way to where the sun dips its fire into the water. The flame, a splinter of green, occurs only at that very moment, yes?"

"You are lucky then. I myself have never seen it. But those who have say that it is very beautiful."

"The lights down there seem to be your only neighbors," observed Amelia Jane.

"Yes, that is very true," replied Maalouf. "And, the most attractive feature of this place, and the main reason we have come here, is that there are only two ways to gain access. The best, and my first choice, is by helicopter, which is why you arrived that way. The original method is via an old skyway tram. The sky cars can only be accessed through the service road located in a secure area behind the resort property. Presently, the casino is putting on a large addition to their hotel," he said, and pointed down the mountain. "See the cluster of lights you refer to as our neighbors? Just this side of those lights is the original tram car access station. The system was installed as the first step in the construction process to bring workers and materials up the mountainside. It's the only other way up here."

"Who controls the tram cars?"

"Both cars are parked somewhere in the middle when not in use. The only operational controls are up here with us. No one can gain access without our permission."

"How do you communicate with the motor controls down below?"

"I have been told it is through a power-line carrier technology. The steel core of the support cables provides the connectivity."

"Sounds secure, but you know what they say: 'where there is a will there is a way'."

"Yes, yes, but the support coupling for each of the cars is rigged with explosive bolts. The same type as used on NASA's Apollo launch vehicle. If the system is accessed in the wrong way, the result will be rather painful and expensive to repair."

"Hmm … this place has the look and feel of a monastery. A special quietness seems to permeate everything," said Mrs. Smythe, changing the subject and hoping she would not be asked to ride on any of the cable cars.

"I think that was the intent of the builder, an old Chinese gentleman named Tan Koon Swan. He told me he found this place too tranquil for his favored lifestyle. Mr. Swan is the leader of the MCA, the Malayan Chinese Association. They are now the main sponsors of all of the construction behind the lights you see down there. Perhaps he will find the balance he desires in his new discotheques and luxury villas."

Amelia Jane turned from the railing to face her host. "Sir, I want to thank you for helping us. Without your support, we would —" she stopped as Maalouf held up both hands.

"There is no need. This is now very, very personal for me, and, even more so for the people who take care of me. Whatever you require of us will be done. I pledge this to you and your partner."

"Is this a private gathering or can anyone join the festivities," I asked as Mike Vaughn, aka the Pilgrim Mugger, and I stepped onto the rooftop veranda.

"Oh, my God, Rick. Hammad told me what happened at the airport. Are you OK?" Amelia Jane cried out. Maalouf didn't say anything but nodded his head as he met my eyes. His expression said it all. He seemed to be as glad as I was that I was still walking on this side of the grass, so to speak.

"Just a little bruising, a couple of bumps is all. Doc Theresa says I'll be fine," I replied. Amelia stepped forward and put her arms around my neck, trying to hide her emotions.

I looked across Amelia's shoulder to Maalouf. "Mike says our friends from Pakistan made it in OK. Did you have any difficulties getting them through Singapore customs?"

"No, it went off without a hitch, I believe is the expression. The flight was diverted as planned. Mr. Vaughn and Amelia took my helicopter and met their plane. My contacts at Changi Airport walked them from their commercial gate to the helicopter. We flew them directly here."

"Do they know what's going on?" I asked.

"Only that there was a problem with the original meeting parameters," replied Amelia Jane, who had finally relaxed her arms from around my neck.

"I'm afraid this operation just got a bit more complicated, Maalouf. Or, maybe from your perspective it may be a bit less risky — depending on our Pakistani friends downstairs."

"I don't understand? What has changed?" asked Maalouf.

"Amelia, Mike, can you give me a minute with Maalouf?" I asked.

"Of course," replied Mrs. Smythe. And with a nod of the head she got Mike to follow her to the stairwell.

"Amelia and Mr. Vaughn seem to enjoy each other's company," commented Maalouf.

I didn't respond because I hadn't noticed until right then the very same thing. Amelia's smile seemed to brighten when Mike was in the room. Well, not surprising: pilgrim muggers are becoming extremely rare. "*Good for you Amelia Jane,*" I said to myself.

"The President, I'm talking about *my* president, Maalouf, has requested, and I'm not convinced that is the word he used, that President Zia's permission be solicited for Stinger weapons to be put directly into the fight. The plan to scrub U.S. markings from each tube before use in Afghanistan has been withdrawn."

"Well then, it seems my brother and I have outlived our usefulness in this endeavor," replied Maalouf.

"Not at all, Sir. We still very much need your assistance," I replied. "The biggest nut to crack is still before us. Two of the largest squirrels that can crack this nut for us are apparently downstairs."

"Nuts, squirrels," repeated Maalouf. "Ha, you're joking, Rick, is at times very amusing, but the older of the two gentlemen downstairs is not someone to joke about."

"Sir, without your backing the past few weeks this entire operation would be dead in the water. And the participation by your nephew, Mustapha, has provided our introduction to his leadership. Things look very good on that front."

"He is a fine young man, a devout husband, and a superb commander," Maalouf said proudly.

"The Mujahideen will get the Russians to rethink their presence in Afghanistan. The Stinger technology almost guarantees it. Mustapha is an important part of our being able to complete this operation."

"Will you be going to Pakistan?" asked Maalouf.

"Yes, if the Pakistanis agree to support us. If they won't, well, I guess my management will play that by ear."

"What can I do to help from this point forward?" asked Maalouf.

"Well, we still don't know what the two gentleman downstairs have in their minds," I said as a starting point for suggestions.

"Rick," replied Maalouf, "whatever you require I will do, and whatever you need it will be provided."

"Thanks, Maalouf, you are a true friend," I responded with a great deal of emotion. "Mustapha has convinced his elders to accept the terms and conditions of our required protocols. All that remains to get started is the acceptance of President Zia and his ISI," I said.

"Our two guests, the generals, you mean?" asked Maalouf.

"The two gentlemen downstairs need to agree with the required handling procedures for the Stinger weapons system. Then all we need to do is show the Mujahideen the best place to stand to kill Russian gunships."

"I will inform my brother that the services of Nasr City are no longer required. But what if the Pakistanis will not agree?" asked Maalouf.

"Plan B," I responded immediately. "Injecting Stinger directly into Afghanistan will not be easy. Nor will the training or managing the supply. But we may not have any choice. Perhaps you should emphasize that point with our guests."

And then I added, gently, "Now that Stinger is no longer requiring space in your special transport channel, the South African Uranium-235 shouldn't draw much attention when it arrives in Karachi next month."

"Hmm mmm, young man you are a constant surprise. How long have you known, Rick?"

"For a while now, Sir. And my immediate management has chosen to look the other way for the moment. Stinger is our only focus. And, in a months' time the delivery will be a moot point."

"Well, I wish I had your confidence on that topic, Rick. But again, what specifically will we do if our guests downstairs won't agree to the terms?"

"We're prepared to set up shop in caves in Afghanistan, near Kohi-Safi."

Maalouf turned and looked out over the valley below. "Then we will convince them, how do you say, to play ball," replied Maalouf, turning back to face me. "However, I'm afraid that only one of the gentlemen downstairs will be able to help us."

"Why is that, Sir?" I asked.

"On their way from Singapore, Mr. Vaughn discovered that only one of them is a real general. General Khan and Mohammad Yousaf Azraq are their names," continued Maalouf. "Mr. Azraq told Vaughn he was formerly a colonel stationed in the southern part of Pakistan. But, he said nothing more after making eye contact with General Khan."

"Rick," called Mike Vaughn. He emerged from the stairwell with a piece of yellow teletype paper clenched in his right hand.

"Mike, Maalouf just informed me that one of the Pakistanis may not be a player. You were going to tell me this when?" I asked.

"I wanted to check with my boss first before I said anything to you. Here, read this. Gust thinks we can deal directly with these guys. He says his source in Islamabad says that President Zia is on board one hundred percent."

"How's that?" I asked.

"The older gentleman downstairs was personally given his fourth Star by Zia and has been recently appointed the Chairman of the Joint Chiefs of Staff Committee for Pakistan. He is also, and has been for the last two years, the head of Pakistan's ISI."

I whistled and asked, "And the other guy?"

"That's a mystery. Our guys on the desk at Langley are at a loss as to how Mr. Azraq fits into this negotiation," replied Mike. "Azraq is or was in the military. In '83 he held the rank of a lieutenant colonel, not a general. His last known assignment was in the city of Quetta which is in Pakistan's southern district of Baluchistan."

"His file came in this afternoon," added Amelia, who had just walked up. "Apparently, Mr./Colonel Mohammad Yousaf Azraq has built quite a reputation as an historian, a writer, and a poet."

"Swell, just what we need," I said. "What is the real general's name?"

"Akhtar Abdul Reman Khan has been the head of the ISI since 1983," said Maalouf.

"Maalouf, I take it that you have a personal history with the General?"

"Indirectly. My association with the ISI has been, how do you say, at an arm's length. My dealings in Pakistan have been brokered mostly through the Chinese and the Egyptians."

"Do you think General Khan knows who you are?" asked Amelia.

"I suspect he does now," replied Maalouf. "When we spoke upon his arrival from the airport he didn't seem to be surprised by my presence. Perhaps President Zia has already made up his mind for him."

"That could be true, Sir," said Amelia, looking down at an open folder.

Mike said, "The background on this officer suggests that he is his own man."

"Perhaps before we get started," I tossed a suggestion on the table, "a private conversation offline would help us avoid any confusion when we formally lay out what we're asking them to do."

"That's a good idea. Who do you suggest?" asked Amelia Jane.

"If you would like, I'll talk to him," Maalouf immediately offered. "May I tell him of the recent decision to provide the Stinger missiles with no change to their outward identification markings?"

"Of course," I replied. And if there appears to be any hesitation on his part—"

"I will make available to him our SAT COMM uplink, to speak directly with his President," interrupted Maalouf.

"Good idea," commented Amelia.

"Where is the ISI hanging their hat these days?" I asked.

"The Ojhri Camp, located outside Islamabad," answered Mike. "Why do you ask?"

"I think we need to be specific as to what we're requesting. But first, if you wouldn't mind, Maalouf, please talk with General Khan. Let's get a read on his frame of mind."

"Certainly, I will do so immediately," confirmed Maalouf.

"Hold up until I call General Bushman. I need to clarify the status of a few things. The Egyptians and the Israelis are now out of the picture. The only part left to firm up is the direct shipment constraints and the associated handling protocols. Can you show me where your COMM center is located?"

"Of course. It is one level down. The communication center, it is directly under that satellite dish antenna," replied Maalouf, pointing across the roof to a cluster of several different flavors of aerial masts.

"Amelia, why don't you tag along? After I talk to General Bushman I think we need to touch base with our boss."

"You think?"

PART IV

The Ojhri Experience

27
A Kabul River Dam

Overlooking Tiber River
3 kilometers from Sufaid Sang
Northwest Frontier Afghanistan
Thursday 3 July 1986 0545 Hours

CWO GARY LAWSON lowered his field glasses and let them fall to the bottom of the leather sling that was draped around his neck. He tapped the shoulder of DELTA-1 (SFC George Angerome) as he turned to retreat from the ledge that overlooked the Kabul River Dam.

"Stay here while I check in with Pezlola."

"Roger that, Mr. Lawson," replied DELTA-1.

Saifullah Khan, Jim Pezlola, (call sign ZERO), and Mustapha Taisei were all seated on the ground behind a large boulder just off the main trail. They were bent over in discussion of the map that lay before them.

"Once you cross the river it is only about three kilometers to the town of Sufaid Sang," said Saifullah, poking his finger on the map directly on top of the Warsak Dam project.

"Is this the best place to cross?" asked Pezlola.

"Yes. The last time we were here there was not anyone from the government at the site," said Saifullah. "Only the workers maintaining the hydro-generation equipment are here."

"I must leave you here and get back to my village," said Saifullah. "I'm sorry I cannot travel with you to the Ojhri Camp, but I have been away too long and the families of the ones who were lost at the mine must be cared for."

"Thanks for all you did for us, Saifullah," said Pezlola. "We owe you a lot for your support but even more for your companionship."

"It has been my honor, Mr. Pezlola, Mr. Lawson," Saifullah said as he rose to his feet, nodding at Gary Lawson who had just walked up to join the group.

"Saifullah," called out Pezlola. "I may call upon you again in the not too distant future."

"Again, it would be my honor to assist, Mr. Jim." With that said, he made a form-up motion to his men with his right hand. The three members of his village, who were sitting cross-legged on the ground directly across the main trail, rose and made their way to the small clearing next to where Saifullah was waiting. With one final pat to the shoulder of his brother-in-law, Mustapha, who had walked with him to the main trail, Saifullah turned and led his group onto the path and down the back side of the mountain.

"It looks quiet off to the east, Jim," said Lawson.

"Good. Saifullah says this is the best place to cross the river," said Pezlola, and pointed to the map still on the ground from the discussion. "The sun will be up in a half-hour. Once we cross the river we'll make our way around Sufaid Sang," he said, running his finger just west of the town. It's about five clicks to this area, a truck stop, just south of Jamrud. Here," said Pezlola, pointing to a spot on the map. We've been promised that the trucks will arrive no later than fourteen hundred hours."

28
Ojhri

ISI Central Command
Ojhri Camp
Chaklala, Rawalpindi – South of Islamabad – Pakistan
Thursday 3 July 1986 1755 Hours

THEY ARRIVED AT the camp Thursday in the early evening just as it was getting dark. The truck convoy had gathered them up at a truck stop located just two clicks (kilometers) south of the town of Sufaid Sang. The passenger list consisted of the CIA operatives Pezlola and Lawson, the seven Delta team members, and the Mujahideen leader Saifullah Khan, plus 14 of his most promising student warriors. The latter, it was hoped, would become seven of the first fully trained, two-man Stinger fire teams.

ISI Central Command and Camp Ojhri were located on a thirty-five-acre complex just south of Islamabad and Pakistan's third largest airport, Islamabad International. The lead vehicle, a Mercedes, and the two five-ton Army transport vehicles pulled completely into the half circle in front of the ISI headquarters building. Three individuals exited the car, Jim Pezlola, Mustapha Taisei, and a Pakistani army captain who, up to this point, had not provided his name. All three of the men took a moment to face the building from the base of the steps. At the very top, just inside the main entrance, stood an individual.

This man, who sported a dark gray business suit, waved them forward. His dark brown hair matched his well-groomed beard. Even though the sun was just about done for the day, a very classy pair of aviator sunglasses hid his eyes.

"Someone forgot to announce that the sun has set," whispered Pezlola. This earned him an unkind look from the Pakistani army captain.

"Welcome, gentlemen. Please come up," said the man in the sunglasses just as all three travelers started up the steps. "Captain, would you please see to our other travelers? If anyone needs to use the facilities direct everyone to the basement entrance on the left side of the building. The Sergeant Major has kept the mess hall open for our guests. Transport everyone over there when they are ready. We will be along directly."

"Yes, Brigadier, I will see to it immediately."

As Pezlola and Saifullah stepped up onto the portico, a hand was offered. "I'm Brigadier General Yousaf Azraq. Please excuse the sunglasses. I seem to have developed an eye infection on my travel back from Malaysia this week.

"Well so much for my rush to judgment on first impressions," thought Pezlola.

"I'm Jim Pezlola, General," replied Jim. "This is Mustapha Taisei, Mujahideen Commander."

"I head up the Afghan Bureau for the ISI," continued the Brigadier. "I've been given the honor by General Khan to set up and coordinate the Stinger storage and training. I have three officers who were trained in the United States at your White Sands base. Also, it is our intent that once the training is completed we will assist with field logistics and transportation. The faster we get Stinger into the fight the faster the Russians will come to understand the true meaning of the word karma."

"Which is what, General Azraq?" asked Pezlola.

"They will come to the realization that unsolicited aggression comes with a price."

"Yes, it does. Payback is a bitch," replied Pezlola.

"I'm not sure what is meant by payback, but I promise you it will be bloody," said Mustapha.

"Yes, I believe it will. Again, welcome. Our summit today has been postponed much too long. Please come in," said Yousaf, indicating they should proceed through the huge, ornately carved wooden doors. "Your friends traveled with us from our meeting in Malaysia. They are waiting for you inside."

As if on cue, the right-hand door, with an impressive height of six meters, was pulled open and held by a uniformed soldier. The Pakistani noncommissioned officer, with his back against the door, saluted his approaching general with his right hand as the group entered the lobby.

"Welcome to Ojhri. How are you Mustapha?" asked General Akhtar Khan, whose uniform displayed four stars on each of its shoulder boards.

"I'm fine, General, Sir. It has been quite a while since our last meeting," answered Mustapha.

"I'm Akhtar Khan. You must be Mr. Pezlola. I'm glad this day has finally arrived," said the head of the ISI. "You have already met my newly appointed head of our Afghan Bureau, Brigadier Azraq. He will coordinate all of your training and operational requirements."

"Thank you, General Khan and Brigadier Azraq. Sir," said Pezlola to Azraq, "you said we had some friends waiting for us?"

"Oh yes, of course. Sorry. They are in the conference center. A Mrs. Smythe and a Mr. Fontain. If you will follow me this way," said Brigadier Azraq, and led the way down the hall.

29

Winds from the Cyclone

Airport Access Road
Near the ISI Ojhri Camp – South of Islamabad
Chaklala, Rawalpindi – Pakistan
Sunday 6 July 1986 0755 Hours

PARKED ON THE shoulder of the airport access road, we watched as the C-141 passed overhead. Its landing gear appeared to be down and locked as the large cargo plane descended on its final approach to Islamabad International Airport. Jim Pezlola was seated next to an empty driver's seat. I was with fellow CIA operative, Amelia Jane Smythe, in the rear of the military marked VW passenger bus. We had just attempted for the second time to call Mr. Lawson on the radio com-link. There was still no joy.

Our driver, a Pakistani NCO, a corporal, was standing outside the vehicle. It was decorated with a professionally applied camouflage paint scheme. I was almost afraid to get out of the car for fear that I wouldn't be able to find it again. Amelia had asked the driver politely but firmly to exit the bus and to go stand by the security fence. He had just turned to face the car and was pointing skyward at the huge aircraft passing overhead. He and his vehicle were on loan from an Army Headquarters support company that was based directly across the highway from the entrance to the ISI's Ojhri encampment.

Pezlola's and Lawson's paid vacation, as Bill Douglas jokingly referred to their role on this mission, had gotten underway late in the previous month. It was 23 July to be exact. Today was day twenty-nine of Delta's assigned duty as watchful angels. The aircraft that had just passed overhead would provide a ride back to their base in Germany and a well-deserved respite for the entire team. As long as there were no unforeseen difficulties, this OP would be in the history books, at least for them, by their supper time.

Earlier in the week, the Mujahideen leadership council had voted unanimously to accept a U.S. Government offer. It would require strict compliance for the transport and the handling of the Stinger weapon. This, of course, included even the return and proper disposal of empty missile tubes. Mustapha had been appointed by Ali Mohsen al-Ahmar, a Regional Mujahideen Commander, to oversee the training for and deployment of the very first Stinger weapons training program.

Although al-Ahmar's headquarters was in the providence of Nangarhar, his command spanned six of the most strategic districts east of the city of Kabul and stretched back through the mountains all the way to the Afghan border and the Northern Frontier boundary of Pakistan. The Mujahideen commitment was firm. The Pakistani ISI commitment would need to be as strong.

Another important piece of good news had come that week via SAT phone. The call had buzzed in the early morning hours on Wednesday the 23rd. The word was that President Zia and the ISI had also given their blessing for the Phase One start of Operation Cyclone. President Zia and his ISI General had pledged their full support for training and the deployment of the Stinger missile system for use against the Russian military in Afghanistan. The operational plan would now have a physical place to work. All that we needed at that point was to work the plan.

As soon as Mustapha was appointed by his leaders, he immediately pledged to them to bring Stinger into the fight. Pezlola suggested they head back to the Peshawar area the very next day. That same night Mustapha selected 14 of his best men to be trained as Stinger sharpshooters. Warrior number 15, Vassar Suleiman, formerly a Terrapin of the University of Maryland, had already submitted himself to take the Stinger training. He also had convinced Mustapha to let him be his team spotter. This Afghan group of volunteers would be the first students to be instructed in the fine art of killing Russian aircraft.

In the VW bus, Pezlola put his thumb and index finger up to his throat and called, "DELTA-1, would you please advise Mr. Lawson that our ride is here? He isn't answering my call."

"Roger that. This is DELTA-1. Stand by," replied SFC Angerome.

DELTA-1 turned, called across the room to SSG Don Goschich (DELTA-3) and said, "Did you copy that? ZERO can't raise the CWO. Have you heard from him recently?"

"Mr. Lawson and Jeff Deccan are down in the quarry near the west gate. They went with Mustapha to assist with setting up the tents."

"The depth of the excavation and its sheer rock walls is a perfect location to choose if a campsite with poor communications was the goal," said an irritated Angerome.

As far as the Mujahideen were concerned, it was the most desirable location on the entire post. According to Deccan (DELTA-2), Suleiman was the only sane one in the bunch. Suleiman elected to make his bed in the barracks.

"In a few hours' time," replied DELTA-3, "it won't be our concern any longer. Let me try them on the alt channel before we send out a search party."

"Have at it," replied DELTA-1 from across the room. Their entire conversation was well within the hearing of Suleiman, who was kneeling by his bunk putting the just-cleaned receiver group back into his AK47.

"Four years at the University of Meerie-land," said Suleiman, entering the conversation, "has forever instilled in me the joys of indoor plumbing, especially as we approach the winter season."

"I find no fault with your logic, Vassar. Break, break for ZERO," DELTA-3 said and released the send switch on his neck.

"Still no joy, Boss," he said, turning back to face DELTA-1.

"Let me try one more time," replied DELTA-1. A double tap on the mic switch was heard and then, "DELTA-2, DELTA-2. DELTA-1, over," called DELTA-1, releasing the switch of his throat mic. There was still no response.

Finally, after several more exchanges took place unsuccessfully, Lawson (ONE) revealed himself, "Breaking camp and proceeding your location in 10 mikes. Come back."

DELTA-1 in the barracks, called out, "Ok people, listen up. As some of you just heard, our transport has just arrived. Get your gear and meet out by the trucks. We will be leaving as soon as Mr. Lawson returns from the pit. Move out."

"All right, 'bout time," was the resounding response in the barracks. The smile on every Delta face could be heard for miles around.

"DELTA-2, this is DELTA-3," said SSG Goschich, releasing the send switch on his throat.

"This is DELTA-2. Come back."

"DELTA-2, be advised that all of your earthly possessions and your 300 copies of Playboy magazine have been packed, as have been our beloved Lawson's belongings. All will be waiting for you curbside. Over."

"Roger that," replied SSG Don Goschich. "ETA five mikes. DELTA-2, out," said Goschich who turned his head towards Mr. Lawson and repeated what had been said. The Chief Warrant Officer gave him a thumbs-up. The batteries in his RAP-4 were dead.

"Did you monitor that, George?" asked DELTA-3 as he walked down the steps of the barracks. DELTA-1 was standing on the grass watching his Delta guys mount the tailgates of the two Pakistani Army five-ton vehicles.

"Yes, clear as a bell," said SFC Angerome. "Our electronics work well at sea level." The front door of the barracks opened and closed with its usual bang as Suleiman appeared and stood with his arms folded on the small wooden porch.

"Vassar, will you be going with us to the airport?," called DELTA-3 from the road.

"No, I'll say my goodbyes here, Sergeant Goschich."

"You take care of your dumb ass, Vassar," said Angerome as he shouldered his gear and passed it up onto the tailgate.

"I will, First Sergeant. My ass is much smarter now that I have access to an endless supply of toilet paper. See you when I see you," said the always-smiling Vassar Suleiman.

Just as Vassar finished his goodbyes, a military scout car containing Lawson, Goschich, and Mustapha pulled up behind the last truck being loaded in the lineup. They all got out of the vehicle and started up the sidewalk towards the lead truck.

"How did things go down in tent city?" Sergeant Angerome asked.

"It will be quite comfortable. Thank you for arranging it with the Brigadier," said Mustapha, who had walked up behind Lawson.

"Do you need any of my men to move the weapons?" asked Mustapha as he climbed up into the rear seat of the crew cab.

"No, I was told the ISI will handle the offloading," replied DELTA-1. "We got the word this morning that the Brigadier's people will also handle the storage and security logistics for the Stingers while you're here. We did a walk-through and checked out their munitions bunker. Their security and facility is top notch. We're leaving you in good hands, Mustapha."

DELTA-1 took his place in the front seat of the first truck in line. He checked the mirror. The road was clear; everyone was loaded. He put his index finger to his throat and said, "This is DELTA-1, breaking camp. Break, Break. ZERO, this is DELTA-1. ETA your location in 15 mikes. DELTA-1, come back."

He then nodded at the driver and extended his arm out the window and waved a winding up motion and then pointed everyone towards the airport and home.

DELTA-1's earpiece clicked. "This is ZERO, DELTA-1. Proceed directly to the hangar. Use same rear gate access as rehearsed. This is ZERO, out."

30
On the Tarmac

Islamabad International Airport
Service Apron – Western End of Runway 26L
Sunday 6 July 1986 0855 Hours

THE HIGH-PITCHED SOUND of the hydraulics ended as the ramp fully extended itself onto the tarmac. Andy Davis, wearing a crew helmet, crossed the rear of the cargo bay just behind the first of six shrink-wrapped pallets of medical supplies. The view out the back of the aircraft revealed the first of four trucks with Red Cross markings. The large panel vans were already fanned out in a half circle, each one backed into position within ten meters of the rear of the aircraft.

Andy continued towards the nose of the cargo bay where he spotted the crew chief kneeling at the base of the cockpit access ladder. A cord from the intercom panel on the wall was connected to the Air Force Sergeant's flight helmet. One final nod of his head signaled to Andy that the conversation with the cockpit had concluded. The man removed his helmet and hung it on a hook next to the panel. As he turned, Davis was walking towards him.

"Sir, we have acknowledged a request from the tower that as soon as the medical supplies have been off-loaded we are to move the aircraft."

"That makes sense, Sergeant. Thanks," said retired CWO Andy Davis, now Head of Security of the Raytheon Corporation. "Can you ask the Pilot in Command if I can use the phone? I need to update my management that we are on the ground safe and sound."

"Sir, we're instructed to provide you with whatever you require. You can make the call from over there," said the airman, and pointed to a place on the bulkhead just to the left of the open, side cargo door.

Captain Nelson was the ODA (Operational Detachment ALPHA) commander of a split team consisting of six, including himself. ODAs provide team support to anyone anywhere on the planet and do so without reservation.

"Captain Nelson," called Andy, as he turned to the leader of the Green Beret team.

Nelson was hunkered down, and out of sight, between the last of the shrink-wrapped weapons and material pallets. The entire team was gathered around him in the center of the bay near the forward-most bulkhead of the aircraft. Their immediate responsibility today was the secure delivery of the uniquely wrapped packages stacked around them.

There were 15 pallets in all: 108 Stingers, 12 training simulators, and 16 cases of spare batteries. Also included were training aids and documentation material (books, slides, and charts), and two 35mm projectors and screens. And last but not least: seven skids, each containing two disassembled target drones, target tow arrays, and three complete launch rail assemblies.

Andy went to where Captain Nelson was kneeling in the middle of his group. They were examining the layout map of this very same airport.

"Yes, Sir, Mr. Davis. What's the word, Sir?" asked Master Sergeant Mike Davis, who stood up from his position on the far side of the circle.

"After the med supplies are offloaded we are to move the aircraft," replied Andy, smiling familiarly at the Master Sergeant.

"Any sign of our crazy friend?" asked MSG Davis.

"No, little brother, but he usually shows up right after an explosion," replied Andy. "The last time we mentioned you in conversation he seemed a little miffed about the time you got him shot."

"I find it hard to believe," replied the MSG, "that he implied that in any way. He was probably upset because I kept referring to his injury as being shot in the ass. He, however, quickly pointed out that no one wears his ass down that low. The reason I know this is because I'm the one who pulled his dumb ass back on the chopper."

"So, you think getting someone shot in the ass should make them all humble and grateful? Is that a common belief among your warrior class?" All the other members of the A-team, including Captain Nelson, seemed fascinated by the exchange between the two brothers.

"I told you I apologized for the ass remark. He took a bullet in his leg, not his ass," replied MSG Davis. And then he turned his head towards the five interested faces. They were enjoying the conversation.

Andy Davis was ready to change the subject. "Captain Nelson, we've just been told by the tower that as soon the Red Cross does their thing the aircraft will be moved. It'll probably be to a hangar on the military side of the field. Keep the thermites on safe until we get the warm and fuzzes from our people on the ground here. Roger that?"

"Will do, Mr. Davis," replied CPT Nelson.

"Belay that 'Mister' shit, please, Sir. Call me Andy or just plain Davis."

"Yes, Sir, Davis, Sir," replied CPT Nelson with a laugh.

"Keep everybody out of sight as much as you can, Mike. No sense in calling attention to ourselves until we get to our final stop. I'm going to call in and see if there are any last-minute changes."

With that said, the four kneeling Staff Sergeants got to their feet. Staff Sergeant Brian McDermott, Operations and Communications coordinator, folded the map and stuffed it into his thigh pouch pocket.

"Mr. Davis—Andy, can I help you make that call?" offered SFT McDermott. "I'm familiar with the COMM systems onboard. We also have SAT phone handsets we brought with us. They're secure as well."

"Thanks, Brian, but the people I'm calling want to see the squawk ID from this particular aircraft."

"Of course, S—Andy," replied McDermott. "They're available if you need them while we're here."

"Denny, Jim, Paul," ordered CPT Nelson, "check the status of the thermites on the Stinger pallets."

Staff Sergeants Dennis Bormann and Paul Murray acknowledged the order and moved down the left side array of pallets. STF Jim Thomas walked across the bay and proceeded down the right side of the cargo line-up. Bormann was trained as a paramedic and was responsible for the team's medical requirements. Murray was responsible for SAT OPS/Intel and Thomas was an engineer — an engineer more in the sense of blowing shit up rather than building things. All the Green Berets were cross-trained as medics.

31

Arrows for the Quill

Islamabad International Airport
ISI Hanger Complex – Building #34
15 Kilometers South of Islamabad, Pakistan
Sunday 6 July 1986 0945 Hours

THERE ARE SEVERAL camps in and around Peshawar that count on the Red Cross for their very existence. On Sunday, July 6, the official flight manifest listed Captain Nelson's flight and its cargo as medical supplies for the Red Cross. For the casual observer, or for that matter, a paid Russian informant, this particular aircraft had fulfilled its mission. It was the main reason the medical supplies were the last brought on board at Frankfurt's Rhine Main AFB. The last-on first-off scenario was played out at Islamabad International Airport.

After the last of the medical supply pallets had been offloaded, the ramp was raised and the aircraft was taxied to building 34. This was on the opposite side of the commercial airport, in the military sector. Anyone monitoring airport radio traffic would have heard the maintenance request made by the aircraft commander of the USAF C141. There was an apparent problem with an oil pressure reading on one of their engines. This behavior, too, would seem normal to anyone looking on. As the giant doors of building 34 slid shut behind the plane, the cargo ramp was once again extended.

The Pakistani major jogged up the right side of the ramp even before it was fully open. His orders were quite clear. He was to greet CWO Davis and his team, and then start the offloading process. His responsibilities also included providing secure transportation, as well as storage and staging logistics for the Stinger munitions and all associated support material.

The major didn't make it all the way into the aircraft. He was met at the top of the ramp, where it was hinged to the main fuselage. The USAF crewman stopped him dead in his tracks. She was facing slightly sideways, but her outstretched left arm, with hand in his face, clearly said "STOP." Her right hand, which was not in his line of sight, was on her sidearm, a 1911 45ACP.

"Good morning, Sergeant, welcome to Islamabad," said the Major, with a pronounced British accent. "I'm here to sign for and offload your cargo. Will you please call the officer in charge?"

"Certainly, Sir. Will you wait here for just a minute while I notify him?"

"Of course. Thank you, Sergeant."

Holding her stance, she used her left hand to touch the send receive switch on her mike boom which was affixed to the right side of her helmet. She turned her head slightly without breaking eye contact with the Major, and spoke quickly into the end tip. The Major cocked his head towards the sergeant but could not hear what was said.

"Mr. Davis is on his way, Major," announced the Sergeant.

"Mr. Davis, you say? That is truly wonderful news," replied the Major.

"How's that, Sir?" asked the Airman, but before the Major could answer, a voice arrived from the shadows.

"There are nine pallets of weapon cases, 14 large crates on seven skids of disassembled drones, and there are six pallets of miscellaneous training supplies. How are you, Ali? I see you got your promotion," said a smiling Andy Davis, who had walked out of the dimly lit cargo bay. An enormous smile erupted on the Major's face. He quickly extended his hand. Of course, this was ignored as the two men embraced. The Pakistani officer was one of (Retired) Andy Davis's most talented former students.

The recently promoted Major Mohammad "Ali" Tariq was dressed in military mountain-desert shaded fatigues. His pants were bloused around his Corcoran style jump boots. ISI's Covert Action Division (Special Activities Division) insignia displayed on his beret flash indicated that he had received

Special Forces training in the United States. Andy was well aware that many of his former students had been cross-trained as covert action experts.

"Mr. Davis, I was not told that you would be coming. It is an honor to have you here, Sir."

"It is my honor, Ali," replied the head of security for the Raytheon Corporation.

Andy Davis, who had just turned 46 the day before, was charged with setting up the first phase of Operation Cyclone. Andy's taste in clothes closely followed the cowboy craze of the late 1970s. His Stetson cowboy hat (black) matched his Western-style shit kickers (riding boots). His Levi jeans, shirt, and vest finished off his appearance that was somewhere between pure folk art and functioning corporate executive.

"Sir, Major, these pallets are all on rollers," announced the newly arrived crew chief. "We can position each one to the end of the ramp. Will you be using lift trucks or breaking the pallets down for transport?"

"My suggestion, Mr. Davis, would be to transport the pallets as configured," said Ali. The munitions bunker at the camp is equipped with the same size forklifts as we have here. We will be able to sort the material any way necessary once we are inside the bunker."

"I think that's an excellent suggestion, Ali. Let me go get the rest of my team and we can get out of the way and let the Air Force and your guys do their thing."

32

Inside the Cyclone

Islamabad International Airport – Building #34
Just South of the City of Islamabad, Pakistan
Sunday 6 July 1986 1005 Hours

PEZLOLA AND COMPANY rolled through the wicked gate (the small door set within a much larger door) of building 34. The 1967 Toyota, Model LA 1-ton, forklift truck, built in Takahama, Japan, was placing the last pallet into the transport closest to the extended ramp of the aircraft. There were four other partially loaded five-ton trucks and an empty bus parked along the wall on the left side of the hangar.

Just as we pulled into the parking lot of building 34, General Khan's staff car arrived and parked in the space between us and the two Delta team trucks. His staff car had followed us onto the airport grounds through the rear service gate. Everyone with me was out of the bus before the General's driver could get around and open his door. Our driver saluted his boss's boss. Everyone waited for the General to speak.

"Good morning, everyone," said General Khan. "We are having good weather for such an important day in our history, yes? Mr. Fontain and Mrs. Smythe, a word if you please before we go inside. The rest of you please carry on."

"Of course, Sir," I replied. "Jim, please take everyone into the hanger. We'll be along directly."

"Will do, Rick," replied Pezlola, and then he shouted across the way. "Listen up, Cinderellas. Your pumpkin awaits. Grab your gear, Delta, and follow me inside."

The U.S. Air Force C-141 cargo plane was parked headfirst almost dead center on the hangar floor. A low-profile tow bar and tractor were still attached to the front landing gear. Building number 34 was the largest of its type on the airport complex. The entrance, 60 meters wide and 16 meters high, had been designed to accept the largest of the world's aircraft.

There was a series of staggered, rolling, door panels, each one hung from a rail system that ran up high across the now closed front opening of the building. Each panel, when fully extended, sealed the hangar entrance from the prying eyes of civilian airport workers, non-authorized military personnel, and the monitoring eyes of multiple Russian surveillance satellites. The latter were a major concern of General Khan and his ISI staff.

"Ali," said Pezlola, offering his hand as he walked up to the ISI Major. "Did everything get offloaded successfully?"

"Yes, Sir," replied Tariq. "We have room to spare on the transports."

"Good," replied Pezlola. "And, I asked you to call me Jim, Ali." As he spoke, the Delta team gathered around in a semi-circle.

"Have you met with Mr. Davis and his security team?" asked CWO Lawson.

"Yes, of course. Mr. Davis was my instructor at Fort Bliss. He and the Special Forces people are using the office and restroom facilities located at the rear, just there," Ali said, and pointed to the left corner of the hangar.

"Are you going to wait for them or are you going to move the weapons now?"

"The plan is to move everything and everyone together, Jim," replied the Major. "The Brigadier General Azraq is inspecting the arrangements at the bunker. He should be here shortly."

"Outstanding," replied Pezlola. "And, Ali, thanks for all of your support this past week. Your words of encouragement to Mustapha's people have really built up their confidence."

"Yes, indeed," agreed Mustapha, who was standing just to the right of Pezlola. "Your support has been magnificent and very much appreciated."

"It has been my honor, Mr. Pezlola. Stinger in the right hands will change the mindset of the Russian military. The occupation of our neighbor will soon come at a very high cost. My General believes that it is only a matter of time until we, Pakistan, suffer the very same fate as Afghanistan. That is, unless we do something to stop them now."

"Speaking of your General, he pulled up as we arrived. Mrs. Smythe and Mr. Fontain are having a discussion with him in the parking area."

"Yes, he told us last night that he planned on meeting the plane."

"Stinger is a game changer, Ali. This moment has been a long time coming, for all of us."

"It has been even longer for some of us," replied Ali.

"I'm sure it has been," agreed ZERO. "Sergeant Angerome, why not walk everybody over to that airman standing by the ramp. Introduce yourselves and see if any upgrades are available."

"Sir?" DELTA-1, not understanding the reference to the term "upgrade" turned to face Pezlola.

"Find out if Rick has booked us in first class and see where we're supposed to store our gear, Sergeant."

"Will do, ZERO," replied DELTA-1, perhaps using the call sign for the last time. He then turned towards the aircraft and followed his team who were already stepping up onto the ramp.

"Mr. Lawson," said Pezlola, "I'll be back after I make my manners with the Pilot in Command. Why don't you go and find Mr. Davis? Tell him I'll be there directly."

"Roger that," replied Lawson.

"Ali, after I speak with the aircraft commander, I'll go and get Mr. Davis. Do you want me to send out the Special Forces guys?" asked Pezlola.

"No rush, Jim. They can take as much time as they need," replied the U.S.- trained Stinger expert.

"By the way, Ali, the new people who just came in? One of them trained in the original Redeye program. His name is Rick. Stay on your toes."

"Thanks, but the Brigadier already gave me a heads-up. Mr. Davis told us in class about the famous Rick Fontain."

"Then you're in for a real treat, Ali. He'll be making an appearance almost any minute now."

"Rick told the General he was coming out here this morning. The General thought that his personal appearance would go a long way in emphasizing the importance of what we are about to do."

"Amen to that, my friend," replied Pezlola.

33
A General Khan Direction

Islamabad International Airport – Building #34
Just South of the City of Islamabad, Pakistan
Sunday 6 July 1986 1025 Hours

AMELIA JANE STEPPED through the tiny gate in the huge hangar door. Our outfits — mountain/desert shaded fatigues — were provided courtesy of General Khan's S-4, Sergeant Usman Farooq. The look and fit of the material was fantastic. I told Amelia at breakfast that she could not have gotten a better fit from a can of spray paint. My rompers, on the other hand, would not get me arrested.

General Khan stepped to one side and waved Mrs. Smythe through the narrow opening. It seemed interesting to me that there is nothing more erotic then a beautiful woman in a well-tailored uniform. Outfitting both of us from the ISI summer battle dress catalogue did not go unrewarded as we followed Mrs. Smythe into building number 34.

The very first thing that struck me as I stepped onto the hangar floor was its sheer size. The U.S. aircraft seemed almost tiny positioned near the exact center of the floor. The plane's ramp was down and several of its crew members were kneeling at the point where the ramp touched the concrete. They were removing the rubber bumper guards placed there earlier to protect the floor from the metal skids. The last of the Delta guys disappeared inside the flying machine while the crew prepped the ramp for its return to Germany. I recognized the officer standing with Jim Pezlola. He had been in the lobby of the ISI Headquarters building the day we arrived from Kuala Lumpur.

"Good morning, General," said Major Tariq as he walked up to us. He saluted and stood at attention awaiting his orders.

"Good morning, Ali. This is Mrs. Smythe," said General Khan. "Mrs. Smythe, this is Major Tariq."

"It is very good to meet you, Major," replied Amelia. "Where did Mr. Pezlola run off to?"

"He indicated he was going to the cockpit, ma'am, and from there to see Mr. Davis, who is at the rear of the hangar."

"And this is Mr. Fontain," continued the General, extending his arm towards me.

"Yes, of course, the infamous Rick Fontain. It is indeed an honor to meet you, Sir."

"Major," I replied, and shook his hand. "I suspect that you have suffered one or more of Mr. Davis's absurd technical presentations."

Laughing, the Major said, "You are exactly how Mr. Davis described you."

"Actually, I have been allowed out in public for some time now. Isn't that right, Amelia?"

"As you will soon find out, Major Tariq, a lot of what Mr. Fontain says is not framed in reality," offered Amelia.

"And this from a lady who has subjected her uniform well past any of the manufacturer's stress parameters," I dryly observed.

"Unfortunately, the supply Sergeant only had small and large sizes to pick from. I am going to correct my situation, if at all possible, this afternoon," Amelia said firmly.

"I think you look very nice in what you have on. I wouldn't change a thing if I were you," replied Ali.

"Thank you, Major Tariq," replied Amelia as she turned her head so no one could see, and wrinkled her nose at me.

"Major," I said. "If we allow Andy Davis to work his magic over the next couple of weeks, as I know he will, the Russians and their Mil Mi manufacturing facility will need to replace a whole bunch of their aircraft this coming season."

"Do you really believe that this Stinger weapons system will be that effective?" asked General Khan.

"The statistics don't lie, General," said Amelia Jane. "Stinger kill ratios are the highest ever registered for any surface to air missile technology. And that goes back to the Redeye program in 1968."

"As you can tell, General," I added, "Mr. Davis has created an entire generation of warriors who believe in this weapon. And, it even includes people who have not attended any of his classes." Amelia could not disagree.

"Major?" I started to ask.

"Please, Mr. Fontain. If we are to be working together please call me Ali."

"OK, Ali, but only if you will call me Rick. Do you know what the schedule is for moving the weapons to the bunker?"

"Mister's Pezlola and Davis and the others are there," he said and pointed to a large glassed-in back office located in the left rear corner of the hangar. "I told them to take their time and we would proceed when they are ready. All of the equipment is loaded on the trucks and is ready to go."

"Ali, we'll meet you back here. If, somehow, we don't cross paths with Mr. Pezlola and he returns to the plane, please tell him not to leave without seeing me." Amelia and I started walking as the ramp of the aircraft started to pull itself back into in-flight position.

General Khan had listened to our exchange and looked at his watch and called after us. "I must leave to catch a flight. You will let me know if you need anything," ordered the General, who then waved his hand towards us and touched the brim of his cap.

"Yes, Sir," I said, turning. "Thank you, Sir. I'll provide you with an update as soon as the training gets under way."

"Very good. I'll be back in my office this Friday," said the General. "Both of you come and see me."

The General then turned to Ali, "Major, please walk me to my car." Both turned and started to leave. The General turned suddenly and shouted my name across the hangar, "Rick, did you know that Congressman Wilson is in town?"

"No, Sir," I cupped my hands and shouted back. "I did not. Do you know where he's staying?"

The General cupped his right hand to the side of his mouth and said, "I was told he is at the Marriott. But it has been my experience that he is not often where he is supposed to be. He is very difficult to keep tabs on."

"Roger that, Sir. Thank you for telling me," I replied and with that both the General and Ali turned back towards the exit and disappeared through the minuscule wicked gate.

34

Five Stars in Islamabad

The Marriott – Front Desk and Lobby
Aga Khan Road, Shalimar 5 – Islamabad 44000 Pakistan
2 Km from the Embassy of United States
Sunday 6 July 1986 1930 Hours

THE FIVE-STAR ISLAMABAD Marriott Hotel pampers its residents. Their world-class spa treatments are completely segregated by gender. Cohabitation with anyone to whom you are not married is considered a complete no-no. Having said that, I remember what Charlie Wilson had once told me about his travel arrangements. He told me that it really helps to have a girlfriend with the same last name as your own. Of course, for Charlie, this was a major concern in terms of putting together a truly great entourage.

Islamabad Marriott Hotel is about 12 miles from both Islamabad Airport and the Rawalpindi Rail Station. Amelia and I were sitting in the lobby with a direct line of sight to the main entrance. We were talking quietly when three black Toyota Land Cruisers pulled in front of the hotel. The middle vehicle's rear passenger door was pulled open by the valet. Out stepped the jovial congressman from Texas. He turned back towards the open door and extended his hand to assist the person who would be charged with this evening's entertainment.

As Charlie came into the lobby he saw us waiting for him. He turned and rested both hands on his good friend's shoulders. He leaned in and whispered something that seemed to disappoint his morale officer. She forced a smile and nodded acceptance to what was said. She then proceeded to the front desk followed by two of the men from their security detail. Charlie walked over and said something that I could not hear to the remaining two security shadows. With that conversation completed, he turned and headed directly towards us. The two men to whom he had spoken remained just on the outer edge of the lobby seating area. They were far enough away that they would not hear our conversation.

"Well, well, well. Fancy meeting you here. How long has it been Rick?"

"It's been way too long, Charlie," I said. "Charlie, I don't believe you know Mrs. Smythe. We both work for a small group of citizens who reside outside the beltway in Virginia."

"Please call me Amelia, Congressman. Rick has told me how you've been fighting to get congress to increase the needed financial support for the Afghans."

"I'm very glad to finally meet you, Amelia. Rick tells me you're a first-class operator."

"Oh, that's funny, Congressman. Rick said the same thing about you. And, just for the record, I have never worked for the phone company."

"Ouch," replied Charlie. "Now that the cat is out of the bag, will you please call me Charlie? Rick, where are we with Cyclone?"

"General Khan just told us that President Zia has approved the use of Stinger with the eradication of manufacturing identification markings no longer being a requirement," I said, offering up this bit information just to see what reaction I would get.

"That was fast," said Charlie, chuckling. "I just met with President Zia last evening. I wasn't sure how thrilled he was with Reagan's decision to present Stinger to the Russians with an in-your-face attitude."

"Everything we need to start has been put in place," Amelia Jane stated. "The ISI has provided us a top-notch facility. Their complex will be partially staffed with a U.S. trained cadre. Day one of the formal training starts tomorrow."

"Are you running the class?" asked Wilson, looking directly at me.

"No, Andy Davis is here. Three of the assigned Pakistani officers are former students of his. The training should go off without a hitch, Charlie."

"Delta Force brought in the first group of Mujahideen to be trained," added Amelia Jane.

"From what I've seen and the ones I've spoken with, they're a highly motivated bunch," I said.

Charlie paused for a moment before asking, "Will the Mujahideen be able to handle the technology?"

"Charlie, when we put a Stinger on each one's shoulders I'll bet you a case of single malt that they will kill *boo-coo* Russian aircraft."

Charlie looked around the lobby for a good long while before speaking. Amelia and I just waited to see what would come next.

"For the last two years," said Charlie in a serious tone that I had not heard before, coming from him, "Congress has tripled the funds to buy weapons and ammunition for the Afghans. Until this very moment, I wasn't sure that they were going to win this battle. Thank you for making today possible. Amelia, Rick, we are finally going to see this fight take a turn for the positive. The Russians, I expect, are going to experience it in a most spectacular fashion."

"One step at a time, Charlie," I said. "But I'll bet you ten bucks on top of the scotch that this time next year Mr. Gorbachev will need a shitload of new helicopter gunships."

"And pilots, right?" added Charlie. "Are you two staying here? I think we should go and get something to drink."

"We just checked out. We're going to camp out with Mr. Davis and his Special Forces angels. But a couple of cocktails sounds brilliant, Charlie," replied Amelia Jane.

"Camp?" inquired Charlie.

"It's a figure of speech, Congressman, and is not as gruesome as it sounds," I explained. "Actually, it's free room and board in a fairly nice barracks provided by the ISI. Besides, I'm really looking forward to sharing a shower with my partner here." This attempt at humor did earn me a raised eyebrow and the usual disgruntled stare. Amelia was deciding how to phrase her next statement.

"Oh, indeed," she said, most precisely. "We should call Hanna tonight and tell her we are taking our mission to the next level."

"Nah, it's not necessary. She's all for conserving Mother Earth's water resources."

Charlie grunted. "If you two are about done, let's go up to my suite. It has a very nice bar."

"Sounds good, Charlie. How long are you going to be in country?" I asked. Everyone got up and the larger of the two security guys put his walkie-talkie up to his lips. As we walked to the bank of elevators located at the far end of the lobby I heard the radio squeal and announce that "five-hall" was clear. This meant, of course, that security had picked up all of the empty scotch bottles from the corridor on the fifth floor and it was safe to walk in.

"We're leaving tomorrow afternoon," replied Charlie. "A Paris stopover for some much-needed supplies," he said, and winked at Amelia.

"All work and no play, right Charlie?" I asked.

"You got that right, Rick. War is hell!"

PART V

Standing in the Cyclone

35

Camping with Class

ISI Headquarters – Ojhri Camp – Day One
Munitions Bunker Complex – AMX #18
Chaklala, Rawalpindi, Pakistan
Monday 7 July 1986 0740 Hours

THE TOTAL SIZE of the Ojhri compound is approximately 156 acres. It's situated just 12 kilometers from Islamabad, and the offices for Generals Akhtar Khan and Brigadier Yousaf Azraq were located there. Yousaf, as the Brigadier told me to address him when we were alone, took me on a tour and quite nonchalantly mentioned that one of the inner Ojhri Camp compounds contained the transit warehousing facilities for over 70 percent of all the arms and ammunition earmarked for the fight in Afghanistan.

There were three main areas of Ojhri. The entire camp's perimeter was encircled with 5-meter-high, dual chain-link fences. The outer fence was equipped with razor wire at the top. The inner space between fences was paved with crushed stone from a quarry located at the far end of the compound. This area between the fences was heavily patrolled with both vehicles and foot patrols. The walking guards were accompanied by a string of man's best friend: the Belgian Shepherd. The term "friend" only applied to people who had a really good excuse to be in this space, which for them was their entire world. Of course, to eat or not to eat someone would always be left to the discretion of their human caretakers.

The Headquarters building was lined up perfectly with the main highway entrance. The huge office building was set back 300 meters at the end of a paved roadway boasting a well-manicured lawn on each side. Three quarters of the way up the asphalt the access road branched off east and west. The end of the drive terminated in a half circle at the main entrance.

This was the first of the three inner compounds configured inside Ojhri. Completely walled in by a brick and block barrier that was five meters tall, this building and the courtyard complex that lay beyond housed the entire 2300 ISI civilian and military staff members.

The second compound I was shown was the home of the ISI's Psychological Warfare Unit. I told the ISI Brigadier, Yousaf, that we have the same type of organization in America called the IRS. We drove through a garage located at the rear of the area. I was told its size was an entire half-acre. There were several levels constructed underground. This garage contained a mixture of several hundred civilian and military vehicles.

The walled complex also contained the base administration and security personnel building, 12 two-story barracks accommodations, a modern kitchen and mess facilities hall, and a very nice service club. The club had been recently renovated to include a well-stocked English-style pub and had the atmosphere of an upscale restaurant. Yousaf told me that this particular compound was sized to support 500-plus student residents.

The third area we visited was by far the largest of the enclosed compounds. It was also the busiest. A wide variety of firing ranges and attached single-story classrooms were pushed up against the entire left edge of the walled fence line. The center of the yard contained a crescent of concrete warehouses. The open end of the horseshoe faced the rear of the compound. A wide, paved road touched the front entrance of each warehouse. There was a rail line that divided the driveway into two equal halves. A huge gate system could be seen where the pavement and rail track left the compound at the rear.

The largest concrete bunker was not part of the horseshoe footprint. AMX #18, as it was labeled, stood by itself and was fabricated out of poured reinforced concrete. The major difference, other than it being a stand-alone, was that it hid three quarters of itself below ground level. Only the huge, concrete, rounded roof was visible as we drove up to its main and only entrance. Designed as a state-of-the-art munitions bunker complex, AMX #18 was the newest of the munitions shelters on campus. This, announced the Brigadier, would be the site of the newly established Stinger Training Command.

The massive entrance could easily accommodate a large multi-ton truck. There were two guards posted on each side of the eight-inch-thick steel doors. A hydraulic motor system pushed the worm gears assigned to each of the doors — a requirement that was due to the massive weight of the metal.

Once inside, I saw that there was a six-meter wide and twenty-meter long corridor. A concrete ramp continued downward at a 15-degree slant. The pathway ended at a copy of the steel doors installed at the entrance. The thickness, I noticed, seemed to be only a fraction of what their cousins were packing at the front. There were two more guards stationed here.

As I stepped into the concrete cavern I was amazed at its size. The dome ceiling was at least 20 meters in height. Although the footprint of this bunker was constructed on a rectangular base, the roundness of the domed ceiling was seamlessly tapered and engineered to fit the floor space perfectly. The high-pressure sodium lamps that hung from the ceiling were evenly spaced and provided an environment that was brighter than natural sunlight.

An array of concrete lockers was constructed on both of the longer sides of the cavern. Each appeared to have an access hatch with the same type of steel hardware patterned after the doors at the entrance. The best and most important feature of this space was the concert hall-like emptiness at its center. It was perfect for the subject matter that was to be taught here.

There was a crowd gathered at the center point on the floor. The group formed a circle around their cowboy instructor, Andy Davis. In his former life, he had been the Army's chief instructor at the White Sands Missile Range. He knew everything there was to know about the weapons system being presented.

On his right shoulder was a long, slender tube. It was not a simulation of what this course was all about. Andy Davis was holding the actual weapon.

On the floor in front of the instructor the empty, all-aluminum, water-proof case was open. Davis's Stetson had been removed and safely laid on the opened lid. In his left hand, he held a round, molded plastic cylinder. When the cylinder was inserted into the well at the rear of the handguard, and the thumb of the shooter's right hand pushed down on the activation switch, a stream of argon gas would be injected into the veins of the electronics. At this same instant, a chemically induced burst of electrical energy would cause the onboard software to ask permission to start the kill sequence.

The acquisition indicator, the hardware, would then seek permission to hold hands with the missile tracking software. Together, they would then conspire to notify the shooter via a confirmation tone. What was seen by the shooter through the sight was verified by the software-controlled sensor array. The tiny power pack breathed life directly into the deadliest ground-to-air missile system ever introduced to modern warfare. The name of this weapon was Stinger.

Amelia Jane and Major Ali Tariq stood slightly behind and to the right of Andy Davis. The 14 citizens of Afghanistan stood in pairs around the circle. Pashto and Dari were the most commonly spoken languages in Pakistan and Afghanistan. Both are officially recognized and were the ones most widely spoken here. Our good fortune was two-fold in the making. Our Major Tariq was not only fluent in both Pashto and Dari, but also in English.

One of the main reasons Bill Douglas had assigned Mrs. Smythe to this project was her Pashto language skill. She was now standing behind Major Tariq verifying Andy's each and every word as it was repeated to the Mujahideen. That was the good news. The really great news was that Major Tariq and two of his people had been trained at the Stinger School located at Fort Bliss, Texas. All three were already qualified as Stinger experts and all three spoke English. This would speed things along nicely.

Andy Davis spoke slowly and distinctly, stopping briefly at the end of each sentence. This was recognizably not his first international rodeo. The Major translated everything. As I made my way over to the rear of the ring of students I saw Amelia hanging on to every word being said by the Major. She was nodding her head in cadence as each translation was being fed to the Mujahideen. The eyes of Andy's students matched the cold smile forming on each face. The solution to the Russian desecration of their country was at hand.

I had personally made the request for Andy to Bill Douglas, and then to General Bushman, DIA. The U.S. President then authorized General

Bushman to direct the 1st/10th Special Forces Command, stationed in Bad Tölz, Germany, to provide A-Team support for Operation Cyclone. They would watch Andy's back for the next three weeks.

Andy had specified that the eight Stinger shooter stations be configured in a circle within the concrete bunker. Captain Nelson and the team's non-commissioned officer in charge, MSG Mike Davis, supervised the entire setup of this state-of-the-art classroom. Eight ringed stations were constructed: each seven meters across, outlined with two layers of sand bags. The height of the bunker's ceiling was perfect for teaching the fine art of identification, tracking, and target sequencing. Everything was laid out in this state-of-the-art classroom to teach efficient killing methods for Russian aircraft.

Three years earlier, in April 1983, the U.S. and the Federal Republic of Germany signed a memorandum of understanding for dual production of the basic Stinger and Stinger-POST weapon systems. The U.S. Army Missile Command (MICOM) placed the procurement contract with the Raytheon Corporation. The procured General Dynamics manufacturing facility was reactivated in California. Production of the MICOM order was completed in March 1984. The more complex version of the Stinger-POST would be produced in Raytheon's Connecticut facility. That production agreement required completion by June 1987. The weapons now stored in AMX #18 had been pulled from the MICOM inventory in Germany the previous week.

In the coming years, the Stinger SAM system, I was told, was scheduled to be developed in four separate variants, including the basic Stinger package. Stinger Passive Optical Seeker Technique (POST), Stinger Reprogrammable Microprocessor (RMP: FIM-92D) and, the Stinger Block I (FIM-92E) would provide enhanced capability for a multitude of complex battlefield situations — such as the one we were facing!

For what Andy and I had in mind, the basic Stinger platform would need only to provide plain-Jane functionality for infrared (IR) reticle-scan and analogue seeker tracking. This, we felt, would be more than sufficient to ambush Russian helicopter gunships and troop transports, a wide range of jet attack aircraft, and cargo airframes of all shapes and sizes.

The IR/UV dual detector feature plus the rosette image scan function were all that would be needed with this standard configuration. Of course, the Mujahideen shooter only cares about the time it takes on each side of 'the moment'. 'The moment' being that blink-of-the-eye result of the missile's warhead penetrating an aircraft's metal skin. In the case of a Mujahideen, this sight ending in a successful explosion was everything.

36

Andy's View

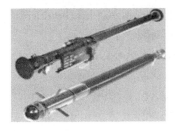

ISI Ojhri Camp – Day Two
Munitions Bunker Complex – AMX #18
Chaklala, Rawalpindi, Pakistan
Tuesday 8 July 1986 0455 Hours

ANDY DAVIS AND I were waiting in the parking area outside of AMX #18. Amelia Jane and Andy's Angels were already inside the bunker classroom setting up for the day's experience. The Stinger training hardware was being prepared for each of the eight shooting stations. Several rope pulley devices were hanging from the ceiling lamp fixtures. Each would dangle an ignited IR pod that would be used to activate the Stinger Tracker sensor array.

"Andy, I got the feeling at dinner last night that you wanted to say something, but you didn't. Am I imagining things?" I asked.

"No, you're absolutely right on, as usual, Rick. I didn't want to say anything in front of the others." He took a big breath. "We won't be able to run this course as originally discussed."

"Amelia said as much to me after class yesterday."

"Interesting. Your partner is a very perceptive woman. She strikes me as one capable lady."

"Our boss, Bill Douglas, refers to her as the trifecta: smart, tough as nails, and gorgeous. Except in this case all three categories are tied for first place."

"Here me out on this, Rick, before you say anything, OK?"

"You got it," I replied.

"When we teach one of our own to do this, and I'm talking about killing aircraft, we are usually well into week number two of the training when the lightbulb goes on in his head and he realizes what Stinger is and what an awesome responsibility is resting on his shoulders. Literally speaking."

"Your point being what?" I asked.

"Hey, I said hear me out, OK? I was going to say that 'most normal people' but that sounds silly for what we have here, doesn't it?"

"Indeed, it does. Sorry, explain what you mean."

"Right. After I dismissed yesterday's class, all fourteen of the Afghans came forward to touch the Stinger tube. This was after I had just described to them what its capabilities were and the projected result."

"So," I said and made a come-on motion for additional information.

"It was in their eyes, Rick. Each one had a look … so cold; well, it made me just a little bit frightened."

"Andy, from what my friend Jimmy Pezlola has relayed of his experience with these men, you have every reason to be scared. These people have been brutalized by the Russians for over six years. And, before that, by who knows who. You had just finished describing a way for them to be able to push the genocide in the opposite direction. The methodical extermination of their people by the Russians will be no more. I suspect you will have their undivided attention from here on out."

"That's exactly my point, Rick. After they understand the basic surface-to-air operational mechanics we should spend the balance of our time with them exclusively on transport procedures and tactical protocols."

"Agreed," I said. "By tactical protocols you mean the best place to stand to kill an airplane driver, right?"

"And, what to do immediately afterward," replied Andy, smiling slightly.

"If you're thinking about telling them to take cover, forget it. They'll scream for their spotter to get another Stinger ready to fire. They're quite fearless. Stinger will make them feel invincible."

"Fine, but I am still going to emphasize that they move to the left or right after firing. Becoming a crispy critter decreases their ability for a second shot."

"The Major has made arrangements to continue the training outdoors at a site 30 to 40 clicks from here."

"Why so far?" asked Andy. "There are plenty of fields within walking distance. Hell, the ranges over by that fence line are perfect for what we need. This is especially true with all of the air traffic going and coming from Islamabad International."

"True, but the prying eyes of those who sell information to the Russians are a huge problem here. More importantly, this is a major concern of our gracious host, President Zia. He wishes for as long as he can to remain militarily incognito."

"And the other reasons?" asked Andy.

"Russian satellite surveillance is a very big worry, possibility the biggest. There are other issues but these are the main two."

"OK, that makes sense," conceded Andy.

"Besides, I've been told that the terrain where we will be doing the strafing exercise will be much more like the environment in which our students will be applying their new skill set."

37
Range at Dargai

The Quarry – Day Seven
41 Clicks from the Ojhri Camp
Khyber Pakhtunkhwa Province, Pakistan
Sunday 13 July 1986 0640 Hours

WE LEFT RAWALPINDI on the N-5 just before daybreak. A quick exit onto the M-1, heading northeast, led us to the last of the paved roadways at Swabi. We arrived just outside of the village of Dargai at 0640 hours. Dargai was part of the Malaccan Agency Tribal area until 1970. Once the hub for trade between the upper regions of Pakistan and the lower regions of Khyber Pakthunkhwa, Dargai was a mere shadow of itself since the depletion of most of its timber.

Of late, most of Pakistan's highway and rail transportation resources were being diverted towards the many passageway requirements in and around Peshawar. For our purposes, the terrain around Dargai would be perfect. And, more importantly, it would not be under any type of Russian satellite surveillance. We hoped!

The range had been laid out the previous day by Andy Davis and Major Tariq. The heavy lifting was provided by a platoon squad of 11 U.S. Army support personnel. They were on loan from a local Headquarters, Headquarters

Company (HHC) based just across the highway from Camp Ojhri. Four of Andy's angels had graciously supervised and even pitched in with the labor. The construction of five sandbagged Stinger tracking circles was completed in record time.

STF McDermott walked-off and arranged the half-moon configuration so that each position would be capable of supporting two shooters and their respective spotters. Surprisingly, there were only a few disagreements about who would be the shooter and who would be the spotter. A quick knife to the throat on day one determined who would be the spotter. This local custom seemed to move things along nicely.

The dead-center view downrange was of a dry riverbed. The foothills off in the distance were at least three kilometers away. This landscape tapered off to the left, advancing easily for over 2000 meters and gradually touching the distant foothills. The jagged cliffs to the left were the remnants of the old quarries that had long since been abandoned. This terrain would lend itself well to the pre-arranged, mock attacks of both jet fighters and helicopters of the Pakistani Air Force.

The large, blue and white 40-seat tour bus followed two Army five-ton trucks into the clearing. One was already parked facing in at the far side of the lot. This natural, ready-made, parking area was located directly in line with, and only 100 meters from, our brand-new Stinger Firing Range.

First out of the bus was Brigadier Yousaf Azraq. Then Major Tariq followed Amelia Jane down the short set of steps. Ali immediately called across the parking area to get the attention of the non-commissioned officer seated in the shade next to the 5-ton truck that had been first on the scene. The Major cupped his hands and yelled, "Did Captain Nelson and his men already leave to place the beacons?"

The Sergeant cupped only his right hand to respond, "Yes, Sir. They have been gone about twenty minutes."

"That's close enough, Sergeant Zahiri," ordered Major Tariq, who had walked around the front of the bus and was now looking directly into the cab of the truck transport. The NCOIC pointed out to the driver where to park.

"Post your perimeter guards as we discussed. Offload the equipment and find Sergeant Davis. He should be out by the pits. See where he wants the equipment you brought to be unpacked."

"Yes, Sir," replied the Pakistani army sergeant who pushed open the door and was already making his way to the tailgate before the truck came to a complete stop.

Andy and I were still on the bus. I put my hand on Andy's shoulder as he was about to stand up. I looked at him and signaled with my eyes to remain seated. When the bus was empty, except for the driver, I said, "We may have a problem."

"What do you mean by 'we', White Man?"

"Listen, Tonto, there was a security breach last week not far from our compound. A sentry just inside the outer fence had his throat cut. They didn't get inside the housing area or the ammo bunkers but someone seems very interested in what we're doing in there."

"Why are you telling me this? If you're trying to scare me, you've succeeded. I'm just a simple instructor working his way through corporate life."

"Andy, it's because of who we are, and especially your unique role here, that a target is painted on all of our backs. We'll need to take extra care from here on out. That means you do not wander out by yourself without at least one or more of your angels in pursuit. I also suggest that you ditch the hat until we all get on the plane home. Understand?"

"Jawohl, mein herr," replied Andy in his best Sergeant Schultz imitation. "You mean back at camp, right? It's okay to wear it out here," he said.

"Have it your way. But the less attention you draw to yourself from the onlookers the better," I replied. "I just want you to be safe, Andy."

"Point taken, Rick. Thanks," replied Andy, placing the black cowboy hat on his head. "Come on. Let's go see how well the Mujahideen have perfected their new warrior skills."

"One more thing," I said. "Put this on before you start class." I reached into my ditty bag and pulled out a 1911 45 ACP in a holster with the web belt tightly wound around both. "You never need a gun until you really need a gun. Better to be safe than sorry, I always say."

"Thanks, Rick, that's very thoughtful of you. But I seldom go anywhere these days without Mr. Glock," replied Andy as he pulled open his jacket and lightly patted the GLOCK 17 9MM semi-automatic pistol on his hip.

"Cool," I replied. "Let's go shoot down some Pakistani aircraft."

"Pakistani, yes, but made in the good ol' U. S. of A.," quipped Andy.

It was just after lunch started that the shot rang out. The second round skipped off a large boulder on the far side of the parking area, just missing Sergeant Paul Murray. He was returning from the tracking range to get something to eat. The mess was being served out of the back of a three-quarter ton van that had driven out from the Ojhri Camp. Tables and benches were located under a canvas fly erected on the side of two of the truck transports. The Afghans had taken their food back to the sandbagged firing stations on the range.

Even before the sound of the first gunshot had started to fade, a hail of fire from automatic weapons rained down on us. Amelia Jane was sitting next to me. Our chair backs were positioned up against the rear wheels of the truck. In what seemed like slow motion I pushed the table away from us and pulled her with me to the space under the truck's undercarriage. The rounds were striking the ground and sending up stone splinters in all directions. The vehicle was also taking hits.

"Well, this was certainly unexpected," offered the cool-headed Mrs. Smythe, as a loud pop was heard and the right front tire sank to the ground on its rim.

"Really," I answered. "Did you ask the mess sergeant what was on the menu for dinner tonight?"

"No, I thought you were going to do that," replied Amelia in a voice that was trying to mask her concern.

Three of the Pakistani combatants, who were caught out in the open, were lying in front of the truck. The closest man to us was lying on his stomach. He was dead. The back of his head had been exploded. The man furthest out from us was dead also. His facial expression with his eyes wide open showed only his surprise at the suddenness of his demise. The third soldier was hit in his thigh and was thrashing around in the stone dust in pain.

"Stay put. I'll be right back," I announced, not quite sure how this was going to go down. I started forward with a maneuver that I hadn't practiced since I was at Fort Bragg in 1968. Amelia grabbed my arm.

"Where do you think you're going, Rick?" she yelled over the sound of the gunfire.

"I'm going to get that man out of the line of fire. When I get him back here to the edge of the truck help me pull him in with us, OK?" I said as I crawled to the low-hanging front bumper. "Here goes nothing."

The Afghans carried their AK-47s with them everywhere they went. They wasted no time in returning fire from their position in the sandbagged tracking pits. For them it must have seemed like just another day at the office.

I scrabbled out into the open, crawling up alongside the injured soldier. I could tell that the sniper fire was coming from the top of the cliff overlooking the quarry. I patted the injured solider on the shoulder and told him that I was going to get him to cover. I grabbed his coat collar and started dragging him back towards the safety of the truck. Several rounds hit the ground near my head. This mode of travel was taking way too long. I got to my feet and dragged the man the last ten feet to cover. Amelia was at the edge of the wheel well and helped me get the Pakistani under the truck.

Amelia pulled the man's hands away from the hole in his thigh to see what she was dealing with. She took a tee shirt from her bag and folded it in a square. She took both his hands in hers and placed them over the makeshift bandage.

"Keep pressure on this, OK?" she said in Pashto. "You're going to be all right," she said, but this time in English. She then proceeded to release his belt buckle and pull the belt from his waist. She quickly fastened it around the leg just above the wound. "We need to release the tourniquet every ten minutes," she announced out loud to herself, and took several deep breaths.

"Good job, Amelia," I said. I looked out across the way to the protected space in front of the mess van. Mike Davis and Brigadier Azraq were hunkered down. One of Azraq's men, who was either injured or dead, was lying on the ground between them. He was wearing a radio backpack. Mike Davis was working the knobs on the top of the radio and the Brigadier was speaking into the telephone-type handset. He was yelling into it with one hand cupped over his right ear. I was too far away to hear what was being said.

"It looks like the General is calling the office to complain about his lunch being interrupted," I offered the comment pointing across to the other vehicle.

"We're going to need a helicopter to get this man to hospital," Amelia said. "Any thoughts on who is shooting at us?"

"It may be that nice S-4 Sergeant," I said. "You know the one that lent us the mountain/desert camo fatigues."

"You aren't serious?"

"Well, he seemed pretty upset about you stretching the uniform material way past the stated thread count stress points," I suggested with a straight face.

"You are crazy, are you not?"

Before I could respond, I saw two Bell AH-1 Cobra gunships coming up the dry riverbed. They broke off, going in separate directions. The ship on the right climbed to 500 meters and headed to an area on top of the cliffs. The other climbed to well over a 1000 meters and circled out of sight over the foothills to our rear. He would probably approach the top of the quarry from the rear.

The incoming fire stopped abruptly at the sound of the arriving aircraft. Then the hum of the Gatling being fired, by the helicopters, across the plateau above the cliffs could be heard by everyone at the range.

"Well, it's nice to see that President Zia is maintaining the hardware we sold them. Hey, Mike," I yelled across the way. "Did you know they were going to strafe us today with live ammo on board? How many you got down over there?"

"There are two down, one killed, one with a gunshot to his hand. Four medivac choppers are inbound. ETA in 20 to 30 mikes."

"Roger that. Sounds like our party crashers have departed. Are you in contact with the Hueys?"

"Wait one, I'll ask the Brigadier," replied Mike. He continued, "Rick, four bad guys are down at the top of the cliff, two vehicles destroyed leaving the back side of the quarry. Our Major Ali is sending four of his guys up there to secure the site. Hold one, Rick."

"Amelia, how is your guy doing?"

"Stable, but he needs a doctor. The sooner the better," she said and took a deep breath.

"You did really good, Mrs. Smythe. Stay with him. I'm going over to the mess van."

"Hey, Rick," yelled Mike across the short space between vehicles. I pressed my ear to the ground and looked in the direction of the voice calling me. "All bad guys are down or gone. All clear. Let's take a quick sweep and see how bad we got hurt."

"Roger that," I said. I slid my body out from under the left side of the truck. The tires were still inflated on this side. I scooped up the AK-47 that had been dropped by Amelia's patient. I was met by Mike as I pulled the charging handle, loading the weapon.

"Let's identify ourselves before we charge in on the Afghans. Although this must be a pretty normal occurrence for them, it would be a damn shame to get shot for not saying 'hi' first."

"Roger that. Excellent advice, Rick," replied the MSG.

We headed off to the right side of the lot, keeping the large boulders spaced unevenly on the perimeter between us and the Stinger shooting positions. In Pashto, Mike yelled out, "Hold your fire. It's Sergeant Davis and Mr. Fountain. We are coming in. Hold your fire."

No response was given. I looked over the huge rock we were standing behind. I could see all five shooting pits. I couldn't see anyone looking back towards us.

"Either no one is home or they're playing possum." I suspected the latter. "You go first, Mike." I waved Mike on as I stepped in behind him.

"Stay behind me. You roger that," ordered Mike with no hesitation as he closed in on the first sandbagged ring.

"Hey, you SF guys are way too serious. We'll do this together," I said and stepped up beside Mike.

The first position was empty. So was the second. We headed towards the center station. As we walked up I could see the heads of five Afghans. The circular position was the largest with sandbags stacked five rows high.

Their backs were positioned towards us. Each man was sitting slouched, arranged evenly in a semicircle. Each man was firmly pressed up against the walls of the station's ringed enclosure. They were silent, with their heads bent down towards the ground. Their weapons were cradled in their arms across their chests. What I saw next made my heart stop. Mike saw it, too, and using one hand as a support, jumped over the wall, landing in a kneeling position at his brother's side.

Andy Davis — husband, father, brother, and friend — lay center stage, face down. His cowboy hat was upside down on the dirt, just inches from his head. A large hole could be seen just below Andy's left shoulder blade. Mike and I rolled him over. His eyes were open but he didn't see us. The exit wound was much larger on this side. Andy never knew what hit him.

"I'm very sorry Mike," I whispered and repeated it to myself. Over and over.

38

A Whole Lot of Sad

Dargai – Khyber Pakhtunkhwa Province
Stinger Training Area – Day Seven Point Five
41 Clicks from the Ojhri Camp
Sunday 13 July 1220 Hours

MUSTAPHA, THE MUJAHIDEEN Commander, Mr. Suleiman, and five of his warriors slipped out the back side of the range. Their destination was the cliff overlooking the Stinger shooting positions. Their instructor had been killed within the first volley of shots. With no vocal commands, Mustapha waved what he wanted done into action.

He left five men to watch over Mr. Davis and two more he sent to the far end of the shooting positions just in case someone tried to approach from that direction. Then he, Suleiman, and the others made their way out and up the back side of the course property. There was plenty of cover all the way up to, and on top of, the ridgeline. They continued along a path that ran all the way around, gradually climbing to the upper heights located across from the excavation's cliff wall. This location, he hoped, would allow them to see who was doing the shooting.

Just as they arrived at a position where they could ascertain what they were dealing with, Suleiman and two others were directed by Mustapha to circle around and approach from the rear. But before they had traveled ten meters, the sound of helos could be heard coming up the dry riverbed. Suleiman turned to see Mustapha wave them back to his side. The Cobra gunship, a recent purchase from the U.S. Government, killed everything living on the cliff's top.

A second chopper was heard. The engine sound seemed to be coming from the rear area behind the cliffs. The first helo, satisfied with the result of its Gatling's fire, dropped down behind the cliff out of their view. A moment later more automatic weapons fire followed by the purring hum of the six rotating barrels of the M-134 mini-gun could be heard again and again. Then there was only the sound of the helicopter turbojet engines. Mustapha signaled for everyone to remain hidden until the birds of prey left the area.

Forty-five minutes later the Mujahideen Commander and his men returned to the center firing position. They stood around the curved wall. They said nothing. They looked down at their fallen instructor. Their faces showed no emotion whatsoever. I looked up at Mustapha who was looking back at me. His promise was silent. The Russians would pay dearly for this. The Afghans would collect this debt in both blood and metal.

"Mike, I need to borrow your SAT phone," I asked. I climbed over the sandbagged wall and stepped towards Mike. He was still kneeling next to his brother. Without saying anything, Mike reached into his thigh pocket and handed me the phone.

"Mike, do you think it would be OK with Andy if I borrowed his hat for a bit?" I asked quietly.

Mike looked up at me and made eye contact. "No problem," he replied. "But why?"

"One, I had just asked him this morning if he could get me one just like his. And, two, I don't want the people who did this to think they were in any way successful."

"You think the hat made him a target?" Mike's voice was flat.

"Maybe, maybe not," I answered. "But, from here on out I'll be wearing the hat. And, I'll kill anybody who tries to remove it from my head."

39

Strength in the Brim

Islamabad International Airport
Parking Lot of Building #34
Located Just Across the Tarmac from the Commercial Terminals
Sunday 13 July 1986 2030 Hours

I SAT ALONE IN the rear seat of Brigadier Yousaf Azraq's staff car. MSG Davis's SAT phone was in my lap. Next to me on the seat was Andy's hat. The call I now needed to make would not be easy. I pulled a small note pad from my pocket. "Bird Farmer" had been his call sign in *Operation Synchronized Sparrow*. All I needed to do was mentally add the year 1968 to the last four digits of his phone number. I used a different year to cross reference each of the listings.

"Mr. Flax's office. May I ask who is calling?" said the executive assistant to Barry Flax.

"Rick Fontain," I answered.

"Mr. Flax is in a meeting. May I ask what this call is in reference to?" she asked.

"No, I'm sorry but you cannot. Please interrupt Mr. Flax and tell him I'm on the line."

"Mr. Flax has asked not to be disturbed. So, if you will call back—" she was saying when I cut her off.

"Get him on the phone now," I said again. "He will take this call. Don't make me ask you again."

There was five seconds of silence before she said, "Please hold."

Almost a full minute went by before Barry came on the phone. "Rick, I sure hope this is important. I—"

I cut him off before he could finish his sentence. "Barry, I don't know how to say this so I'll just say it. Andy was killed earlier today. Andy is gone, Barry," I said and my eyes began to tear up. "I'm so very sorry."

"How did it happen?" asked Barry in a whisper after several moments of silence.

I told him.

I had just finished the call when a civilian van pulled into the parking lot to my left and stopped in front of the center hangar door. The side door slid open and out stepped Captain Nelson. He saw me, and nodded in my direction. I got out of the car, putting on my new hat with both hands as I walked over to him.

"Did everything go OK at the embassy?" I asked. Through the open side door, I could see a flag-draped coffin. Mike Davis was sitting on the floor beside it with his back pushed up against the front passenger seat. His right hand was resting on top of the flag.

"They were very accommodating," replied Captain Nelson. "General Khan met us there and personally escorted us to a funeral home in the suburbs of Islamabad. Andy was placed in the casket by their staff. An army doctor was summoned. All the required paperwork was provided for his trip home."

"That was very gracious of the General," I said. "The Brigadier and the Major are inside. I'm waiting for a call on the ETA of the aircraft."

"Rick," called Mike Davis. "A word if you please."

"Hey, Mike," I said gently as I walked to the open door and sat on the edge of the carpeted floor, facing him.

"The hat looks good on you," acknowledged Mike. "Thanks for arranging all this so fast. I haven't been very much of a help, have I?"

"Nonsense," I said immediately. "Your sole responsibility, Sergeant, is to take your brother home to his family." As I said this to him the center door to the hangar began to open.

"Sir," I said to get Captain Nelson's attention. "I think we should move everyone inside." I pulled my legs up inside the van for the short trip. "Corporal," I said to the driver, "please move us inside the building. Park over there." I pointed to the left. The airplane would be here soon.

"Rick," asked Mike in a whisper of voice. "I need a favor."

"Name it Mike. If it's within my power, you've got it."

"I need your help in getting assigned back here. Can you see what you can do in making that happen?"

"Of course," I said immediately, not really sure how I could. "Call me when you get back to Germany, OK, Mike? On another note, Captain Nelson picked up another SAT phone from the embassy. I need to hold on to this one a little while longer," I said, holding up Mike's phone. "The coordinating brass have all been given this telephone number."

"Fine ... I'll call you when I get back to Tölz." Mike was referring to the Special Forces Base at Bad Tölz, Germany.

"You do that, but I plan on seeing you before then. I'd like to attend Andy's service. You let me know when and where that is, 10-4?"

"Will do," he replied as another vehicle pulled into the lot. It followed us into the hangar and parked directly behind us. Amelia Jane jumped down from the cab on the passenger side of the truck and headed toward Captain Nelson. I got out of the van to join them.

"Captain Nelson," she said. "Your Green Berets went to the barracks to pick up everyone's gear. They'll be here directly, Sir."

"Thank you, Mrs. Smythe," replied the Captain. "Is that the Stinger class I hear in the back of the truck?" Amelia laughed at the comment. The Afghans barely spoke amongst themselves. They seemed to prefer to communicate through eye contact and the use of slight hand gestures — mostly stabbing motions. Eight hundred years of fighting has that result.

"Yes, Sir, minus Mustapha and Suleiman. They were summoned to the ISI HQ."

"What's all that about?" I asked.

"I don't have a clue," replied Amelia. "But I did overhear part of a conversation between General Khan and our Brigadier General."

"And?" I asked.

"It seems that there was a survivor among the people who attacked us at the range."

"No shit," I said. "That's good news. But, not for him, I'm sure."

"Apparently, Suleiman pulled the man from one of the shot-up vehicles that attempted to flee the area. The helos had killed all the others."

"It's a wonder Mustapha didn't execute the guy on the spot."

"Before returning to the range, Mustapha had him tied up and left for whoever came to clean up the mess. The Major found him when he and his guys arrived on the scene a few minutes later. Here he is now," Amelia said, as Major Tariq returned to the Brigadier's staff car.

"I've been called to Headquarters," offered the Major in a very sobering tone. "Please wait in the barracks until I come and get you. It may be late but I will collect you as soon as I can."

"Will do. Delta's return is expected on this incoming aircraft. I'll get them settled and wait for your call, Ali."

"I can't tell you how sorry I am that this has happened, Rick. Please know we will not stop until those responsible are found and executed."

"Thanks, Ali," I relied. "Please allow me to be there when you do, my friend."

40

Staying the Course

US Embassy London – 6 Hours Earlier
Office of Bill Douglas – 5th Floor
25 Grosvenor Square, London – United Kingdom
Sunday 13 July 1986 1030 Hours

BILL DOUGLAS ROSE from his desk and walked to the window. The rain had stopped but the sky was still overcast. The statue of Franklin D. Roosevelt was still standing in the downpour. It was positioned in the gardens very near that far building whose entrance was marked with a brass plate displaying the number 9. This was the site of General Dwight D. Eisenhower's headquarters during the Second World War. Douglas shook his head from side to side.

He turned from the window and returned to his desk. As he took a seat he picked up the phone. With his right index finger he pushed the COMM center's intercom button.

"Who's this?" he asked, and was told it was Specialist-7, Dennis Anderson. "Dennis, place a call to General Bushman in D.C. He's probably at home. Do you have that number?"

"Yes, Sir."

"Good. If he's not available ask whoever you talk with to get word to the General to call me as soon as possible. Thanks, Dennis. I'll be here for a couple more hours," said Douglas and ended the call.

Thirty seconds later the intercom buzzed. "Anderson, Sir. I have General Bushman on the line."

"That was quick. Thanks, Dennis. Please put him through."

"Hello, Bill, it's been a while," came the sober voice of LT General Gerald Bushman, Retired. "What's on your mind?"

"Rick just called. Andy Davis was killed at the Stinger training range this morning." There was silence on the line. "... Sir, are you still there?" asked Douglas.

"Yes. Did we lose anyone else? Is Rick OK?" asked Bushman.

"Rick and Amelia were not injured, nor were any of our Green Berets."

"How about the Afghans?"

"The Afghans didn't suffer any losses. There were, however, four Pakistani military killed in action and three wounded. Sir, SF Master Sergeant Mike Davis was there when his brother was killed. He was part of his brother's protection detail."

"That's tough," replied the General. "What do you need?"

"Sir, Rick has requested transport for Mr. Davis. He is also asking for the return of Pezlola, Lawson, and Delta, as soon as possible. I said I would call you and make the request."

"I'll make the arrangements for the aircraft as soon as we hang up," answered Gerry Bushman somberly. "Did Rick say why he wants to push up the timeline on Phase 3?"

"No, but I'll hazard a guess that he wants to get Stinger working in Afghanistan as soon as possible."

"Bill, call Rick and tell him ... tell him he has my deepest sympathy for the loss of his friend. Please extend the same to Master Sergeant Davis for the loss of his brother."

"I will, Sir," replied the CIA's London HOS. "Should I alert Pezlola and Lawson?"

"Where are they right now?" asked the General.

"Lawson is in Bischofsgrün. He'll know how to get hold of Pezlola."

"Good, get them to Rhine Main. We can at least get them delivered with the airplane this evening. Delta may take a bit longer to arrange but I have a couple favors that I can call in. Tell Rick the wheels are turning. They'll be there as soon as orders allow. Anything else you need, Bill?"

"No Sir. Thank you, Sir," replied Douglas.

"It never gets easy does it, Bill? I'll let you know the flight info as soon as it's arranged."

"Thank you, Sir," replied Douglas.

It was only three hours and 37 minutes after Douglas's call that the Lockheed C-130 Hercules lifted off from Rhine Main AFB. On board were four pallets requested for Phase 3 of Cyclone. In the airline-type seating at the front of the aircraft were CIA members Jim Pezlola and Gary Lawson. Also flying this night were SFC George Angerome and his entire Delta Force team.

41
Understanding Evil

ISI Headquarters & Administration Building
Ojhri Camp – South of Islamabad – Sub-Basement Level 2A
Chaklala, Rawalpindi – Pakistan
Monday 14 July 1986 0330 Hours

SUB-BASEMENT LEVEL 2A could only be accessed from the boiler room on Sub-Basement Level 1B. A large steel door located on the back wall between two of the boilers was propped open with a folding chair. Major Ali Tariq waved me into the stairwell, such as it was. There was one light bulb located at the 90-degree turn in the stairs. As we made the bend I could see one more light burning at the bottom step where it touched a large puddle of water.

The air was heavy with moisture. There were wet patches of water all along our route across the large open space. We came to a double-wide set of steel doors. Most of the paint was peeling and any exposed metal was well rusted. Ali banged on the door with the butt of his pistol. We waited a full 30 seconds before the left door was pushed outward by a corporal. I recognized him from his assignment at the firing range.

We crossed the room to the opposite wall. The only light in this compartment was coming from a framed windowpane that was set into the concrete block wall. The one-way mirrored glass, 12 feet wide by 4 feet high, was obviously designed for large group entertainment. The view into the adjoining chamber revealed its purpose. A man was hanging by his hands — which were bound together — from a chain attached to the ceiling. His legs were spread apart. Each foot was secured to either side of a metal grate that was positioned directly under the man's body. Apparently, this featured convenience was being used to manage and remove all types of fluids.

There was a hose lashed to the chain just above the man's hands. It was spilling large quantities of water, under considerable pressure, onto the man — completely encasing his head and body in water. He was naked except for his underwear but, even so, these were pulled down and were stretched between his knees. Go figure!

"Rick, sorry for the delay in receiving you — and the hour," said Brigadier Yousaf Azraq as Ali and I walked up. Mustapha and Suleiman were standing to the side, away from the others. Suleiman had his arms folded across his chest, watching with fascination the interrogation process. Mustapha's face did not show any emotion at all. He just stood there cradling his AK-47.

"That's OK, Sir," I responded. "Major Tariq kept me informed and it gave me a chance to bring Mr. Pezlola and his team up to date on the current conditions. Who is the gentleman being showered in the other room?"

"His name is Anam Kashif. He works here as a sanitation worker, a garbage man. He has admitted providing information to the Russians. He is responsible for telling the local KGB contingent about your group." Just after the General finished his statement the lights in the room dimmed. I turned my attention back into the chamber.

The interrogator standing in front of Mr. Kashif had an electric cable in each hand. He was wearing thick rubber gloves that covered his arms up to his elbows. He was holding a cable on the man's left nipple and the other was securely clamped to his testicles. A helper on the far side of the room was operating a large knife switch. The "on" position was what was causing the lights to dim. Well, that wasn't entirely true — Mr. Kashif was helping also.

"What's become of the man captured this morning at the range?" I asked.

"He is no longer among the living. However, he did share with us the names of some of his friends before leaving this world," replied the Brigadier.

"Oh, is this gentleman one of the named?" I asked.

Without answering me, the Brigadier explained that Anam Kashif was 34 years old. He was married and had lived with his wife in Islamabad. She had been killed in a freak accident two years before. Freak in the sense that she was found unconscious at the bottom of the basement stairs of the apartment building where they lived. A man in a Pakistani Army uniform had been seen leaving the building just minutes before. Kashif told the police that his wife had never been in the basement before that day and had no reason that he knew of to be there. There was no follow up investigation. And that, as they say, is how hatred manifests itself.

I continued to question the Brigadier. "Did he tell us who he's working for? Any names or addresses that would warrant a house call?"

"Both, actually. We were just trying to verify what was told to us before calling it a night."

"Was it anybody you know?" I asked.

"Yes, it is someone we have been watching for some time now." The door to the right of the viewing port opened and the man with the rubber gloves stood with one foot in our room with his back pushed up against the door, holding it open.

"I'm sorry, Sir, he's dead. However, I believe he told us everything he knew," offered the interrogator.

"Very good, Sergeant. You two go and get some sleep. I'll have the infirmary send their people to collect the body. We can write our reports tomorrow."

42

Dance of Incompetence

Ojhri ISI Inner Compound

ISI Ojhri Camp – Outside the Outer Wall
South of Islamabad – Chaklala, Rawalpindi – Pakistan
Friday 18 July 1986 2210 Hours

MOHAMMAD ESCRIAH AND seven Russian Spetsnaz (Russian Special Forces) soldiers were dropped off on the highway near the outer fencing of Ojhri Camp. They moved quickly to a position at the base of the first of the two fences. They were well hidden from any traffic passing on the main road. Mr. Escriah was a KGB field operative who reported to the 2nd Secretary of Culture Attaché for the Russian Embassy located in Islamabad. Up until four months earlier, the seven Spetsnaz operatives with him this night had been the guests of the Pakistani Army at the facility known as the Badaber Fortress.

Fabricated in plain sight, Badaber was advertised, and given the same appearance, as many of the relief centers sprinkled in and around the Peshawar District. Typically, these centers were established to provide relief services to Afghan refugees. In actuality, this particular facility called Badaber was a class one, high security prison.

Some 40 Russian soldiers and as many as 400 supposedly disloyal citizens of Afghanistan were housed there. Most were captured in the fighting in the mountain villages surrounding the city of Jalalabad. Being sent here by the Mujahideen leadership was not a happy experience. The purpose of Badaber was a closely-guarded secret until many years after the Russians withdrew their forces from Afghanistan.

The Fortress was staffed partly by the Pakistani military, partly by the Mujahideen, and even included a small contingent of American CIA. The Americans were there only to provide logistical support for the Mujahideen leadership in Peshawar. The Russian captives were held in high contempt and suffered immeasurably at the hands of their captors.

It was a Russian soldier, Victor Duhovchenko, who planned and led the mass escape attempt in early 1986. The endeavor stalled at the only exit to the complex. The local army security showed up in force and pushed them back to the center of the compound. Seeing that their escape was being thwarted, Victor pulled everyone who could still walk into the administration building. With failure just hours away, Victor helped a small group of Spetsnaz operatives — whom he had taken a liking to — access the sub-basement level. The room was located directly under the prison armory.

Six months earlier, the KGB man, Mohammad Escriah, was returning in his car from a meeting in the North. Escriah was also a member of the KHAD, the Afghan Secret Police. His agency was dedicated to the complete devastation of President Zia and his government. A terror campaign of bombing civilians was in the works. For this reason, he had driven all the way to the town of Gilgit. The Afghan Secret Police were trained and advised by the KGB, where he already enjoyed membership.

The meeting was a bust. However, good fortune was about to smile upon him. A huge explosion and fireball appeared in his windshield. The fiery event seemed to be happening miles away. Towards the west perhaps, "in the vicinity of Peshawar," he whispered to himself. He drove on for another 20 minutes before he came upon an unconscious man lying half in the road with his legs submerged in the water of a drainage ditch. With the car's headlights trained on the man, Escriah got out to see what the man might possess. A Good Samaritan Escriah was not.

He rounded the front of his car and stepped into the narrow beam of the headlamps. As he bent down and touched the shoulder of the unconscious man six other males came out of the darkness and surrounded him. The seventh man, the injured one, stood up and spoke to the others in Russian. It was Mohammad's good fortune that night that he also spoke Russian. The order to kill him and get into his car was quickly modified to allow him to drive them to a safe place.

In the following days, Mohammad learned that his newfound friends had escaped from Badaber through a sewage pipe. He was told that once the prison break had been thwarted by the responding Pakistani military the remaining Russian prisoners broke off from the main group of rioters.

Twenty-one of their comrades had survived the initial efforts of the overwhelming firepower of the military to retake the prison. They retreated to the basement of the main building in the center of the Fortress. This building contained the Armory, they explained. Victor Duhovchenko, realizing the end was near, gave the order to set fire to the armory. He also helped the seven Spetsnaz warriors to access the sewer pipe and reseal it after their departure. The resulting explosion removed all evidence of their exit. It also provided the desired result — a proclamation that all prisoners were killed in the explosion. The fortress was totally destroyed.

This night at the Ojhri camp, the proclamation report that listed the number and the names of the dead at Badaber prison would finally be made whole and truthful. The van had returned to almost the exact same spot where Ali Hastani had climbed into the Ojhri Camp compound the week before. He had made it a full 500 meters into the compound before being shot to death by one of the ISI security force.

He had killed an Ojhri guard just inside the second fence not 10 meters from where he had cut his way into the compound. His handler, Mohammad Escriah, had watched the entire event unfold from a position on top of this same fence that they would carve their way through tonight.

Escriah was confident that the Ojhri security force would not be expecting another attack so soon, and in this same area. What he had witnessed firsthand the previous week and what he had been told by his contact inside Ojhri made him feel confident. His Spetsnaz force was well trained for this type of operation. They should be able to get in and out of the housing compound before the Pakistanis and the Americans knew what hit them.

From his position hanging just below the top of the inner chain link webbing he could very clearly see his objective off in the distance. A path to the secure space inside that inner walled area was right in front of him. The foreigners, their housing quarters, and the Officers Club where they spent the evening hours were located behind that second walled compound. He could see his prize just 800 meters from where he hung. His plan called for his Russian Spetsnaz operatives to access the inner sanctum, regardless of the obstacles put before them, and kill everyone they found.

He knew he could do this. He also knew this would finally get him the recognition he deserved at the highest levels within the KGB. It would not be easy but his team was well trained and they would cut a path directly to those he needed to kill. His informant was a garbage man. The man had told him that he couldn't say for sure who these foreign persons were but several of his coworkers had been told that the mysterious group in question was most likely American CIA. He also was told that this group could be found at the Officers Club in the evenings.

He had been watching the compound for the past several weeks. The previous Sunday a bus and truck convoy had departed Ojhri for parts unknown. Escriah ordered eight of his men to follow in two vehicles at a safe distance. Their orders were to find out where the convoy was going and what it was up to. And, if the opportunity presented itself, they were to kill as many of the foreigners as possible.

That was five days before. His eight men and the vehicles in which they rode had not been seen or heard from since. There were, however, whispered rumors circulating in and around Islamabad. In the haunts of the Pakistani military, there were murmurs of a firefight that had taken place about 40 kilometers to the north of Ojhri. But that limited bit of information was all that could be gleaned by his people. Tonight, he intended to even the score: locate this group of foreigners and kill them all.

It would have been nice if he could have touched base with his garbage man one more time. Just to see if everything seemed to be proceeding normally on post. But the man suffered from severe depression and was unstable at times. He had disappeared in the past. Sometimes it would be for days at a time. However, since he had first been recruited his information had been solid. No matter, they would strike the Officers Club hard and fast, kill everyone inside, and exit through the rear of the compound. They would be gone before anyone knew what hit them.

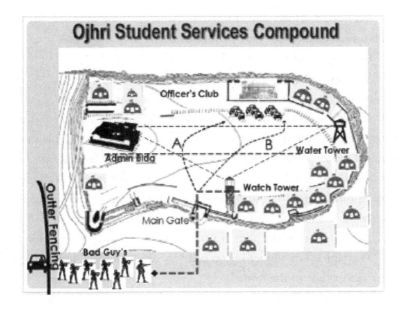

Officers Club Main Dining Room
ISI Ojhri Camp
Friday 18 July 1986 2215 Hours

My earpiece clicked and the voice of Major Mohammad "Ali" Tariq was soft but excited. "Outside the compound wall near the gate entrance … eight targets … single file … wait … they have now just separated into two groups of four at the gate. Both of these groups are still for the moment. They seem to be sizing up the situation … hold one."

"OK, everyone," I said as I stood up from a table at the center of the room. "As you just heard, the Major has identified eight bad guys on their way here. If for any reason their Plan A succeeds, one or more of the assholes will be allowed to come up the steps and through that door," I said and pointed towards the front entrance to the club. "You are to hold your fire. If by chance, and pay close attention to what I'm saying, if they get by me … then and only then are you authorized to engage. Is that clear?"

"Hooah," was the simultaneous response from the three Delta Force operatives seated at a table closest to the bar at the rear of the room.

"Rick," offered Mustapha, "if you don't mind, we'll stand right here behind you?"

"Very good, Mustapha," I replied. "Same goes for you, Mr. Turtle. You will do nothing unless they get by me. Understand?"

"Of course, Rick," answered Suleiman.

"Whatever you wish," replied Mustapha.

Jim Pezlola didn't respond verbally; he just shook his head from side to side in mock disapproval of the instructions. Everyone got up, including Jim, and fanned out around the outer edge of the room. Mustapha, Suleiman, and I moved towards the front entrance. There were two columns, one on each side of the hostess desk. From here I would have a direct view of the two sets of spring-hinged glass entrance doors. The interior doors could be pushed in either direction. The outer ones only opened outward. (Note: this is an important feature to make note of when designing a proper execution.)

"Mustapha, I'm going to prop open the inside doors," I said. "This will give us a clear shot to the front."

"Yes, I agree. Good thinking," replied the Mujahideen Commander.

"You see that knob on the wall there to your right?" I asked Suleiman. "It controls the volume for the music. Turn it all the way to the right. Let's get this party started," I said and went to the front and pushed each door to a fully opened position. The sound of Frankie Valli and the Four Seasons' "What About Tomorrow" was now flowing, pushing through the front doors, down the steps, and into the parking lot.

The Brigadier, Yousaf Azraq, had come to the club earlier that evening. He was all decked out in his very natty looking camo fatigues. He promptly announced that the club was closing. He then asked the 70-plus patrons to gather their things and to exit into the parking lot. Everyone cooperated without complaint.

A five-meter block and brick wall surrounded this part of the camp. The Brigadier raised a bullhorn. The Sergeant he was aiming to contact was over 100 meters away on the steps of the ISI's Security Military Police Administration Building.

"Sergeant, bring in the selected vehicles from the motor pool," he said and waived his left arm towards the parking lot in front of the officer's club.

Forty plus cars and vans of various makes and manufacture were led through the gate by his own personal staff car. These vehicles were sourced from the large under cover transport facility. I had been shown this facility two weeks before. The Brigadier's intent was simple. These vehicles would provide the appearance of a target, the Officer's Club, well stocked with opportunity.

After Azraq was satisfied with the placement of the props, he turned and walked up the stairs and into the club. He started to pull the bullhorn towards his face but halted and laughed at this attempt at humor. None of the Green Berets cringed from his threat to their eardrums. With a big smile of anticipation for tonight's entertainment, Azraq proceeded to lay out the game plan for us.

Our assigned task this night would be to remain in the club. We would welcome any of the 'wannabe' assassins who were lucky enough to survive traveling across the courtyard.

"Roger that, Sir," I said. "Where will you be during the festivities this evening?"

"The roof of the Admin building," he replied. "Play it safe tonight, Rick."

"Yes, Sir," I replied as the Brigadier turned and left the club.

At the appointed time, Mrs. Smythe, Staff Sergeant Dennis Deccan, and Major Ali Tariq were nestled out of sight on top of the water tower at the far end of the courtyard.

Thirty-five meters to the right of the main gate was a watchtower that rose five meters above the inner wall that it was designed to survey. This post was seldom staffed. DELTA-3 (Pat Goschich) and Gary Lawson were lying alone on the forward side of the tower roof. Their reward: a commanding view of the entire courtyard. The newly promoted SFC Goschich was equipped this evening with a recent gift: a McMillan Tac-50. Produced in Phoenix, Arizona in the United States by McMillan Firearms Manufacturing, it was perhaps the most accurate of all in the long-range .50-caliber class.

Brigadier Azraq, DELTA-1 (MSG George Angerome), and three Pakistani MPs (Military Police) who were trained sharpshooters were on the roof of the three-story Administration Building. Three layers of concrete block extended past the roofline. This would provide the perfect cover for concealing DELTA-1, the Brigadier, and his shooters.

George Angerome was resting with his back up against the block wall with the second McMillan TAC-50 nestled in his arms. Besides the three sniper teams, there were 21 squads of military police well-hidden around the perimeter of the compound. Nineteen units were positioned in the barracks buildings located in a horseshoe configuration at the far end of the plaza. Two more squads were positioned on the first floor of the Administration Building. The triangle of death was complete.

ISI Ojhri Camp
Outside the Gate of the Inner Compound
Friday 18 July 1986 2220 Hours

"DELTA-3, this is STING-1," I called to SFC Pat Goschich, on the roof of the water tower. "Do you have eyes on our arriving guests?" I asked, releasing the switch on my throat mic. One click came back indicating that he did indeed.

"STING-1, this is DELTA-3. They are at the gate. Four bad guys just crossed the opening but are still outside the fence. Wait one. We have one inside moving right, towards DELTA-2 at the tower. Stand by."

"DELTA-2, this is STING-1. You are to remain stoic. These guys are supposedly Spetsnaz. They will probably check out your house before committing to coming inside." One click was returned.

"DELTA-3, this is STING-1. You give us two clicks when they commit inside the wire." I turned towards Jimmy Pezlola, call sign ZERO. He nodded his approval towards me. Jim had moved behind the bar in the Officers Club and stationed himself next to the large cash register. Jim held a Beretta M9, semi-automatic, 9×19mm Parabellum in his right hand. He held it closely against his chest. His finger was outside the trigger guard, paralleling the barrel.

On the roof of the Admin Building, "What does it mean 'inside the wire'?" asked the Brigadier of no one in particular. The young General was wearing one of the RAP-4 digital COMM units.

"In this case, Sir, it means the area inside this compound." Offering the explanation was DELTA-1. Angerome snuck a peak over the wall using his scope to sight-target the area by the main gate. He immediately moved his hand to his throat switch. "DELTA-2, this is DELTA-1. You are about to be boarded. Stay very, very still." One click was returned.

One man armed with an AK-47 had come through the gate and made his way up the right side of the inner wall. He kept in the darkness until he got even with the base of the watchtower. After pausing for almost a full minute he stepped up onto the staircase and climbed, cat-like, two steps at a time, up the 37 steps, arriving on the boarded platform at the top. The boardwalk footpath completely surrounded the glassed-in guard station. Satisfied that no one was home he retraced his steps and disappeared back through the gate.

"DELTA-2, this is DELTA-3. Your visitor has returned to his friends at the gate."

"Stay frosty, everyone," ordered DELTA-1. A series of single clicks was heard by all.

It was a full three minutes before a single file of eight men moved through the gate onto the parade ground. At 30 meters the group broke into two groups of four. Staying in the shadows as much as possible, both groups were heading directly towards the Officers Club on the far side of the yard.

"DELTA-1, this is DELTA-2. Be advised that the group on my left, your 12 o'clock, second from the front, is armed with an RPG and an AK. I suggest he be dispatched numero uno. Their backs are to me. Would you like me to make the recommended assignments, DELTA-1?"

"This is 1. Affirmative DELTA-2. Call the plays. Snap count will be by 2. Confirm," ordered Angerome.

"DELTA-3, this is 2. At your 12, tag items from front to back: 3, 1 and 2 in that order. DELTA-1, on your 12, tag items 2, 3, and 1. Copy that."

Delta-1 slumped down with his back against the Admin Building roof's rise. He looked to his left and snapped his fingers to get the attention of the Pakistani sharpshooters assigned to him. All three of the NCOs looked towards him. DELTA-1 flashed three sets of the pre-arranged hand signals. Three, one, and two was the order given. MSG Angerome would share the bad guy carrying the RPG with the number three sharpshooter.

"DELTA-2 has both groupies marked as number 4. Stand by." Angerome was referring to the last combatant in each of the groups of four men.

"DELTA-2, this is 3. Tag number 1 in my group is only advertising a pistol. This must be Escriah. He'll be cleared all the way to the big party inside the Officer's Club. 10-4 ... Confirm 2. This is DELTA-3. Come back." One large click was returned by three.

"Confirmed DELTA-3, this is DELTA-1. Number 1 in front of DELTA-3 is not to be molested. Confirm." A series of clicks confirmed the order. "DELTA-2, this is 1. Start your snap count."

"Roger, 1. On my count. 3 2 1 … execute," ordered DELTA-2. DELTA-1 looked to his left and snapped his fingers as the count hit 2. The Pakistani shooters rose up on their heels, charging their weapons as the count went to one.

All three corners of the triangle fired at the same time. Targets 2 left, 4 right, and 3 right were dead before the report of the weapons had caught up with the rounds fired. The Russian shooter marked as 4 left had turned completely around and found DELTA-2 on the roof of the watchtower just as his entire head disintegrated. Sergeant Goschich paused after completing his part in this mission, watching the spray from the torso that stood motionless and bewildered in the dimly lit courtyard. It was for just that one moment. It then fell backwards into eternity.

The Pakistani MPs were firing Heckler & Koch PSG1s. Their targets were all in the closest group coming up the left side of the yard. The targets were numbered 3, 1, 2. Three and one were down but not quite dead. These Russian death squad members were thrashing around on the ground, screaming in pain. Target number 2, hit from two separate angles, lay motionless on the cobblestones — very dead.

As planned, target number 1 of the group making its way up the right side of the courtyard was allowed to escape into the maze of parked vehicles in front of the Officer's Club. Target number 2 of this same group wasn't that lucky. The extra time and effort he expended utilizing a well-practiced zigzag evasive maneuver cost him his life. The .50-caliber round from the Barrett barked three more times. The third projectile entered just below and on the side of the Russian's right knee. It struck with such force that the entire leg was severed. Flying almost straight up in the air, the calf somersaulted with its black leather boot and came to rest on the cobblestones a good 10 meters away from its former owner. He would bleed out in less than two minutes.

"ZERO, this is DELTA-1. All the bad guys are down except who we think might be Mr. Escriah. All teams hold your fire. All teams hold your positions. STING-1, come back."

"Roger that, DELTA-1. I'm holding his table in reserve. This is STING-1."

"Mr. Escriah, this is Brigadier Azraq." The voice came through the bull-horn propped on the edge of the roof of the Administration Building. "Please put your weapon down and proceed to the front entrance of the building behind you. We will hold our fire. You have one minute to comply."

ISI Ojhri Camp
Inner Compound Office's Club Parking Lot
Friday 18 July 1986 2240 Hours

A voice inside his immortal soul was now screaming at him for an explanation. His rapid breathing could not be quieted sufficiently to allow his mind to fathom what had just transpired. He was crouched down on his knees between two of the parked vehicles. He moved his head slightly to the left to look back towards the gate — the very same gate they had come through only minutes before. His narrow line of sight revealed only two of his fallen comrades. He suspected the same fate had befallen all of the others. The loud, metallic voice again broke the silence.

"Thirty seconds, Mohammad Escriah. Put your weapon down, raise your hands, and walk up the steps to the building behind you." There was a pause. "Twenty seconds, Mohammad. Do it now," said the Brigadier, who was now standing erect on the roof of the Admin Building. The silence that rained over the yard was complete. The screams of the suffering had ceased. The courtyard had become as still as a photograph.

"Hold your fire, I'm coming," yelled the completely disheveled Mohammad Escriah. He slowly rose up with his hands pointing skyward. His right hand still held a pistol. At the base of the water tower, several vehicles started their engines, turned on their headlights, and started forward towards the front of the club.

"Toss the weapon, Mr. Escriah, and walk to the steps," repeated the Brigadier.

Without putting his hands down, Escriah flung the pistol to his right as he continued his journey to the steps. His mind kept repeating the same two questions over and over. "How did this happen? How did they know me by name?" All in good time he thought. Perhaps the answer was at the top of these steps. Maybe there was still a chance for a successful mission outcome. "I just need to get close," he thought.

The first scout car reached the base of the steps as Escriah reached the glass doors at the top. DELTA-3 stepped out onto the pavement from the passenger side. He was cradling the Barret like a hunter on safari.

"Go right on in, Mohammad," yelled DELTA-3. "Your table reservation has been confirmed."

Mohammad Escriah, with his hands still pointing skyward, turned slightly to see who was speaking. "Who are you people?" he screamed down the steps.

"All in good time, Mohammad," taunted CWO Lawson in English. He had walked up from the second vehicle to arrive on the scene. Amelia Jane had gotten out at the same time. She was standing between the headlights, leaning slightly back against the bumper.

"Now open the door and go in," yelled Amelia Jane through a set of raised, cupped hands. Andy Davis had been a friend of hers, too.

"The party can't start without you, dirt bag," said DELTA-2, who had trotted up from the front gate. "Get inside. Now, or I'll shoot you where you stand."

Mohammad started to lower his right hand to pull open the door. "Left hand, asshole," called DELTA-3. "Keep your hands up." Mohammad complied and entered the space between the inner and outer doors. The inner doors were propped open and just 5 meters beyond them was a man wearing a cowboy hat standing in the open. Just behind him there were two other individuals. They appeared to be Afghans.

In my right hand, pointing at the floor, was a chrome-plated Colt Commander, a 1911 4.3-inch 45 ACP. It was a gift I received in 1970 from General Gerald Bushman, the then assistant director of the CIA .

"Good evening, Mohammad," I said with my biggest fake smile. "Before I invite you the rest of the way inside, I think you should know that if you have any weapons, such as guns, knives, or even a grenade or two, you should leave them right there on the floor. I promise you, you will not live to regret doing so."

With his hands still raised towards the ceiling, Mohammad asked, "You are American?"

"Unfortunately for you, Mr. Escriah," I replied, "what country I hail from is the least of your concerns this evening. Are you a Star Trek devotee, Mohammad?"

Escriah was silent.

"No matter. I thought you might be familiar with one of my favorite quotes from the movie *Revenge of Khan*. You seem to have a good command of the English language. This is good because my Urdu sucks. And I didn't want to have to bring my partner in here to explain why a small detail like a language barrier was slowing down my need to kill you. But I digress."

"You're American CIA?"

"Tonight, I'm just the boogieman, Mohammad. But, I'm *your* boogieman. Be grateful for that. If I had turned you over to my friends outside, your experience … well, let's just say it would be a hundred times more terrible than anything I am capable of providing you."

"You do not frighten me, American."

"I told you that where I reside on planet earth is not up for discussion. Let's get back to the topic of revenge. There's a quote that has stuck with me over the years. It was just recently that I finally understood its true meaning."

"You are crazy," replied Mohammad.

"Revenge, Mr. Escriah, is a dish best served unemotionally in our business. But I *gotta tell you* I'm having a tough time here."

"I demand to be turned over to the Egyptian Embassy."

"Aow, Aow, Aow." I did my very best to imitate the James Brown Auto Alarm. "That's the wrong embassy, Mohammad. Strike one. What will Victor say when he finds out how bad you have fucked this up?"

"I don't know anyone named Victor," replied Mohammad.

"You're probably right. Why would Victor Pavlovich Yakunin, the Soviet Ambassador to Pakistan, personally know a terrorist low-life like you?" Mohammad went wide-eyed with that bit of information. "How anyone at the Russian embassy would associate with the likes of someone of your character … well, actually, that's not too hard to understand. But fortunately — unfortunately for you, the ISI is very good at what they do."

"That is a lie," replied a noticeably shaken Mohammad.

"Which part?" I responded. "That the ISI is good at what they do, or that Andre Gomickovitch, 2nd Secretary to the Attaché for Culture, who was assigned, until this evening that is, to the Russian Embassy here in Islamabad, has been declared persona non grata and is being driven to the airport as we speak."

Mohammad's facial expression changed from that of a confused man to a guy who knew he had no future here on earth. "Strike two, Mohammad," I said and grinned.

Mohammad started to shake, and was starting to lower his hands. "No, no, no," I said. "We still haven't determined if you have relinquished from your person any and all other weapons. Please, and very slowly, lower your hands and open the front of your jacket."

In almost slow motion, Mohammad pulled open his coat and held it open.

"What have we here?" I said. On Mohammad's right hip was a belt holster with a pistol. "Good boy," I said. "Now pull the coat up higher and turn around so I can see your back."

Mohammad did as he was told. There weren't any other weapons on his belt as he completed the 360-degree rotation.

"Now, with your left hand, reach over and slowly pull the pistol and drop it on the floor."

Mohammad complied.

"Good man," I said. "Now kick it towards me." He did.

"Now take off your coat and toss it over here." The jacket hit the tiled floor of the vestibule with a heavy metallic thud. "Why do I suspect that you have stolen the Ambassador's silverware? Or is it perhaps another weapon?"

"Hand grenades and some Semtex," croaked Mohammad.

"Well, Mohammad, no one can say you came to the party unprepared. Of course, there is your lack of mission planning skill that seems to have got everyone with you killed tonight. But, all in all, from *my* perspective everything has worked out. Don't you think?"

Mohammad gathered his last bit of confidence and said. "This conversation is beginning to bore me. Just arrest me and let's get on with it."

"Arrest you! Arrest you!" I laughed. "My dear Mohammad, you're one sick son of a bitch." I reached up and touched my mic throat switch. "Mr. Escriah has just been called out. Strike three! Please move, everyone who might be in direct line with the front doors of the club."

Amelia Jane, Mr. Lawson, and the others gathered at the steps moved off to the side. The drivers backed their vehicles off at an angle.

"What is this meaning, 'Strike'? It is a reference to your American baseball, yes?"

"It is a line item on the final checklist."

"A checklist," replied Mohammad, who saw my eyes go cold. The chill reached him in that same instant. The end to everything was not far behind.

"The hour is growing late and not to say I haven't enjoyed our short time together — I actually have not. You ordered the murder of a friend of mine. Shot him in the back, they did. Your people," I whispered. My eyes started to tear up. My right hand with the 1911 Colt pointing at the floor was gently tapping my pants leg.

"Blood and Guts, Mohammad," I said and in the same breath my hand flashed up and I triple-tapped the target in the chest.

The glass doors were flung open as both sides exploded with the force of Mr. Escriah's person being propelled backwards at an amazing speed. Tiny pieces of glass showered the front steps and front sidewalk of the Ojhri Officers Club. Mohammad, spread-eagled, lay upside down with his head resting on the fourth step from the bottom. His eyes were wide open with a look of sudden amazement. There wasn't much blood. All three shots had penetrated his heart and had immediately stopped the flow.

I walked out and stood at the center of the destroyed door frame. I put the pistol away at the small of my back. Pezlola walked out and stood beside me.

"Nice grouping, Rick," he said and continued on down the stairs followed by Mustapha and the other Delta guys who had been inside with me. They passed Mrs. Smythe on her way up the steps. She took my arm when she reached the top and we walked together down the steps and out into the parking lot. DELTA-1 and the Brigadier were waiting by his staff car.

"Rick," said the Brigadier and then added, "Mrs. Smythe," and briefly touched the brim of his cap.

"Brigadier," I responded. "Sorry about the mess, Sir."

Ignoring the obvious, he continued. "The General sends his compliments. He assures me, and now I will assure you, that what has transpired here tonight, well … this night never happened and you were never here," said the Brigadier. "Mustapha, a word if you please."

I turned and started to head back towards the club. Suleiman emerged at that very same moment and stood at the top of the steps. He had his AK slung upside down on his left shoulder, Escriah's jacket draped over his left arm, and the pistol, a Russian PSS 7.62x42mm, equipped with the new noiseless cartridge, was balanced nicely in his left hand. He spotted us and skipped down the steps and into the parking lot.

"Mustapha, are you leaving?" he called out to his Commander, who was walking with the Brigadier towards the Admin Building.

"Yes, I'll find you later at the barracks," answered Mustapha, who went up the steps to the building and disappeared inside.

"DELTA-6 told me this handgun doesn't make any noise when it is fired," commented Suleiman to no one in particular. "He was right. I fired it into one of the tabletops. No noise at all. It is simply amazing."

"I'm glad you didn't shoot the jacket," I said. "The General would need to build an entire new facility for his officers. As for the table cloth, it will be deducted from your government stipend."

Suleiman, not concerned with references to either the possibility of an explosion or the penalty of a stipend, asked, "Do you know where I might be able to get ammo for this pistol?"

"No problem," answered the Major, who had walked up on the conversation and recognized the weapon Mustapha was holding. "We have several of those pistols in inventory and a good supply of this type of ammo. I'll bring a few boxes to the range tomorrow. We are going to the range tomorrow, yes?"

"Yes, we most certainly are," I replied. "My friend Andy Davis would expect us to finish what he started."

43

After Glow

Ojhri Camp's Inner Services Compound
Quarters – Guest Cadre Barracks
Friday 18 July 1986 2325 Hours

AS THE EVENING'S festivities were winding down, a military transport shot through the inner gate. The glare of the headlights at first made it difficult to determine what type of vehicle it was and, more to the point, who was at the wheel. It was Major Ali Tariq who recognized the vehicle and prevented its destruction. And, thank God, he did. The ISI MPs were still a bit hyped from the recent activities that had taken place in their front yard.

The Pakistani military transport pulled up to where we were standing. Almost in the same instant that it came to a full stop the right front passenger door opened. A burgundy loafer with a U.S. penny at its center was planted firmly on the ground.

"Amelia, Rick," said a smiling Ed McCall, "you are a hard bunch to find. I tried to call but—"

"Let me guess. No answer," I said.

"There was no answer," he finished his sentence.

"Ed that is my fault. I left the SAT phone in the barracks." I had done this on purpose. The GPS global positioning chip would confirm, if ever queried, that the phone had been in the barracks for the entire evening, and hence, so had I.

"Major Tariq, may I present Ed McCall," I said. "Mr. McCall is from our Embassy in the U.K." Misters Pezlola and Lawson were standing in the headlights of one of the ISI scout cars. They knew Ed and nodded their greeting from where they stood. Ed proceeded to shake hands with the ISI staff as the military police and medical transports started to fill the area.

"Major," said Ed affably. "It's good to finally meet you in person."

"It is my honor, Sir," replied Ali.

"Jim, Gary, I see you've been taking good care of Amelia and Rick." Both men nodded and moved closer to the conversation.

"How long have you been in country, Ed?" I asked.

Ed examined his watch and said, "One hour and thirty-seven minutes. Is there somewhere we can talk?"

"Of course. Let's go over to the barracks. Ali, I'd like the use of one of these Land Cruisers." I pointed to the back row of vehicle props. "We'll be in the barracks, if anybody asks."

"OK, Rick," replied Major Tariq. "I think we are good here. I also need to leave."

"Ali, we may need to go the airport later," I said.

"Of course," said Tariq. He had just walked around to the driver's side window of the ISI airport transport. He spoke to the NCO who had brought Ed from the Islamabad international terminal.

"Sergeant, park this vehicle in front of the Admin Building. Take one of these Land Cruisers and drive Mr. Fontain and his party wherever they need to go. Stay with them until they release you."

"Yes, Sir," replied the sergeant. He put the truck in gear and drove across the courtyard.

"Rick," called Ali, "I'll see you at breakfast if not before. Have a good rest of your night."

I replied, "Thanks, Ali." I thought some of his parting comment was strange. "Jim, Gary, are you ready? Amelia, you good to go?"

Pezlola called out to DELTA-1, "Sergeant Angerome, is Delta hanging here awhile?"

"Yes, Sir, I offered our help to the Admin NCOIC."

"Make sure Suleiman gets home. 10-4."

"No problem," replied MSG Angerome. "We'll see you back at the ranch."

"Thanks, George," replied ZERO. "Mr. Lawson, Amelia Jane. We're leaving. Let's take a ride. Ali, thanks for the use of the wheels." Ali touched the brim of his beret on his way towards the Admin Building. The Brigadier and Mustapha had already disappeared inside the building. I imagined that no matter what government was involved in these types of operations the required paperwork would result in the demise of several large trees.

"Rick," called Lawson from the steps of the O Club. "I need a few minutes here. I'll give DELTA-1 a hand and bring everybody home afterwards."

"Roger that, Gary," I replied. Jim and Amelia got in the far back seat of the closest Cruiser. The driver returned from parking the truck and got in behind the steering wheel. Ed got in behind the driver and I slid in next to him from the other door. "Take us over to our barracks please, Sergeant."

"Rick, I would suggest everyone do a quick change into some civilian clothes. We need to go into the city," said Ed.

I held my finger up to my lips.

"Sergeant, I just need a quick change of clothes and then I need you to give us a ride into town," I said.

"Yes, Sir," replied the Sergeant. "That will be no problem. While you are changing, Sir, I'll go top off the petrol."

Ed's eyes flickered towards the driver. We arrived in the parking area at the rear of the barracks.

"I see you know where we live, Sergeant," I probed, with just a hint of suspicion.

"Yes, Sir, the Major gave me the directions," replied the ISI NCO. "I'll be back here directly after I fill up." His English was excellent, spoken as if he was a distant cousin of Amelia Jane.

We climbed the seven steps to the rear entrance of the barracks. We stood in the tiny vestibule directly across from the main latrine assigned for residents of the first floor. I suspected we were the only ones in the building. Even so, I signaled for everyone to follow me into the giant tiled room. I went down the line of sinks turning the handle for the cold water to the fully opened setting. Everyone, but Pezlola, was looking at me with curious eyes.

"Ok, Ed," I made a come-on motion with my hands. "Let's continue, shall we?"

"Congressman Wilson is here and would like a word with you. He's the one who sent me out here," replied Ed. He reached into his inside jacket pocket and retrieved a large, brown manila envelope. He held it out towards me.

"This came in the pouch from State just before I left the office. It's from General Bushman. For your eyes only."

"Swell. It's always nice of the General to give a heads-up when a hit on you has been sanctioned."

"A hit…" repeated Ed.

I tore the end of the envelope and pulled out a single sheet of paper. I shook my head from side to side. "I was being metaphorical, Ed. Charlie is staying in town tonight?" I asked, while I finished reading the General's note.

"Oh, I see," replied Ed. "Yes, I believe he will. I was told the plane will remain overnight and leave tomorrow at 1600 hours. The Congressman said he would return to Islamabad in a couple of hours. He wants to meet us at the Marriott. I think that's where he's staying."

"Where did Mike and Charlie run off to?" I asked.

"I wasn't told but I heard Mr. Vaughn — Mike — tell someone at Langley on a SAT phone just before we landed that he and the Congressman were going to meet with someone named Avrakotos."

"Hmm. Gust is here also. Ok, Ed, what brings you to sunny Islamabad," I asked, "besides a Gulfstream-IV? Mike, the Pilgrim Mugger, could have brought the General's envelope." This earned me a raised eyebrow from Amelia Jane.

"A very nice way to travel for sure," replied Ed. In a more serious voice he said, "The service for Andy Davis is on Monday in San Antonio. Charlie Wilson's office asked Bushman for guidance. He in turn called Douglas, and here I am. The boss said it would be up to you if you wanted to attend. He knew you and Mr. Davis were quite close."

"We were. The General's note asks me to make the time and come for the service," I said, controlling my voice.

"So, the ride is yours if you want it. I was told I could stay on until your return. That is, if you need the help."

"Thanks, Ed, but everything here is in a wait-and-see state. Amelia, Jim, and Gary can handle whatever comes up while I'm gone."

"Roger that," replied Ed.

"Amelia, did you catch what Ed just offered up?"

"Yes, I agree with you," replied Amelia Jane. "You should go back and help the boss, Ed. Lord knows with everyone gone he must be close to tears."

Ed picked up on the sarcasm in her voice. "You didn't hear this from me," offered Ed, "but Mrs. Flouts told me that most mornings she can hear him pawing the carpet in his office."

"Seriously, Ed, when you get back to London you should pick up a bale of hay in duty free. Sprinkle it around Bill's office before he gets in." I offered this advice in a tone that sounded completely serious. Amelia thought this was hysterical. Ed did not. He had no idea where to purchase hay at Gatwick.

"Ed, you started to say something else in the car," I prompted.

Ed continued, "Not sure what the Congressman is up to, but he seemed upset about something. Both he and Mike took off immediately after we landed. Mike told me they were going to meet some people and wouldn't be long."

"Did Mike say what the meeting was about?" I asked.

"No, but when he was on the phone I heard him say something about a problem with the mules, whatever he meant by that."

"Interesting, and perhaps a bit of luck for a change," offered Pezlola. "The Brigadier told us two weeks ago that there was a huge shortage in pack animals. Apparently, the ISI and our local CIA have gotten together and bounced the issue to Langley."

"If Mike is here," suggested Amelia, "his boss, Gust Avrakotos, is probably coordinating the terms and conditions, and probably the purchase and delivery method."

"Have you spoken to Mike since KL?" I asked Amelia Jane, resting my butt on the edge of a sink.

"Yes, a few times," replied Amelia, searching my eyes for any additional meaning to the question. "He met with Maalouf Torki bin Taisei in Abu Dhabi last weekend. David James made the request and arranged for the briefing update."

"Besides moving Stinger by mule, the Brigadier told me that there are plans to move huge quantities of equipment, medical supplies, and food once the pack animal shortage is fixed. At this point, the Afghans are hurting for supplies."

"What caused the problem in the first place?" asked Ed.

"Disease," replied Pezlola. "It's killed most of the in-country herds. Other pack animals like horses and camels weren't affected but they're also in a very short supply. But mules are the preferred mode of transportation to move weapons and ammunition. An enormous number of them will be required going forward."

"Interesting. I had no idea how bad it had gotten," I replied. "Cyclone, at this moment, has only half the necessary mules to carry out Phase 3. The move across the border is scheduled the week after next. I hope the transport problem will be resolved before we go."

"We … I'm glad you said we, Rick," said Pezlola. "The Delta guys have all volunteered to go in with Mustapha. They want to see this operation to completion."

"Yeah, well, don't hold your breath for a decision on that just yet," I reacted. "There seems to be some confusion as to when Cyclone will be considered complete."

"Oh?"

"Some of our internal management is pressuring Bushman to end this operation when the Stingers are loaded onto the mules and are passed over the border. "The Afghan mindset doesn't plan very far into the future," I added. "They tend to stand and celebrate the moment."

"What's the problem with that?" asked Ed.

"What the Mujahideen does after firing a Stinger missile will determine whether Operation Cyclone lives or dies. The protection of an empty Stinger tube is every bit as important as having the discipline to reposition for a second and third shot. That's why we need to go with them on their first mission."

"Who will make that decision, Rick? General Bushman?" asked Ed.

"No. The President will make the final call," I said. Everyone was quiet. The sound of running water filled the room.

"If the first time Stinger is used in Afghanistan," I started the thought and paused slightly, "with an unproven or haphazard game plan, well … it would be game over. Phase 3 will be cancelled like a stamp. There's no way that we can let Stinger loose in Afghanistan without the proper field evaluation and assurances that the weapon systems handling protocols will be followed."

"Rick, I agree wholeheartedly," said Pezlola. "We need to get Douglas to get us a buy-in with the General."

"Agreed, but the decision to proceed with Cyclone will also depend on the long-term security protocols put in place by Pakistan," I added.

"You mean acceptance by the ISI?" asked Ed.

"No, we have their acceptance. The gamble we face is their commitment for the long haul. We'll need to closely monitor the arrangement for the entire life cycle of the agreement, and that hasn't been well defined."

"We're going to need people here, on the ground, for the duration," confirmed Jim Pezlola. There was no question about it, in our minds.

I looked around the room. I then went to each sink and shut off the water. "Let's change clothes and go see what Charlie wants."

"I'll think I'll pass," said Pezlola.

"Suit yourself, Jim, I replied. "Ed, there's a Day Room out front. Make yourself comfortable."

44
Top of the World

Islamabad Marriott Rooftop Lounge
Islamabad, Pakistan
Saturday 19 July 1986 0135 Hours

A CONVOY OF ONE vehicle was formed after a quick change of clothes at the barracks. Our driver dropped Amelia, Ed, and me off at the main lobby entrance of the Marriot Islamabad. He then pulled the Land Cruiser to the far side of the half circle. He parked behind three other identical Toyotas, all with government license plates. When we entered the atrium, we encountered a view of Mike Vaughn, his elbows resting high on a counter top. Mike was conversing at the front desk with someone on the Marriott staff.

"Well, things are looking up for you," I said to Amelia Jane. This earned me a frown and an elbow to my rib cage. "Hey, I told you I don't have any problem with the guy. If you're smitten with a person who mugs pilgrims for a living, well there isn't anything left to say."

"Except," prompted Amelia, with her hands on her hips.

"I think he's a good guy, Mrs. Smythe. I'm glad you two have found one another."

"Thanks ever-so-much, Rick." She gave a forced, fake grin. "Where are we supposed to meet the Congressman?"

"Beats me. Let's ask your boyfriend. Come on Ed, I'll introduce you to Amelia's beau."

"I met him on the way here."

Mike turned towards us as we walked up to the front desk. With a great big smile, he hugged Amelia and kissed her on the cheek. He then offered his hand to me and then shook hands with Ed.

"Rick, I was so sorry to hear about Andy," said Mike.

"He was special. However, he left us in very good shape, Mike." I changed the subject. Where will we be meeting?"

"Everyone's up on the roof — just like the song," replied Mike. "The General got here about 30 minutes ago, and closed the lounge. I just came down to get you."

"Which General?" I asked.

"I believe he said his name was Khan. The ISI 4-star."

"You look like you've lost some weight," Amelia said to Mike as we started towards the elevators.

And before Mike could reply I said, "You sound like Hanna." This earned me a dirty look complete with Amelia sticking out her tongue.

"Children, there will be no fighting in the elevator," said Mike, laughing.

"Come on, Mike. Let me buy you an oyster milkshake," I said as the doors began to close. "I spoke with Mr. D just before we left the barracks," I started.

"Mr. D?" asked Mike.

"Our boss, Mike. Bill Douglas" I said, motioning to Amelia, Ed, and myself. "He said to tell you and yours that Mr. Reese, the mule trader in the U.S., has agreed to the contract terms. The mules will be made available."

"Yes, Gust got the call on the way back from the border."

"What's Charlie got to do with the mules? The last I heard most of his scotch was being delivered via the Flying Tigers."

"Not so," replied Mike, laughing. "But it seems the Tigers do also provide transportation for all sorts of cargo, including all types of four legged critters."

"Who else is upstairs with the General and Charlie Wilson?" asked Amelia Jane. The elevator chime signaled our arrival before Mike could answer. The doors opened to the Top of the World Lounge.

"Never mind, Mike. Part of my answer is in plain sight."

Mustapha and his uncle, Maalouf Torki bin Taisei, were seated just inside the main entrance of the outer bar. They did not hear nor even notice that we had come into the room. I had wondered where Mustapha had disappeared to after this night's trial and tribulations.

From the elevator landing we stepped down six carpeted steps into to the plush décor of the salon, with a bar that ran the entire length of the wall to the right. There were sofas and leather chairs sprinkled at the center of the room. The clusters were separated only by small tables each accommodating up to eight people. Maalouf and Mustapha were seated in the last of the booths installed along the left wall. The entrance to the outside dining room of the Top of the World lounge was just a few meters away.

Mustapha hadn't bothered to change and was still wearing the same borrowed Pakistani warrior outfit. His uncle was wearing a charcoal gray business suit. A white open collar dress shirt provided the appearance of both business and casual. The men were deep in conversation. When we walked by them, they didn't even look up. They were sitting close together. Maalouf's hand was resting on Mustapha's right shoulder. I nodded to Amelia to keep going towards the entrance to the outside dining room.

This part of the lounge was open to the sky all the way around. The edges of the roof were lined with panels of glass one meter tall that were designed to buffer umbrella-equipped tables from the wind. Three of the tables at the center contained a total of seven ISI security men. At the far end of the deck there was a panoramic view of eastern Islamabad. A large conference table was set there by itself. No other tables were located nearby. Gust Avrakotos and Dr. Theresa Asghar were seated with a direct view of the entrance, and us, as we approached.

Mohammed Abu Ghazala, General Akhtar Abdul Rehman Khan, and our own Brigadier Mohammad Yousaf Azraq had their backs towards us. Everyone looked up as we approached the table. General Khan nodded his head but remained seated. I shook the hands extended by Ghazala and Azraq, who pushed their chairs back to greet us. Amelia went around to Theresa and exchanged kisses and then turned and introduced herself to Mr. Avrakotos.

"Good evening," I said. Those who knew us responded in kind. "Most of you already know my partner, but for those of you who do not, this is Mrs. Smythe and I'm—"

"You're Rick Fontain," exclaimed Gust Avrakotos. "Please have a seat and make yourself comfortable. It's great to meet the both of you. What would you like to drink?"

"Hemlock would go down nicely about now, Gust," I said, laughing. General Khan, may I present Ed McCall? He came in with Congressman Wilson." The three of us took seats facing the window. Not my first choice to put my back to the door, but I suspected I wouldn't be there long. I hoped.

Major Tariq joined us on the deck. "Mr. McCall, it is a pleasure," he said. He went to the Brigadier and whispered into his ear. Azraq nodded and pointed to an empty chair next to me.

"We need to stop meeting like this, Ali," I said with a smile.

"You know who I am?" Avrakotos asked me from across the table.

"Yes. You are Mike's boss and you do not suffer fools," I answered.

"Do I detect a hint of mild disapproval?" Both of the Generals had turned their attention to our exchange.

"On the contrary, Gust. Everything I know about you is five by five. Mike thinks the world of you, so, that's good enough for me."

"You're right, Mike," said Gust. "He says exactly what's on his mind."

"It's true, Mr. Avrakotos. He is not shy, this one," interjected Amelia. "Would you like to tell us how we might be of service?"

"Actually, I come bearing gifts for your project."

"Not to look a gift mule in the mouth, but where is Charlie?" I asked.

45
Coming Home

Andrews Air Force Base
Silver Spring Maryland
Sunday 20 July 1986 0300 Hours

THE AIR FORCE C-20J (Gulfstream-IV) landed at Andrews Air Force Base at 0200 hours. The smell of the air and the sensation of putting your feet on U.S. soil, has never and will never get old for me.

I hadn't been home for a few months. Hanna's temporary duty assignment to the German Embassy in London had been postponed to mid-August. Charlie wanted to stop in Washington, D.C. to take care of a few alligators who were about to escape from the swamp that was his office.

I bummed a ride with a duty NCO who was leaving the base at the end of his shift. He dropped me off at home in Silver Spring. I walked up the driveway, bending at the waist just low enough to pick up the newspaper. It was just a little past 0400 hours. All I had to do now was get into bed without Hanna shooting me. She kept a loaded three five seven in a holster. The gun was installed on her side of the bed with the business end down. It was held steady by a long and wide flat metal tong inserted between the mattress and the box spring.

I tiptoed into the bedroom holding my shoes in one hand and my diddy bag in the other. Hanna was sleeping on her side with her back towards me. I rounded the queen-size bed and bent down to place my shoes under the closer of the two chairs. I dropped the diddy bag in the second chair as I took a seat next to Hanna. I placed one hand on her shoulder and the other hand over the butt-end of the pistol.

"Honey bunny, I'm home," I whispered. Startled, Hanna's hand shot out and grabbed my hand that rested on top of the holstered weapon.

"Mein Gott, Rick, you are really making a habit of this. Why didn't you call?"

"We landed just after 0200. I didn't want to wake you."

Hanna yawned, and with her free gun hand started to rub the sleep from her eyes. "Well, now that you have, why are you still dressed?"

The Fontain Residence
Silver Spring, Maryland
Sunday 20 July 1986 0730 Hours

I got out of bed and pulled on a pair of sweat pants. They were hanging on the back of the closet door just where I had left them a few months before. I went to the kitchen to start the coffee and flicked on the TV as I walked around the counter. Actress Hayley Mills was being interviewed. I never told anybody that I had had a squirreled-away crush on Hayley growing up. Her starring role in Walt Disney's film *The Parent Trap* had hooked me but good. This fascination had started the summer of '61. "My, my," I thought, looking at the screen. She was still very pretty.

Both Hanna and I drank our coffee black. This not only saved us time but also unnecessary calories. It also protected the true taste and purpose of the coffee.

"Hanna," I said, poking my head around the corner and calling down the hallway. "What do you have planned for this morning?"

"I was supposed to get my hair cut. What are you going to do?"

"I wanted to go over and see Mom. And if I can get a hold of Daryl I thought we could get together with him and Darcy for dinner tonight."

"That would be nice. Darcy calls every other day to check on me. Let me call and see what they're doing this evening."

"Have you sent this week's mail to London yet?"

"No, it's all still in the basket by the front door. I'm going to jump in the shower."

The words to the Hayley Mills song from *The Parent Trap* popped into my head: "Let's get together, yeah, yeah, yeah." I filled the thermal flask with freshly made coffee. I pulled a tray down from the top of the fridge, putting two mugs and the flask on it, and made my way to the master bath. Saving water was not my main concern as I pulled open the shower door.

"What took you so long?"

"We need a faster coffee machine. Have you washed behind your ears yet?"

"No, I have not. Yet," whispered Hanna. She snuggled up, putting her arms slowly around my neck. Our lips were just barely touching as I wrapped my arms around her middle, holding her tightly. Hanna leaned back and lifted up her body locking her legs behind me. We kissed as the water cascaded down our backs.

"Mr. Fontain, I think something has come up," giggled Hanna. I pulled her frame up a few inches and then let her back down. Her eyes closed and a deep sigh escaped from her lips. Slowly Hanna climbed up and down, gathering purpose with each effort.

"Who says couples don't enjoy good, clean fun?" I said as my breathing started to require more oxygen.

The Kings Contrivance
Ellicott City – Maryland
Sunday 20 July 1986 2250 Hours

"So," I paused, formulating my response to the question just presented by Darcy: when had I met Andy Davis for the first time? I smiled across the restaurant table as the day in question was yanked to the front of my mind.

"I figured about 10 seconds after the drone was destroyed that my instructor/spotter, Sergeant First Class Andy Davis, would run from the firing station toward the grandstands. Everything that morning seemed to be taking place in slow motion. I imagined Andy would start yelling at the top of his lungs: '*I told him not to fire, I told him not to fire.*' But he didn't. Instead, he calmly spoke to me, telling me to secure the weapon back in its case."

"What happened to the drone, Rick?" asked Daryl.

"The drone caught on fire and went down. Crashed," I said. "That much was obvious at the time but we couldn't see exactly where. But there was a series of loud explosions coming from behind the grandstands.

"Was that the first time you and Andy met?" asked Hanna, who was seated to my left. Daryl was sitting across from me and Darcy was opposite Hanna. We'd just ordered some coffee and dessert. We were getting ready to call it a night; Hanna and I were going to San Antonio in the morning, to attend Andy's service.

"No," I said. "Not really. I mean, he didn't teach any of the classes at Bliss but I spoke to him a couple of times. He would stand in the back of some of the classes. I asked him if there were any techniques to avoid being targeted by the vapor trail pointing to the shooter's position after firing. His response was short and absolutely of no help."

"What did he say?" asked Hanna.

"He said to me, and I quote, 'You noticed that, did you?' "

"After that encounter, we would see each other around the school. He would nod. The only other time we spoke was the day I shot down Barry's drone."

"Who is Barry?" asked Darcy.

"Barry was a corporate VP at General Dynamics at the time. Anyway, Andy was the real deal. Whenever he came around, everyone was always asking for his advice. If you looked up *leadership* in the dictionary you'd find Andy's picture."

"How did you wind up with him as your spotter?" asked Daryl.

"You know, I've often wondered how that happened. I was the only one he spotted for that day. The live fire was the first time we'd formally been put together. I was the last to shoot. The other four shooters were coached by the classroom instructors, but Andy stepped in beside me. And as it turned out, it changed both of our lives. It was my first real glance of what leadership was all about."

"Did you stay in touch with him after you got discharged?" asked Darcy.

"No, it wasn't until '82 that we met again. It had been, what? 14 years? Jesus, 14 years," I said, shaking my head slightly. The majority of the conversation this evening had been centered on my good friend Andy Davis. Up until this evening I hadn't allowed much time, if any, to reflect on his loss and even less time to think about how much Andy had influenced my life.

"So the drone crashed and I was the one who had fired, so all I could think of was that my ass was grass. But thanks to Andy, it didn't turn out that way at all," I said and looked around the table. I had never told anybody about that day in the desert.

"After the drone crashed, Andy and me … well, we were soon summoned to the throne room. We walked alone up the hill from the range. The runner had told us to get our asses up to the General Dynamics pavilion. I remember whispering, "That didn't take long" and Andy didn't respond but gave me a very stern look. We could see the smoke spiraling upwards behind the spectator's grandstand. As we got to the top of the rise we could see the flames coming from the destroyed aircraft."

"You were expecting a court martial followed by firing squad, no doubt," interrupted Daryl, laughing.

"Just as we entered the pavilion we heard words of pure joy being proclaimed by someone. It was Barry Flax. We could hear him but couldn't see him at first because he was at the center of a small huddle of reporters. He sounded delighted with the current series of events. Everyone in the gaggle was writing feverishly on their notepads.

"The group parted a little as we got nearer and this gave us a full view of who was speaking. I still remember Barry's facial expressions as if it was yesterday. As he listed his talking points he was waving his hands around, imitating a missile in flight. He ended his recap by clapping them together loudly to imitate the sound of the explosion that had destroyed his very expensive jet drone."

"'Blowing up heat pods,' Barry was saying, 'is boring at best, but shooting down a jet airplane demonstrates the real capability of the Redeye weapons system.'"

"If I'd had the money I would have bought one of them myself, right then and there." I paused and smiled as everyone laughed.

"I remember the look on Andy's face as we turned to look at each other. Andy couldn't believe what was being said. Barry continued on with his conservative philosophy of changing the world one explosion at a time. He droned on — no pun intended — continuing to regale the press. He said, 'I'll bet none of you will forget today anytime soon,' and I turned to Andy and said, 'I know I won't, Sergeant. And that would be the understatement of the year if the out-of-control, flaming jet had crashed into the grandstands where they were sitting.' That wasn't word for word but it's close enough for government work," I said and continued. "So, Andy puts his right index finger to my lips and says, 'Keep your comments to yourself.' He pauses long enough to look down at my name tag and continues with, 'until I find out how much trouble we're in, Fontain. Are we clear?' The key word being 'we're'. So, I said, 'Clear, Sergeant.' "

"My friend Andy was a class act." No one said anything more for at least 15 seconds. All the eyes at the table were waiting on me. But there was nothing else that needed saying. Both Hanna and Darcy knew that Andy had been killed on assignment, but they didn't know where, how … or why. God was the only one who knew why, and he hadn't shared much with me since this whole nightmare started to play out.

Andy's Day
San Antonio International Airport
Air Force C-20A
Monday 21 July 1986 0910 Hours

We landed at 0835. The pilot taxied us to a spot on the apron just inside the service ramp. We were a football field distant and directly across from Terminal-B, Gate B-1. Out the porthole located just across the aisle from us I could see the main airport complex. The Control Tower, a new 221-foot structure, was positioned just beyond the new terminal B complex. Andy had mentioned at dinner a week or so before that his father-in-law had told Nancy, his wife, that construction was just about complete. He told me he was looking forward to seeing it the next time he got home.

Congressman Charlie Wilson came back into the cabin after conversing with the pilot. As one of the flight crew opened the cabin door and pushed out the short set of steps, the heat immediately charged into the cabin.

"It'll be a few minutes before our transport arrives. And, oh by the way, I've been told that Air Force One is on the ground here," said Charlie.

Before I could respond to that bit of information, the co-pilot, an Air Force Captain who had followed Charlie back into the cabin, put his hand on Charlie's arm for him to pause.

"Sir, this just came in for you," he said and handed him a printout from a fax machine. Charlie took his reading specs from his shirt pocket and held them up to his eyes without putting them on.

"Speaking of the devil, we just received a directive from Air Force One. They're requiring us to remain on board. We're to await further direction. Booboo, did you know about this being in the works?"

"Not a thing, Sir," replied Booboo.

"Booboo" was really Cath Franklin, who was Charlie's office affairs manager. Many believed there was more emphasis on the "affairs" part of her title than the manager label. But in all fairness to Cath, their relationship was actually strictly platonic. And managing Charlie's social schedule would certainly earn her a special place in heaven.

"General Bushman is probably accompanying the President," I suggested. "This must have been a last-minute decision by the President. I talked to the General last night and he didn't let on that Rawhide was thinking about attending."

"Who's Rawhide?" asked Hanna.

"That's the Secret Service's code name for the President, honey," I replied.

Charlie went to the galley fridge and pulled out a bottle of water. He then twisted off the lid, flung it in the sink, and went to stand in the open door of the aircraft.

"Perhaps the gentlemen who are coming at a fast clip towards us will propose some guidance on how we are to proceed," said Wilson as he took a swig. The three men reached our aircraft. Two remained at the foot of the stairs, while the shortest of the three came up the squat set of steps and pursued a backward moving Charlie into the cabin.

"Good morning, Congressman," he started. "And you must be the Fontain's?" he asked as he moved deeper into the seating area.

"This is Ms. Franklin. She works for Congressman Wilson," I said.

"Ms. Franklin," he said, nodding his head towards her and then looking around at all of us. "The President would like you to join him on Air Force One. When you're ready I'll guide you over there."

"And you are?" asked the perplexed Congressman.

"Christ's sake, Charlie," I said. "Who the hell do you think he is?"

"It's OK, Mr. Fontain," he replied. "I'm Sanders, Congressman. I'm assigned to the President's protection detail." He then held up an open leather wallet just six inches from Charlie's face. A picture ID on one side and a badge on the other showed "Secret Service" printed plainly on both.

"Now, if you'll gather your things and follow me," said Special Agent in Charge Sanders.

As our little group walked across the tarmac towards Air Force One I saw another Gulfstream, a G-IV, with what looked like the Raytheon logo, coming in for a landing. Barry Flax was here.

Air Force One
San Antonio International Airport
Monday 21 July 1986 0940 Hours

"General," I said as we entered the rear area of Air Force One. "Sir, this is Congressman Wilson and Ms. Franklin."

"Ms. Franklin, Congressman," replied LT General Gerald Bushman. Bushman shook hands first with Ms. Franklin and then the Congressman.

"We seem to have successfully not met over the last several years, Sir. Perhaps that has been a blessing for us all," said Charlie Wilson.

"Jesus, Charlie," I murmured.

"Perhaps," replied Bushman, amused. "Mike Vaughn filled that void and did a great job for both of us." He then gave Hanna a hug and a kiss and shook my hand. This he held a bit longer than expected. I could tell he was deciding whether or not to say something but opted not to at the last moment. He turned and waved everyone into the main cabin at the center of the aircraft.

This part of the Boeing 707 was configured with cubicle type seating. Four sets of tables, two on each side of the aircraft, were configured between two seats facing forward and three slimmer versions aimed towards the rear. "Please take a seat and make yourselves comfortable," offered an Air Force steward who appeared magically out of the forward passageway.

Hanna and I took seats that were facing across a table looking towards the rear. Charlie and Ms. Franklin selected the tabletop opposite us. They selected seats that were facing forward. Sanders returned from the front, whispered something in the General's ear, and turned and went back to the front of the aircraft.

"I was just told that Mr. Flax's plane has landed," said General Bushman. "He'll be escorted here in a few minutes. The President would like a few minutes of your time. As soon as he returns to the aircraft he'll come back here and greet you."

"General," I said and started to stand, "can you please ask Mr. Sanders to meet me at the rear of the aircraft?"

"There's no problem, Rick. Mr. Sanders has added your name to the authorized list."

"Roger that," I replied and relaxed into the seat.

Hanna asked me what that was all about. I told her that carrying firearms around POTUS was not usually allowed by the Secret Service. Actually, it was never permitted. It must have been one of my part-time charades that listed me as a member of the U.S. Secret Service and, hence, allowed to carry a gun around the President. Hanna agreed that strangers with guns should not hang with the Pres.

The steward returned with a tray containing two carafes of coffee, fresh cream, sugar, spoons, and eight mugs. I looked over at Charlie, whom I knew was wondering when happy hour would start.

I could see the Raytheon G-IV taxi in next to the aircraft we came in on. Sanders rushed by and picked up two of his posse at the foot of the stairs as he exited Air Force One. The General put his hand on the tabletop and slid into the seat directly opposite from Hanna.

"Are you two going back to D.C. after the service?"

"Yes, Sir, that's the plan. Why do you ask?"

"I'll ride back with you."

"Yes, Sir. I talked to Nancy on Saturday. I asked if she needed anything. She said her family was hanging close and she had all the support she needed at the moment."

"We'll ask again, of course, at the service," added Hanna.

"Knowing Barry Flax as I do," I said, "Andy's family will want for nothing. So, I suspect we'll also be returning with Charlie."

Nancy was Nancy Davis, Andy's wife. They had two children: Sara and Billy, who were 16 and 13, respectively. Both were in school in El Paso, where the family lived.

Andy was born and raised just outside of San Antonio in the town of Boerne. This was where he had grown up. This is where his parents had lived and died. Nancy's parents lived in the town of Gruene, located right outside of New Braunfels and 25 miles north of San Antonio. Large numbers of relatives on both sides lived in the immediate area.

The day Andy was killed I spoke to Nancy. She confided in me that Andy and she had planned to return to San Antonio after the Army. This plan was put on hold when Andy took the job at Raytheon. She would make the move tomorrow but it wouldn't be fair to Sara. Not being allowed to graduate with her friends in El Paso would be too much to ask of her after her father's death.

I returned to the present. "General, where do you think the President is?

"He and the First Lady have gone to pay their respects to Mrs. Davis and the children. They should be back here in just a few minutes," replied Bushman.

"That is a very nice gesture by the President and the First Lady," commented Hanna.

"Very thoughtful," I added. "Andy's family will cherish the visit. I'm sure of that. Will he be speaking at the service?" I asked.

"No," replied the General. "He can't be here officially. The circumstances surrounding Andy's death are classified Top Secret White House/Cyclone."

"I see," I said softly.

"I'll be speaking," said General Bushman after a brief pause. "I was asked to speak by the President — in his absence. And, I think it would be fitting if you also said a few words to the family, Rick, especially the children. You and Andy were serving together and you were there when he was killed."

"Sir," I answered. As I turned my head I could see out the window next to Cath Franklin's head. A convoy was approaching Air Force One. Four black late-model Suburban's with a limo sandwiched in the middle had passed by and pulled up to the forward hatch on Air Force One.

The General knew I would do what he requested. He also knew from my short response that I was not thrilled with the task. It wouldn't be easy for me — especially to talk about a series of events that could not include any detail of how my friend Andy Davis had met his maker.

"General, Sir," the steward announced from the aisle passage, "the President and First Lady are back on board."

"Thank you. Please pass the word that everyone is here except Mr. Flax. Oh, he's walking up to the aircraft as we speak."

"Yes, Sir. I'll let the Chief of Staff know."

Barry Flax had come on board and walked up to where we were seated just as POTUS arrived. "Mr. President, it's an honor. I'm Barry Flax," said Barry, who was perspiring after his jog across the tarmac. Swiping his palm on his pant leg he extended his hand to the President.

"Mr. Flax," replied POTUS, shaking his hand. "Please have a seat." With that, Barry slid in across from Cath.

The President was wearing a light gray suit with a white dress shirt. A red and gray striped tie completed the picture. A smiling POTUS scanned our group and immediately leaned across our tabletop with a hand outstretched to Hanna.

"Mrs. Fontain, I'm so glad to meet you," said the President. Hanna smiled as the President turned his attention towards me.

"Mr. Fontain, — Rick. Is it OK if I call you Rick?"

"Of course, Sir. I'm very glad to meet you, Mr. President."

Reagan turned and slid into the seat beside Barry. "Hello, Charlie," he said, nodding his head towards Wilson.

"Mr. President," replied Charlie, "may I present Cath Franklin?" POTUS had already reached across the table to shake hands with Cath.

"It's an honor to meet you, Mr. President," said Cath, visibly thrilled to be meeting POTUS.

"Charlie, I'm glad you came. Your efforts with President Zia are starting to bear fruit."

"Yes, Sir, and in a few weeks, you should have the result you're looking for," replied Wilson in an uncharacteristically serious tone.

"So, I've been told," responded Reagan, getting back to his feet. "Could you all follow me up to the front? Nancy would like to meet Cath and Hanna. I need a word with you three in private," he said, making eye contact with Charlie, the General, and me. "That includes you, too, Gerry."

"Of course, Mr. President, that would be lovely," replied Hanna. Ms. Franklin, on the other hand, got to her feet and just smiled.

I got up and grabbed Andy's Stetson off the far side of the tabletop.

"That's a very good looking hat, Rick," said POTUS. "I have one almost as nice but I don't get much of a chance to wear it these days."

"Yes, Sir. It belonged to a friend of mine. I wear it everywhere now."

Reagan waved us up the passageway. We came to a large conference area on the right side of the aircraft. Mrs. Reagan and Chief of Staff Don Regan were seated on a couch in front of four windows. The President entered and said, "Nancy and Don, this is Hanna and Rick Fontain, Cath Franklin, and of course you know Charlie Wilson. Please have a seat Hanna, Cath. We won't be long, I promise." The President then indicated that the rest of us should proceed into his private office. Hanna took a seat between the First Lady and the Chief of Staff. Cath took a seat in the chair at the head of the table.

POTUS stepped through the door to his office and sat down at his desk. Charlie and General Bushman followed. As Barry and I entered POTUS asked us to close the door and be seated.

"In the next few weeks a decision must be made on Phase 3 of Operation Cyclone," said Reagan.

"Sir—" I started to respond.

"Hang on, Rick," said the President. "What I had hoped could be accomplished through Operation Cyclone has become a political football."

"Mr. President," I again interrupted.

POTUS held up the palm of his right hand. "The CIA has successfully dragged its feet on this for well over three years. It's a shame, because deep down I know if it had been properly addressed at the beginning it could have hastened the end of the invasion of Afghanistan and, for that matter, the end of the Cold War.

Reagan leaned back and folded his arms, scanning the cabin. He pushed back deeper into the leather of his executive chair and looked directly at me.

"Gerry tells me Phase 3 of Cyclone is ready to go."

"Yes, Mr. President. We're ready. It will depend on the mule situation, Sir."

"Mules?" asked Reagan, as if he'd misunderstood.

"Yes, mules, Mr. President. It's a transportation logistics problem," I explained. "I've been told that it will be solved in the next few days."

"And why did you say '*we* are ready', Rick?"

"Mr. President," answered General Bushman. "Phase 3 will require Special Forces hands-on involvement."

Reagan turned to me again. "I was also told you've requested permission to accompany the Mujahideen into Afghanistan."

"Yes, Mr. President," I said, glancing at the General. "I've asked for that privilege."

"You don't trust the people you helped to train?" asked the President.

"It's not that at all, Mr. President. I would trust these people with my life. But I need to put my eyes on their performance and verify that the protocols we have mandated will work for them and for—"

"You think there'll be a problem, Rick," interrupted Bushman.

"Sir, Standard Operating Procedures are just that: standard. They apply to most situations, but they aren't guaranteed to apply to *all* situations. All battlefields have a dynamic personality of their own. We need — I need — to ensure that the protocols and procedures we've predetermined will indeed fit both the Mujahideen and the battlefields they'll be fighting on, while at the same time ensuring that Stinger is used wisely while its potential is realized."

"And if you find the situation untenable?" asked POTUS.

"I don't think that will be the case, Mr. President. But, if the weapon can't be protected, it would be my recommendation that Stinger be removed from play, immediately."

No one said anything or a full ten seconds.

"It's been a long time getting to this point," said the President, who had turned slightly to look out the porthole behind him.

"And Andy Davis is who we can thank for getting us this far, Mr. President. He alone deserves the credit," I quickly added.

"Today is all about Andy Davis's family. Tomorrow, well, I've just decided to play this out to the end." Reagan looked back at us. He placed both palms face down on the desk. "First, and this isn't any real surprise to us, to me in particular, Zia has moved the goalposts yet again. In a recent speech, he's declared that Islamic Law will be the law of Pakistan. This in itself is not unexpected, but the timing of his announcement is curious. From a U.S. support perspective, the funding for Afghanistan will be difficult. Congress will view Zia in the same way they view the Ayatollah Ruhollah Khomeini. So, we need to finalize Cyclone, one way or another. And we need to do it as soon as possible."

"Sir," I took the opportunity to jump in. "We're prepared to implement the final phase in two weeks' time." I looked over to Charlie and then to the General. Both were silent and both wore expressions indicating they knew what would come next. When the President processed what I had just said, he smiled his famous smile and was about to continue. But before he did the General spoke up.

"Mr. President, Mr. Fontain has requested the participation of Special Forces in Phase 3."

"That's why I wanted to talk with you, Rick," said Reagan. "Destroying Russian aircraft is not as important as protecting the Stinger technology. Don't you agree?"

"Absolutely, Mr. President," I said.

"You have a plan to accomplish this?" asked POTUS.

"Yes, Sir, I do. Both Special Forces and Delta Forces have volunteered to go. With their support, we'll be able to teach, evaluate, and maintain the required Stinger protocols. We'll have complete oversight of the operation, including personnel — the ISI and the Mujahideen."

Reagan leaned back, refolded his arms and said, "You're not concerned with what Zia will do once we commit?"

"Mr. President," offered General Bushman, "General Khan, as you are aware, is the head of Pakistan's ISI. His profile indicates that he is his own man. President Zia relies on him to conduct all internal military operations. His counsel remains important to Zia."

"And, Mr. President," I added, "Brigadier Azraq was hand-picked by Khan. He was brought in at the very beginning of Phase 1. He has personally promised to do everything in his power to protect Stinger. I believe him."

I pressed on. "The Pakistani ISI, their people on the ground at Ojhri, have pledged their support to us. I believe we can trust them. If in the future, they are ordered to violate that trust I have General Khan's personal assurance we will be given ample opportunity to shut down Cyclone."

"Good," replied POTUS. "We're all on the same page. So the staffing of Phase 3 is what needs to be finalized?"

"Mr. President, General Khan has assigned his best people for this project. We're dealing with very smart and very capable individuals who are both dependable and truthful. They'll be the ones we must rely on to enforce the protocols we require. They have also volunteered to participate in Phase 3."

"But," the President waited for the other shoe to drop.

"Mr. President, Cyclone can't be completed without Special Forces."

"I see," said POTUS. "You say Special Forces has volunteered to go?"

"Yes, Mr. President," I replied. "Delta has also asked to participate."

"Well," replied Rawhide, who stood up and came around his desk and rested his butt on the edge, "it will all come down to whether or not Zia is trustworthy. This is a long-term concern. Let's proceed with Phase 3. General, you're authorized to use Special Forces in the final phase of Cyclone."

"Thank you, Mr. President," said Charlie Wilson, who had been silent up to now. "Stinger is very important to them. Unless the Mujahideen start winning, Pakistan will suffer the same fate as Afghanistan. I expect they'll work very hard to comply with our requirements."

"I hope that will be the case, Charlie," said POTUS. "Gentleman, thank you for coming here today." Rawhide pulled open the door and stepped into the conference area and addressed the entire group.

"Nancy and I were heartbroken when we learned of the loss of Andy Davis. That's why we came down here today to meet his family and to tell them how much his country honors their sacrifice."

"Mr. President," said Hanna, "it's a wonderful gesture for you and the First Lady to come and console Nancy and the children."

"It's our honor, Hanna," replied the First Lady. Everyone moved to the open cabin door.

I used both hands to put on Andy's hat as Hanna and I descended the short staircase at the front of Air Force One.

San Antonio National Cemetery
517 Paso Hondo
Bexar County, Texas
Monday 21 July 1986 1240 Hours

San Antonio National Cemetery is located in Bexar County, Texas. The General, Gerald Bushman, was finishing up his remarks to the gathering.

"Thank you, Mrs. Davis, Sara and Billy, for allowing me to be here today to honor your husband ... your Dad." He paused and made eye contact with all of the Davis's. Both Sara and Billy were looking back at him.

"Our country will be forever in his debt ... forever and ever." He paused again for slightly longer and then continued. "May God always protect and bless you." And with that he stepped to the side of the gravesite and said, "Rick."

It wasn't an excessively large gathering, nor was it small. Two hundred and fifty people had filled the church. Over a hundred of them had followed Andy to the cemetery. Everyone stood in a half circle that was five deep. The journey from Saint Peters Catholic Church located in Boerne had taken almost three quarters of an hour. The procession of cars was over a mile long. MSgt Mike Davis stood and shook my hand with both of his as I arrived in front of the seated family. Mike had spoken to the gathering just prior to the General's remarks. He had broken into tears before he finished.

"I know it's hard to understand, but painful times, like this one, happen. Your husband, your Dad, your brother, your son-in-law...." I paused and looked out over the group. "Our Andy, for most of his life, did — to the best of his ability — whatever was necessary to keep us safe." The realization hit me like a ton of bricks.

"I met my friend Andy, your Dad," I said looking towards Sara and Billy, "in 1968. I'd been in the Army for only a few months. I was pretty wet behind the ears when I showed up on his doorstep at Fort Bliss. Little did I know that he would change my life forever. Andy played a big part in who I've become in this life. He was there for me from the very beginning. I was with him in the very end. And in that end, he provided a way for a great number of people to have a better way of life. Not many of us will be able to make that claim. God bless my friend Andy Davis. And God bless the United

States of America, which he served so well. Billy smiled back at me while Sara still stared off to some place in the distance.

My voice stopped working and my eyes went immediately to Hanna, who was standing beside General Bushman. Her face forced the strength back into my voice.

"The world is a better place because of my friend Andy. I will miss him very much."

Not only was there still no noise, there wasn't any movement within the ranks, either. "Sergeant, please sound Taps," I said and walked to where Nancy and the children were sitting. I put one knee to the ground and placed my hands on hers as the bugler played the well-loved notes. I stood and pulled Billy to me, giving him a hug. At the same time, I leaned in and kissed Sara on the forehead. I then returned to my seat between Hanna and the General.

The honor guard didn't miss a beat. The four Army representatives, one Airman, one Naval Commander, and a retired Texas Ranger fired the three sets of rifle shots to mark the importance of the folding of Andy's flag. Nancy had flinched only with the first volley. She fully understood and embraced the following two reports of seven shots each. She made eye contact with, and graciously accepted the perfectly folded flag from, the Chief Warrant Officer, who told her it was given on behalf of a grateful nation.

46

Andy's Notes

Rhein-Main Air Base

Hangar Complex – Building 549
Frankfurt, Germany
Thursday 24 July 1986 2140 Hours

THE LOCKHEED C-141 Starlifter landed on the shared main runway. A follow-me vehicle was parked on the perfect circle at the end. The pilot was directed to follow along the service road to a secure area on the parking apron in front of building 549. The flying time from Dover AFB with the headwinds this time of year took nine hours and 54 minutes. The flight's cargo was mostly reconditioned aircraft engines and landing gear parts.

I exited the aircraft through the left front hatch. Only the lights from the aircraft and one spot-lamp mounted on the corner of the building provided a break in the darkness. The concrete under my feet felt good. I stood for a moment in the semi-darkness looking at the front of building 549. I could be wrong, I thought, but this was the same hangar from which my Redeye group staged *Operation Sparrow Signature* in 1969.

The left side hangar door was being pulled open. As I approached, Ed McCall came into view. He stood alone under the only functioning light in the bay.

"Hi, Ed," I said. "You do get around, don't yah? If I'd known you hadn't paid your electric bill I would have brought candles and some flashlights."

"Our hosts apparently like to operate in the dark. Go figure," he said seriously.

"Hello, Rick. Put your bag in this jeep," called out Staff Sergeant Dennis Bormann, pointing to the vehicle snugged in behind a canvas clad three-quarter ton truck. Both vehicles were parked head-in next to a wooden staircase. Seated in almost complete darkness, with their backs against the wall just to the left of the stairs, were some very special forces: STFs Paul Murray, Brian McDermott, and Jim Thomas.

"Hi, Dennis," I said. "Paul, Brian, Jim," I added, nodding at the others huddled by the stairs.

"Everyone's up in the mezzanine," Ed continued. "The Major and Captain Nelson went up just a few minutes ago."

"Who's the major? Where's the rest of your team?"

"The Major just arrived about 15 minutes before you, direct from Langley." Ed still hadn't told me who the major was. "The rest of my guys are in the back of that three-quarter."

"And you know this how, Sergeant?"

"It's been just a half hour since I saw them climb in. Oh, you meant the Major? Believe me, he is, and I do have my sources. I could tell you how I know, but then I'd have to kill you."

"Ha, ha. That's the oldest one in the book. Careful DELTA-2, I'll have Suleiman steal all of your toilet paper. Who else is up there?"

"The boss — that is, *your* boss, your Uncle Max, and our own beloved Captain Nelson."

"You're just a fountain of knowledge, Dennis. We'll have to have a drink one of these nights so I can know how this war can be won. Mike Davis is still on the plane. He's talking to someone in Bad Tölz. He's probably trying to find out where you guys are hiding."

"You want me to go get him?" asked Jim Thomas, poking his head out of the shadows.

"No, I'll get him," offered Ed, turning to go back outside. "You go on up, Rick. They seem anxious to get started."

"Roger that. Is that the way up?" I asked, pointing to the steps.

"One level up, go through the repair shop. Conference room is all the way in the back."

"I think I know the room. OK, see you guys up there."

"No, we were told to wait here," said STF Murray. "It hasn't been decided if we'll be going with you."

"You should check with Dennis. I'll bet he knows," I said. "And hey, worst case they let Mike go, right?" I climbed the stairs two at a time.

"Whatever the decision," called STF Sergeant Thomas, "do us a small favor. See if they'll let us break out our night vision gear while we wait down here in the dark. 10-4?"

"Will do," I said, laughing. "Or at least," I paused on the landing and leaned back over the railing, "if they won't go for that, I'll try for a bigger light bulb."

"Roger that," replied the Staff Sergeant in a most serious tone.

I pushed the door open and entered what appeared to be the very same electronics repair shop I had walked through in '69. Talk about déjà vu. I could swear that not only was this the same room but nothing on the work bench seemed to have been disturbed in all of the time that had passed. Even after 17 years the soldering iron seemed to be in the exact same position. I continued through the shop and saw Bill Douglas in the conference room through the window in the wall. Sitting across from him was Captain Nelson, the Special Forces B-Team commander, and a Marine officer I didn't recognize. Uncle Max was coming out as I reached the door.

"Hi Rick, I was just going to use the rest room. Go on in. I'll be right back."

"Good to see you Max. Ed and Mike will be up in a minute. Anybody else coming?"

"No, this is it," replied Uncle Max. "This shouldn't take long. You have a plane to catch."

I walked into the conference room and placed my briefcase on the table. "Hi, everyone. Ed and Mike are coming right behind me."

"Rick," Douglas acknowledged me. "Good flight?"

"Yes, although my ass will never be the same. How are you, Sir?" I asked Captain Nelson.

"I'm good, Rick, and I asked you to call me Greg."

"Sorry, Greg," I replied. "It's been a long week."

"Rick, this is Major Bill Harris," said Bill Douglas, indicating the Marine officer. "Major Harris will remain in Ojhri during the Phase 3 operation. He and Major Tariq will formalize the storage and distribution protocols for Cyclone going forward."

I reached over as the six-foot, two-inch Major stood up and leaned in to shake my hand. "Rick Fontain, Major," I introduced myself. "It's very good to have you on the team, Sir."

"Rick, please call me Bill, and I'm glad to be assigned to this operation." We both took our seats.

"I just talked to Amelia Jane," said Bill Douglas. "She said the mules are being staged outside the town of Mardan."

"That's good news. Is Mike Vaughn still in country?" I asked.

"Yes, he personally went to the depot in Peshawar and selected thirty animals for us. Major Tariq arranged transport and had them delivered to the rally point yesterday."

"What did Mrs. Smythe say about our request to have Saifullah be a part of the team?"

"Mustapha spoke to Saifullah this past weekend," said Max Gresonine, returning to the discussion. Following him into the room were MSG Mike Davis and Ed McCall. They took seats at the far side of the table.

"Saifullah has agreed," added Douglas. "However, Amelia says he wants the authority and control to pick the entrance and exit points for each of our mule trains."

"Makes sense," I said. "General Bushman told me before I left Dover that two of the seven recent supply strings were intercepted and destroyed by the Russians. I suspect that is a major concern to Saifullah."

"And, of course, the mules," said Captain Nelson with a rueful smile.

"Both of the attacks," said McCall, "occurred in the same area in which you'll be traveling."

"I just spoke to Gary Lawson before I left the plane," Mike added. "He and Major Tariq went to Peshawar to speak with two of the men who survived one of the attacks."

"Bill," I said, looking towards Major Harris, "Major Tariq is the number two man at Ojhri Camp. You and he will coordinate the rear support activities during Phase 3." I then turned back toward Mike. "And what did the two men say?" I asked.

"They said that the Russians stopped the convoy using three helos. There were four gunships reported on the second attack. In both cases one or more of the larger gunships, probably 24s, would fly overhead while the smaller transports landed at each end of the convoy."

"Smart and efficient," commented Ed McCall. "The smaller ones were most likely Mil Mi-8s."

"Are you thinking what I'm thinking, Mike?" I asked Andy's brother.

"Hell, yes," replied Mike.

I clicked both tabs on my briefcase and pushed the lid open. I reached in and took a thick notebook out and tossed it to the center of the table.

"It was the first week of class," I said. "Andy confided in me that the traditional classroom approach would not work with this type of student. He said that once the basic understanding of the operation of the weapon was solid the focus needed to be entirely on tactics."

"And he did just that," added Mike. "He spent almost every evening after dinner talking shop — mostly with Suleiman."

"He's the one who was educated in the United States?" asked Douglas.

"The University of Maryland," I responded. "Suleiman saw from the very beginning what Stinger brought to the party. And, if there is one person in all of Afghanistan who has ever thought up more creative ways of killing Russians than Suleiman, well, that would truly surprise the hell out of me."

"What do you suggest, Rick?" asked Bill Douglas.

"No need for suggestions at all, Bill. Andy wrote it all down for us," I replied and placed my hand on the notebook at the center of the table. Pages 16 through 29 described various methods and procedures for attacking Russian truck convoys in and around the major cities.

"I studied most of this on the way over. It was in Andy's things that were sent home. Mike found the book and gave it to me. With a few modifications and slight reverse engineering I think we can overcome any objections the mules may be having about traveling through mountain passes. We can hunt down the Russians who will think they're hunting us down."

"So, your idea is to turn the tables and trap the Russians in their own game? Very clever, Rick," said my Uncle Max.

On the advice of Mustapha's brother-in-law, Saifullah, I had elected to use the Northwest Frontier Province territory to enter Afghanistan. There were several reasons for this choice. The most important being that the multiple trails were all suitable for travel by our pack animals. Additionally, this area of Pakistan was not usually monitored by Russian satellites; we should be able to come and go across the border without being seen.

"The elders of the Mirdadzai Khudiadadzai tribe have a good working relationship with Saifullah," mentioned Mike Davis.

"Jim Pezlola has worked with them in the past," I added. "He told me they were not friendly with the Russians. The control of this and the adjacent districts to their village, Kakar Sunzer-khels, would offer us several choices once we cross over."

"Each trail," said Ed McCall, "has terrain that is perfect for the mules. This has been verified via the latest SAT imaging."

"These routes offer us the best access," I said, "and the most direct path to the Bagram area."

"Also, General Khan's S-4 has supplied us with camo covers," said Mike. "These tarp nettings will allow us to hide in plain sight, if necessary."

"Captain Nelson, sorry, Greg, do you want to bring your guys up here for this discussion?" I asked. "They seemed unsure about their upcoming travel arrangements."

"Rick," said Nelson, "MSG Davis will brief and assign responsibilities to my guys on the ride over. We'll divvy up the responsibilities based on what we decide to take into Afghanistan."

"Roger that," I replied.

"Bill," I asked Mr. Douglas, "did you and General Bushman have that discussion on Phase 3?"

"Per your recommendation, the objective will be the Russian air base at Bagram," replied Douglas. "The problem to solve is how to get 30 mules, 24 Stingers, and a large group of Mujahideen shooters into position on the plateau four kilometers northeast of the airfield."

"Mustapha," I started, "has told us it would be wise to solicit, one more time, the services of Saifullah. This we have done. It will be a zigzag travel plan. Not a straight line but a route providing cover most of the way, and through areas that are not usually surveyed by the Russians."

"Suleiman said it would be a piece of cake," I added. "This made me wonder if he'd attended one too many toga parties at Maryland." Everyone laughed. "Whether he did or not I plan on sticking very close to his counsel. He has an intelligent hatred of the Russians. This makes him a very important resource for all of us."

"Even if he decides to wear his toga into battle?" Mike Davis imagined that ridiculous sight.

"As long as he keeps his underwear on we should be fine," I said in the most solemn tone I could muster.

Major Bill Harris spoke up next. "It's very refreshing to be part of a group that really has their shit together ... even though some of your men wear togas." Everyone laughed, including Bill Douglas.

"Ed, did you bring the map of the area around Bagram?" I asked.

47

Packing for Success

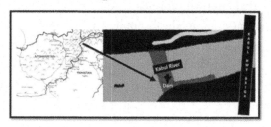

Crossing the Kabul
Warsak Dam – Northern Pakistan
Thursday 31 July 1986 0430 Hours

W E LEFT ISLAMABAD on the M-1. At Mardan, we turned north on the N-45. Our trucks arrived in the district of Chitral, Pakistan, where we unloaded in an out of the way staging area. We could see the top of the walled Chitral Fort from our location on the side road. We were taking 24 Stingers on this first outing into Afghanistan. Approximately one half of the pack animals would be assigned two weapon cases each. The balance of the mule train would include Mustapha's supply wish list. This had been compiled and passed to him indirectly by the organization of Mujahideen fighters residing near the Bagram Air Base. We felt the Mujahideen fighting forces residing in the cave system above the air base would be key to a successful assault. Therefore, we would come bearing gifts.

The wish list size and content was almost comical. The number of items alone would require a minimum of 6,000 pack animals. Mustapha asked me what he should do. I had smiled and told him to flip a coin and roll up his sleeves, metaphorically speaking. We re-engineered the list of items to fit the reality of having only 12 mules available. We packed what we thought any well deserving band of mountain warriors would welcome with open arms: sixty AKs with several thousand rounds of ammunition, 100 pounds of engineering charges (C-4) equipped with the new wireless detonators, 24 LAWs rockets, 20 cases of C-rations, and other miscellaneous items such as fuel sticks, batteries, signal mirrors, binoculars, four M-64 megaphones, and some very expensive spotter scopes. We were now packed for our first journey into harm's way.

I decided that our own miscellaneous items, needed to sustain ourselves (including spare batteries, medical supplies, ammo, food and feed) would be distributed across the animals carrying the 24 Stingers. Our Special Forces guys had suggested that five M183 satchel charges be included. An additional 100 pounds of the ever-popular Claymore mines is always a hit when planning a party. So, we packed 20 of the little guys.

The entire 30-mule string ensemble, which included very few musicians, was completely outfitted with the new Fall Line of camo netting tarps. These were supplied by Amelia's favorite outfitter and tailor, Sergeant Farooq, the ISI's S-4 clothier. Each tarp was matched perfectly on one side with the valley floor vegetation and the reverse side with the rock material of the mountains. Perfect for the type of terrain we would be traveling through. We hoped.

Living on the Edge
Kabul River
Thursday 31 July 1986 0455 Hours

The Warsak Dam was located on the Kabul River in Pakistan. A mass concrete, gravity structure, it was constructed in 1960 and modernized in 1981. It was located approximately 20 kilometers northwest of the city of Peshawar. Our access west into Afghanistan required us to cross the Kabul River Bridge and approach the dam from the north side. The south end of the dam's structure was tied into the mountain; there was no way to access this part of the dam from the south side of the river.

There was a series of tunnels built during the construction of the dam. Their purpose was the diversion of the water while the concrete was being poured at the main site. A narrow catwalk notched into the rock wall angled upwards from the river for well over 200 meters. The last of the three tunnels carved into the side of the cliff was the one we needed. This structure was cut through the mountain to the foothills beyond.

They say every journey begins with the first step. It was footstep approximately two thousand something that made my heart stop. I was walking in front of Amelia Jane. The Brigadier was in front of me and he had a hold of mule number five's tail. As we stepped from the concrete stability of the dam onto the rock shelf of the cliff we turned 90 degrees towards the right. We walked a full 50 meters along the cliff wall. At this point we were still even with the top of the dam.

The stone shelf we were on turned downward. The path widened at the entrance to the first of the tunnels. The pathway narrowed again as we started a steep climb upward to the mouth of the second tunnel. This part of the cliff wall had seen better days. There were places in the path where large chunks of the rock were missing. Mother Nature had taken her toll. As Mr. Saifullah Khan led us all onto the 30-inch wide rock catwalk it was Amelia who spoke first.

"Rick, when you booked this trip, did you get the feeling that Saifullah was upset with us?"

"Whatever would make you think that," I grimaced, my mind carefully placing each step before I took it. It was just starting to get light. This was both good and bad.

"Oh, I don't know, it was just a thought. It probably has something to do with the height, the raging river below, and the fact that the path we're on seems to be crumbling with every step."

"I have had these same thoughts, Amelia," the Brigadier joined in. "Perhaps a small prayer is in order."

"Perhaps a very large prayer," I said, "and a parachute. Both would be of comfort right about now."

"Amen," replied Amelia and remained silent until we reached the end of the catwalk and the entrance to tunnel number three.

The fact that this trail was less than a yard wide, and large pieces had crumbled from its outer edge, didn't seem to bother our tour guide Saifullah in the least. Nor did it seem to bother the mules. I now understood why the pack loads were redistributed before leaving the staging area. The left side of each mule was freed of any items that would hinder the animal from staying as close to the cliff wall as possible without touching. So that they could maintain balance, the heaver items were placed at the center of each mule's back.

Saifullah had marched us down the full length of the path from hell and successfully delivered each and every one of us, two-legged and four-legged alike, into the third tunnel framed in the cliff wall. This particular tunnel had not been used to divert water during the construction of the dam. It was cut through the mountain to the foothills beyond just in case the two adjacent tunnels were not able to handle any additional water diversion requirements. The first two tunnels were cut through the stone paralleling the river. Our tunnel opened onto a hillside. We were standing about halfway up from the valley floor. My first impression was that we were standing at the end of a boxed canyon. Saifullah had already started to zigzag his way down the slope.

"Well, this is an improvement," remarked Amelia, who had remained silent for the entire journey through the tunnel.

"Yeah," I said. "It's starting to get light. You'll notice that there isn't much cover down there. So, I'm reserving my right to scream."

As we reached the floor of the canyon I looked back up the hill to see that the end of the mule train had exited the tunnel. Mustapha was walking down the line towards us. He had walked the entire way behind his brother-in-law. As he reached our place in line, he pivoted on his right foot and fell in between us.

"Once everyone is down there on flat ground we will pause briefly to redistribute the pack loads. We will leave this trail and climb towards the west in about 40 minutes more. We are making good time."

I asked, "I thought we chose this route because it would offer us cover to hide if needed?"

"Of course, but the thinking was that early on in this part of our travel it is not so necessary. This part of the border is not usually under surveillance. As we get deeper into the mountains there will be plenty of places to hide if necessary."

"Usually, huh? Are you going to check things in the rear, Mustapha?" asked Amelia.

"I'll walk with you," I said to Mustapha. "Captain Nelson wants to drop a team to our rear as we go. Sergeant Angerome was curious if Saifullah's people wanted some company out in front."

"Both good suggestions," Mustapha responded. "Suleiman and two of Saifullah's people are a half a kilometer out in front now. He said he would welcome a couple of his Delta buddies to join him if ZERO thought it a good idea."

"Done. I'll tell Angerome on our way. The Green Beanies are holding two Stingers at the ready under the camo netting. Just in case there are any unscheduled flyovers."

"Amelia, would you run a COMMs check?" I asked. Just as I said this, our ear buds came to life. It was DELTA-1, George Angerome, running a test with 2 through 7. Amelia and I were designated call signs STING-2 and STING-1, respectively. The remaining CIA were ZERO (Pezlola) and ONE (Lawson).

"ZERO, this is STING-2. Over," barked Amelia, squeezing her mic throat switch.

"STING-2, this is ZERO. Go," replied Pezlola.

"COMMs check. Read you five by five, over," said Amelia.

"Same, same. Out," answered Jim.

The COMMs check continued, concluding with STF Jimmy Thomas.

I found SFC Angerome marching behind mule number 12, the last of the pack animals carrying the Stingers.

"Hey, George, how's it going?" I asked.

"So far, so good. So far, that is."

"Suleiman says a couple of his Delta buddies are welcome up front, if you want to join him," I said.

"Who's with him now?" asked DELTA-1.

"Two of my men," answered Mustapha. "Plus, two of Saifullah's guys."

"Sounds about right for now. Suleiman has a radio, right?" asked Angerome. "How about we do a couple of flankers while we're strolling down here in the open. One shooter, one Delta flanked on each side."

"Do it," I said. "Mustapha, get two of your guys and have them pull out two Stingers and come back here to George."

"OK, it will just take a minute," replied Mustapha. He walked off towards the front. Mustapha's people, except Suleiman and himself, had refused to wear the RAP-4 COMMs gear.

"What is Vassar's call sign?" asked DELTA-1.

"Who is Vassar?" I asked. "Oh, Mr. Turtle you mean? Mr. Suleiman's call sign is TERRAPIN-1," I answered.

George squeezed his throat mic and spoke quickly, "One Big Turtle, this is DELTA-1, come back."

"Very funny, George, but I'm glad you called," said TERRAPIN-1. "There are engine sounds, just now, towards the west. Could be three or more gunships. Suggest you stop and cover up, over."

"Roger that," replied DELTA-1. "Send me an update every 60 seconds. Roger that?"

One double click was a response in the positive. "COMMs Alert, the word is COVERUP, I repeat COVERUP. Just like we practiced people, now move. ZERO, did you monitor COMMs with TERRAPIN?"

"Affirmative, DELTA-1."

"ZERO, GB-1 confirms," Captain Gregory Nelson jumped in.

"DELTA-1, this is ZERO. TERRAPIN-1 reports three helos traveling north to south about one mile perpendicular to our nine o'clock. Expect in two mikes. Cover up and remain very still. Come back."

"Roger that," replied DELTA-1. "Count down status every 30 seconds." One double click was returned.

I touched my mic switch, "Stay very still people, and check your covers." I found Amelia hunkered down under mule number five. I took one last look up and down the line before ducking for cover. What I saw made my heart stop. But it was too late to do anything about it. The engine sounds were pounding across the valley floor.

"Holy Christ," I said as I got down beside Amelia Jane.

"What?"

"One of the Afghans has put up the wrong side of his tarp. It's going to look damned peculiar to the Russians that in this whole fucking valley there is only one rock with snow on it."

"You're kidding."

"You know I don't joke about end of the world scenarios." The engines were getting louder and more pronounced as they bounced around on the valley floor.

Suleiman's voice came back online. "Helos crossing your 12 o'clock at a point two-five kilometers. Speed approximately 100 to 125 KPH. Altitude is

500 meters. Standby … Standby … Standby … OK, we are good. They are gone. All clear."

I touched my throat switch to transmit but DELTA-1 beat me to it.

"TERAPIN-1, good job son. DELTA-1, out."

"DELTA-1, this is STING-1, meet me at Mount Everest. Over," I said.

"STING-1, DELTA-1 here. Say again."

"Just walk towards the front, George, and stop at the huge rock with snow on it. Out."

Shut Eye
35 CLICKS to Bagram
Saturday 3 August 1986 0325 Hours

It was day three and we were approximately 35 clicks from the caves that overlooked the Russian air base at Bagram. It had been very slow going. We were only traveling in the light of day as we got close to our destination. The terrain, in places, was way too treacherous to attempt any travel in the dark. Dennis Bormann, DELTA-2, had stumbled the previous day in the dark and really fucked-up his ankle. There was also a cut on the back of his calf that was deep. He could still travel under his own power but I could tell that he was in pain. In the dark, walking on the so-called trail was like rolling through the bumper guards inside a giant pinball machine. The mules, however, still thought they were on vacation.

The messenger came in the middle of the night. He found our point man, Vassar Suleiman, nestled between two huge boulders. Neither warrior had seemed surprised to find the other. Apparently, the Russians had recently caught and destroyed two of the three supply shipments intended for this district. The Afghan military commander for this entire area was a man named Ahmad Shah Massoud. A written order from Massoud was produced by the visitor and he made a verbal request to Suleiman.

Mustapha awoke moments before Suleiman reached to touch his shoulder. He had bedded down just off the main trail with the rest of the convoy. His AK was cradled across his chest.

"Careful, Vassar, it is dangerous to be sleepwalking this time of the morning. What do you need?"

"There is a messenger here to see you. He has been sent by Massoud. He has a written message for your eyes only."

"Where is he now?" Mustapha asked.

"I am here, Commander," replied the warrior who stood in the shadows just beyond Suleiman.

"You have a letter for me?"

With that said, the man stepped forward, holding the message. "Our situation is urgent. Commander Massoud would like your counsel."

The base of operations for the Mujahideen force was seven kilometers to the north. Mustapha found me with just one of my eyes sound asleep. Once he was sure I was wide awake he asked me if I would be interested in a field trip. I then asked him if he really understood what a field was. He didn't respond.

"Tall, soft, waving grass with daisies growing everywhere does a field make." He looked perplexed as I pressed my throat switch. "ZERO, wake up FATHER and come up front. We have been asked out on a date." FATHER-1 was the top man in Pakistan's ISI part in Operation Cyclone: Brigadier Yousaf Azraq.

"I'm awake, STING-1," replied FATHER-1.

"Good morning, Yousaf," I said. "You want to take a walk with us?"

We (Brigadier Azraq, Pezlola, my favorite Terrapin, and I) followed Commander Massoud's messenger-warrior down the trail before first light. Amelia Jane, DELTA-1, CWO Lawson, and Captain Nelson were not thrilled with this alteration to our travel plan.

The two-hour journey ended as we entered a well-camouflaged door installed in the face of the mountain. We were met by this area's supreme leader, Ahmad Shah Massoud, who greeted us with folded arms just 10 meters inside the mine's entrance. Massoud was gracious and pumped each of our arms with a firm handshake. The hum of a gasoline generator could be heard in the distance. He told us as we walked through the tunnel that we were in an abandoned gemstone mine. The tunnel led into a large bubble in the rock. This auditorium-shaped room seemed to be the center for all of the activity inside the mountain. The cavity was well lit and completely decorated out of stone.

The ceiling at its center was over 10 meters in height. The great hall measured a good 30 meters square. There were numerous shaft openings in the walls of the room. Not all of the portals were at floor level. There appeared to be several hundred Mujahideen milling around — some going and coming out of the multiple tunnels that peppered the walls. It was a good bet that there was more than one way in and out of this place.

"Welcome, and thank you for coming here on such short notice. We have suffered some serious setbacks in the last few weeks. I was told that Mustapha might be able to help with our problem."

"Commander," began Mustapha, "how may we be of service?"

The commander, an older man, took hold of his walking stick and motioned everyone to a place on the floor that had a soft, sand-like surface.

"We are here," he said and punched a hole in the earth. "Here is Peshawar and these are the main routes through the mountains that are used to supply us." He drew several lines out from the Pakistan city. "Twice in the last three weeks we have had convoys on these routes intercepted and destroyed."

"Your messenger," Mustapha asked for confirmation, "said that there were three supply trains?"

"Yes, the second, the one that made it without incident, had been delayed leaving the warehouse complex for six hours. We observed the Russians waiting at the place that the supply train would have been if they had left on time. You see this place here," he poked his stick into the sand. "This canyon is what is called a choke point. Most travelers must use this pass to get to the west."

"Most, but not all?" I enquired.

"There are other trails, of course. The added distance and the condition of these paths are a hardship for most. Adding one or more days to a journey would increase the danger of being caught out in the open unnecessarily."

"You obviously have a tattletale feeding info to the Russians." I added, "They don't have a direct view of the depot. Nor could they ascertain when each train actually leaves from the station without being told."

"I do not know what a tattletale is, but you are correct. The Russians have eyes on our supply line schedules."

"Apparently they only have access to the proposed schedule," I pointed out. "Perhaps we can use that to our advantage."

"But how?" questioned the elder. "They attack us from the sky with their iron monsters. Our weapons can't effectively penetrate the skin of their larger gunships. Only the heavier caliber machine guns are effective, but there is seldom enough time to position them."

"Can you describe for us how the attacks are staged?" I asked.

"I can," replied Massoud. "But our immediate concern is that another supply train left Peshawar yesterday — on time. That is why I sent for Mustapha. I was told there is a weapon that will kill these gunships."

"When do you expect this supply train to be inside the targeted area?" asked ZERO, speaking for the first time.

"In two days' time, anytime starting from noon on that day. The attack will most likely be here," replied the commander and stabbed another hole closer to the first one he had made in the ground. He left the staff sticking in the sand, standing there like an exclamation point at the end of a sentence.

"Perhaps we can provide a cure for the Russian bad behavior," I said.

"That is the place where it will most likely happen." Massoud pointed at his staff. Speaking through clenched teeth he added, "They seem to prefer this area."

"There is no escape when each end of the pass is blocked," replied Mustapha, using his finger to draw the canyon's shape in the sand. "I suggest thunder followed by lightning as a solution," he said as stood back up.

"Perhaps we can do even better than that," offered the Brigadier. "I'm Brigadier Yousaf Azraq. You know who I represent, Massoud?"

"Yes, of course I do, Sir. It is a great honor to meet with you face to face," replied Massoud.

"The honor, Sir, is all mine."

Four Hooves and a Great Attitude
The Peshawar Mule Train
28 CLICKS This Side of Heaven
Friday 1 August 1986 0630 Hours

Runners were sent. The Peshawar mule train was stopped in its tracks just 28 clicks (military slang for "kilometers") shy of the pass where the scheduled ambush was to take place. They were quickly diverted from the main trail just after the sun set on the very next day. The convoy leaders told us that three Russian gunships had flown high over them earlier the previous afternoon. Their leader had a premonition of what lay in wait for them at the canyon pass. He had all but made up his mind to return to Peshawar.

Mustapha talked to some of the men in the convoy. Most expressed a fear that the same fate that had befallen their friends on previous expeditions would befall them also. They were well aware of the brutality shown previous convoys. We, in turn, suggested an alternative action. We told them about our plan and laid out what we wanted them to do. The good news was that they would have the entire morning off — with pay.

Suleiman had backtracked slightly and angled our mules away from their northern hideout. Mustapha and his men merged with the Peshawar cooperative at noon. A deep, wooded gap in the mountain was found off the main trail just four kilometers from the expected ambush site. The tall trees protruding out of the gorge provided the necessary cover from the prying eyes of Russian aircraft.

We pulled 20 of the 46 mules and redistributed the bundles of both of our convoys. The loads would be heavy but the distance we needed the mules to travel would not be far if all went as planned. Suleiman whispered great things, mostly food related, in the ears of each of the lucky 20.

"Is this place safe enough to wait?" I asked, looking up the path of the narrow gorge selected as a hideout. "What if the Russians walk a patrol into here?"

"Not likely," replied Suleiman. His reasoning was sound. The trail into this ravine was a dead end and seldom, if ever, visited.

"I don't see any other place on the map to wait while we take care of business," I said.

"No," replied Mustapha, who had just released the bait for our trap at the canyon ambush site. "There is not any real cover for this many animals between here and the canyon pass. So, they will have to wait here until we give the all-clear."

"Once the ambush is complete we'll need to move through the canyon before the Russians respond with more aircraft," I said.

Our Stinger animals and the 26 remaining over-packed Peshawar mules would remain there in the tall pines until the Russians were neutralized. The faux convoy proceeded to 1.5 clicks from the canyon and slowed to a crawl, waiting for Russian gunships to put eyes on them.

Earlier that morning I had sent the advance teams to prep the canyon. Mustapha, seated on a fallen tree trunk, had looked up from the notebook that I had given him. He said, "Mr. Andy seems to address this very situation. With a little, as you said, engineering in reverse, we should have a good result."

I had responded, "Mustapha, the correct term is reverse engineering, and I think the plan is a good one."

Twenty of the Mujahideen warriors sent by Massoud now manned the convoy being used as bait. Their AK-47s hung on slings under each of the mules they were leading.

"Suleiman," Mustapha called, "the Brigadier and ZERO took a look at the top areas overlooking the pass. They just radioed. Did you hear? Only the left side of this canyon's roof will provide required concealment for the Stinger teams."

"How about the areas at each end of the canyon where the main trail enters and exits?" I had asked. "These two points are described as being extremely narrow."

"Yes, they are," answered Suleiman, who had just returned from the far side of the canyon. "The exit is slightly smaller than the entrance but not too narrow that a helicopter could not land. We saw marks on the ground where the gunships had previously set down. We can do this one of two ways," Mustapha had said, formulating a plan. This was a good thing. This was what Phase 3 was all about.

Baiting the Trap
Turning the Tables
Friday 1 August 1986 1430 Hours

There were two helos that came out of the west and circled off to the north. They were cruising at about 700 meters. At their height and speed they had an excellent view of the entire canyon. On their present course, they would have no problem spotting the arriving faux supply convoy.

"ZERO, this is STING-1, come back," I called from an elevated position at the far side of the canyon. We were on a rock shelf 100 meters from the western exit of the pass. A direct line of sight into the center of the canyon gave us the opportunity to follow our convoy's progress. DELTA-1 (MSG Angerome) and STING-3 (Mustapha) were working a spotter scope nearby.

The first in the parade to run out on the field was a single horse and rider. Next came the 20 mules loaded up with a whole lot of nothing. Their speed could only be described as steady and slow. The packs strapped to their backs consisted mostly of branches and pine needles, and gave each mule the appearance of a fully laden beast of burden. A Mujahideen warrior accompanied each of the four-legged soldiers. A well-concealed AK was in easy reach, lashed to the belly harness of each animal.

"ZERO here. Go, STING-1," replied Pezlola, who was at ground level just inside the east entrance to the pass.

"Two more choppers, 8s probably, are trailing the 24s by a half a click. Do you have eyes on STING-2?"

"Roger. STING-2 is directly above me about halfway up the wall. Amelia, do you copy STING-1?"

"I'm here, STING-1. What can I do for you?" responded Amelia Jane, all business.

"Be safe. Things are going to get noisy. Break. TERRAPIN-1, you got your ears on?"

"Suleiman here, Mr. Rick. What do you need?" he asked, releasing the switch at his throat.

"Just remember not to get too close to the helo after it lands. And, please don't start the entertainment until the gunship settles in at the rear. 10-4?"

"Of course, it will be just according to plan, yes. We are ready here. I'll await your signal."

"Mr. ONE, STING-1, over," I called.

"STING-1, this is ONE. Go," replied CWO Lawson from his spot overlooking the pass.

"How's the weather up there? Come back."

"It was fine until the additional 24 showed up. We're all set here. Just say the word."

"Roger. Stand-by everyone."

"Hey, George," I called to DELTA-1 who had taken a knee a few meters away. He and Mustapha were looking at the trail map given to us by the Peshawar convoy commander. "You sure your guys are down there at the west exit? I haven't seen any movement at all."

DELTA-1 touched his neck and called, "DELTA, confirm position." The response was an immediate click.

"GB-1, this is STING-1. Last call. Come back."

"We're all set at this end," replied Captain Nelson on the ground outside the east entrance to the pass. He and the Brigadier, call sign FATHER-1, had selected much the same view as ours. The majority of the Green Berets were waiting to bring the real convoy into the canyon after the Russians were cleared from the premises.

"GB-2, this is STING-1. Are you copying our traffic? Over." There was no response.

"GB-2, this is ONE. Come back."

"STING-1, this is ONE. I have GB-2 on the line. What is your message?"

"Gary, just tell him we're starting here. Tell him to get ready to start towards us when we call. This is STING-1, standing by."

"STING-1, this is FATHER. Over," called the Brigadier. He and Pezlola watched the Mil Mi-8 slowly lower itself into the east end of the canyon.

"Go, FATHER," said DELTA-1, who beat me to the mic switch.

"You have a helo arriving low over your six. Entire convoy is now inside. TERRAPIN is just past the mid-point. Copy all that?"

"Roger. Ditto on a helo at your 12 o'clock," I said and re-keyed my mike switch. "OK, everybody, standby," I said and took a deep breath.

According to the eyewitness reports given to us by Massoud's people, the Russians had used multiple aircraft for each attack. One or more gunships would remain above, flying cover. Two of the less armored, troop-carrying helos would land, one at each end of the convoy. This would block any chance for escape for the members of the supply train.

The Mil Mi-24 was truly an evil piece of hardware. Although it was capable of transporting up to eight fully equipped solders it was seldom called upon to do so. A crew of three was its usual load, as well as an 80-millimeter (3.1 inch) S-8 rocket pod that ranged in capacity from seven to 20 depending on what the day required. The 23-millimeter (0.91 inch) gun pod was also popular with most of the murdering flight crews.

The Mil Mi-8 was a true troop transport that could do double duty as a weapons platform. It could carry up to 24 armed combatants but seldom carried more that 16 at a time. The characteristics of a balanced flight plan were fuel, weight, and distance, all in the appropriate amounts. This helo was typically armed with the same 23 mm gun platform as its wicked stepmother, the Mil Mi-24.

Suleiman was only halfway up the canyon trail when the first of the 24s flying at 50 meters passed overhead. The engine noise was deafening as the sound bounced from the walls and rained down on the pack animals. It had come out of the east and proceeded down the center of the route. But before reaching the western exit, the pilot pulled up sharply with full military power. Next came the second gunship, flying in from the west and making its way along the top of the cliff, zigzagging from the north to the south roof areas of the gorge. Satisfied with what it had scanned, it also went to full power. It disappeared towards the east. It did this even before completing the full length of the canyon. Because of the abrupt departure Pezlola thought our group had been detected.

The motor sounds returned and could be heard everywhere in the canyon. The two gunships took up overlook positions at each end of the canyon, hovering at approximately 200 meters. Apparently satisfied with the reconnaissance, the Russians were proceeding with the holdup. The low flying Mil Mi-8 at my end of the playing field swooped up and over the entrance to the canyon. Once inside, it immediately flared out and came down, almost touching the ground. Slowly the pilot walked the aircraft to the spot containing the existing wheel marks from a previous visit. Hovering at two meters, the pilot was staring at Suleiman who was standing still on the trail just beyond the halfway mark.

"Everyone, this is STING-1. Hold your positions. We're still waiting for the west 8 to settle in. Suleiman, wave a friendly greeting and move up another 25 meters. The rear of the convoy is too close to the east end landing zone. Over." And with that said, the second Mil Mi-8, with its rear ramp being lowered, touched down.

"STING-1, this is GB-1. Our guest has put down. What say you? Come back."

"GB-1, STING-2," interjected Amelia Jane. "Helo is right where he needs to be. Standby."

The Russian pilot at our end hovered at the same height as its twin, which was over two football fields away. Both ends of the convoy were now a safe distance from the expected touch down of both aircraft.

"OK, people, this is STING-1," I started. "By the numbers. As soon as both 8s touch, take out the 24s. TERRAPIN, please direct everyone to *hit the dirt* as soon as the 24s are attacked. Roger that?"

One click came back as the helo in the rear settled in a cloud of dust. Then, as if on cue, the other helo landed with a slight thump and bounce. Both kept their engines running at a fast idol.

"Shoot, Gary," I called into the mic. The Mujahideen Sting team leader on the roof of the canyon directed his four shooters and their spotters into action. They threw off their camo tarps and shouldered their already powered-up Stingers.

"Number one, target right. Number four, target left. Aim correct. Tone lock, tone lock ... elevate ... fire, fire, fire." Shooters two and three, were told to standby. The command sequence had been initiated by yelling and hand singles and, of course, the clapping of Gary's hands to provide the required cadence. Eye contact was not practical in this type of combat. Number four was the first to get a tone lock, elevated an additional 10 degrees, and pulled the trigger.

The aiming technique for Stingers was vastly different from that of its predecessor, Redeye. The result was not. The mach-2 plus speed offers little chance for a target to escape. In just 3.5 seconds after the trigger-pull the warhead entered the left side air intake of the hovering Mil Mi-24 gunship. The resulting explosion not only killed the engine but also vaporized the fuel cell on that side of the aircraft. The orange fireball dropped out of my line of sight before the final result could be realized. However, the thick black chimney of smoke quickly appeared in the skyline, marking the unseen result.

"GB-1, STING-1. You have a visual on the 24?"

"Affirmative, STING-1. No survivors. Over."

"STING-1, FATHER-1. We are clear this end to address the 8."

"Roger that. Stay frosty. Watch the back door for any unfriendlies trying to leave early from the party."

In almost the same instant, as shooter number four's Stinger completed its life's purpose, shooter number one accomplished tone lock and fired. Because of the longer distance, the missile took a full five seconds to reach its digital mark. Because the airship was facing almost straight on to the shooter, the missile's payload struck high up on the right side of the fuselage. The explosion caused the main power transfer shaft to seize. The huge blades froze in place as the engine roared to full power, accomplishing absolutely nothing.

The tail rotor, still functioning as designed, caused a series of 360-degree corkscrew-type maneuvers. The trip back to earth was interrupted as a large rock shelf reached out and flipped the airframe into a series of somersaults. This result ended violently on the unforgiving rock-laden surface below. The airship collapsed and the rotor blades on the left side shattered. Surprisingly, it did not explode, and came to rest just 30 meters outside the east entrance to the pass. There was no sign of life within the aircraft.

"Go on the 8s. Fire in the hole," I said and let go of the mic switch.

Ten seconds after halting the faux convoy, the Mil Mi-8 was still crouched facing Suleiman at the western exit. The Russian pilot saw the missile strike the gunship that was hovering over the east entrance. He recognized an ambush. He immediately went to full takeoff power and had gotten only five meters above the ground when the C-4 charge was detonated.

An hour before, Special Forces engineer Jim Thomas, call sign DELTA-5, had placed the charges below the ground where the Russian helos had landed on previous holdups. Suleiman found the site prep remarkable. He watched DELTA-5 dig the bowl-shaped depression in the canyon floor. It was shallow, only 1/3 of a meter deep with a one meter circumference. He then directed his Mujahideen helpers to line the bowl with multiple slabs of flat rock.

STF Thomas took one of the two satchel charges (M83s) from the canvas pouch strapped to his favorite mule. He walked the short distance to the prepared hole and knelt down. He removed the trigger transmitter from the side pocket of the military bag. He put this in his left front shirt pocket. Next, he dumped the bag containing the 16 C-4 block charges into the bottom of the hole. He fanned all but one evenly into a circle around the flat sides of the wok-shaped depression.

The soft, putty-like material of the C-4 was molded into the shape and size of a slightly curved salad dish. The wireless detonator was pushed into the center of the charged array. Thomas carefully laid the thin antenna wire up and facing towards where Suleiman would be sitting on his horse. Satisfied with his creation, he pushed the loose sand back into the hole. He would duplicate this same setup at the other end of the course.

Wireless detonation was all the rage that year. Suleiman was given one of the devices and Amelia Jane the other. The hand-held device had a trigger-type switch and a theoretical range of 50 meters. There was a cover that protected the trigger. This was flipped up and out-of-the-way when the time came to detonate.

"Mr. Suleiman," started Jim Thomas, "and Miss Amelia, these triggers are wireless. They each have a unique address," he had explained. "Unfortunately, they are new and not completely field tested. I tell you this because they have not always just detonated their assigned frequency. So, keep a respectful distance from the explosives at all times. Even though the charges are shaped, you will want to keep well back when you pull the trigger. Understood?" Both Suleiman and Amelia Jane nodded their understanding.

The mystical chimney of death rose up in a blink of an eye. The aircraft designated for Suleiman disintegrated into a pile of molten metal. The fact that the helo was not on the ground at the time of detonation actually enhanced the chemical reaction. The extreme temperature generated out of the ground immediately penetrated the metal surrounding both fuel cells. The result vaporized the contents, which in this case was aviation grade JP (jet propellant) fuel. It was a good thing that Suleiman had his back turned and was pushing his horse and everyone else back to the center of the pass when he squeezed the wireless remote. Even with this attempt for additional distance the heat from the fireball singed the hair on the back of his neck.

Although the triggers should have been pulled within moments of each other, Amelia Jane was faced with a slightly different situation.

"STING-2, this is Father-1. Your helo has opened his ramp. Prepare for the discharge of ground forces upon landing,"

The rear ramp on the helo with Amelia's name on it had dropped down even before the transport touched the ground. Several of the Spetsnaz storm troopers were about to disembark. The Russian pilot overreacted to the event he was witnessing at the other end of the canyon. He violently jerked the aircraft from the ground, causing several of his passenger soldiers to be thrown into the air from the open ramp. They would be dead before what remained of their bodies hit the ground.

Two of the three Claymores discharged; the third one failed. The two that did work sent 1400 steel balls into the rear cabin and ramp areas of the aircraft. The shaped charge installed under the helo's proposed landing erupted a fraction of a second later. The fiery funnel came out of the ground missing the bulk of the airframe. The pilot had jerked the helo violently to the right side of the landing zone. The wave of the energy whipped skyward, catching only the left landing strut. Even so, it was more than enough force to throw the aircraft end-over-end across the canyon like a child's toy.

Amelia Jane had depressed both triggers at the same time. The wireless device detonated a split second behind the wired detonator attached to the Claymores. In the end, this didn't matter at all. The mortally wounded copter lay on its side at the base of the rock wall on the far side of the canyon. There had been no fire as a result of the impact. Those who survived the Claymores died when the airframe was abruptly stopped by the stone surface of the canyon wall. Everyone on all four choppers was dead.

The scoreboard, if there were such a thing in combat, would have displayed: Mujahideen 4/Visitors 0. The Mujahideen's next performance would be the Russian air base at Bagram.

Our Perfect Hideout
Just .7 Km from the Ambush Site
Saturday 2 August 1986 1245 Hours

Traveling through the night, we had come directly from our perfect hideout. It was located just down the trail from the ambush site. The Russians never suspected that we would be so bold as to stay in the area. The hide and wait strategy had worked. The angry response from the Russian air base at Bagram crisscrossed the skies for well over three hours. If we had been caught out in the open it would have certainly upset the mules.

As we gathered inside the canyon pass minutes after the attack, the gamble to bring everyone up one hour before the ambush was complete had paid off. The Brigadier had ordered it, saying it was worth the risk. The dead Russian patrol would be expected to check in within a certain timeframe. Once their command realized communications were lost a response in force would be forthcoming.

Our departure time from the scene was important for us to maintain.

The true Stinger convoy had moved into the canyon just 15 minutes after the final explosion. We nestled up behind Suleiman's almost empty mule train. There was a slight delay in getting around the burning wreckage at the canyon's western exit. The heat and flames from the pile of molten metal were impressive. The puddle of what was once a Mil Mi-8 Russian troop transport finally cooled enough for us to make our way safely around it.

We trotted out of the canyon in double-time. At mile marker .7 Suleiman turned us sharply north onto a pre-scouted side trail. Mustapha came to the front and tucked each of us in under the tall, dense, pine trees. It was because of the expected Russian air force response times that he had chosen this particular site. It contained the best cover and it was the closest choice to get everyone out of Dodge.

From the time the attack had ended until the first Mil Mi-24 was heard overhead, only three quarters of an hour had passed. Two more Mil Mi-24s flew over us a few minutes later. We were snugged in under the tall pines only a couple hundred meters off the main trail. Five minutes later there were two more flyovers, but this time they were much further north. Fifteen more minutes went by. We heard the engine sounds, but no more sightings of any aircraft. They seemed to be concentrating on widening the search area outward from the ambush site. The engine noises finally faded and it became very quiet. We waited three more hours before moving on.

It was Suleiman's voice in my ear at the end of the first hour that broke the silence, "How about we kill the next helo that comes around?"

I started to key my mike but before I could, Mustapha's voice came on. "TERRAPIN-1, this is STING-3. MIGS circling at 1500 meters at the northwest. That is exactly what they are waiting for. No shooting and do not point any shiny objects towards the sky. Come back."

"Sorry, Commander. TERRAPIN out," replied a slightly subdued Suleiman.

"I had turned to DELTA-1 and said, "I think these guys are going to be just fine."

48

The After Party

Mujahideen Providence Basecamp
Near the District of Kohi-Safi
Parwan, Afghanistan
Saturday 2 August 1986 1540 Hours

W E ENTERED THE mine on the southern side of the mountain.
The mules were parked in a tree-lined gorge several clicks to our
rear. The mules would bring their loads into the mountain as
soon as it got dark.

The corridor was well lit with incandescent bulbs. The lamps installed
in this access tunnel seemed brighter than the ones we encountered on our
first visit. Massoud had not met us at the door, so to speak, as he had on our
first visit. We walked for what seemed to be a quarter of a kilometer. Finally,
we arrived in the same open chamber as before. The occupancy seemed to
have doubled since our last visit. There were also a number of women in the
crowd mix this time around.

Massoud had his back to us as we were directed from the tunnel. The
man standing in front of our host nodded his head and pointed in our direction. The Commander for all of the districts surrounding Bagram and the
mountains to the north turned and walked quickly towards us. The grin on
his face was one of joyous acceptance.

"Welcome back," offered Massoud, with outstretched arms. "Your success has changed the way we will fight the Russian murderers for all time."

"Massoud," replied the Brigadier, "your support has made this first step possible."

"Come with me into my quarters. We will sit and have some refreshments," Massoud said.

As we were ushered into a surprisingly well-furnished chamber, he continued the conversation. "The Stinger missile is the equalizer we have needed since the beginning. Now we will be able to push the Russian invaders from our country."

"It certainly is a start," I said. I looked around. "This is very nice. Who is your decorator?" The question was meant to be rhetorical and I continued with what was really on my mind. "What we need now, Commander, is your assistance with our next project."

"My wife has provided this sanctuary. You will have whatever you require — within reason, of course," replied the obliging commander, with a smile.

"Of course, Massoud," said the Brigadier. "You sent me 30 of your fighters to be students last year. In exchange, we supplied you with a large cache of the Chinese MBRL launchers and rockets. We would like you to assist us in deploying a number of these rockets in our next attack. That is, if they are still available?"

"I was told you have used the rockets against Bagram on several occasions," said Mustapha, who had not spoken to anyone since we arrived. He spoke softly, but there was no mistaking that he was demanding an explanation regarding what he had been told. Regardless of the answer, Mustapha would require the Commander's complete cooperation. This next attack had too many moving pieces for us to do all alone.

Massoud and Mustapha locked eyes for a full ten seconds. Finally Massoud answered, "Yes, but the result was not a good one. A number of our people were killed."

"What went wrong?" I asked. "Were the weapons defective?"

"Were the men, the men we trained, were they injured firing the weapon?" asked the Brigadier.

"Yes and no," answered Massoud. "The Russian counterattack killed some of our shooters. But one was killed when the rocket was ignited during the launch."

"Isn't that controlled by a hand-switch, a push button? The shooter is afforded a certain degree of safety well clear of the launch tubes," I said. We had captured several of these launchers in Vietnam in '69.

"We weren't using the wheeled launchers, nor the tubes," said a man who had entered the room from the other side of a curtain behind Massoud's desk. "The wheeled base units were too heavy to manage for any great distance. However, it was discovered that individual rockets could be fired by laying them on the ground, propping them up slightly, and lighting a make-shift fuse."

"Gentleman, may I present Commander Nabi?" said Massoud, making the introduction. "I sent for him when I heard you were on your way back here."

The former Captain Amar Nabi was part of the Russian-trained Afghan puppet air force. He had been taught to fly in the Soviet Union. He had brought his SU-22 into an airstrip near Peshawar and surrendered it to the CIA. When his copilot objected, he had taken out his pistol and shot him in the head. He now was the leader of a 400-man force located near Kohi-Safi and the plateau caves that overlooked the Bagram air base.

"You found this method of firing the rockets effective?" asked the Brigadier icily.

Not intimidated by the Brigadier General, Nabi answered, "As a matter of fact, I did not. They are all but worthless and a waste of time when fired this way."

"Then why do it?" I asked.

He eyed me carefully. "And, you are?"

"My name is Fontain. We're here to attack the air base at Bagram, and we'll require your assistance."

"You have brought us the Stinger weapons, yes?" Nabi was good at controlling the conversation.

"Yes and no," I said. "If you can assist us in getting close to the approaches of the air base runways, then we can have that discussion. Do we understand each other?" I asked.

"Okey dokey, Sir," replied Nabi, who sounded very much like our own Mr. Suleiman.

"How do you know about Stinger?"

"I used to be a pilot in my previous life. Let me say that my instructor was much impressed with this technology."

"Then you understand my concern," I replied. "The Stinger technology is too important to be exposed to capture or to be misused in its deployment."

"Good philosophy. I think you and I are going to get along very well. How do you say, no bull-ship between us?"

"That remains to be seen," I said, chuckling at this man's self-assurance. "And the word is 'shit', not 'ship'. Please answer Brigadier Azraq's question. Why did you waste the Chinese rockets?"

"I was ordered to use them. How I used them was left up to me."

"Certainly, the men trained on this weapon told you that this was not a wise thing to do," said the Brigadier.

"Out of the 30 men you trained, Sir," Nabi addressed the Brigadier, "only five were still among the living. And, none were in the district at the time the attack was ordered."

"Who ordered you? Massoud?" asked the Brigadier in a low voice that was almost a whisper. He was looking directly at the Area Commander.

"No, he did not," Nabi replied firmly. "It was my predecessor. This event we are discussing was the main reason he was removed."

"So, Commander Nabi, what went wrong?" I asked.

"The shorter answer would be to tell you what went right. My orders were to cause a diversion on the western fence as darkness fell. It took a full two days just to get into position. We arrived in the darkness the day before. We remained covered up all the next day until it got dark."

"You still haven't explained why you did not use the launcher firing tubes."

"As you may or may not be aware, there has been a shortage of pack animals. If we had mules, we could have moved the rocket launchers in close. But we did not, so I ordered what I thought was the next best thing. This, as it turned out, was a near tragedy."

"You know," I said, "the range on the MBRL is well over eight clicks. Why not manhandle the tubes and shoot at a distance?"

"Clicks?" asked Nabi.

"Kilometers," I answered.

"Oh, I see. It is slang, yes? Why not shoot from a distance? Good question — except for the fact that I couldn't figure out how the damn things came apart much less how I was supposed to aim them. No, I decided to take the individual rockets and set them off close to the fence line."

"Did it work at all?" I asked. I was beginning to like this guy. He didn't back down; nor did he get defensive when confronted by management. He appeared to be able to adapt regardless of the situation.

"No. Not at all. We were lucky to escape with our lives. The main attack force failed to show up. We found out later that they had been ambushed the day before. In either case, four of the six rockets did make it into the compound. One hit the fence, bounced, and exploded, injuring the three men who fired it. One blew up immediately when the fuse was ignited. That man was killed instantly."

"Any idea what the four rounds hit? Any of them make it to the center of the compound?" I pushed for more details.

"No, there were not any secondary explosions heard. We sent several thousand rounds of automatic weapons fire into the base before we withdrew towards the west. All in all, a complete waste of blood and treasure."

No one said anything for a while. Then I asked, "Massoud, where are the MBRLs being stored now?"

"They are here," replied Commander Nabi. "And the men who were trained on them, only three remain, they are here also."

"Outstanding, Commander Nabi," I said, and winked my approval of his after-action report. "We have another plan and we'd like your assistance with it. This time the mules will do the heavy lifting."

"Wonderful, and please call me Amar. Will it involve great danger and heroic sacrifice?"

I laughed and said, "My name is Rick Fontain, and yes, Amar, it will be exciting for everyone. There's someone I'd like you to meet. His name is Suleiman."

"Oh, Vassar and I have been friends since childhood. Our parents were quite close. Is he here?"

"Yes. I should have seen the resemblance," I answered.

"Resemblance you say? What do you mean by this?"

"Cut from the same cloth, a professional approach to killing every Russian you encounter," I replied. "Am I close?"

Amar Nabi examined my expression before responding. "Perhaps the CIA does understand what is being done to my country. The Stinger will be the answer to our prayers."

"Of course, I can neither deny nor confirm what the CIA believes. However, I can guarantee you I do understand. The Brigadier will help us all focus our prayers on this next operation."

The Brigadier smiled dryly and offered a bit of levity, "This time there are more than enough mules for you to consult with before firing the rockets, Amar Nabi."

49
Fire on the Mountain

Mujahideen Area Headquarters
Abandoned Gemstone Mine
Panjshir Province of Afghanistan
Friday 15 August 1986 1955 Hours

FOUND THE AREA commander, Ahmad Shah Massoud, to be a most accommodating fellow. It probably had something to do with the rescue of the recent supply of beef jerky. The killing of a whole bunch of Russians in the process was just icing on the cake, so to speak. Why we had come to his mountain put a smile on his face.

The Russian air base near the town of Bagram was well protected he told us. We would have the help of the local combatants if we so desired. Massoud used a well-worn set of Michelin road maps to give us a very detailed briefing of the entire area.

Via an analysis he made from a very large stash of captured charts, maps and documents, FATHER-1 (Brigadier Azraq) ascertained that Bagram had initially been set up as an all-Soviet operation. The base was designed to be a northern oasis for controlling this part of Afghanistan. There were two, full, fighter regiments based there. The metal birds parked on the weathered tarmac were MIG-23s, Russia's most modern. According to Pezlola, who was fluent in Russian, one of the documents indicated that a large formation of the older MiG-21s and the Su-25s were scheduled to arrive in Bagram in the coming months. These aircraft were among the most efficient of Russia's fixed-wing killing machines. Of course, the topic of mass murder in 1986 was seldom discussed by the international community.

There was one full squadron of the iron monster known as the Mil Mi-24 stationed at Bagram. The only prerequisite to pilot the 24 was that you needed to possess homicidal tendencies or be a devout sociopath. Possession of both credentials was preferred and assured rapid advancement in rank. This aircraft and its crew were of particular interest to the Mujahideen Stinger class graduates of 1986.

We were told by a local villager, who worked in the kitchens at the Bagram base, that a large quantity of different looking helicopters was bunched near the warehouse storage facilities. She pointed out their location to us on a captured diagram of the airfield. I showed her the transparency silhouettes that were tucked in the flap at the rear of Andy's notebook. She fingered the aircraft marked as a Mil Mi-8.

Mujahideen observers positioned on the mountain east of the airfield had been monitoring the traffic in and out of Bagram for the past several weeks. The steady stream of AN-26 cargo aircraft was a recent development in the normal traffic patterns. The village woman told us that most of the much-needed food and medical supplies were being brought in by air. This, she had been told, was a direct result of the stepped-up ambush actions of the Mujahideen. There were only two roadways that connected Bagram from the south. Both required travel through the mountain passes. Only one of the roads was suitable for heavy truck and armor traffic.

We thanked the village woman for her help. She started towards the main tunnel but stopped suddenly. She turned to face us and cocked her head to one side and spoke to Mustapha.

"I do not know if this is important, but last week a group of Afghan pilots landed their planes." She walked to the map table and pointed to a spot on the same diagram used previously.

"They are parked here," she said. "I was told by a fellow worker that he had spoken to one of the pilots. He indicated that their entire air group had been transferred to Bagram. This Afghan pilot was not happy about not being allowed to commingle with the Russians. That is odd, yes?"

"Yes and no. The Russians have trust issues for all Afghans," I said after Mustapha translated what had been said. Nabi, standing to the side with his arms folded across his chest, gave me a big smile. He had been a pilot in the Afghan Airforce. He had flown his SU-22 to Peshawar and turned it over to the American CIA.

"The spotters on overwatch," I then commented, "saw these aircraft arrive and assumed that they were Russian."

"We were wondering why they were located so far from the main group," added Pezlola. The Afghan Air Force for the puppet government in Kabul consisted of a mix of 27 of the older Su-7 and Su-22 aircraft.

The village woman nodded her farewell for the second time and turned to leave.

"Thank you again for all of your help," I said, and Mustapha started to translate. The woman stopped and turned towards me.

"No, it is we who thank you for coming to help us get rid of this evil," she replied in English, turned on her heels, and this time made her exit into the main tunnel.

The Russian and the Afghan air forces had very little, if any, real combat experience. Flying around the Afghan countryside bombing and strafing its inhabitants did not a combat pilot make. The true meaning of combat was about to be experienced by both governments, big time. Operation Cyclone was poised to stab the invaders. A new page in Russian military history was about to be published.

Phase One of Three – A Canyon Ambush
Abandoned Gemstone Mine – Central Chamber
Sunday 24 August 1986 1545 Hours

Ahmad Shah Massoud stood in the center chamber of his abandoned gemstone mine. Gathered around him were all those who would participate in the coming ambush of a Russian convoy headed towards Bagram Air Base. The ambush would serve as an immediate prelude to the attack on the air base itself.

"'The time has come to provide the Russian murderers a taste of their own medicine," he said.

Massoud leaned on the top-nob of his well-worn walking stick. Leaders from the surrounding districts had been summoned. Some were sitting cross-legged, while others stood just behind them. Their presence here today was mandatory but none of these men would have missed this conference for all the tea in China. The word had spread about the new weapon. The Russians had been ambushed and they had been destroyed. Mustapha and I took turns explaining what we would require in the coming week.

Almost 40 minutes later, as the presentation was nearing its conclusion, I said, "After this week the Russians will give pause before they fly over your villages."

Mustapha, who was standing beside me, had repeated my words so that everyone present had a complete understanding of what would be required of them. What we were about to undertake — and its end result — had been embraced by all. What we did not realize was from that moment forward the Afghans had no intention of waiting for Russians to fly over their villages. From that day on, Russian pilots would risk their lives every time they took off. The Mujahideen would seek out and kill any aircraft wherever it might be. It was up to Mustapha to make sure this was done with proper planning and that every trigger-pull yielded the optimal result.

Massoud poked his walking stick deep into the sand diagram that had been created on the cavern floor.

"If a Russian convoy headed to Bagram comes this Wednesday, as it has for the last several weeks, you will stop it. If one does not come you will remain in place until you get the word to withdraw. This is important."

"Yes, it's a very important part of this operation," I added. "You will be joined by several of Mustapha's Stinger teams and the American Delta Special Operations men. The two roads used for travel from the south are over eight kilometers apart. However, this one," I said and dropped to one knee and stabbed my finger into the sand, "is the only suitable choice they have for large trucks and heavy armor." The Mujahideen commanders leaned in and were nodding their heads in agreement.

"So," I continued, "we need three Stinger teams on the ridge of the canyon: here, here, and here." I pointed to the preselected rooftop areas on both sides of the gorge.

This caused some muted conversation to occur. The conversation ended in agreement and they became silent to hear what came next. I then explained that each team would have sufficient Stinger missiles to deal with multiple aircraft.

"What of the tanks that sometimes accompany the supply vehicles?" asked a man standing near the front.

"Several teams, assisted by Special Forces experts embedded with your men, will be down on the canyon floor. Here," I pointed again to the diagram, "and here at the exit end of the pass. From what we have learned from the previous convoy behavior, the lead and trailing vehicles are always armored vehicles." This time the gathering grew silent.

"We will kill the lead vehicle first to stop the convoy, here," I said and marked the second sand diagram that had been constructed a few feet to the left of the Bagram drawing. Mustapha was very familiar with this highway. He recommended this location because it allowed the entire convoy to be fully committed inside the canyon when stopped. Because of the narrow width of the roadway at this point it would be impossible for any of the trailing members of the convoy to escape around the disabled lead tank. As soon as the line of vehicles stopped moving the rear vehicle would be disabled. This would trap every vehicle inside the canyon.

An older man, pushing forward from his position against the wall, asked with concern, "How to you intend to stop the armored vehicles?"

Mustapha answered this question but first repeated it for my benefit. "We will use a weapon called M72 LAW," which had no translation into the local language. "It is very small but very powerful. The rocket it shoots will penetrate small, but kill big. These weapons are specifically engineered to disable the largest of the Russian heavy armor." The man who asked the question nodded his head in acceptance and returned to his position against the wall.

"Also," I added, "we will have placed shaped charges under the roadway beforehand should the rockets fail to completely disable the armor."

"Sometimes their tanks ride inside the line of vehicles," noted an elder seated to the right side of the group. "How will you deal with those?"

"I was told of your usual methods to improvise explosive devices to deal with their armor." I paused. "However, there will be ample rockets to shoot the center of the vehicle lineup should it be necessary."

A leader at the back offered this comment: "Our devices, sometimes they disappoint. Sometimes they even kill us. These new weapons are very welcome."

"Our Special Forces engineer will design, and give instruction in the placement of, shaped charges under the roadway in key areas should the rockets fail to halt the heavy tanks." I added this point to the ambush scenario to emphasize the importance of backup planning. If any of these tracked vehicles were to reach Bagram during the main attack our Stinger teams, positioned close along the southern fence, would be put in harm's way.

"Also," added the Brigadier, who had not spoken since his introduction at the start, "we have brought with us anti-personnel mines, called Claymores. These devices will kill every living thing residing inside a canvas-covered truck. They will be placed along the entire length of the kill zone."

I nodded my concurrence and continued with the last of the ambush requirements. "There will be 60 elevated shooters hidden in the cliff walls. Once the vehicles are halted, the truck cabs — the drivers mainly — will be taken under small arms fire." I explained that if all additional passengers could be taken down by the sharpshooters the Claymores would not be necessary. I went on to say, "The use of the mines would destroy the cargo. If any of the trucks contain large numbers of troops, those vehicles should be singled out and destroyed with the mines. One squeeze of a Claymore's wired remote trigger will shred everything in its path."

"This Claymore, it only explodes to the front, you are saying?" asked the man sitting cross-legged in front of me.

"Yes, only to the front," I replied. He nodded his head and smiled.

"Are there any other comments or suggestions?" I asked. The main attack on the Bagram air base would start in 68 hours.

"You mentioned training on these new weapons in the coming months," remarked another man who had stood up as everyone was preparing to gather their things and leave.

"Yes, the Stinger course at the Ojhri Camp will be made available," answered the Brigadier. "Mustapha has been given the responsibility to coordinate this for you."

"Yes," replied Mustapha, holding up his arms for everyone to pause. "After this operation, I will take eight men from each of your districts to be trained on the use of our new weapon. Our goal is to have four Stinger teams in each district before the winter storms come."

This same man asked, "What about the training for the anti-tank weapons?"

I smiled after that was translated and told him, "The Mujahideen will have no problem with OJT, excuse me, I meant to say on-the-job-training." After only one demonstration our Mr. Suleiman had told me that there would be no need for formal training for the M72 LAW rockets.

There were no more questions. The ambush plan was now in play.

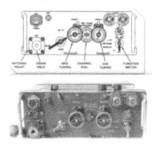

Setting the Stage
Assigning Responsibilities
Sunday 24 August 1986 1845 Hours

The details for the main attack on Bagram had been discussed for the last several hours. The main purpose and focus of our mission was providing the Mujahideen with the means to become proficient with the Stinger weapons system. To accomplish this, we were in the process of designing the best way to solicit a sufficient number of test subjects. The Bagram Air Base contained more than enough aircraft to meet our requirements. All we needed now was a plan to draw them out so that the Mujahideen could practice killing them. The plan needed to be designed to draw them out in groups of three and four — not the whole fucking air base emptying out all at once.

Commander Nabi had committed all of his 400 warriors up on the plateau for the coming bout. The attack was scheduled to begin on Wednesday. In attendance that evening were 75 of the Commander's senior group leaders. Their assigned duties were many and would require hours, and in some cases days, to implement.

I called out a reminder as the men got up to leave. "Please see Suleiman on your way out." I pointed to an opening in the far wall where Mr. Turtle was beckoning those group leaders with an assigned task utilizing a digital COMMs system called PRC-77.

"If you are involved on the plateau with the rocket launchers, or if you have an assignment on the highway canyon, the radios and the spare batteries are ready for your overview. Please spend a few minutes to learn the basic operational features. Communicating this week is vital to our success."

This was repeated in Pashto by Mustapha. Again, the Mujahideen leaders turned to Suleiman, who was dispensing the backpack radios. One of the elders passing near me turned to examine my face. As if on cue he touched my shoulder, smiled his acceptance, and continued into the main tunnel.

When the room was almost empty I asked the Brigadier, "How do you think it went?" The Brigadier, who had walked over and was erasing the sand diagram with his right boot, nodded his head but said nothing.

A messenger arrived through the east tunnel. He immediately walked to Massoud. A short whisper to Massoud's cocked head and they walked off towards the area commander's office quarters. Brigadier Azraq and I stood, not saying anything. We were alone at the center of the chamber.

Finally, after almost a full minute, and Azraq's satisfaction with his footwork, he said, "The assurance in your voice came through loud and clear today, Mr. Rick. These men will all take with them a feeling of confidence. A feeling that most of them thought would not be possible in their lifetime."

"That good, huh?" I replied. "Well, we'll see, won't we? Nabi asked to see us as soon as we are free here. He has some issues with the way the Chinese rockets have been stored."

"Yes, he told me last night," replied the ISI General. "Apparently, the dampness has found its way into their makeshift armory. This has caused his concern."

"The rounds we trained with last week all worked as advertised," I commented.

"Let's go and see what his disquiets are." The Brigadier led me to an opening in the north wall. This was the tunnel that ran to a whole other part of the mountain. This tunnel opening was oval — much different than the others. The other portals were all squared, and framed with large pieces of timber. Tilting at a downward angle, we walked with flashlights for 45 meters to a tee junction. We turned to the left and walked up a slight incline this time into a large room with a dome ceiling.

"Good. You are here," called Commander Amar Nabi from the far side of the hall. "I take it my warriors were all enthusiastic with our plan?"

"Our plan?" I asked in a rhetorical sense. "I thought when I didn't see you at the meeting that you might have changed your mind."

"No, not in the slightest. I had seen signs of water damage to the rocket crates when we were here last week. I had my men restack each of the pallets that were nearest to the rear wall. If you remember, we pulled all of the practice rounds from the top of this section," he said and pointed to the center stack of wooden ammo cases with Chinese lettering on the end of each box. An old oil lamp was sitting in the top of an open crate. One of the crates on the top of the recently restacked pallet was open. Its sides were discolored with what appeared to have been a dampness injury.

"I see you've found a way to dry up the moisture problem," I said, pointing to the device that was providing most of the light in the room. "So, if the top of this mountain blows off then we can safely say that there hasn't been any long-term damage to the rockets from the dampness. Yes?"

"Oh, I see you are very security conscious. Not to worry. I have found that you can actually throw these into an open fire and they will not explode," replied the Commander.

"Interesting. What does your doctor say about this fixation on death? That must have been one hell of a party when you tested that piece of logic."

"Perhaps we can get back to why you asked us to come over and look at what you suspected may be a problem with the rockets." The Brigadier gently got us back on track.

"As you can see, I had my men restack the crates, putting the bottom containers on the top. I then opened one case from each pile. No water contamination on the inside. The rockets look OK — no sign of water damage was found in any of these boxes. Sorry, for the false alarm."

"Hey, no apology necessary. Now was the time to find out the shape the rockets are in," I said.

"Not when we are lined up for the attack," agreed the Brigadier.

"Did you get the four launchers disassembled for transport?" I asked Nabi.

"Of course, and the harnesses for the mules are being made ready as we speak. We will leave tonight for the caves above Bagram's high plateau."

"Check in with Captain Nelson before you leave," I said. "He may have some requests for transport space."

"Greg and his special guys are already making plans to travel with us to the caves tonight. We are taking the Stingers with us," replied Nabi.

"Good. And if I were you, I'd relocate that lamp. There's no sense in tempting the fire gods."

Preparing the Bull's Eye
A Game of Lethal Lawn Darts
Monday 25 August 1986 2040 Hours

The mules were loaded late that evening. The 26 mules, four Green Berets, and 53 Mujahideen warriors left the gemstone mine through the north shaft. They walked out into the coming darkness onto a winding and well-worn path. The four disassembled MBRL artillery pieces and 160 rockets were being transported for a distance of 7.3 kilometers.

The caves located above the northern plateau would be their first stop. They would stay there until darkness returned the following day. Then they would walk down into the foothills and out onto the huge plateau.

I was told that if one looked out of the front of the larger of these caves one would have an excellent view of the Bagram Township. The military complex and airfield were located 1.6 kilometers further to the southwest. A game of lethal lawn darts was being planned by the Mujahideen management.

The calibration notes taken by Suleiman at our MBRL range orientation class the previous week indicated a very fast setup time. Each rocket's elevation wheels had quarter kilometer markings scratched onto its elevation control knob. The distance to target from the plateau was 4.8 kilometers.

A large, almost white, jagged rock protruded out of the rock wall directly above the cave entrance where they had spent the night. The entrance looked down the valley across the Bagram base, to the mountains 9.5 kilometers to the southwest. If lining up the white rock with the point halfway between the two mountain peaks, one could draw a straight line directly through the main runway at Bagram. Not the most scientific approach of setting up a mortar attack — but more than sufficient for this government's planning requirements.

There were 11 hash marks etched perpendicularly around the center plate supporting each rocket tube. The zero-mark indicated that the artillery platform array was pointed straight forward. Each tick to the right or left corrected the rocket impact in the respective direction by 10 meters.

Suleiman had come up with the slang nickname *lawn dart* for the MBRL rockets. He explained that in his freshman year of college this popular pastime made him aware of his gift: projectile targeting was a game he was born to play. Putting a rocket on target was an important skillset in the neighborhood where he had grown up. None of his former classmates at the University of Maryland would ever have understood the importance of his talent.

Commander Nabi had over 400 men under his command. His area of responsibility for this operation would take place on two important fronts. The first mission responsibility for the majority of these men was the transport and positioning of the rockets, and the protection of the launching sites. The 144 Chinese 107mm skyrockets would target the main runway at the Bagram airfield.

The second responsibility, being handled by 130 of Nabi's shooters, was the protection of the forces on the mountain as well as those down on the ground near the southern security fences. The four MBRL units would be manually programmed by remote observation. The 107mm projectiles would be walked, one at a time, onto and across the center of the Bagram military complex. This would require perfect execution from well-positioned forward observation teams.

A high mesa, touching the mountain to its rear, was chosen as the MBRL launch platform. The front of the plateau dropped off sharply at first, but then cascaded gradually down to the flat valley floor. The military complex was located very near the valley center.

Commander Nabi had placed 50 shooters a quarter click out in front of the MBRL positions. Staff Sergeants Dennis Bormann, GB-3; Paul Murray, GB-4; and Brian McDermott, GB-5 were embedded with the shooters down in front, a half a click from the leading edge of the plateau. Captain Nelson, GB-1, would run the main PRC-77 COMM center located near the picket line set up to amuse the mules during their short break in the activities. GB-2, MSG Mike Davis, had wormed his way in with Suleiman's group. They were located down on the valley floor just outside the Bagram Air Base's southeast security fence.

Commander Nabi had dedicated a hundred of his people to positions to the front of the MBRL batteries. Twenty-five shooters were protecting each flank, while 50 men were fanned out across the rear of the plateau. Fourteen men from a local village were keeping watch over the 34 mules that would move the MBRLs back up and into the mountain, situation permitting.

The eyes for the overall attack would be two strategically placed observation posts (OPs). Each post would be installed on the mountain that was 1.6 kilometers east of the Bagram Air Base and 5.3 kilometers from the centermost MBRL battery, high up on the plateau. The higher of the two posts would be the eyes for the MBRL rocket attack.

Commander Nabi graciously assigned 60 of his warriors to carry the required weapons and equipment to each of these sites on the west side of the mountain. Once the posts were up and running, the Mujahideen shooters would provide the perimeter protection down in front of the lower post. A splinter group, containing an unmanaged Stinger Team, would take a position on the mountain between the two posts.

The entire Russian air base complex could be observed from either platform. Each position would serve a dual function. The upper OP installation, located at an elevation that was just short of 1500 meters, would direct the MBRL batteries.

A secondary responsibility of the higher OP, should it become necessary, would be the overwatch of the Stinger teams. Five Stinger teams were installed on the valley floor near the south end of Bagram's main runway. There was a control point 1.3 kilometers to their rear. This command point had Stinger capability and was manned by FATHER-1 (Brigadier Azraq) and STING-3 (Mustapha Taisei).

The lower OP, located at an elevation of 1175 meters, had the primary overwatch responsibility for all air traffic leaving or approaching the Russian air base, which was ringed in its entirety by inner and outer security fences. This OP was occupied by me (STING-1), Amelia Jane (STING-2), and Brian McDermott (GB-5). McDermott would work the four assigned frequencies of the PRC-77s stacked at the rear of the post, designated OP#2. The secondary responsibility for the lower post was to provide MBRL support, should the upper position be compromised. Redundancy and more redundancy was always a good thing when attacking an enemy of superior strength.

50
Inside the Cyclone

Posting the Observation
Overlooking Bagram Air Base – 7 Hours to Zero
Near the Town of Bagram, Afghanistan
Wednesday 27 August 1986 0459 Hours

THE SUN WAS just now bringing us its light. The zero hour would be at high noon. This meant there would be a seven hour wait for the forward teams under their slightly modified camo-tarps. The overwatch from the upper OP reported the situation layout at the center of the Russian compound unchanged. Row after row of planes were parked close together in groups. Each cluster was being presented as a large target of opportunity.

The airplane parking lot at Bagram bore a striking resemblance to the 1941 U.S. Army Command, Pearl Harbor. At Pearl Harbor there had been a mandate for all aircraft to be reconfigured into tight centralized clusters. On the morning of December 7, it became apparent that this had not been a good idea. Now the Mujahideen, just as had the Japanese, gazed in disbelief at the flawed layout of the planes. Now, all we needed to do was reach out and touch them gently with the rockets.

Massoud had ordered the surveillance on the mountain the previous month. His men's abilities were limited to what their captured, low-powered Russian binoculars could see. Their duties mainly consisted of counting the incoming and outgoing aircraft.

Each of the observation posts would be equipped with state-of-the-art optical gear; specifically, M151spotter scopes — light and powerful, as well as weather resistant and fog-proof. Delta had brought several of these with them. These particular units would provide an excellent view of the Bagram base. The M151s had the longest reach of anything on the market.

Bagram could be watched up close with these tools. It was what we saw through the lens of the M151 that caused us to question the sanity of the Russian command. Tightly clustered aircraft were displayed at the center. What in the world were they thinking?

Sure, a ground force commando attack was much more probable than a coordinated airstrike. Even a Mujahideen well-orchestrated mortar attack would not warrant the spreading of aircraft over the 5.4 jeribs (roughly 12 acres) of the Bagram base. Or would it? In any event, we were shocked by what we saw.

"STING-1, this is TERRAPIN," called Suleiman at less than half his usual volume.

"Good morning, Mr. Turtle," I replied. "You're up early. This is STING-1. Come back."

"Funny man, STING-1," replied Suleiman. "I'm flashing your position. Can you see me? TERRAPIN, over." Suleiman had a small mirror I had given him after supper the night before. I told him it would be an attention getter if something happened to his radio.

"STING-2, this is STING-1, avert your eyes," I said and released the throat switch of the RAP-4.

"The Turtle man is flashing us," I called over to Amelia Jane, then added, "TERRAPIN, STING-1. That's affirmative, Mr. Turtle. Looks like you've snugged in very well with your surroundings. This is STING-1. Come back."

"Very funny, STING-1. I do not know how STING-2 puts up with it. STING-2, if you are listening, mark the following positions on your chart. Let me know when you're ready. TERRAPIN holding."

"TERRAPIN, this is STING-2. You have to consider the fact that he is insane. Wait one. OK, ready to receive. This is STING-2. Go."

"Straight line to my 10 o'clock. This is our center point at 35 meters, 10-4. STING-2, are you with me so far? Come back."

"Roger, TERRAPIN, 35 to your 10. Come back."

"Excellent, STING-2. Draw a concave arc through that center point from my seven o'clock to my one o'clock. Come back."

"Affirmative, TERRAPIN."

"Two shooters located each side of center point. Stations are numbered 1 through 4. Locations are as follows: on the bend, 1 at 8, 2 at 9, 3 at 11, and 4 at 12. Copy that. This is TERRAPIN, standing by."

"This is STING-1, Mr. Turtle. STING-2 is eyeballing your clock. I say again, your clock. Wait one."

The plastic covered map spread across the large boulder now contained the necessary grease pencil markings identified from Amelia's compass. She carefully checked the position references with our M151. When satisfied, Amelia held her right thumb up, pointing towards the sky.

I reached to my throat and called, "I thought the University of Maryland would insist on the use of the Pythagorean Theorem for all wartime attack logistics. This is STING-1. Come back."

"STING-1, GB-2," called MSG Mike Davis, who was partnered with Suleiman. "How about eyeballing this right triangle, STING-1? GB, over."

Amelia Jane looked up from the spotter scope, laughed and said, "Mike is holding up his middle finger towards our position."

"No shit," I replied. I keyed my mic. "GB-2, STING-1 here. Displaying your IQ is not recommended while serving in combat. You could panic the men under your protection. Suggest you use both hands to complete the required right triangle. This is STING-1 standing up for all of those who support the use of higher mathematics for a better war. Over."

"Knock it off you two. This is ZERO," called Jim Pezlola, laughing. "Scanned STING nest positions. Everything is well hidden. You are good to go, GB-2. This is ZERO, standing by."

"Ditto, this is STING-2. You are well hidden. Good job. STING-2, out."

"GB-2, this is STING-1. Let the games begin. Stay invisible, Green Beret. STING-1, out."

"GB-2, this is ONE," called Mr. Lawson from the upper OP. "ZERO took another scan, says all your guys are ghosts. Good hunting today. This is ONE. Out."

"Roger that," replied Mike Davis. "Thanks guys. Keep us up-to-date. If you see any unfriendlies in our part of the yard, pick up the phone. This is GB-2. Out."

One Year Earlier
China Pakistan Railway
October 1985 Pakistan

The China Pakistan Railway had been constructed all the way from Kashgar, mainland China, to the port city of Gwadar, Pakistan. It was in October 1985 that the rear gates of the Ojhri Camp were cranked opened to receive the first of the Chinese MBRLs. A spur from the main rail line had been constructed in 1984 to provide direct access into the ISI's warehouse complex.

Thirty Mujahideen were solicited for MBRL training that year. The instruction was held at the Ojhri Training Complex in Pakistan. It was partially hands-on. I say "partially" because Suleiman had told me that the Mujahideen shooters sometimes opted to strike the firing button with the bare heal of their right foot. This, of course, allowed both fingers of the shooter to be placed into their ears. The MBRL was a very loud son-of-a-bitch.

The Ojhri Camp's MBRL Rocket Munitions School also provided basic proficiency training in assembling and disassembling the artillery's carriage and its very heavy platform. As for the preparation and storage of the rockets, that fell mainly on deaf ears. (No pun intended.) However, in the mind of the Mujahideen warrior, anything that could blow up and kill Russians was to be valued and protected.

The breakdown for transport was limited to a tear-down into three main components: the wheeled-axle assembly, the solid metal carriage platform, and the 12-barrel launch tube ensemble. Each component had a different weight, but they added up to significant poundage. This important issue was not addressed in the procurement process. In mountainous terrain three men and seven mules were required to deploy just one MBRL. All in all, this weapon system could only be used for short distance excursions or, God forbid, one way missions.

In 1984 the 107mm Chinese MBRLs had been acquired under a secret purchase agreement. The Pakistani ISI and the American CIA had arranged to receive 24 of the artillery pieces. Included in the sale were 3000 of the 107-mm rocket-type shells. The wheelbase boasted a super rugged frame that would support 12 launch tubes.

Individually, each cylinder was capable of delivering pure terror up to a range of 8.5 kilometers. The only drawback was the conservative design, which limited launches to one skyrocket at a time. This would actually turn out to be a blessing. In the early months of 1986, six of these units and 900 of the rocket shells were transported into Afghanistan. The Mujahideen Area Command directed that the weapons be stocked-piled within its gemstone mine headquarters.

The Kickoff – Toll Booth Management
Canyon Pass 7Km's South of Bagram
Wednesday 27 August 1986 1159 Hours

The incoming Russian convoy increased their speed as they approached the canyons. STING-2 (Amelia Jane) and I were in the lower observation post on the mountain when the call came in. The caller, DELTA-1, notified us that he had been alerted by STF Chas Mackenzie, DELTA-7, that one of Nabi's shooters reported that a large motorcade had entered the outer access road leading into the canyons. This particular stretch of highway twisted and turned through three contiguous sections of the narrow-walled passage. This canyon roadway was the most improved and therefore the preferred route for the heavy Russian trucks and armor.

The ambush would be held in the last section of these huge stone gullies. The location was chosen because it was configured with the narrowest choke points. Its only shortcoming was that this section of canyon was the shortest in length. The announced ETA was two minutes. Earlier that morning, at 1115 hours, I had notified the Delta group at the canyon site that two Mil Mi-24s had left the Bagram Air Base. Minutes later two Mig-23s also took off. All four of these aircraft headed south towards the direction of the incoming convoy. An obvious protective umbrella was being put up to shield the incoming Russian supply train.

Master Sergeant George Angerome, call sign DELTA-1, located in the center of the canyon, would coordinate today's ambush. All of his Delta guys were deployed across the ambush site. Their responsibility this day would be to assist in the complete destruction of the incoming armor and the capture of as many of the transport vehicles as time and circumstance permitted.

Using the PRC-77 COMM unit set up at the rear of the OP I called, "DELTA-1, this is STING-1. DELTA-1, STING-1, come back." No joy. Just for the hell of it I touched the mic switch on my RAP-4.

"STING-1, go," replied SFC George Angerome.

"DELTA-1, our private line sounds 5 by 5. No new fast birdies have departed here. What is your SITREP? Come back." I was asking him for a situation report, a "SITREP".

"STING-1, MiGs arrived earlier, still circling northeast at 1500. Helos have cruised the roof once from the north, moving slow across both roof areas at 300 meters. They came back heading south towards the incoming convoy at 800 meters. Moving fast with no attention to detail. This is DELTA-1. Come back."

"Roger, DELTA-1. Understand ETA of supply train is imminent. This is STING-1."

"STING-1, engine noises arriving now. Gun-tube of the first land shark just pushed through the entrance. Hold one, STING-1. DELTA-4, your 12 o'clock chunk of iron has just arrived. DELTA-8, get ready to slam the back door." Two sets of predetermined double clicks were heard.

The first static hiss came to everyone's earpiece. "Break, break, this is DELTA-1. DELTA- 2 and 3, keep watch for troop carriers." DELTA 2 and 3 were down on the ground on the canyon floor.

"DELTA-1, this is DELTA-7. Two of the 24s have followed the trucks into the canyon. One just passed over my six up here. One is coasting over the convoy. He's about even with us up on the roofline. This is DELTA-7 firing 2, and we be gone. Out."

"Roger that, DELTA-7. Break 1, this is DELTA-4. Hold one for the boom. My guy here is waiting for his shoulder tap. Counting down." It was just a half a breath later that the swoosh of the LAWs rocket was followed by the impact explosion at the ass end of the Russian tank.

Engine noises from the trucks and both helos were now bouncing off the walls. DELTA-8, located at the south end of the canyon floor, watched as the convoy abruptly came to a halt.

"DELTA-1, this is 8. We may have a problem back here. Not all of the convoy is inside the kill zone. Come back."

The lead vehicle in the convoy, a 12-year-old T-72B3M Main battle tank, had passed DELTA-4's position at the canyon's exit. The overwatch had reported that 26 Ural-4320 heavy truck transports were following this tank. The trailing vehicle of the convoy was reported to be a second battle tank. The model number was not known by DELTA-7's Mujahideen spotter; however, he did report that the turret's gun tube was pointed towards the rear.

"DELTA-1, this is STING-1. When the lead armor is killed, use the most distant Sting team to shoot both helos. This should draw at least one of the MiGs down to see what they can see. You with me so far, George?"

"Yes, STING-1, I follow. Your advice sounds very exciting. Especially for the DELTA-7 fire-team. This is DELTA-1. Come back."

"Hey, trust me on this, the Sting team with the longest shot has the best chance for a positive result. Stinger needs a big gulp of freedom to get up to speed. Stinger shooters should pack it up before they shoot, then get out of Dodge ASAP. The other teams can deal with a miss and the MiG's possible curiosity. Copy that? Come back."

"10-4, STING-1. Break. DELTA-7, this is DELTA-1." DELTA-7 was on the west canyon roof just above DELTA-1, to the far left.

"DELTA-7, you hear all that? Come back." All of the Delta guys who were down on the canyon floor were receiving only one side of this conversation that was generated by me and my friends, who were eight kilometers away on the mountain to the north.

The planning for today's ambush called for all COMMs to be run through the PRC-77s. DELTA-1 and DELTA-7 were the only ones in possession of the PRC-77s. It was a surprise that the RAP-4s were working as well as they were. Everybody on the roof was good to go.

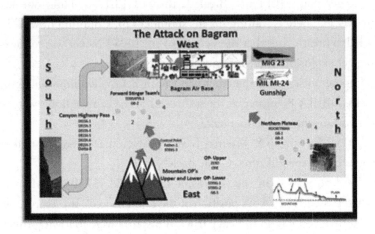

"This is DELTA-7. Second arrow poised and ready. DELTA's 5 and 6 watch for our result. Good luck all. DELTA-7, ready to boogie."

"Pick up the phone if things get too exciting over there. George, let us know if any of the aircraft leave the party early. This is STING-1, standing by."

"10-4, STING-1. See you after the revelry. Break, break."

"This is DELTA-4. Front door is locked. DELTA-8, you are clear to block the rear entrance."

"This is DELTA-1. Kill the drivers. Execute, execute, execute."

The muted thud of the M72 LAW rocket had immediately halted the T-72 armor halfway through the canyon's exit. DELTA-1 was tucked in three quarters of the way up on the west cliff wall. He was well hidden at the halfway point with a good view of the entire canyon floor. The crevasse behind him would allow both shelter and easy access to the canyon roof. From there, if necessary, he could use the trails leading down the back side of the mountain as a means of escape.

"DELTA-8, this is DELTA-1. Brian, waiting on your solution. Come back."

"DELTA-1, this is DELTA-4. Lead vehicle is dead. I repeat, lead is dead. Do you copy that DELTA-1? Come back."

"Roger that DELTA-4, DELTA-8, valet parking is now in play. DELTA-4 is blocking the exit. DELTAs 2 and 3 … you got troops pouring out of positions 7 and 9. I say again, truck transports in positions 7 and 9."

"DELTA-8, this is DELTA-1. The order is close the back door. Close it now. Come back."

"DELTA-1, this is DELTA-8. Not all of the Russian vehicles made it inside. Anyone got eyes on this?"

"This is DELTA-1. Can't see past the entrance from where I sit. Break. DELTA-7, are you eyeballing this situation? Come back."

"This is 7. No eyeball on the back door. The angle is too sharp."

"This is DELTA-5." Breaking into the conversation and with a better view was Sergeant E-5 Donny Mathews. He was located on the west canyon roof directly across from DELTA-1. "Three vehicles didn't make it all the way in: two trucks, and bringing up the rear is a T-72 or maybe it's a 62. Over."

DELTA-8, who was down on the canyon floor just 15 meters from the paved road surface, mouthed just one word under his breath. "Swell."

"DELTA-8, this is DELTA-1. Execute Plan-B. I say again … execute Plan-B. Come back."

"This is DELTA-8, executing plan-B. Stand by."

There were three Stinger teams located up on the roof for the operation. The first of the three teams was located almost directly across the pass from MSG Angerome. Sergeant Mathews, DELTA-5, was on the west canyon roof. DELTA-5 had the best view of what was caught in the back door.

Each Stinger team had a DELTA member assigned. Two of the teams above DELTA-1's position were at each end of the east canyon roof, respectively. On the spot, it was decided that DELTA-7 would draw the first blood. A really important feature of the east canyon's roof was that it was chock full of large fractures in the rock. Most of these spaces were large enough to conceal a three-man Stinger team. These foxholes manufactured by God had provided ample cover thus far. The teams would remain hidden until the Mil Mi-24s came down to play.

Valet Parking
Applying the LAW
Wednesday 27 August 1986 1145 Hours

The hardest part of operating the M72 Light Anti-Tank Weapon (known as the LAW rocket), according to Suleiman, was removing it from its waterproof pouch. The demo we provided the Mujahideen could have been limited to the simple procedure of extending the launch tube before firing. From that moment on, the inventory list for intact Russian armor in Afghanistan would need to be revised.

Just moments before, the M72 LAW rocket launched at the front door of the canyon pass, with a whoosh. The result was immediate. The rocket struck the tank in the rear, just below the eight-inch exhaust port. The explosion was a muffled thud, with most of the sound directed inside the crew compartment. The warhead had bored a small hole in the metal. It passed through the engine compartment missing the bulk of the engine. The hole created was perfectly round and measured six inches in diameter. Once safely inside, its purpose — destroying all human life — took only a fraction of a second. The rocket's red glare had stabbed one of the fuel cells. The white-hot, molten metal delivered into the crew space resulted in an explosion that pushed out in all directions. The gun turret was separated from the main body of the tank, lifting it skyward a full five meters.

"DELTA-1, this is 4. Front door is closed. Gunships directly overhead. Both hovering at 200 meters."

Slamming the Back Door
Reach Out and Touch Someone
Wednesday 27 August 1986 1148 Hours

"DELTA-8, this is DELTA-1, status on B. The clock is running. DELTA-8, do you copy?"

"DELTA-1, this is 8. The good news is that the convoy is stopped. The bad news is the armor is free roaming outside the back door." The number of vehicles was longer than our estimate. The really bad news was that there were gunships eyeballing the situation at the front door.

"This is 8 at the back. Heads up, DELTA-4. It's about to get exciting down your way."

"DELTA-5, are you going to shoot this son-of-bitch? Come back."

"DELTA-8, this is 5. There's a second 24 on the roof above you. You should move now if you're going. Break, break. DELTA-7, hold your shot until both 24s get farther north. 10-4."

"DELTA-1, this is 7 up on the roof. Second gunship just passed over our six. He's moving towards the north. DELTA-6, get very skinny and do it now. I have clear shots to both boogies, one high and one low. Firing now. Stand by."

The gunship, a Mil Mi-24, was hovering at 200 meters over the fourth truck from the front. The smoke from the destroyed tank began to fill that end of the canyon. All of the Mujahideen shooters were still well hidden. The gunship had no targets. The pilot must have panicked. He went to full military power, pulling the aircraft almost straight up and angling off to the west. He had just about escaped the area when the Stinger found its mark. His escape attempt was too little, too late. The missile hit the turbine exhaust port at a slight angle. Motor noises were heard, and some black smoke was seen, as it disappeared over the western roof. This ambush was now in full motion.

"DELTA-7, firing two. We be gone. This is DELTA-7, beating feet off the roof." Not waiting to see the result, DELTA-7 followed his two Stinger guys deeper into the fissure and out onto the reverse east slope of the canyon.

"All DELTA, this is DELTA-1. Convoy is parked. Release the Claymores on positions 7 and 9. This is DELTA-1. Execute now. I say again, execute."

AK-47 small arms fire erupted all along the canyon floor. Activity around the destroyed tank was probably what had panicked the first gunship driver.

"Roger, DELTA-1. This is DELTA-3. Good to go. Triggering now." Two loud booms were heard up and down the canyon. The Claymore mines were evenly spaced along the canyon roadway. The handle of each trigger switch was marked with the estimated position of a parked convoy vehicle. Triggers 7 and 9 were squeezed simultaneously — one in each hand. The remaining Russian soldiers who had survived the shotgun effect of the Claymores were quickly dispatched by the closest of the assigned shooters.

"DELTA-8, this is 5. You're clear to the entrance."

"Roger 5. This is 8, moving now. Standby." DELTA-8 tapped the shoulders of his two Mujahideen shooters. They jogged from their hideout, turning left at the edge of the paved roadway. The first of the two transports stopped in the canyon entrance had managed to get only its front wheels inside. Small arms fire to its windscreen from the AK-47s produced two dead Russian soldiers. They were slouched over in the cab, the motor still running.

DELTA-8 signaled one of his shooters to take up a position on the opposite side of the first vehicle. They moved to the last of the trucks in the lineup. This transport was not visible from inside the gorge. The passenger door sprang open and a combatant made a dash towards the rear. DELTA-8 double-tapped him in the back of the head with his silenced Beretta M9. The driver was killed by the Mujahideen warrior on that side of the truck. Half a clip from his AK-47 on full automatic hurled through the windscreen made quite a mess. The face of the driver disintegrated, leaving the body almost headless. Now unmanned, the tank revved its engine and swiveled its turret back towards the front. The convoy was now completely captive inside the canyon. All that remained was the destruction of the trailing tracked vehicle. Easier said than done!

"DELTA-5, this is DELTA-8. Can you still see the giant piece of metal at the back door? Is he still parked in the driveway? Come back."

"10-4, Tom. He's back about four meters now. Turret is moving around to the north. They are buttoned up tight. I think he's trying to size up the situation. Be safe. DELTA- 5, standing by."

"Roger that. If he changes position, get on the horn. DELTA-8 is on the move," replied DELTA-8, letting his hand fall from the mic switch.

DELTA-8 (SPEC-5 Tom Truscott) sent a shooter up each side of the second transport. Using hand signals and whistling, he directed them to kneel by the rear tires. The width and angle of this part of the entrance made it difficult for those in the tank to see into the canyon.

"DELTA-1, this is 8," called Truscott. "Two down, moving on the 72."

"Copy 8. This is DELTA-1 standing by."

DELTA-5, looking through his binoculars, saw DELTA-8 disappear under the front of the second Russian transport. His two accompanying shooters confirmed that the tank had not moved. Tom Truscott reached his hand out the left side just as he arrived at the rear wheels. Three more shooters had run up and crouched by the tires.

An M-183 charge assembly was passed to Tom's outstretched hand. He transferred the wireless trigger into his chest pocket. The third shooter had dragged a very long pole with him and was in the process of feeding it at an angle under the front bumper of the number-two truck. DELTA-8 draped one of the straps of the satchel charge on a hook fastened to the end of the pole. Crawling low and dragging the M-183 and its attached rod, he stopped about two meters from the daylight at the rear bumper of the truck. He touched his throat mic.

"DELTA-5, Donny, any change in the tank? Come back."

"Eight, no change. He just swung the turret back towards the south. Suggest you do whatever you are going to do quickly. DELTA-5, holding for the boom. Break, break."

"Roger, 8 is moving." DELTA-8 took a deep breath and let half of it out as he pushed the explosives out the back end of the truck. He could see the tank's turret moving back towards the north and the truck he was hiding under. He hoped its field of vision wasn't angled enough to see under the truck.

"DELTA-1, this is DELTA-5. Be advised incoming MiG from the south." DELTA-5 heard the jet before he had a visual. He raised his binoculars to the northwest. Sure enough, it was true. Curiosity would kill the cat.

"DELTA-5, this is 1. Gunship wounded over DELTA-6's location. Do you have eyes on result? Come back."

"Roger that, 1. This is 5. Tail rotor took a solid hit, some smoke on egress. Moved off to the northeast. Appeared to have controls badly damaged. No visual on final result. Explosion heard and smoke now rising visibly in that same direction. Comeback." That end of the roof got sprayed pretty well by the gunship before DELTA-7's Stinger hit. There had been no joy calling DELTA-6 after that.

"DELTA-1, this is 5," called SGT Mathews from his position located at the center of the west roof. "Helo over convoy jumped over me pointed to the northwest. Helo was hit, threw smoke, moved towards the northwest. No eyeball on 6 since last transmission. Watch the MiG coming down from the south for a look-see. Everybody button up. 5 clear."

DELTA-8's pole wasn't long enough. The package attached at the tip was about one meter short of reaching the underbelly of the targeted tank. With one giant lunge forward, DELTA-8 extended his body a full two meters out into the open. This propelled the M-183 a good two meters under the T-72. As if attached to a bungee cord, DELTA-8 shot backwards under cover and back-crawled to the midpoint under the truck. He rolled out from under the transport on the left side just past the rear wheels.

The Mujahideen shooter closest to him offered his hand to pull him up. DELTA-8 accepted the assistance. DELTA-6's static voice burst into the clear as he came back on the line. "DELTA-1, this is DELTA-6. Had to use the fire escape momentarily. We got two killed in action up here. Gunship did a number on us. MiG coming down this side. We will kill him on the pass. Tone lock confirmed. Firing 1…"

The MiG flew across the west canyon roof much too fast to see anything of importance; and after all, seeing is believing. However, in this case, hearing would trump seeing. The sound of acquisition tone lock has a horrifying effect on a pilot, especially when flying so close to Mother Earth. Full military power was applied by the MiG. Stinger didn't seem to notice, or care, one way or the other.

"This is DELTA-5. MiG blew up on its climb to the north. Second MiG still circling to the southwest. This is 5, standing by." Neither DELTA-1 nor 6 responded. The smell of vaporized JP was thick in the air.

"This is STING-1, calling DELTA-5. Understand two gunships and 1 MiG KO'd. Come back."

"This is DELTA-5. We had a visual on the MiG. Both gunships were hit but no confirmation on result of either. Come back."

"Roger that. Let us know if remaining MiG leaves the party. This is STING-1, standing by."

The Green Beret call sign GB-6, STF Brian McDermott – Demolition Engineer, had taken DELTA-8 aside over the previous weekend. Six M-183s with wireless remote detonators had been included in their combat inventory. They were listed as engineering tools. When the canyon ambush was being designed, GB-6 asked DELTA-8 if he would like a gizmo that could be used to kill a tank. So, they spent a half hour discussing how an M-183 was constructed and, more importantly, how it could be detonated without anyone being anywhere near it.

DELTA-8 popped to his feet at the end of his roll with an assist from the closest shooter. He motioned everyone to move quickly back into the canyon. As he picked up the pace he went to his breast pocket and grasped the device that would make the whole effort worthwhile. Raising his right hand high over his shoulder he flipped up the safety cap and placed his thumb on the red trigger button. His left hand went to his throat switch. "This is 8. Fire in the hole."

The resulting explosion pushed the tank upwards to its pivot point. It paused just for an instant before falling backwards onto its turret. The fires began immediately and the secondary explosions were a result of cooking off the ammo from the intense heat. The entire convoy was now dead.

"DELTA-1, this is DELTA-5. Tank is destroyed, no survivors. For the moment, the canyon is ours. This is DELTA-5. Did you copy that also STING-1?"

51

Observing the Rain

Over Watch from the Side of the Mountain
Lower Observation Post
4.3 Km's Due East of the Bagram Air Base
Wednesday 27 August 1986 1146 Hours

AMELIA JANE, CALL sign STING-2, and I were nestled on the mountain at the front of OP#2. From our fissure foxhole, we could look down into the Bagram Air Base. We checked the layout one final time before the rockets would start their march across the base. Just then, DELTA-5's voice came in to our earpieces.

"Say again, DELTA-5. This is STING-2. Transmission garbled on first part."

"STING 1 and 2, convoy killed 1159 hours. Two Mil Mi-24s took Stinger hits. One MiG vaporized. No visual on gunship results. Large smoke plume to the northwest suggests at least one has crashed. Convoy is being looted as we speak. Clean up underway. DELTA-1's COMMs is down. The MiG sprayed the entire east roof before trying to escape. This is DELTA-5, standing by."

"DELTA-5, STING-1 here. That's very good news, Donny. This is STING-1. Break, break. ZERO, did you copy DELTA-5's last transmission? Comeback."

"Well, that seemed to go by the book, Rick." Amelia Jane was relieved.

"STING-1, this is ZERO. Affirmative on DELTA-1. Lawn darts will start their zero in one mike. Standing by."

"STING-1, FATHER-1 here. DELTA-1's message not received, only your side of the call. Status comeback. This is FATHER-1. Over."

Before I could key my mic switch, Pezlola, call sign ZERO, answered the Brigadier.

"FATHER-1, this is ZERO. Convoy halted. Two 24s hit, one MiG destroyed. The canyon is ours. The DELTAs are standing by. Over."

"Roger, ZERO. Only getting one side of the conversation down here. This is FATHER-1. Out."

Wayward Bird – A Delayed Result
South East End of Bagram's Main Runway
Valley Floor 100 Meters from Outer Security Enclosure
Wednesday 27 August 1986 1158 Hours

"STING-1, this is TERRAPIN. We got a wounded gunship, looks like a 24, inbound coming from the south. Black smoke and engine sounds are irregular … suggests they are in trouble. Should we kill it? Comeback."

"TERRAPIN, STING…" Tracking with my binoculars I stopped mid-sentence as the Mil Mi-24 stopped flying and hit hard on the valley floor.

I raised my binoculars a second time and adjusted up to get a closer look. Amelia Jane looked back over her shoulder and said, "Rick, tell him to send someone out to check the status of the crew. The Russians will be all over Suleiman's position in short order. Tell him to make it quick."

"TERRAPIN, STING-1. Send two shooters to investigate from your closest nest. This is STING-1, standing by."

"STING-1, GB-2 here. I'm on it," replied MSG Mike Davis, who was embedded with TERRAPIN.

"Mike, take two guys with you over there to help that crew into the afterlife if necessary. Don't linger. You can expect company will be sent to your location. Make it quick."

"Roger that."

Amelia Jane was monitoring the activity through the spotter scope. I pushed on my mic key, "GB-2, STING-1. I say again, don't dilly-dally. Mike, I suspect his mother will be sending his siblings very soon. STING-1, standing by."

Two Mujahideen warriors emerged from the closest of the Stinger nests just as GB-2, Mike Davis, rushed past their position. Their AKs held at port arms (straight out in front of them), they jogged the short distance towards the downed aircraft. GB-2 and the two Mujahideen shooters arrived together at the crash site. The Mil Mi-24 was nose down and pitched to the right at a 15-degree angle. The left side cabin entrance was open and offered easy access. The co-pilot's windscreen at the nose was bright red with tissue and blood. As they got closer it was apparent that he had died on impact.

"DELTA-5, STING-2," called Mrs. Smythe. "I think we have found one of your missing gunships. Hold for a re-cap. This is STING-2. Wait one."

"STING-2, DELTA-5. DELTA-1's COMM link is still down. I have a visual on him. MiG strafed roof area from DELTA-7 to 6. 20mm cannon fire ruffed up DELTA-1's guys who were topside at the time. No one was home at 7. DELTA-6 is back in coverage. Two KIA with 6. This is DELTA-5 standing by."

"STING-1, this is GB-2," called Mike. "The Ivan co-pilot and the one crewman were DOA. Double-tapped the driver trying to exit the right side of the aircraft," continued Mike. "Thumbing thermos times two. Fire-in-the-hole. Posse beating feet back to nest. GB-2 back on break. Out."

I suspected that the Russian command was in complete disarray at this point. Our plan to divide and wreak havoc had been successful so far. We had stopped and killed the incoming convoy. The air support sent to overwatch the incoming supply train had been seriously compromised. Only one fighter jet remained. And, from what he knew had happened to his friends he was probably thinking long and hard about his next move while cruising northeast of the canyon highway.

Meanwhile, back at the ranch, a massive rocket attack was underway. For sure, the cat was now out of the bag. The rumors were true. The American CIA was now actively involved with these so called primitive insurgents.

"STING-1, DELTA-5," called Sergeant Donny Mathews from the canyon ambush site. He was still located on the east roof above and directly across from DELTA-1's former position. "Surviving MiG circling north-northwest. Appears he is a bit cautious about coming down to play. If he leaves, you'll be the first phone call. DELTA-5, standing by."

At 1750 meters, directly above us, were CIA case officers: the recently promoted LTC Jim Pezlola, call sign ZERO, and CWO Gary Lawson, call sign ONE. They were snugged in with an even better view of the Bagram airfield than Amelia and I had. Ten more of Nabi's men and a Mustapha Stinger team had hidden in the rocks sprinkled between the two observation posts. Perhaps hidden was a poor choice in describing this group — looking at them standing out in the open on the side of the mountain, well, you would think they were attending any normal stadium sporting event.

Payback's a Bitch
Canyon Pass – The Chasm was Quite
Wednesday 27 August 1986 1159 Hours

"STING-1, DELTA-5. Heads up. MiG just bolted north. Sky is now clear. No bad birds in sight. DELTA-1 signaled that he has five people down. DELTA-7 is back in position. His wounded and dead have been moved out and down the back side of the mountain. This is DELTA-5 on the east side above the chasm. Standing by."

Major Andria Gogoro was assigned that morning to provide air cover support for the 35th Guards Air Assault Brigade's scheduled incoming convoy. His unit, the 368th Assault Aviation Regiment, had been assigned to Bagram in November of 1985. There were two squadrons of SU-25s, and one full complement of Mikoyan-Gurevich 23s. These aircraft were more commonly known as the MiG-23 Flogger.

Created as an upgrade to the MiG-21, the MiG-23's description as a variable-geometry fighter aircraft had earned it a ferocious reputation. However, with the slaughter of unarmed villagers, including women and children, in its record, it was not a reputation that many wanted to claim.

The morning had started off like most. Gogoro and his wingman had been assigned to overwatch the incoming convoy.

Two gunships, Mil Mi-24s from the 35th Guards, were also assigned to provide close-in air to ground support for the convoy. This was a routine they had practiced and participated in many times over the past several months. However, there were now reports that the insurgents had attacked several aircraft in the mountains to the east. From the descriptions of the eyewitnesses, it almost sounded like a type of guided missile was now in play.

"Control, this is Wolfhound," called the Russian major. "Convoy has been halted. Insurgents well hidden in the last section of the highway pass. No movement visible. Both Hinds took fire from canyon overlook. Insurgents appear to be using some sort of a missile lock system. One Hind and Wolfhound-2 are down just west of canyon exit. Suggest SU-25 scramble. Wolfhound standing by."

"Wolfhound, Control. Scrambling SU-25s. Wait one. Wolfhound, we are now taking fire here. Main runway has taken several hits. Return this location and advise when you are over us. Control over."

"Control, Wolfhound. Understood. Returning base. Wolfhound out."

The Rockets' Red Glare – A Game of Lawn Darts
Up on the Northern Plateau
Wednesday 27 August 1986 1206 Hours

Commander Nabi and Brigadier, Azraq (call sign FATHER-1), had agreed that the higher OP could better control the walking of the MBRL rockets, nick-named *lawn darts*, through the strategic areas on the Bagram complex. As in all well laid plans, there was a hitch.

"STING-1, this is ONE, over," called the CIA's Gary Lawson.

"Go, ONE," I replied and released the touch switch on the RAP-4.

For internal communications, the short range RAP-4 digital COMMs were being used for talking amongst ourselves, both here on the mountain and down on the valley floor. Special Forces and Delta were also using them to communicate within their assigned locations. However, because of the height and line-of-sight capability of the mountain observation posts, the RAP-4s were working better than expected. We were told these devices only worked well in close proximity to each other. The fact that the mountain offered an optimal position to send and receive to both the Special Forces on the northern plateau and the Delta group located on top of the southern canyon highway was just icing on the cake.

It was a good thing the RAP-4 communicators were clear as a bell in both directions. Mustapha, Suleiman, Brigadier Yousaf Azraq, and Commander Nabi were all wearing our spare RAP-4 COMM units.

The call came in just moments before the rocket attack was supposed to start.

"STING-1, ONE here. ROCKETMAN-1 reports one of his 77s is down. Come back." Gary Lawson was trying to tell me that one of Commander Nabi's radios was not functioning. I was not hearing all of the 77 traffic being announced over the speaker arrangement located at the rear of the OP. The PRC-77 (pronounced "prick 77") radios were dedicated for fire direction of the MBRL rocket launchers. The exchange of information for each of the artillery pieces needed to be closely coordinated. The seven-kilometer distance between the OPs and the batteries on the northern plateau, would require the digital features and distance capability of the PRC-77s, we assumed.

"Calling Mr. ONE. This is STING-1. Not sure what you're telling me. Over," I replied.

"STING-1, this is ONE. Number 3 MBRL's 77 is down. Come back."

ZERO and ONE had already guided six rockets from MBRL units 1 and 4 onto Bagram and into their assigned quadrants. The main runway had been hit by at least three of the 107mm projectiles.

"Copy ONE. MBRL's 2 and 3 are waiting for a fix. Come back," I replied and turned to GB-5, Staff Sergeant Brian McDermott. He was kneeling next to the radios, connecting the last of the bridged antenna array.

"Brian, ROCKETMAN has a problem with one of his PRICKs," I said. "Not your guys — it's one of his radios. Any suggestions?"

Laughing, GB-5 replied, "I heard. Let me ask Captain Nelson what's up." Brian touched his throat mic, and called out, "GB-1, GB-5. GB-1, GB-5. Come back."

"Roger, this is GB-1. Brian, we lost one of the 77s. Over," replied Captain Nelson. He had come forward from his rear watch position near the mule picket line. He and his Special Forces were embedded with Commander Nabi's people. The Green Berets were providing security out in front and for each individual battery across the entire launch site.

"I'll be damned," I said to myself. "Brian, are the RAP-4s up there working 5 by 5?"

"Yeah, I was talking to Captain Nelson on the way up here this morning. I even talked to DELTA-1 when they walked up on the canyon roof this morning. Let me ask the Captain about the 77 on number 3."

"Hey, Boss, what's the problem with the 77? Come back," asked GB-5.

"It came off the mule and bounced pretty good getting down onto the plateau last night. I described what had happened to the commander this morning. His only comment was in Pashto. The closest translation I could determine was that he said, "shit happens". We hadn't tested it at that point. Changed the battery twice this a.m. but still no joy. It be dead. Over."

"Roger that. Wait one," replied McDermott and then turned to face me. "We could take him a spare but it'll take well over an hour to get over there."

I keyed my mike. "ROCKETMAN, STING-1. Mr. ONE has concerns. How do we call the game without proper ID and timing on one of your units? Any suggestions? Over." Gary Lawson had volunteered to coordinate the fire placement and timing for the four MBRL units spread across the northern plateau.

"STING-1, we are spread wide up here," replied Commander Nabi, keying his personal COMMs. "We're the ones looking for suggestions. ROCKETMAN, standing by."

"Pardon the interruption, STING-1. This is TERRAPIN-1 down at the fence. ZERO, be advised, MiG approaching Bagram from the south at my 10 o'clock, moving fast at about 1200 meters. Uh oh, make that my 12 o'clock, soon to be my six. MiG has changed direction and heading due east," called Suleiman. "That will be a clock reading of your high noon. Straight at the mountain. Come back." The MiG-23 was heading directly at us.

"Everybody pucker up. This is STING-1. FATHER-1, this may be your big chance to be a hero. Did you copy traffic from TERRAPIN? Come back."

"This is STING-3. Hold one for result." STING-3, Mustapha, and FATHER-1, the Brigadier, were embedded at the base of the mountain.

Jim Pezlola pulled both spotter scopes off the rock and took one final glance down the mountain. What he saw caused him to immediately grab his throat.

"STING-1, this is ZERO. The Stinger team and friends, positioned right above you, are standing in the open. I suspect the reflective glare from their gear, or the Russian traffic control tower on the base, has caused the unwanted attention. Our protection team is not answering their 77. This is ZERO. Come back." Pezlola let his hand drop and called over to his partner, Gary Lawson.

"We better get small, Gary. That MiG seems to have somebody's number up here. Did you get anybody on the 77?" asked Pezlola. "I bet you 10 bucks that they haven't even got the damned thing powered up."

Off in the distance a faint announcement was being yelled up the mountain in Pashto. Upon hearing my exchange with Jim, Amelia Jane had grabbed the hand-held M-64 megaphone, a voice-powered, cone-shaped amplifier. Andy Davis, instructor extraordinaire, who left nothing to chance, had called for four megaphones in the original equipment configuration for the first Ojhri Stinger class. Amelia climbed to the top of the rock shelf, keeping a large boulder between her back and the incoming MiG. She pointed the M-64 up the mountain and screamed in Pashto, "Incoming, incoming. Get the fook down, NOW, you assholes." Of course, cursing in Pashto with a British accent didn't diminish its meaning.

"STING-1, this is ONE. All of the groundhogs have covered up. Recommend you put your fingers in your ears now." The familiar strafing sound of an incoming jet engine was getting louder. Amelia returned to the front of our rocky layer and knelt beside me. I was looking out between the two huge boulders.

"STING-1, this is TERRAPIN," called Suleiman. "He either sees something up there with you or the Russian control tower has directed him to take a look. Say the word and we will shoot him dead. TERRAPIN-1, standing by."

I pressed the mic button, "TERRAPIN, hold one. Let's see what he's up to. This is STING-1."

The MiG passed just 200 meters to the south of the heavily camouflaged position of Brigadier Azraq, and our beloved Mustapha. They were located 600 meters to the rear of TERRAPIN-1 at the foot of the mountain.

Mustapha had shouldered a Stinger tube as soon as the MiG had been sighted. As the aircraft screamed past his position and started up the mountain, STING-3 stepped out into the open area. Already powered up, he acquired the target just as it reached the foothills. Raising the sight up 12 degrees, he fired. He raised his left hand to the mic switch and started the count.

"STING-3 counting down 1001, 1002, 100 ... target destroyed. This is STING-3, standing by."

The Stinger missile hit the rear exhaust port and stabilizer of the aircraft and exploded. The hit caused the MiG to cartwheel into the solid rock face of the mountain. A huge fireball shot up over 100 meters into the air. Amelia Jane and I could feel the heat and smell the burning jet fuel.

The groundhogs were out in the open again. Several of them were holding their AKs in their right hands, high over their heads, pointing at the sky. On full automatic the AK makes quite a racket. I depressed my mic switch to see if ZERO and One had survived this particular celebration.

"ZERO, this is STING-1. Are you taking fire? Come back." But as quickly as it had started, it stopped. The Mujahideen disappeared back under cover.

"Funny, someone probably told them that the MBRLs can land on them as well as the Russians. This is ZERO."

Next, TERRAPIN-1 broke into the conversation with the following announcement. "STING-1, this is TERRAPIN here. Starting phase two; three gunships, 24s, just jumped the fence in front of us. They appear interested in their flaming comrade." And as soon as they passed over his head he continued, "STING-1, this is TERRAPIN. They are heading straight for the mountain." Suleiman also had one of Andy's megaphones. He pushed it under the tarp, raised it up slightly, and yelled through it to his forward Stinger positions. "One, three, four: power up." He swung around to see the progress the Russian gunships were making. Turning back to the Stinger teams he yelled again into the M-64.

"Shoot right to left. Acquire, acquire, acquire. Elevate 10. Shoot, shoot, shoot. Position 2: tube up, power up, stand by."

The right side of the Russian triangulated formation took the first hit. The missile penetrated the metal skin just below the air intake cover on the right side of the aircraft. Large quantities of thick black smoke began to emerge from the turbine. The Mil Mi stopped flying and plowed into the valley floor. It skidded into the soil, striking a large boulder. The sudden stop flipped the aircraft upside down. As dumb luck would have it, the Russian pilot hit the only Mujahideen landing aid within several hundred meters.

Stinger team number 3 fired a defective missile at the center aircraft in the combat cluster. The projectile sailed only 25 meters before falling harmlessly to the valley floor.

"Team 2," yelled Suleiman into the M-64. "Acquire middle gunship. Elevate. Sh— WAIT. Stand down, team 2. Go on, kill it Mr. Mike."

GB-2, Mike Davis, brother of Andy Davis, had stepped out of his hideout and pointed his already powered-up Stinger tube at the middle, now serpentining, gunship. There would be no escape for this aircraft. The trap that TERRAPIN and company had set had just been sprung.

The third missile fired by team 4 exploded at the base of the main rotor assembly. This caused the pilot of the third helo to attempt an escape towards the north. However, the damage to the hydraulics caused the rear rotor to lock up. Steering of the aircraft was no longer possible. The helo turned 180 degrees twice — once in each direction — before hitting hard on the valley floor. The sheer power of the gunship's momentum made it corkscrew deep into the valley's dirt and rock landscape.

The fourth backup shot by Mike Davis, would be one for the record book. Once the shooting had started, the middle gunship started a series of quick jerking maneuvers. It was on its second jog towards the north that the missile arrived. It did not explode on the outside of the aircraft. Instead it dove into the open portal located on the left side. It entered the rear cabin space directly behind the dual cockpits.

The missile detonated on the forward bulkhead. The shrapnel from the explosion killed both pilots. The gunship pulled sharply up at an almost 90 degree angle. It stalled at a height of 60 meters. It fell back immediately, tail first, to the ground. The fuel cells ignited on impact, and the flash of fire was immediate and spectacular. Just as thunder follows lightning, the booming sound of the gunship's last breath was heard moments later up on the mountain.

52
Fine Tuning

Meanwhile Back at the Ranch
Up on the Plateau
Wednesday 27 August 1986 1208 Hours

"ROCKETMAN...," I STARTED to talk but decided to un-key the mike ... gathering my thoughts; I muttered *Jesus* under my breath to no one in particular...."

"Rocketman, this is STING, sorry STING-2 was showing me something in one of her Hollywood gossip magazines...." This earned me a negative shaking of her head which immediately turned into the sound of an outright English chuckle, as she turned back to the spotter scope.

"Commander," I said to restart the conversation. I suggest the following. Pull your two inside units closer towards the center, close enough so that you and GB-1 can control each other's lawn darts if necessary. Do you concur, ROCKETMAN? This is STING-1. Come back."

The original launch and control plan for the MBRLs called for them to be coordinated utilizing the PRC-77s guided by just one person, CWO Lawson. In a previous life, Gary held a primary designation as a cannonfire ranging expert, and was fully trained as an FO, a forward observer. This skill-set would lend itself very well to the task at hand. With one of the 77s out of service, zeroing (fine-tuning) the center two batteries was a problem.

The transmission protocols established in the planning process called for utilizing four PRC-77 digital radios — one embedded with each MBRL unit. Utilizing a very powerful set of spotter scopes, Gary would direct and correct the delivery of the MBRL rockets. He would do two units at a time. The goal was first to zero each rocket launcher and then to provide a play-by-play result for each of the lawn darts arriving for a landing on the Bagram base. The failure of the PRC-77 for lawn dart machine number 3 rendered it deaf, dumb, and blind in the grand scheme of things. Of course, this was delaying both inside MBRLs, designated with the position numbers 2 and 3, from getting into the game.

"Affirmative STING-1, this is GB-1. Suggest we only move MBRL number 3. MBRL 2 is already just to the left of center. Come back."

"Makes sense, Captain," I said to Captain Nelson, who had come up from his position in the rear staging area.

"STING-1, GB-1. ETA on the reposition is 10 to 15 mikes. Over."

"Roger that, GB-1. Break. ZERO, I'm waiting on ROCKETMAN's reset. Suggest you fire for effect with volleys from MBRLs 1 and 4, so they keep their heads down. How about it? This is STING-1. Come back."

"STING-1, this is ZERO, 10-4. Starting up again now."

"Roger that, ZERO. I'll inject 2 and 3 into the mix from lower OP. Come back."

"STING-1, ZERO. Same protocol for station designation?" he asked.

"ZERO, affirmative. Suggest cadence modification once batteries 2 and 3 are fine-tuned. Switch from 77s to RAP-4 once all of the lawn dart machines are fine-tuned. Come back."

"STING-1, this is ZERO. Confirmed. COMMs for the two center MBRLs will utilize secondary channel on the one working PRICK-77. Come back."

"Negative, ZERO. Suggest ROCKETMAN and GB-1 use this private line. Keep director's role for target and timing of MBRLs 1 and 4 on the 77s for the time being. Once 2 and 3 are tuned everyone can talk on the RAP-4 COMMs. This is STING-1 standing by."

"Jesus, Rick," called Lawson, quickly keying his mike. "Nothing like a major change in procedure 10 minutes into the second quarter. Who is on the private net at launchers 1 and 4? Come back."

"GBs 3 and 4 will be in position by the time center units are zeroed. 10-4. Come back."

"This is ONE. That will work, Rick. This is ONE."

"This is STING-1. Mr. Lawson, the really good news is because we are using the runway's center as ground zero, we have kept their fixed wings from responding. We can continue to use the main runway to split assignments. The bad news will be when more of the helos escape during a reload at half-time."

"This is ONE. Enough with the football analogies. If TERRAPIN is correct, we'll need to kill the Russian eyes — the traffic control tower — ASAP. This is ONE standing by."

"This is ZERO, PRICKs one and four are sounding loud and clear. Break. GB-1," ZERO called by depressing the throat switch of his RAP-4, "call STING-1 when 3 is in place. Come back."

"This is GB-1, continuing with the 77s for lawn dart pods 1 and 4. ROCKETMAN and GB-1, on the RAP-4 for the zero. Out."

"STING-1, ROCKETMAN here with unit 3. Your transmission is coming in loud and clear. We will be in position in 2 mikes. Over."

I decided to ask TERRAPIN-1 to pull the plateau Stinger teams from forward positions to be in line with the rocket launchers. I knew that this modification would give ROCKETMAN and GB-1 some peace of mind, plus we would be able to use their COMMs during the grand finale. Should some Russian birds escape the nest and come to visit, well, GBs 3 and 4 would just have to do double duty.

"ROCKETMAN, this is TERRAPIN," called Suleiman. "Amar, can you send someone out to get a message to GB-4?"

"Standby, TERRAPIN," replied ROCKETMAN-1. He processed the request, and immediately started to order a jogger to the front to get GB-4 to come to the phone. But before the runner had taken two steps GB-4's voice came into Suleiman's earpiece.

"TERRAPIN, this is GB-4," called Staff Sergeant Paul Murray. "What's up? Come back." The COMM link was working well from the mountain OPs to most everywhere on the northern plateau,

"GB-4, this is ZERO. I wasn't aware that the internal COMMs were working up there. Are you in contact with GB-3? Come back."

"ZERO, this is GB-3. Been listening in all morning to your traffic. Over." There were four Stinger teams positioned on the plateau. One, a half click out in front with GB-6 on the forward edge, and one at the rear with the reserve supplies and the pack animal line. And now, GB-3 and GB-4 would be positioned to the right and left of lawn dart machines 1 and 4, respectively.

In our weekend planning session we had identified the Russian control tower as Ground Zero. We drew a large cross on the site diagram. We used the tower location as the center point. Starting in the upper left quadrant and moving in a clockwise direction, each quad was marked 1 through 4. The 4 MBRL batteries were given the number associated with their respective assigned quadrants (1 through 4).

Quad areas 1 and 4 had the majority of the important infrastructure: hangars, mess and kitchens, and living quarters. Quad areas 2 and 3 contained the majority of the parked and closely clustered aircraft, as well as the tank farms.

"Lawson now spoke up. "STING-1, this is ONE. First field goal attempt in 4 mikes. Suggest we halt 1 and 4 at 50 percent expenditure. Call a timeout when you start the reload. 2 and 3 should be ready to rock in two mikes. Come back."

"This is STING-1, ROCKETMAN. Kickoff now in 1 mike. GB-1, run COMMs check with the ROCKETMAN. Call for snap count. This is STING-1, standing by."

"TERRAPIN," called GB-1. Suleiman was down on the valley floor close to Bagram's southeast security fence. "You are sounding 5 by 5. Stinger teams repositioned. GB-3 inline and to the right of MBRL 3. Break. GB-4, you on the line? Over."

"Roger, GB-1. GB-4 here. Relocation complete. Settled in to the left of MBRL 2. Over."

"GBs 3 and 4, sounds like our private line is 5 by 5. Four is left, three is right. Stinger teams have eyes on the skies. TERRAPIN-1, down in front, standing by."

Singing in the Rain
Lower OP – Walking the Dog
Wednesday 27 August 1986 1210 Hours

All and all it took only 16 minutes to reposition the number 3 rocket launcher. Four mules were brought up from the line. The MBRL unit 3, fully assembled, was dragged by one mule to its new position. The other three mules were loaded with the loose ammo from the lawn, and, led by their handlers, followed the tire marks to the new location. Training mules to carry live ammo was, in and of itself, one for the record books. Only 15 meters now separated the MBRLs designated as 2 and 3.

"STING-1, ROCKETMAN," called an excited and slightly winded Commander Nabi. "Reposition complete. MBRLs 2 and 3 ready to go. ROCKETMAN-1 standing by."

"STING-1, TERRAPIN. Counting the bang of 22 rocket hits. We may be pressed for time. Come back."

"Roger, Mr. Turtle. Several hits on main runway will buy some time. Hang tight. Break. ZERO, request update on runway status. Please feed lawn dart results to TERRAPIN. Come back."

"Roger that, STING-1. Suggest third and fourth quarter be called on internal COMMs. Status and results will be fed directly to TERRAPIN as they occur. This is ZERO. Come back."

"Roger that, ZERO. Break, break. GB-3, GB-4, come back."

"This is 3. 4 is on the line. Go."

"This is STING-1. Take a position with your closest rocket launcher. As soon as the zero is complete on machines 2 and 3, remaining rockets will be coordinated over the RAP-4 COMMs. 10-4?"

So far, the Russian aircraft utilizing the runway had been limited to one AN-25 cargo transport. The decision to let it go unharmed was well founded. Keeping the location of the Stinger teams secret for as long as possible was important, but the plan had been thwarted when the three gunships had jumped the fence. If the Russian tower had seen the locations from which the Stinger teams fired their missiles, the next wave of gunships could be much more exciting for our people near the fence. What Suleiman did not want to occur was a mass exodus of warplanes. This would spell disaster. The forward Stinger teams had a limited amount of war shots remaining in their inventory.

"Mr. Turtle, STING-2," called Amelia Jane. "Only 11 hits on the runway so far. I imagine the rain of rockets is causing all sorts of flight delays. Stay close to the phone. STING-2, standing by."

"Thanks OP#2. Keep us appraised. Turtle, standing by."

TERRAPIN, this is ZERO. Confirming 15 rounds now at runway center, no new aircraft activity. Smoke at the center of the compound is hiding latest rocket results in quads 1 and 4."

Pezlola looked up to where his partner, Lawson, was stretched out on top of a large boulder. One hand was resting on the spotter's scope. The other was working the mike extended on a long, coiled cable stretched from a PRC-77 propped against a boulder to his rear.

"STING-1, this is ONE. Batteries 1 and 4 have 12 more rounds, six each, before reload. Suggest your zero-start time in five mikes. Reload will require minimum of 12 to 15 mikes. This is ZERO, standing by."

"Roger, ZERO. Break. ROCKETMAN, GB-1, STING-1 here. Are you ready?"

"STING-1, GB-1 here. MBRL 2 ready," replied Captain Nelson.

"STING-1, ROCKETMAN here. Three is ready to shoot. Standing by."

"Roger. Break. ZERO, batteries 2and 3 are good to go. 2 will fire first, 3 will fire on fourth one thousand count — as in1004. Standing by."

At the nine-minute mark my ear piece announced, "STING-1, this is ZERO. We are at recess … reloading. Two more hits scored on the runway, one direct hit on the control tower roof — dead center. You are clear to proceed. Over."

This was truly good news. Fighter aircraft feel safer when they have eyes up high — looking through a pane of glass. The bad news would be if the gunship drivers got together and decided to pop up and over their security fence in a mass exodus. Helicopters do not need an intact runway. Even so, jumping out of the playpen blind would make them extremely vulnerable.

"Roger, ZERO. Break, break. TERRAPIN, did you copy ZERO? Over."

"10-4, this is TERRAPIN. Copied ATC destroyed. Keep feeding us the runway status. This is TERRAPIN. Out."

"GB-1, this is STING-1. Fire one rocket. Please confirm trigger and count down. Standing by. Break, break. ROCKETMAN, standby to fire. On the thousand count of 4. Acknowledge."

"Roger, STING, on one thousand four count. ROCKETMAN, standing by."

"STING-1, battery 2 firing NOW. Counting 1001, 1002, 1003, 1004."

"ROCKETMAN, fire one. Confirm. Break. GB-1, this STING-1. Boom in quad 2. Long 100, right 75. Copy. Come back."

"STING-1, this is GB-3 firing 1. Counting down now: 1001, 1002, 1003, 1004."

"GB-2, fire second round on your count. ROCKETMAN, this is STING-1. Short 500. Repeat, short 500, left 125. Break."

"STING-1, this is GB-2 firing now. 1001, 1002, 1003..."

"GB-1, Quad 3 at the bottom. Go left 20. Suggest you add 50. ROCKETMAN, go with second launch. Confirm with count. Come back."

"STING-1, this is ROCKETMAN. 3 firing ... now. 1001, 1002, 1003, 10..."

"ROCKETMAN, bullseye Quad 4. Suggest you work a tight circle around this setting. Break. GB-1, fire one more into quad 3. Fire minus 20. Confirm."

"STING-1, GB-1 here. Dropping 20. MBRL 2 firing now."

"Boom GB-1. Looks like a hit on a JP fuel tank! Both batteries fire for effect. ZERO, recess in eight mikes. Over."

"Roger, STING-1. Nice shooting. Confirm recess now in seven. Over."

"Affirmative. Break. FATHER-1, STING-1. Come back," I called.

"STING-1, go," the Brigadier replied from his hideout at the base of this mountain. He released the switch at the center of his throat strap and waited on the reply from his favorite systems engineer from AT&T.

"FATHER, you and STING-3 still in shock from your lucky hit? Everything copacetic down there? Over."

"STING-1, this is STING-3. Not sure what is copacetic, but we are looking at a lot of black smoke over at the air base. I assume you will announce if the morning sky is about to become filled with our Russian friends. This is STING-3 saying come back."

"STING-3, STING-1. ATC tower destroyed. Suggest we start to leap-frog TERRAPIN back to your six. Do you concur? Come back."

"10-4, STING-1. Break, break. TERRAPIN, this is STING-3. Are you on the line? Come back."

"STING-3, this is TERRAPIN," called Suleiman.

Breaking the Bad – Silent Convoy
Canyon Ambush Site
Wednesday 27 August 1986 1202 Hours

"STING-1, DELTA-5. South canyon highway approach quiet. No new traffic. Convoy stripped of all usable items. DELTA-1 has moved to the roof with 7. This is DELTA-5, standing by."

"STING-1, this is DELTA-7. DELTA-1 is with me. Mujahideen ground force has moved out of the canyon, withdrawing towards the west. Roof teams will remain in place until they are at a safe distance. This is DELTA-7 standing by."

The Grand Finale
Fire for Effect
Wednesday 27 August 1986 1247 Hours

"This is ONE, calling ROCKETMAN and GBs 1, 3, and 4. COMMs check. Come back."

"This is GB-1 alongside ROCKETMAN, ready to receive your transmission. Over."

"Hello ONE, GB-3 here," replied Dennis Bormann.

"Ditto ONE. GB-4 ready to receive. Over."

"This is ONE. COMMs check 5 by 5," announced CWO Lawson. "All batteries are zeroed. GBs 3 and 4 monitor operation of your assigned lawn dart generator. Commence firing all batteries."

"ROCKETMAN, this is STING-1. Send for the mules. Pull back to the rear of the plateau upon expenditure of all rockets. 10-4. This is STING-1. Break, break. DELTA-6, SITREP. Come back."

"STING-1, this is GB-1. Mules coming up now. Full expenditure in 16 mikes. This is GB-1. Out."

"STING-1, this is DELTA-7. We are descending east on back side of canyon. DELTA-6 has linked with 5. Next COMM check in two hours from Eagle's Nest at Charlie-Peter. We be ghosts and gone. This is DELTA-7. Out."

"Roger that, 7. ZERO, you copy all that? This is STING-1."

"Roger, STING. Ambush site vacated 1241 hours. This is ZERO. Break. FATHER, this is ZERO. Come back. Over."

"ZERO, FATHER-1."

"FATHER, canyon operation complete. DELTA moving to Eagle CP. This is ZERO."

"Roger that. Executing leapfrog of TERRAPIN teams now. This is FATHER-1, standing by the back door."

The Brigadier and Mustapha were positioned on the ground level a half-kilometer directly behind the Stinger fire teams. They were nestled in on a slight rise near the base of our mountain. The valley floor ended just behind their hideout.

We had decided not to station the Brigadier, FATHER-1, up high in the OPs. The reasoning, as I explained it to him, was simple. The foothills offered a direct avenue for escape. The OPs did not. The trails in the foothills wound their way gradually upwards almost a full kilometer. The terrain offered plenty of cover and safe passage into the surrounding mountains towards the east.

Mike Davis, GB-2, had told Mustapha at the end of our first planning session that he desperately needed to look some Russian gunships in the eye. When Mr. Turtle heard of Mike's request, his immediate response was a very big, shit-eating grin. He and his four Stinger teams had welcomed Andy's brother into their group, no questions asked. The very next thing TERRAPIN-1 did was assure GB-2 he wouldn't be disappointed. And, as it turned out, he was not.

By the Dawn's Early Light
The Rocket's Red Glare
Wednesday 27 August 1986 1312 Hours

Earlier that morning, at 0330 hundred hours, Suleiman had arrived with four Mujahideen Stinger teams. Their task was undertaken in complete darkness. They dug in 500 meters from the south corner of Bagram's security fence. Once in position, they quickly covered themselves as the sunlight marched across the valley towards them.

The Stinger shooters had been arranged in a half circle facing the outer security fence. The south end of the main runway was only 100 meters inside the inner ring of the security fencing. Suleiman, his spotter MSG Mike Davis, and the PRC-77 radio operator were at the center, behind the curved array of shooters. Suleiman would, if necessary, direct these teams with hand signals and shouts. Suleiman's RAP4 Special Forces throat mic was courtesy of Mike, GB-2. Their sheltered hideout was fastened out of a large set of camo tarps, courtesy of Ojhri Camp's S-4. A good amount of hastily cut plant material from the valley floor was also used. The OPs above had guided them flawlessly. Only one action item remained. It was called Leap Frog. Just like the kid's game, we would have our teams take turns moving forward (and, in this case, take turns covering for each other).

It was Mustapha who had voiced his concern the evening before. Commander Nabi and the Brigadier agreed: the first rockets from the MBRLs would target the central runway and, if God was on their side, the air control tower would be destroyed. He was, they did, and history was changed.

The initial rocket launches were directed to the tarmac at the center of the complex. It was important that the MiG and SU fighters not be allowed to get into the game after the rockets started to fall. None did. The fate that befell the control tower was just icing on the cake. This piece of good luck not only allowed additional time on-site, but would cause any escaping aircraft to emerge from their base blind as bats.

Breaking Camp
All's Well That Ends Well
Wednesday 27 August 1986 1320 Hours

The most important result we had hoped for had been achieved. Stinger, in the trained hands of the Mujahideen, would make the liberation of Afghanistan possible. As the lawn dart players providing the half-time show were retiring to the locker room, I keyed my mic to end the fourth quarter.

"STING-3, this is STING-1. Angels to the front. Execute Leap Frog. TERRAPIN, state status for the first jump. This is STING-1. Come back."

"Roger, STING-1. This is TERRAPIN. Angels moving to us now. Break. FATHER-1, this is TERRAPIN. Are you with the incoming angels? Come back."

"Sorry, TERRAPIN. Jogging to you lost my ear piece. This is FATHER-1. ETA in five mikes. Come back."

"Roger, FATHER. Five and counting."

"STING-2, this is Turtle. Team one will jump first. Watch our backs."

"Roger, Mr. Turtle. This is STING-1. Please pick up all of your empty tubes and the misfires on your way east. This is STING-1, standing by."

"Roger that, STING-1. This is TERRAPIN, already packed. Waiting on our escort. Standing by."

Suleiman yelled to team number three to power up and keep an eye on the fence line. Mike Davis slapped a battery into a Stinger tube but did not power up. His group would be the last to depart.

"Roger that. Wait one, TERRAPIN. Angels are in place. This is STING-3. Execute Leap Frog. Come back."

"STING-3, Team 1 vacating and moving into protected area. Team 4 will jump on your signal. Come back."

"Roger, TERRAPIN. Team 1 is in sight. Send all teams at your own cadence. This is FATHER-1, standing by."

"ZERO, this is STING-1. Break camp. Leap Frog is in progress. Start your way down here. Pick up the masters of stealth on your way. 10-4. Come back."

"STING-1, this is ONE, what is a 'master of stealth'? Come back."

"STING-1, this is ZERO. I'll gather them up on the way. See you in 20. This is ZERO shutting down the upper. ZERO signing off."

Pezlola called over to Gary Lawson. "Rick was referring to Nabi's shooters and Mustapha's Sting team. They seem to be again sunning themselves on the rocks below us. Rick was dishing out his usual sarcasm."

"No! Not Rick! He would never kid around in a combat situation," replied Lawson, laughing. Rick was never serious about anything — until he was.

"Are you all packed? If so, I'm ready when you are," said Pezlola.

Gary was quiet. He was still contemplating how someone could just pick up a microphone and a spotter's scope, and skillfully direct men firing a Chinese MBRL rocket launcher eight kilometers distant like he had been doing it all his life — and then proceed to walk the rockets to within meters of where they were needed. This was something that had taken Gary over six months to perfect in a classroom environment. He finally answered Jim.

"Yeah, I'm all set. Did you ever work in the field with Rick in '69? I can't get it out of my head how he zeroed the MBRLs with just a few shots."

Jim Pezlola grinned. "No, but Douglas told me that he has a natural ability to put people where they need to be, with or without a radio."

"What he did today was pretty amazing, making each and every one of us feel like we were in charge," Lawson said as he swung his backpack up to his shoulder. "Christ, he had to know in his head exactly where each of us was standing today. More importantly, he knew what each of us was facing and what we needed to do. Every one of us."

"That in a nut shell, Mr. Lawson, describes our Rick to a tee. Plus, I understand they are still running his OPLAN Synchronized Sparrow at Fort Bliss.

"No shit," replied Lawson.

The not-yet-announced, but newly promoted Lieutenant Colonel James Pezlola pulled on his pack and clipped the stability strap of his M-16 to his vest. He nodded and said, "Well, we still need to get down off this mountain,

Gary. So, I suggest we hold off calling him the Pope until we are safely back inside Massoud's mountain palace."

"Ha ha," replied the CWO. "Don't get me wrong, Jim, I'm not complaining. As a matter of fact, I'm feeling very blessed at this moment."

"Gary, the After Action Report on this operation will be interesting to some, maybe terrifying to most. Be careful with your footing on your way down. The Afghans are utilizing their mule protocol."

Gary picked up his weapon and turned to face his partner. "What the hell is that supposed to mean?"

Jim smiled and led them out onto the jagged mountain pathway. "Do you remember the pack animal that slipped off the trail and broke its leg the second day out?"

"Yes, they … no shit. You're not suggesting that the Afghans apply that same logic to people, are you?"

"Is a frog's ass water-tight? Just watch your step, Gary. Watch your step," repeated Pezlola, who was now facing forward with a great big grin on his face. It had been over 15 years since they had made the acquaintance of Rick Fontain. It was truly rewarding to be able to get the band back together from time to time.

53

Scribing the Whirlwind

US Embassy
Conference Center – 3rd Floor
25 Grosvenor Square, London
Monday 1 September 1986 1015 Hours

M
R. DOUGLAS, MR. McCall just rang me. Everyone is here," announced Mrs. Flouts over the intercom.

"Thanks, Carrie, I'm on my way," replied Bill Douglas, rising from his chair.

"Mr. Douglas." Mrs. Flouts's voice again came over the intercom speaker. "The front desk also called. You have a visitor in the lobby. It's a man named Mohammed Abu Ghazala. He doesn't have an appointment, but is asking for a few minutes of your time. What should I tell security?"

Douglas sat back down, leaned in, and pushed the lever down to talk. "Call down to Ed. Ask him to fetch Mr. Ghazala and take him to ... where's the meeting being held downstairs?"

"Conference Center 3A, Mr. Douglas," replied Mrs. Flouts.

"Yeah, have Ed take him there. And Carrie, I've asked you to call me Bill when we're conversing amongst ourselves."

"Yes, Mr. Douglas."

Bill Douglas looked down at the center of his desk and smiled, shaking his head. There was no changing the proper English manner of this lady. Bill pushed the lever to the talk position one more time. "Carrie, please ask Ed to find an open room on three and come and get me. I'll be in 3A. Thanks, Carrie."

Douglas got up again, snatched his suit jacket from a hook on the coat rack, and rounded the front of his desk. He heard Carrie talking to Ed as he left the office. He pushed open the right side of the floor-to-ceiling glass door, entered the hallway, and made a bee-line straight to the stairwell.

Moments later Douglas entered the third floor. He turned to the right. Conference Center 3A was at the end of the hallway behind an opaque glass wall. He walked to where the two Marine guards were standing by the door. His ID badge clipped to his lapel was electronically read and a faint click was heard in the door's hardware. He pushed the chromed bar that was fastened to the glass. Douglas walked quickly across the vestibule and pushed open the heavy wooden door on the opposite wall.

There were over 15 individuals in attendance today. Over half were based outside the U.K. All but seven of them were CIA. Two participants that were not in "the company" were from the DOD, the Department of Defense. Five were from the State Department.

The lights were down low. A map of Pakistan and Afghanistan was being projected onto the large screen at the front of the room. The briefing binders were still stacked neatly on the table next to the projector. Each attendee would be given one once the introduction was complete. The spine of each binder displayed a label stating: Operation Cyclone, Phase(s) I – III. Section (IV) was in parentheses and would not contain any pages. At the conclusion of today's meeting the contents and any notes scribbled in the page margins would be gathered up and put in burn bags. All material would then be taken to the basement for disposal.

Bill Douglas walked to the front of the room and slid into his saved seat. "Sorry I'm late, Rick," he apologized. "There was a last-minute visitor who needed my attention."

"Good morning, Bill." That was all I could think of to say. Some of the people in the room I didn't know, and the ones I did were way above my pay grade. Well, not as far as they use to be. Anyway, my usual touch of smartass didn't seem appropriate, especially since my role within CIA as a NOC was most likely over. I had been unofficially counseled as to that fact on my way out of Pakistan.

The door at the rear of the room opened and Ed McCall walked in, marching directly to Douglas. Bending slightly at the waist, he whispered something in Bill's ear. Bill Douglas got up and Ed sat down. Douglas disappeared through the same door through which Ed had arrived.

"Ladies and gentlemen," I concluded my introduction, "that completes the scope of what will be discussed in today's after action accounting. The details of the Bagram operation that we discuss this morning will exemplify how technology and technical support will change … have changed, the war in Afghanistan. Although Operation Cyclone was born in 1981, the program was not feasible until this year, until July of this year, to be precise. The result, I believe, and I think you will agree, justifies the recommendation to continue with Phase III protocol and implement the Phase IV managed overview if the President authorizes the continuation of Cyclone. A firm commitment of the Pakistani ISI and the Mujahideen leadership has been carefully garnered. Our mandated protocols will be maintained by both parties."

"Mr. Fontain, why are you opening this discussion? How do you fit into all of this?"

"And you are, ma'am?" I asked with my best smile. *Does it matter now how I answer that?* I asked myself.

"Lisa Meerdter, State Department. What part do you or have you played in all of this?"

Ed McCall and I made eye contact. He was shaking his head, ever so slightly, from left to right.

"Thanks, Lisa," I started, and dialed back my expression. This well-dressed lady in her chic power suit projected all of the charm of Genghis Khan answering questions at his first and last press conference.

"The Army sent me to Redeye missile training in 1968. After separation, I was hired by The Bell System, AT&T in particular, and Bell Laboratories, specifically."

"You're not answering my question," she said and folded her arms across her chest. Too bad, I thought. The lady was equipped with some very nice groceries. I quickly refocused my attention to her face.

"My company's relationship with Raytheon and General Dynamics resulted in a DOD request that I be brought in to consult on the Stinger technology and its deployment. Does that answer your question, Lisa?"

Before she could respond, a male voice added to what I had just said. "Ms. Meerdter, Rick was one of the first to use this technology in the service of the United States in the early months of 1968. When the President issued the order for Cyclone in '82, Rick's name was submitted to be read-in on this Presidential finding. I hope that answers your question."

"Yes, thank you," she said and smiled at me. Next, she turned towards General Bushman, who had added the additional information.

"And you are?" asked Lisa.

The man who had remained seated, who was dressed in a gray striped three-piece suit, stood up. "I'm Gerald Bushman, DOD/DIC. I represent the Whitehouse." With that said, he sat back down.

"As stated, the goal, the focus, this morning will be to describe the result of introducing Stinger technology into the game in Afghanistan," I tried to continue.

Lisa quickly interrupted again. "Is that how the CIA refers to this program, as a game?"

"That's hardly the issue, ma'am," I fired back instantly at Lisa's second interruption.

"And what is the issue, Rick?"

"The mass murder of thousands of women and children is certainly only a sport to the Russians who have invaded Afghanistan," I stated strongly, beginning to lose my patience.

And Amelia Jane added, "The game Mr. Fontain refers to is the logistics board created to combat the Russian military. I suggest we all hold our questions until the overview is complete. This will insure we keep to the proposed schedule." Everything always sounds better when the British say it.

"Lisa, Amelia Jane Smythe is one of the case officers who took part in the Bagram attack." DIA Bushman nodded in Amelia's direction. "There were both American and Afghan casualties in the implementation. It is not a game to us."

"I'm sorry. I'll hold my questions until the end. Thank you." Well, at least Amelia got her to unfold her arms. I made eye contact with Amelia and raised my eyebrows in thanks.

"Colonel Pezlola will now walk us through the attack on Bagram, the events leading up to it, and the exit strategies utilized. This portion of the after action is classified Top Secret – Cyclone/Whitehouse."

Lisa's hand started to go up again but she quickly withdrew it. Her smile was genuine.

Reborn: Rick 2.0
Conference Center – Room 319
25 Grosvenor Square, London
Monday 1 September 1986 1245 Hours

"Mohammed," said Bill Douglas as he entered room 319. Mohammed Abu Ghazala was a member of the Egyptian Defense Ministry, based in London, and, the brother of Maalouf Torki bin Taisei. Maalouf was a Malaysian citizen and one of the largest, if not 'thee' largest, arms dealer in the Middle East. Operation Cyclone would not have been possible without his assistance. I had saved Mohammed's half-brother's life which probably had a great deal to do with his visit here today.

"Mr. Douglas, thank you for receiving me on such short notice."

"Mohammed, I've asked you to please call me Bill. And, you have a standing invitation to come to the Embassy anytime you want. What can I do for you, Mohammed?"

"This is for you, the CIA that is, it has to do with our mutual acquaintance, Rick Fontain."

Douglas held out his hand as the folder was handed over. "Dr. Asghar told me to convey to you that her boss, Nahum Admoni, personally gathered this information. He also told her to assure you that this file is complete and the information contained in it does not, I repeat, does not exist anywhere else. My brother insisted on this … and, Theresia made it happen."

Douglas flipped open the cover. There was a familiar photo stapled to the inside of the folder. It was a photo of Rick Fontain at 20 years old in the field at Fulda, West Germany. The file had been kept current, even including a listing of Fontain's recent degree from the University of Baltimore.

"I don't know what to say, Mo. So, I'll just say thank you. Rick will be elated, I'm sure."

"Max Gresonine has verified that all records referencing Rick Fontain have been deleted by German intelligence. All that remains is what I'm handing to you now. Max is available to discuss if you require. Anyway, thanks for meeting. My brother sends his regards."

"That is very gracious of Maalouf. Please tell your brother that I owe him one."

"Maalouf suggests that AT&T send Rick to Dubai next month to accept the contract on the Etisalat High Rise Office Building complex. This will cement his role with AT&T in the Middle East and the Pacific Rim."

Bill Douglas didn't say anything for over five seconds. "Outstanding. Please tell Maalouf I owe him twice."

Pilgrim Mugger Comes to London
US EMBASSY – Conference Center – 3A
Monday 1 September 1986 1245 Hours

Bill Douglas had excused himself at the break. Amelia Jane, Jim Pezlola, and Mike Vaughn were gathered by the windows at the rear of the room. I had called my office and given the good news to Joe Hauf. Joe, in London, and two other individuals in New Jersey were the only ones at AT&T who knew of my connection to the CIA.

I walked over to Amelia and the others. "So, Colonel, how come Gary didn't come?" I asked the recently promoted Jim Pezlola. "Do you have him polishing your car, or perhaps just doing some light yard work until he proves himself?"

Pezlola choked slightly on the sip of coffee he had just taken. "His Mom is ill. He grabbed a flight to the States."

"Oh, I'm sorry to hear that. Is there anything we can do?

"Gary said he'd call when he got there."

"Did Delta and the Special Forces guys get back in country without any hassles?" I asked.

"Oh yeah, you should have come with us to Germany. It was like landing in the middle of Mardi Gras. The C-130H received quite a homecoming from their respective groups. The hangar at Ramstein looked like New Year's Eve in Times Square."

"So much for a low profile on their return, huh," I commented.

"Cummings, the two star, had reserved the hangar under the pretense of their having a base picnic," explained Mike Vaughn. "Everyone in attendance was told to stick with that particular story."

"Who in the hell thought that one up?" I asked.

"It was Bushman," said Douglas, walking up to us. "He and General Cummings served in Vietnam together. Delta Forces and the Green Berets will be well taken care of. Rick, let's you and I go grab a cup of coffee."

"Yes, Sir. I'm supposed to close the meeting — will this take long?"

"Mike, you work here now. You finish up," Douglas commanded the startled Mike Vaughn.

Mike was silent for a moment. He had been told in the morning that his request for transfer was still in the works. "Yes, Sir. I'll take of it."

Douglas had asked me what I thought about Mike working with us in London. I told him they didn't come any better. Just as important, Amelia Jane thought so, too.

"We'll be back upstairs in about an hour," Douglas said. "Good job, everybody. Let's go, Rick."

Barley Mow
82 Duke St
Mayfair, London
Monday 1 September 1986 1305 Hours

Bill and I left the embassy and walked casually to the corner of Upper Brooke. We crossed over midway and turned left on Duke Street. Barley Mow was popular for its dinner menu, not supper. This was true for most pubs that served food in this city. An American living off the land in London town needed to understand that having supper at a pub meant risking eating food that had been sitting out since noon. Having said that, a luncheon menu need not be gourmet, but it certainly should offer some choice other than bangers and mash (sausages and mashed potatoes). What a pub like Barley Mow did extremely well was offer a wide selection of locally brewed refreshments.

"Is this a good father and son get-together or just your average pull-the-pin and come to Jesus verbal memorandum?" I asked and slid into the half-booth with a full view of the entrance to the room.

Douglas was in the process of sitting down but stopped midway at my sarcastic insinuation.

"You know, Rick, when you first told me you worked for the Ray-Ban Corporation I thought you were just another draftee pissed off at your present predicament."

"Well, if memory serves, it was Foster-Grant, and I was upset at the time about not being assigned a single room in the practically empty Armed Forces hotel."

"The hell, you say," replied Douglas, laughing.

"But after spending the next two days in country with you, I realized I would never need a good pair of sunglasses, here in the U.K. that is. It seems silly to purchase expensive sunglasses for just two days a year."

Douglas smiled and looked down at the tabletop and fingered the menu. "Then you told me that you were here to address the Association of Blind Fighter Pilots. That bizarre attempt at misdirection caused me to rethink my first impression of you. You do remember saying that?"

"No, but you do realize that there was no such organization, in the U.K.? They were based in Los Angeles and hadn't branched out internationally at the time."

Douglas laughed. "I did realize that it didn't exist at all. What caught my attention was that you were making the shit up as you were talking to me. Our meeting that day prompted a telephone call to your buddy Doc Lattermire. The rest, as you say, is history.

"So, is this the meeting where you tell me all this spy shit has gone full circle?"

Bill laughed again, "Oh ye of little faith." Douglas slid the folder from under his menu and pushed it across the table.

"What's this, and why are we here walking down memory lane, Bill?"

"It hasn't been officially blessed, but your Mossad girlfriend, Dr. Asghar, has arranged an unprecedented coup within her organization."

"The Mossad?" I asked, my eyes popping just a tad.

"Your very good friend, Maalouf the arms dealer made the ... I was going to say request, but it was really more in the way of a demand to her boss. Theresa and your Uncle Max have verified that Israeli intelligence, Admoni himself, complied with Maalouf's wishes."

"Complied with what, Bill? I wasn't aware I had been put on any Israeli hit list."

"Your antics in Dubai exposed the fact that your identity was known to the Mossad. The leak had come from someone in Germany's Federal Intelligence Service.

"Did Max say who in his shop sent my info to Tel Aviv?"

"No, but you can bet that whoever it was is sorry he or she did. The point in all this is that you are now able to continue as a NOC inside AT&T. And, all extracurricular activities from now on will be conducted under an assumed name, like you and Amelia used in Kuala Lumpur."

"What about our friends in Islamabad?"

"Bushman and General Khan have come to an understanding. You entered Pakistan under the Siemens Telecom profile. Brigadier Azraq assures us that none of the American identities were or will be recorded by the ISI, nor were any passed to the Russians. The people who could have done so are all dead."

"So Rick Fontain, Intelligent Building expert, lives on to continue AT&T's quest for total domination of the world's tallest buildings?"

"Almost. Bushman is waiting to hear back from Bill Casey. But that part should be just a formality."

"Hmm … why do I get the feeling that they are sealing up the entrance to the bat cave as we speak?"

"It could be because you're in the CIA," replied Douglas, and then changed the subject. "Charlie Wilson is in the hospital. When you're in Washington you should go see him."

"I'm going to Washington? What about AT&T and Maalouf's UAE building project?"

"I thought you'd welcome the opportunity to help your beautiful wife with moving. She is still coming?"

"Yes, and yes. And what is wrong with Charlie?"

"Heart attack, and several other complications brought on by certain lifestyle decisions."

"When do I go?"

Douglas reached into his jacket pocket and handed over an envelope.

"Travel documents?" I asked. I then peered into the envelope and whistled. "First class, British Air. Very nice," I said and added, "What's the catch?"

"No catch, have a good flight, and the two of you hurry back. We have a lot on our plates."

"You mean a buffet?" I chuckled. "And, Maalouf?"

"No rush. The 16th of this month is the tentative date being suggested. The meeting will be held in Abu Dhabi."

"You know Maalouf has appointed us as the GC, the General Contractor."

"Is that good?" asked Douglas.

"Well, in the high-rise construction market the GC has total control over who plays."

"That good, huh?"

"That, and the assignment of a $39 million dollar management fee — to get started. The really good news is that there is another $400 million to be allocated once the foundation is poured."

"You are in the wrong business, Rick."

"That, Sir, has crossed my mind."

54

Foggy Is the Bottom

Harry S. Truman Building
2201 C Street, NW
Monday 8 September 1986 0215 Hours

T HE TRUMAN BUILDING was located in the Foggy Bottom neighborhood of Washington, D.C. George Pratt Shultz, U.S. Secretary of State, was driven down the ramp into the underground parking garage. The Chevy Suburban stopped near his usual drop-off point. This area of the garage was situated directly across from Shultz's personal entrance to his private elevator. He exited out the rear door on the other side of the vehicle from where he'd been sitting. This deviated greatly from his usual routine.

His handlers recovered quickly and followed him by circling around the Chevy, but the Secretary quickly halted their advance. He continued onward across the concrete and the painted yellow lines to an all-white, parked Lincoln Town car. I jumped out of the front passenger door of the Lincoln and immediately pulled open the rear passenger door for him. I gave the Secretary the appearance that I had been doing this sort of thing all of my life.

"Good morning, Mr. Secretary," I said to the back of his head as he turned to enter the vehicle. I pushed the door shut with both hands and got back in the front seat. The Secretary's people were standing around the Suburban with folded arms.

"Gerry, what's so goddam important that it couldn't wait until morning?" asked the Secretary.

Gerald Bushman, DOD's Director, Defense Intelligence Agency, turned towards him and handed him a folder banded with yellow and blue stripes.

"What's this?" demanded Shultz.

The front cover had "Russian/Egypt Desk" printed in the upper left corner in big bold letters. "Egyptian President Hosni Mubarak has finalized arrangements for a meeting with Israeli Prime Minister Shimon Peres this Wednesday," answered Bushman.

"Interesting, but what has this got to do with us? Has the CIA struck out again trying to get in bed with the Egyptians?"

"Funny, I should ask you that same question, George. A channel to send arms directly into Pakistan without any U.S. fingerprints on them has been a long time in the works. Or, am I missing something?"

Shultz laughed. "No, Gerry, I just find it a bit unusual to meet in the middle of the night about a meeting in Cairo. A meeting we are not invited to attend."

"What if we were, George? Suppose we received an invitation? What would you like to see on the agenda?"

"I suppose Mubarak is looking for certain sanctions to be lifted."

"Rick's friend in Malaysia has insisted that the Israeli transports be made available to the Egyptians. All arms into Afghanistan will be sent through Israeli controlled channels."

"Who in the hell is Rick? And who's his friend?"

"George, may I present Rick Fontain? Rick's a member of the Technical Staff of Bell Labs."

"Sure he is, and I'm a personal friend of the Tooth Fairy."

I turned around in my seat and stuck out my hand. "How do you do, Sir?"

Schultz shook my hand but didn't let go right away. "You're that Redeye guy?"

"Not anymore, Sir. Stinger is what we use now."

"Then you're that Stinger guy I've been reading about in the After Action Reports.

"Sir, we buried that man several weeks ago, in Texas. His name was Andy Davis."

"George is read-in on Cyclone, Rick," Bushman informed me.

George let go of my hand.

"Rick ran Phase 1 and 2 of Cyclone in Pakistan," added Bushman. "And oversaw the Phase 3 activities in Afghanistan. He just got back. Phase 4 is under study by the Whitehouse."

"Who is this so called 'friend' in Malaysia?"

"Sir, he's in the Malaysian Ministry."

"Hmm. Changing the subject: did the required protocols for Cyclone work?" asked Shultz. "I ask the question because, well … if that technology gets out in the open…."

"Yes, Sir, the protocols have all worked as designed. They will continue to be enforced with the people we have there, that is, if Phase 4 is approved. Our Pakistani partners are first-rate and can be trusted to keep the weapon secure."

"Are you looking to put Stinger into the Israeli pipeline? Is that why you're here?"

"No, Sir. We fly them in direct with the Red Cross re-supply."

"Then back to why we are meeting at o-dark-thirty. What's in it for the Israelis? Why is Peres all of sudden willing to cozy up with Cairo?"

Bushman started to answer but I broke in. "Sir, we believe — the CIA believes — that Admoni is trying to mend some fences over the damage caused by his shenanigans with that spy shit he pulled last year. Also, we believe this arrangement will allow the Mossad to get their camel's nose deeper under the flap of Zia's tent in Karachi."

"Our nose also, I'll bet." There was a good 10 seconds of silence before Shultz spoke again. "You remember meeting Secretary Rogers? Now I remember where I heard your name. I was Secretary of Labor in '69 … *Operation Sparrow 'something'.* You made quite an impression on him."

I laughed, "Yes, Sir, in '69. Rose Island, just outside of Munich. Sir, I'm not sure how I could have made an impression. We only met that day for what must have been a full 30 seconds."

"There's a file on that meeting in Germany. There are background pro-files on everyone who attended," said Shultz. Bill was disappointed that you didn't come see him after you got out of the Army."

Gerry and I made eye contact.

Shultz continued, "Wait until I see Bill Rogers, he won't believe—"

"George, Mr. Secretary," said General Bushman, stopping the Secretary mid-sentence. "I would ask you not to tell Bill Rogers that you saw or met with Rick … or to tell anyone for that matter — at least until Cyclone com-pletes. We're presently dealing with another issue with Rick's cover at AT&T."

"Of course. So I'll ask again. What is it you need from State?"

"I would like for you to send a representative, Lisa Meerdter, to the meeting in Cairo."

"Why Ms. Meerdter? What purpose will her attendance serve?"

"She was in London for the After Action overview. She's up to speed on Cyclone. And, she did a tour at the Embassy in Cairo. She knows the lay of the land."

"OK. And our motive for going?"

"There is a certain U.S. citizen being held by the Egyptians," replied Bushman. "We'd like him released."

"One of yours?" asked Shultz.

"No, he's FBI. Got caught up in a bank fraud investigation during the coup attempt last year."

"Is that it?" asked Shultz, looking at his watch.

"Not quite. I'm sending Mike Vaughn with Lisa. He works for Gust Avrakotos."

"And his function, Gerry? Look, it's late or very early, ok? And I'm tired, so let's stop beating around the bush, shall we?"

"Mike will let Peres know that the tent flap will need to be pulled up far enough for both of our noses."

"And why would the Israelis agree to that? Sharing INTEL isn't in their nature."

"True, but in this case, they'll cooperate. If they don't, we'll tell the world that they sold 112 tons of weapons grade uranium to Zia."

"Why haven't I been told about this?"

"No one knows about this except the Pakistani ISI, the Mossad, our friend in Malaysia, and the people in this car. Rick found out when he was leaving Pakistan."

"We knew that Zia had started development of a bomb? Jesus. You want Admoni to share information so that we can slow down the Pakistani program? That about it?"

"Yes, Mr. Secretary," replied Bushman. "Mike and Lisa need to start moving today to be in place in time. Sorry to rob you of your beauty sleep, George. This couldn't wait."

"Understood. Keep me in the loop, will you? During daylight hours is preferable."

"Oh, and one other thing, George, that was uncovered during Cyclone," added Bushman. "Captured documents by the Mujahideen show an appeal to Moscow from the military command in western Afghanistan requesting permission to use tactical nukes: suitcase sized atomic weapons. Someone needs to tell the Russians that this is a very bad idea."

We sat in silence while the Secretary digested what he had just been told. Finally, he responded with only two words. "You think?" With that said, he opened his door and left the car.

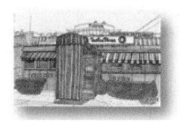

All Night Tastee Diner
8601 Cameron St
Silver Spring, MD
Monday 8 September 1986 0425 Hours

"Do you feel confident about getting the State Department to put on the proper face with the Russian ambassador?" I asked. We had stopped at the

Tastee Diner in Silver Spring a little after four in the morning. General Bushman was quiet most of the way back from Foggy Bottom. His mind was obviously examining the records posted there over the previous 16 years. We took a seat at the end of the counter that faced the entrance.

I started again. "A penny for your thoughts, Sir." The waitress brought us two coffees. The General looked at me and smiled. "In '69, the only foreign government meeting you attended was Rose Island, correct?"

"Yes, Sir, all other functions were CIA hosted."

"The file with you in it that George Shultz referenced — it was the guest list for the West German security forces. State was asked for the list of attendees and their bios. I doubt the file will show any information on you other than your assigned unit inside 3rd Armor."

"I'm sorry, Sir, I'm not following."

"I'll still get Joe Wilson to go over and redact the CIA info from the file, but I think we're good as far as the information they have on you."

"Sir, are you referring to Rose Island?"

"Sorry, Rick, but when George mentioned the file I thought we were facing another problem with your cover. But it's not a problem. When are you and Hanna flying out?"

"We're booked on TWA direct out of Baltimore to Gatwick on Tuesday evening." I looked at my watch and continued. "What was POTUS's response when you told him about the uranium and the suitcase nukes?"

A nod and a smile was all that was returned. "You are to be promoted to GS-12 Step 10. The President told me to tell you, a job well done."

"How about the Delta and Special Forces guys?" I asked.

"They were all bumped one pay grade. Captain Nelson is now Major Nelson, MSGs Davis and Angerome are presently changing their insignias to the rank of Warrant Officer, CWO2."

"Well, that probably ruined Mike's day but would certainly put a smile on Andy's face. Thanks for arranging the promotions. They did a great job, all of them."

"When you see your Uncle Max, you might want to ask him how your NOC info got compromised and into the hands of the Mossad. Let me know what he says."

I nodded.

"You want another coffee?" asked the General.

"I'm good. I've got to get home and help Hanna finish packing. You wouldn't believe what a German lady thinks 'pack light' means."

Bushman laughed and said, "There's one other thing I need to tell you. Charlie Wilson is out of the hospital and recuperating at home. He asked to see you. If you have the time."

55

The Best View in DC

The Watergate
2500 Virginia Ave NW
Washington, DC 20037
Tuesday 9 September 1986 0915 Hours

HELLO CHARLIE. WE didn't wake you up, did we?" I asked. Charlie Wilson answered the door wearing khaki slacks, a blue dress shirt unbuttoned at the collar, and what could only be called a smoking jacket. The last part of the door chime melody, "Anchor's Away", faded as he pulled open the door. In his left hand Charlie held a coffee mug displaying the U.S. Congressional seal.

"Hanna, Rick. It's really good of you to visit. Come on in and make yourselves at home."

Charlie looked well, but I could sense something was off. He seemed somewhat guarded. Whatever had put him in the hospital had scared him, but good. I picked up the long cardboard box I had balanced on top of my right shoe. It wasn't at all heavy, but its unusual shape made it necessary for me to use two hands. The carton was a little over five feet in length and had the same perimeter as a 5-inch square.

I walked with Charlie past the entrance to the kitchen to the center of the upper living space. I propped the package against the railing that overlooked the lower part of the condo and the entrance to the outside balcony.

"What's in the box?" asked Charlie.

"It's from the Department of the Navy — a torpedo from the USS Nautilus," I joked, but I was curious myself. All that Wilson, CIA's Joe Wilson, had told me, was that it had been sent by his favorite CIA guy, Gust Avrakotos. How Gust got access to a nuclear submarine seemed to give Charlie pause.

"No shit," replied Charlie in a whisper. And then he called, "Hanna darling, come on down here. I want to show you the best view in all of Washington." He waved us towards the stairs and the living room. "Bring the box, Rick. We'll do the honors on the terrace."

Joe Wilson had walked me to his car earlier that morning. Our Langley meeting had been brief. The envelope for David James was tucked safely inside my sportcoat breast pocket. We picked up Hanna on the way through the lobby. In his car trunk was this neatly boxed package. Gust Avrakotos had sent it from Islamabad. Joe told me it was for Charlie. Then Joe told me I could give it to Charlie when I visited later that morning. Because Joe was in the CIA I didn't bother to ask him how he knew I was going to see Charlie.

All three of us stepped up to the balcony railing, like pigs to the trough. It truly was an amazing view. The Iwo Jima Memorial was directly out in front of us, on the other side of the Potomac River. Way to the left and in the distance was the Lincoln Memorial. Charlie told us that Lincoln would have waved to us if only he had arms that *moved*. He went on to say that the Afghanistan supply lines were still experiencing the same type of design defects. The metaphor went entirely over Hanna's head, but not mine. Well beyond the Lincoln Memorial, and also on the other side of the river, we could see the Pentagon.

"Very cool," I said.

"Magnificent," replied Hanna. "You are very fortunate to have such a beautiful sight to greet you every day."

"Oh, where are my manners? Would you like some coffee, juice, scotch?" Hanna and I both laughed at the ladder of the refreshments being offered, but Charlie seemed serious. We declined.

"How about we open the package from Gust?" I suggested, and pulled a small blade from behind my belt buckle. Charlie didn't notice but Hanna's eyebrows arched up slightly at the sight of the knife.

"Sounds like a plan," replied Charlie.

I cut the tape at one end of the carton, pulled back the flaps and tilted the open end towards the floor. A Stinger tube slid out onto the balcony floor. The tube did not have the sight assembly, nor did it contain a missile. A plain white envelope was taped to the middle of the cylinder. Printed in bold capital letters was the name CHARLIE.

"It's not loaded," I observed. "I guess Gust knew you lived near an airport."

Hanna knelt down next to the tube and asked, "What is it?"

"It's a poster case," I replied. "Charlie can use it to mail out his re-election posters to the voters in Texas."

Charlie laughed at my answer and handed me the note that was in the envelope. He got down on both knees next to Hanna and picked up the tube to examine it more closely. "This is a Stinger missile launch tube."

"And, according to Gust," I added, "this was the first one fired by the Mujahideen in Afghanistan. This is *very* cool."

56
Full Circle – Abu Dhabi Do

Sheraton Abu Dhabi Hotel & Resort
Penthouse – Level 2 – 3rd St – Corniche Road
Abu Dhabi – United Arab Emirates
Tuesday 16 September 1986 1815 Hours

E VERY TIME I visit this city I think of Fred Flintstone racing off in his car. I pushed open the glass shower door and snatched a towel from the heated bar. I wrapped it around my waist and walked into the bedroom to dress.

"You do realize that there is a concerted effort to conserve water here," chided Dr. Theresa Asghar. She was seated on the closer of the two chaise lounges. "Ten minutes is a bit excessive, is it not?"

"Dr. Theresa, I suspect you have not conquered your '*listening to men in the shower*' fetish."

"Aren't you worried about turning into a prune?" she asked.

"I'll default to your expertise, Doctor. However, there is scientific evidence that wrinkled skin makes it easier to grab and hold onto wet objects."

She laughed, "How are you Rick? Good flight?"

"Any landing you can walk away from is good. What's up? Is Maalouf stuck in the elevator again?"

"He asked me to extend an invitation for cocktails, just you, up in the private residence, before dinner."

"How is he doing? I understand he got you to beg your boss to erase my face from every water closet in Israel?"

Smiling she said, "It wasn't, how do you say, a big deal. As a matter of fact, at first we couldn't even find your file."

"Max Gresonine told me it was kept on the magazine rack in Director Admoni's personal head."

"Head?"

"Personal bathroom," I clarified.

"I hope you never lose your levity, Rick, playing on this stage day in and day out with the truly evil. Well, sometimes this darkness is...." We locked eyes for a moment and then I changed the subject.

"Is Hammad available? I have something for him."

"Yes, he is downstairs making preparations for our dinner this evening with your Ambassador, I have been told."

"How is Hammad? Is his brother's family doing OK?"

"Hammad is Hammad. His family has been well comforted. He asked me last week when you would be here. I think he likes you."

"I'm teaching him Spanish. Can I go down there?"

"I'll ask him to come and see you. You know how cluttered his work area gets at times." Theresa got up to leave. "He should be up here before you finish dressing."

I laughed because the last time I saw him entertaining guests in his office at the hotel in Dubai it got quite messy. "Theresa," I called. She turned in the doorway. "I forgot to ask, how are you and Caitlin getting along?" Theresa cocked her head to the side trying to read into the question.

"How long have you known?"

"About what?" I asked in a tone that said I knew they were lovers but had absolutely no problem with it. As a matter of fact, I was happy for both of them.

"She is very well. She will be at dinner."

"I'm glad to hear that. I'm happy for you both."

With a slight smile Theresa turned and left the suite.

Sheraton Abu Dhabi Hotel & Resort
Penthouse – Level 2
Tuesday 16 September 1986 1835 Hours

The door chime sounded as I finished buttoning the cuff on my shirt. I heard the lock click and the door being pushed open. A voice called out, "Mr. Fontain, it is Hammad."

"Hammad, come on in. I'm in the bedroom."

Hammad walked into the room. "Hammad, Como esta usted? And belay that Mr. Fontain crap. I asked you to call me, Rick."

"Mr. Rick, it is good to see you again. The doctor told me you wanted to see me."

"You didn't answer my question, how are you? How's your family? I'm sorry about the death of your brother."

"My brother's family is handling their loss. Me, it's one day at a time. I suspect it will never really ever go away — the pain, that is."

"No, Hammad, not ever. But it does get," I paused, "quieter." I looked at Hammad and he understood what I meant.

"I come bearing gifts," I said, changing the subject in an attempt to change the mood. I went to my garment bag and unzipped one of the larger outside pouches.

"My Uncle Max has access to Glock's, their manufacturing facility. The Glock 18 is a 9 mil sister product to the 17." I walked towards Hammad and handed him the cherry wood gun case. The manufacturer's name and the gun model were etched on the lid. The indentations were painted in black.

"This is unexpected, M ... Rick. Thank you very much," said Hammad in a subdued tone.

"It was the least I could do for breaking the grip on your Walther. Apparently, the damage happened when I fainted in the garage at the airport in KL." Actually, I was referring to being shot in the chest by a Russian KGB operative trying to exit his car. At Doc Theresa's suggestion, I had been wearing a vest. Hammad was still processing the fainting comment.

"This model was just released. You'll need to be extra careful when you pull the trigger on this pistol. Unlike the model 17, the 18 can operate in a full automatic mode. You may find that beneficial when the people who work for you ask for extra vacation days."

"How? Oh, you are again being ironic. Dr. Asghar said I should be careful in my understanding when you speak. Workers asking for additional vacation would be considered impolite."

"Yes, they would," I said with an extra touch of solemnity. Hammad saw this and decided to offer a solution.

"I could display the case open on my desk, to ensure politeness. This response is a good attempt at being ironic, yes?"

"Not if you don't fire a couple clips into the ceiling every so often," I said ever more seriously. Just kidding. Yes, it was a very good attempt at *ironic-ness*," I smiled. Are you going upstairs?"

"Yes, I'll take you up."

"The rooms on this level don't have any number assignments. What's that all about?"

"Everything above the 12th floor is part of Mr. Taisei's residence."

"No shit. I guess he must like me a lot, huh?"

"Yes he does, very much. And I do also, Mr. Rick."

"Just plain ol' Rick, will do, Hammad." I pulled the opposite pocket open on my suitcase. "This can be specifically shaped for the model 17. After dinner, I'll show you how to shape it." I had been assured that it could also accommodate the frame of the model 18.

"The 18 has almost the same frame dimensions as the 17," I continued. "Armadillo leather shoulder holsters are the best. There are two spare magazines in the pouches attached on the opposite side of the harness. They can accept both the 17 and the 33 round sized mags."

"It is an amazing gift. Thank you very much."

"Maybe after you practice your quick draw in the mirror we can go out and kill a few KGB guys?"

"It will be my honor, Mr. Rick."

"That was me being ironic again, Hammad."

"Of course. What time should I pick you up, just plain ol' Rick?"

Lobby Bar
Sheraton Abu Dhabi Hotel & Resort
Wednesday 17 September 1986 0005 Hours

Joe Wase came through the hotel's main entrance riding the wave of the revolving glass doors. He was followed into the lobby by Ambassador David James, and bringing up the rear were two more of Wase's people. From my seat at the bar I could see three parked embassy vehicles in the circle at the front. Joe spotted me on his second head swivel. He headed towards the salon's bar. He nodded at me and turned quickly from the entrance to face the trailing Ambassador. He waited until the Ambassador walked past the point where the marble tile met the plush carpet of the salon. He then turned his full attention back towards the expanse of the lobby.

"Everybody catch their flight OK?" I asked David as he walked up. Joe Hauf and Sal DeLacaro had flown in to attend the formal award of the AT&T contract. The GM, DeLacaro, was not a happy camper. The award of this contract was going to cause a lot of problems for him — and in his mind — the corporation. He told his resident account manager that he had been stabbed in the back. As soon as he got back to Hong Kong he would start the ball rolling to have me fired. Apparently, the award of the UAE office complex was huge and way beyond AT&T's capabilities, at least from DeLacaro's perspective.

David had overheard Joe Hauf, my boss, say he needed a ride to the airport right after dinner and offered his car to take him. Sal, who was seated next to Joe, asked if he could get a ride with them. David had just returned to the hotel from dropping them off at the airport.

"You know Rick, if I didn't know better, I'd think you had given up your day job with the Agency."

I laughed and replied, "That was the purpose of the dinner and the dog and pony show this evening, was it not?"

"Touché," replied the Ambassador. He waited for the bartender, who was coming towards us, to continue down the length of the bar. Once we were alone again the Ambassador said what was on his mind.

"First things first. You have a boss who is completely in love with you."

"Oh, I knew Douglas would come around one of these days."

James laughed and said, "Not Bill. Your AT&T boss, Hauf. He thinks you can walk on water. Douglas is still of the opinion that you are insane."

"No shit. He thinks I'm insane? A man who jumped out of a perfectly good helicopter in Laos? Okay, I admit that there's some partial truth to what was said."

"Which part?" asked James. "Walking on water or the insanity?"

"I've ordered wooden shoes from the Netherlands. Each one is the same size as an Iroquois Indian war canoe."

James watched my facial expression for a moment not quite knowing how to address the last comment. "Bill, our Bill Douglas, told me a while back about your BSP DO. Until this moment, I never fully realized what he meant."

"Sir, what is a *bisp-do*?"

"It stands for Bull Shit Persona Disorder," replied James.

"Yes, Sir," I replied, because I sensed he was considering giving the order to have Joe Wase shoot me or, even worse, drive me to the nearest all night golf course. David smiled at me and continued.

"Mr. DeLacaro, your boss's, boss's, boss, would like to have you fitted for a set of concrete galoshes." This was said in all seriousness. "He told me this in strict confidence tonight on our way to the airport. He went on to say that he was going to have a hard time convincing his corporate overlords about the scope of what was sold here. Plus, he said you have gone off the reservation for the last time. You have doomed the group here to a scope of work with which the company cannot possibly comply."

"Mr. DeLacaro will have an even more difficult time convincing his boss why he should keep his job out here. Coover, my Bell Labs handler in New Jersey, passed a personal invitation through Carly Fiorina's shop to AT&T's new Chairman, Jim Olsen. He's accepted. The invite came directly from his Eminence Zayed bin Sultan Al Nahyan. The discussion will include, but will not be limited to, AT&T's role in the purchase of satellite communication services for the entire UAE. Relationships are everything in this part of the world, Mr. Ambassador."

Ambassador James first whistled and then said, "Jesus."

"No, Sir, not Jesus. The name of the person who made it happen is Maalouf."

"Hmm. Well answer me this. How do you expect the 15 or so AT&T guys over in Dubai to support a project of this size? And, why didn't you tell DeLacaro what was going on?"

"You met him. What do you think? The Ove Arup Group, Limited, based in Hong Kong, will be here next week to discuss their contract with AT&T, as the Systems Integrator. They offer engineering, design, planning, project management, and consulting services for all major building systems. Maalouf has already mandated that the selected architectural firm pass their requirements through the Systems Integrator. AT&T will also have a say in choosing the construction contractors and all matters pertaining to infrastructure product selection. All cable delivery design must be blessed by the Systems Integrator."

"I'm curious, why would Ove Arup want to partner with AT&T? Why not go directly to the client?"

"Simple. The contract the UAE signed with AT&T assigns them as the general contractor. That and the $39 million-dollar honey-pot. AT&T now controls pretty much anyone who participates in this project."

"Jesus," said the Ambassador again.

"Sir, believe me when I say this: I gave the son of a bitch every opportunity to be the hero in all of this. He told me to go fuck myself."

"I believe you. I was going to ask, if this was your real day job, and I'm choosing my words carefully here, would you have behaved in the same way?"

"And what did you decide?"

"I'm quite sure you would have attacked the problem in exactly the same way."

I didn't know what to say or how to respond to that, so I didn't. Besides, it wasn't my real day job. The Ambassador's comment had a double-edged feeling to it. If I was willing to freelance outside the box with my AT&T assignments, how loyal could I be considered as a spy?

"Sir," I started to respond but James held up his palm for me to stop.

"Rick, don't over analyze what I said. Ready for another drink?" he asked, closing the subject.

"No thanks. I've got an early flight."

"Going back to London?"

"Yes, Sir. I'm going with Maalouf to KL, and then on to London." I couldn't decide whether or not to tell the Ambassador what we were going to do in Malaysia. If he had the need to know he would already have known. I gave a half laugh at that thought.

"Something funny, Rick?"

"No, Sir," I replied.

"Are you ready to perform your next string of miracles?" asked the Ambassador.

I laughed again. "You'll have to call my office for an appointment, Mr. Ambassador."

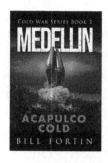

Medellín: Acapulco Cold

Snakes in the Temple – Five Months Later
Batu Feringgi Main Road – Jalan Batu Feringgi
11100 Batu Feringgi – Pulau Pinang, Malaysia
Sunday 10 January 1987 1940 Hours

NAMED PRINCE OF Wales Island by the British in 1786, Penang Island is part of the Malaysian State of Penang. The island's city of George Town is the second most populous in Malaysia. I had been here a few years ago, for a cabling bid for the tallest building in the city, the Komtar Tower. We were not the highest bidder, but we were not even close to being the lowest. And when your product has no voice in the solution then you had better be the cheapest guy out there.

Hammad told me on the way to Penang Island that Maalouf Taisei had several properties on the island. We were taken directly from the airport and driven up the J6. We were going to a place that was described to me as one of the best and most expensive resorts on the Pacific Rim. The Shangri-La's Rasa Sayang Resort was located on the northern tip of the island. When I walked through the lobby it was apparent that no expense had been spared in the decor.

The concierge who greeted us walked us past the smiling faces of the front desk. The view was breathtaking as we walked out onto a large garden veranda. The moon was almost full and was positioned, floating, just above the water on the far horizon. The Andaman Sea reflected in its light for as far as the eye could see. This part of the island pointed directly into the Malacca Straight. I recognized Maalouf, who was seated at the forward edge of the terrace. There were two other individuals seated with their backs towards me. Trusting souls, I thought.

The two strangers stood as Hammad and I walked up. Maalouf remained seated. I bent down slightly and took his, the owner's, hand. This I turned into a gentle embrace. It was then I saw that Maalouf's foot was in a walking cast. I then turned to the two individuals standing next to their chairs.

"Rick, this is Jeffery Chew," said Maalouf, pointing to the gentleman closest to me. I shook his outstretched hand.

"It's very good to meet you, Jeffery," I said.

"And, this is S.T. Lee." Jeffery took a step back, giving S.T. an avenue to extend his hand. "Jeffery is from Singapore. S.T. hails out of Seoul."

"S.T.," I started, keeping a firm grip on his hand, "we met in Mexico City in '85, yes?"

"Yes, it was a project meeting for Torre Chapultepec. The owner was interested in intelligent building technology. You were the only one there who seemed to know what he was asking for."

I let go of his hand and gestured for both men to take their seats. I sat so that I could see both the water and the hotel's portals. Hammad took a seat not far from us where he could keep an eye on everything.

"Mr. Somona, the owner, wanted an integrated solution, a nontraditional approach for his construction project. Most Mexican construction company managers don't have a clue," I said.

"I wasn't aware you two had met," remarked Mr. Taisei. "It is a small world, wouldn't you agree?"

"You and Walt Disney, Maalouf," I joked. "Why did you call this meeting?" Maalouf knew I was not a great believer in coincidence. My radar was booting up.

Jeffery started the conversation. "There has been an incident in northwestern Afghanistan. Up near the border with Iran."

"That, Sir, is not for public consumption," I said and made eye contact with Maalouf.

"I planned on meeting you at the airport and bringing you up- to-date, Rick. I slipped this morning on the wet tile in my bathroom," Maalouf said, sliding his foot from under the table so that his cast was on full display. "These gentlemen have something to offer you in the way of information on that incident." I glanced over at Hammad who indicated that was not the whole truth. Which part was not true? I wondered.

"OK," I said. "Have at it, S.T., Jeffery."

Jeffery spoke again. "The Afghans got careless and got pushed across the border, my source says, by a Spetsnaz patrol. The Iranians detained them and confiscated their weapons: four loaded Stinger launch tubes and 12 separate missile reloads." As the Stinger program matured at the Ojhri Camp in Pakistan the training now included the procedure for reloading the firing tubes. This solved a whole host of bulky resupply issues. It also created several more.

I was quiet for the moment, digesting what had just been said. It pretty much matched what I'd been told by the recently promoted LTC Mohammad "Ali" Tariq, leader of the Stinger field operations at the Ojhri Camp. The district Commander, Tooran Ismail of Herat, commanded the area where the missiles were lost. The first Stinger shipment had been successfully brought through by his deputy, Colonel Aladdin.

Subsequent resupply of Stingers in the later months was given to a lieutenant from the Khalis group. He was personally given instructions to not go near the Iranian border by Major Bill Harris, who was our CIA liaison at the Ojhri Camp. It was unclear why the lieutenant abandoned the supply patrol the second day out. His men became disoriented when confronted by a Russian Spetsnaz patrol. They were forced to cross the Helmand River at a point unfamiliar to them. When the patrol reached the other side of the river they were arrested by the Iranian border scouts. They had crossed the border into Iran.

"S.T. has spoken to the Iranians," Maalouf spoke up. "They have no intention of returning the Stingers to the Mujahideen."

S.T. then added, "The Iranians are being pressured by the Medellín Cartel. They wish to purchase the Stingers."

"Interesting," I said. "How are they involved with the Iranians?" I asked.

"The Cartel is a major distributor for the heroin coming from this part of the world. Even the Mujahideen has done business with them," explained Maalouf.

"S.T., do you have anything to add? How do you figure in all of this?" I asked.

"The Cartel was the reason I was in Mexico when you and I met. My role is to act as the go-between between the Cartel, the Golden Triangle — which is Myanmar, Laos and Thailand, as you know — and the Golden Crescent: Afghanistan, Pakistan and Iran. I just happened to be in Iran when the captured missiles were mentioned to Jorge Luis and Pablo Escobar. They are, I think you would say, at the top of the food chain in the alliance."

"What does the Medellín Cartel have to do with Torre Chapultepec?"

"Absolutely nothing. I was there to help my cousin. He needed a ride to the meeting. Rather than wait in the car he told me to come up with him."

"Good answer. I hope it turns out to be true. Jeffery, where are the missiles now?"

"As of twelve hours ago, they were still in Iran. The two Cartel members are returning to Columbia on Tuesday."

"I would guess they won't be transporting the missiles as carry-on luggage. Any idea how the weapons will be sent?"

"The decision on the transportation method," replied Maalouf, "is held solely by the Cartel."

"Swell," I replied. I then asked, "Jeffery, S.T., did either of you get a sense of why, actually more importantly, what, the Cartel is going to do with the Stingers? Any comments they made or any particular targets mentioned?"

"No," replied Jeffery without delay. "The Stingers were mentioned when they met. Señor Escobar immediately said they would buy them. No price was asked, but there was no doubt that the sale was made.

Everybody remained quiet for almost a full minute. Finally Maalouf said, "Rick, the immediate problem the Cartel is facing in North America is in Mexico. The Mexican government has clamped down on both its southern and northern border surveillance."

"The Cartel has threatened violence in response to the government interventions," said S.T.

"Blowing things up is the Cartel's preferred method for convincing those who cause them problems," said Hammad. He had walked over to our table and leaned in to whisper in my ear. He said I had a phone call and I could take it in the business center.

I stood up to excuse myself. It would be the airlines that the Cartel would target. I started to move towards the lobby. I stopped and turned towards the table. "I'll be back in a minute. In the meantime, see if you can brainstorm on how the missiles will be transported." As I walked, my mind yelled at me. This was exactly the concern we had had from the very beginning of the operation.

As I walked away I heard Jeffery say, "We have upset him very much, yes?"

Maalouf paused slightly before answering. "Mr. Fontain set up the Pakistan protocols to prevent this type of event from occurring. He feels personally responsible."

"What can we do to help, Mr. Taisei?" asked S.T.

Maalouf laughed slightly and then said, "I suggest we examine how the drugs are typically transported. The missiles would more than likely be included with a drug shipment."

"And if they are not?" queried Jeffery.

"Where are the drugs sent for pickup?" asked S.T. "Is the method of transport usually by water or air?"

"All good questions," replied Maalouf. "Jeffery, any suggestion as to where to start?"

"Last year there were eleven shipments by water. Three or more were sent by air. The majority of the shipments were received in Veracruz, Mexico. There are several other ports used in Central and South America."

"Maalouf," I said as I returned and stood at the edge of the table. "Could you ask Theresa to help with gathering a list of the ships leaving Iran this week?"

"Of course, she and Caitlin are here. I will ask."

"Typically, they use the large containers," said S.T. "So the list should probably focus on ships capable of carrying large containers."

"Why are you helping us at this point in time, S.T.?" I asked. "Why the change in sides?"

"They, the Cartel, murdered my cousin and his entire family."

"I'm sorry," I replied. I meant what I said, but I would check this out for sure.

"The other destinations," added S.T., "were Tolú in Columbia, Trujillo in Honduras, and Belize City. These received the smaller type containers, but containers none the less."

"What if we are not able to find these missiles before delivery, Rick?" asked Maalouf.

"I suspect Aero Mexico, Mexicana, and several other airlines are going to have some very upset passengers."

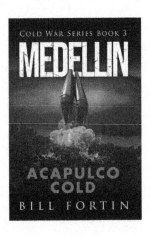

Characters, Places and Terms

Afghanistan

- **Ahmad Shah Massoud**   Afghan political and military leader. He was a powerful military commander during the resistance against the Soviet occupation between 1979 and 1989 and in the following years of civil war, during which time he became known as the Lion of Panjshir

- **Amar Nabi**   Commander, Bagram District; Russian trained pilot — defected with SU-22; call sign ROCKETMAN-1

- **Anam Kashif**   Ouija Camp base garbage man — spy for the Russians

- **Brigadier Mohammad Yousaf Azraq**   ISI Commander; born 5 October 1937 Logar, Afghanistan — noted Afghan historian and writer of Afghanistan's history

- **Captain Gregory Nelson**   Special Forces team leader (Green Beret) — call sign GB-1

- **Gary Lawson**   CWO — CIA — call sign ONE

- **Jim Pezlola**   LT Colonel — call sign ZERO

- **MSG/CWO Mike Davis**   Green Beret and brother of Andy Davis — NCOIC — call sign GB-2

- **Mirdadzai Khudiadadzai tribe**   Arranged CIA meeting with Mujahideen Commander Mustapha Taisei

- **Mustapha Ismail Taisei**   Afghanistan Mujahideen Commander

- **Sergeant E-5 Donny Mathews**   Delta Forces; call sign DELTA-5

- **Sergeant First Class George Angerome**   Delta Forces Team Leader; call sign DELTA-1

- **Staff Sergeant Dennis Deccan**   Delta Forces; call sign DELTA-2

- **Spec-5 Sandy Johnson**   Delta Forces; call sign DELTA-4

- **SPEC-5 Tom Truscott**   Delta Forces; call sign DELTA-8
- **Staff Sergeant Brian McDermott**   Special Forces (Green Beret); call sign GB-5
- **Staff Sergeant Chas Mackenzie**   Delta forces; call sign DELTA-7
- **Staff Sergeant Dennis Bormann**   Special Forces (Green Beret); call sign GB-3
- **Staff Sergeant Jim Thomas**   Special Forces (Green Beret); call sign GB-6
- **Staff Sergeant Pat Goschich**   Delta Forces; call sign DELTA-3
- **Staff Sergeant Paul Murray**   Special Forces (Green Beret); call sign GB-4
- **Staff Sergeant Randy Boston**   Delta Forces; call sign DELTA-6
- **Field Marshal Mohammed Abu Ghazala**   Egyptian Defense ministry
- **Vassar Suleiman**   Mujahideen — Mustapha's second in command; educated at the University of Maryland; call sign TERRAPIN-1

Germany

- **General Cummings**   U.S. two star — arranged home coming for Delta and Special Forces at Ramstein AFB
- **Karl Guntur Schmidt**   Deceased husband of Hanna Schmidt; agent for the West German organization known as the Bundesnachrichtendienst, the Federal Intelligence Service or BND; killed in the line of duty
- **Max Gresonine**   German BND, Federal Intelligence Service officer; contact/coordinator with the Bundesnachrichtendienst — Federal Intelligence Service

London

- **William (Bill) J. Douglas**   U.S. Cultural Attaché to London Embassy; Actual position — CIA Station Chief in London
- **Rick Fontain**   CIA/Bell Labs (London Office); formerly Redeye team leader; call sign STING-1

- **Amelia Jane Dancer Smythe** Subject matter expert on Russian Mil Mi 24 — recruited by David James in 1982 — present assignment CIA Field Operations Officer; London — reporting to Bill Douglas
- **Ed McCall** CIA Executive Case Officer
- **Mohammed Abu Ghazala** Egyptian Defense Ministry; half-brother to Maalouf Torki bin Taisei
- **Joe Hauf** 3rd level manager, AT&T London office
- **Carrie Ester Flouts** Personal secretary to Bill Douglas; 43 years old, married and the former personal secretary to David James

Israel

- **Nahum Admoni** Former Israeli intelligence officer who served as the Director-General of the Mossad from 1982 to 1989

Malaysia/Singapore

- **Ahmad Haqq** Hammad's driver at the airport in Kuala Lumpur
- **Jeffery Chew** Cartel scheduler and broker
- **S.T. Lee** Korean National Cartel go-between

Pakistan

- **Captain Amar Nabi** Mujahideen, Pilot and Commander — Bagram Area
- **Ahmad Shah Massoud** Mujahideen district commander near Bagram
- **Brigadier Mohammad Yousaf Azraq** ISI — Inter-Services Intelligence — Command of the Stinger training and distribution; call sign FATHER-1
- **General Akhtar Abdul Rehman Khan** Head of the Pakistani ISI
- **Major Bill Harris** CIA; Marine Officer; 34 years old; works for Joe Wilson and a dotted line to Gust Avrakotos; married, two children
- **Saifullah Khan** CIA-solicited guide services; wife is sister to Mustapha Ismail Taisei

- **Sergeant Usman Farooq**   General Khan's S-4 at the Ojhri Camp's headquarters
- **Major Mohammad "Ali" Tariq**   Head of ISI Ojhri Stinger training — former student of Andy Davis
- **Mohammad Escriah and six Pakistani men**   Attacked ISI Ojhri Camp

Russia/Soviet Union

- **Leonid Ilyich Brezhnev**   19 December 1906 — 10 November 1982); General Secretary of the Central Committee (CC) of the Communist Party of the Soviet Union (CPSU), presiding over the country from 1964 until his death in 1982
- **Alexei Grigory Lysotovich**   Russian economist and politician

United Arab Emirates

- **Abu Dhabi**   The capital and second most populous city in the United Arab Emirates
- **Caitlin**   Daughter of Maalouf Torki bin Taisei; cousin of Dr. Theresa Asghar
- **David James**   US Ambassador to the UAE
- **Theresa Asghar, MD**   Israeli, thirty-six years old; attended Harvard Medical school; two-year residency at Johns Hopkins Hospital; Maalouf's personal physician and niece; Caitlin Taisei's cousin
- **Joe Wase**   HOS for David James, US Ambassador to the UAE
- **Maalouf Torki bin Taisei**   A Malaysian citizen, member of their cabinet, and probably the largest arms dealer in that part of the world
- **Hammad abid Ndakwah**   Head of security for Maalouf Torki bin Taisei
- **Patrick**   Smartly dressed door-keeper at the Sheraton Dubai
- **Sal DeLacaro**   AT&T Asia Pacific General Manager
- **Sir Ove Nyquist Arup**   16 April 1895 – 5 February 1988) English engineer who founded Arup Group Limited, a multinational corporation

offering engineering, design, planning, project management, and consulting services for building systems

- **Zayed bin Sultan Al Nahyan** The Supreme Council of Rulers of the United Arab Emirates; elected to continuous five-year terms as President of the UAE

United States/ North – Central – South America's

- **Andy Davis** Head Of Security for General Dynamics / Raytheon Corporations; Former CWO Instructor Fort Bliss
- **Barry Flax** Vice President, Research and Development: General Dynamics
- **Carly Fiorina** AT&T 1986 Network Systems
- **Cath Franklin** Charlie Wilson's Office Staff
- **Charlie Wilson** Texas congressman; a swashbuckling lawmaker played a major role in getting the Soviets out of Afghanistan
- **Daryl Russell** CIA — Office of Mid-East Analysis (OMEA)
- **Dave Shatner** 1985, Charlie Wilson's office manager
- **Don Coover** Director, Research and Development: Bell Labs
- **Don Regan** President Reagan's Chief of Staff in 1986
- **Ed McCall** CIA Field Support Analyst — direct report to Joe Wilson at Langley
- **George Pratt Shultz** President Reagan's Secretary of State in 1986
- **Gustav Lascaris "Gust" Avrakotos** January 14, 1938 – December 1, 2005 — American case officer and Afghan Task Force Chief for the United States Central Intelligence Agency; Avrakotos was little known to the public until the publication of the book *Charlie Wilson's War: The Extraordinary Story of the Largest Covert Operation in History* by George Crile
- **Hanna Gresonine Fontain** Wife of Rick Fontain; niece of Max Gresonine
- **James Baker** President Reagan's first Chief of Staff, 1982
- **Joe Wilson** Department Head, Central Intelligence Agency; Office of Russian and European Analysis (OREA)

- **Lisa Meerdter**   State Department
- **Lt. Gen. Gerald Bushman**   The Director, Defense Intelligence Agency (DIA) Department of Defense (DOD)
- **Major Bill Harris**   CIA on-site Phase IV Coordinator — Ojhri Camp — Operation Cyclone
- **Mike Vaughn**   CIA Langley — analyst — Afghan/Pakistan Desk; works for Gust Avrakotos
- **Nancy Davis**   Wife of Andy Davis
- **Nancy Reagan**   First Lady — wife of President Ronald Reagan
- **Peggy Grande**   President Reagan's personal assistant
- **Ronald Reagan**   40th President of the United States of America
- **William Joseph "Bill" Casey**   March 13, 1913 – May 6, 1987 — Director of the Central Intelligence Agency from 1981 to 1987